THE PIRATE'S LOCKET

Legends of Calverique, Book One

BY KATARINA D'BEERS

ISBN: 978-1-968857-05-9
First Edition

Cover Design by Azraelle Rumple
Edited by Katie Evans

Published by Siren's Lantern Press
An Imprint of Escape the Classroom
PO Box 746
Coleman, FL 33521
www.escapetheclassroom.com

DEDICATION

To my grandmother, Carolyn

Who taught me to love books and kept stacks of adventurous romances wherever she went. I do not know if this book would make her proud or embarrassed, but I dedicate it to her all the same.

CONTENTS

PREFACE

Brackwater Hall, Cornwall
Spring, 1793

Her wedding dress hung from the armoire like a shroud. Its lace and silk were meant to smother her into silence. Beatrix's gaze lingered on it longer than she wished. Behind her, the fire snapped in the grate. It made a sound too alive for a room otherwise complicit in keeping her secret.

She drew a long breath and set the cravat at her throat neatly. She tugged once at her linen shirt's cuffs. The shirt's fabric hung strangely. It fit like a short chemise, and it was as coarse as sackcloth when it touched the insides of her wrists. The breeches were worse still. They bound her thighs tightly, in a way that made her gait awkward.

Beneath the discomfort, something unexpected stirred. Unlike the wedding gown, these garments did not seek to confine her. They *armed* her.

She put her gloves in her pocket, and then fastened the locket around her neck and hid it beneath her shirt.

She had known grief, but what she felt now was not grief. Grief was stillness. This was thunder that rose behind her ribs, threatening to break her open if she stayed.

They believed she would bend. They thought she would don the exquisitely adorned gown, smile for the ceremony, and then disappear into submission. They were wrong.

She could hear the whispers of her mother's still unanswered secret calling her to chase it. She crossed to the window and pushed it open. Cold spring air cut across her face. She could smell the sea salt on the wind as it climbed up the cliffs.

The sea waited for her. It was neither safe nor kind, but it was her freedom.

She took one last look around her bedroom, then turned toward the open window. She threw her pack to the ground, dropped into the garden, and ran.

Part I: The Labyrinth of Lies

CHAPTER 1

Brackwater Hall, Three Days Earlier

The rain had slicked the stones of Brackwater's drive to a mirror-dark sheen. Ambrose Drake left his coat dripping in the hands of a footman and strode down the corridor with the slow, unhurried gait of a man accustomed to forcing doors open. His dark blond hair was damp and wind-tossed from the ride in. His deep brown eyes, the color of wet earth, swept over the hall with measuring calculation. He carried himself like a man whose presence was tolerated out of obligation, not affection, and he savored the discomfort it caused.

Lord Alexander Wrenwood, the first Earl of Saltash, looked up from the papers on his desk as the study door opened. His expression did not shift, though his fingers tightened imperceptibly around the quill in his hand. Drake's presence struck like a shadow from the past. His height, the dark blond hair, and those hard brown eyes echoed his father so vividly that Lord Wrenwood felt the years burn away—like the sea had sent a wraith to remind him of the life he had buried beneath a title, fine clothes, and the stone walls of Brackwater.

"Captain Drake," Wrenwood said. The title, *captain*, was edged with formality rather than respect. He did not rise from his chair, but his gaze measured the younger man as one might study a storm on the horizon when it was too distant to feel its thunder, but close enough to demand attention. His gaze caught, involuntarily, on Drake's cravat. There gleamed a black opal; its dark heart burned alive with spectral fire. Its colors shifted as though restless within the stone. Wrenwood forced his eyes back to his visitor's gaze. "To what do I owe the pleasure of this unexpected call?"

Ambrose smiled without warmth and reached into the inner pocket of his coat. He placed a small, oilcloth-wrapped parcel on the desk between them. "I've come with a proposition, my lord."

Wrenwood made no move to touch it. "And what is that?"

Ambrose unwrapped the parcel himself, revealing a worn leather logbook. Wrenwood's gaze flickered.

"This," Ambrose said softly, opening the book to a page thick with salt stains and spidery ink, "is the log of the *Maiden's Cutlass*. You remember her, don't you? She's the ship you captained before the Crown saw fit to grant you an earldom and a new name."

Wrenwood's pulse quickened, but he kept his expression blank. "That name has been dead for thirty years."

"Names don't die, my lord; they only sleep until someone with the sense to use them comes along." Ambrose leaned forward. His voice dropped to a purr. "You were a pirate in the Seven Years' War, and one of the best, if these pages are to be believed. The Admiralty pardoned you, but I wonder what the Lords of Parliament—and your dear neighbors—might think of their venerable Earl once they read of the *Maiden's Cutlass* plundering French and English merchants alike."

Wrenwood's hand clenched around the cane. "Spanish ones, too, if we're telling the truth." He spat back at Ambrose. "What is it you want?"

"A simple thing," Ambrose replied smoothly. "Your daughter's hand in marriage. I want a marriage contract that is signed, sealed, and binding, with a dowry worthy of the fortune you stole to earn it."

"And if I refuse?"

Ambrose smiled again. "Then with the next tide, these pages sail for London, to the Admiralty, the courts, and the press. The name you've so carefully buried will rise again, and when it does, your daughter's marriage prospects will sink to nothing. No man of standing will touch her, and your title will go down to the depths with her."

Lord Wrenwood's gaze hardened. "You would do well to remember, Drake, that if you drag my name through the muck, you'll take your own family's down with it. Many of those sailings you threaten to parade before London were carried out under Lord Falmouth's own orders. You think anyone will spare the Drakes when the scandal breaks?"

Ambrose's smile did not falter. "I have no illusions about what it will do to my father. Let it burn him. I'm not here to protect the Drake name, my lord. I'm here for what I want—and I always get it."

Wrenwood's eyes narrowed. "Then why my daughter? Of all the heiresses you could bully into your grasp, why her?"

Ambrose's answer came without hesitation. "Because she has… certain qualities. Qualities I value." His gaze lingered, sharp as a drawn blade. "She is more important than even you realize."

A flicker of unease crossed Wrenwood's eyes, but he forced his expression into the same cool mask he had worn since the first volley. "Name your terms," he said evenly, though the weight behind the words betrayed his reluctance.

Ambrose leaned back in his chair. He looked as relaxed as if they were discussing nothing more consequential than the weather. "As I said, I want a marriage contract that is signed, sealed, and binding. Your daughter's dowry will reflect the gravity of this union; I want twenty thousand pounds, in coin or property. She will retain the jewels from her mother's collection. All of them."

Wrenwood's jaw flexed. "You act as though you mean to buy her outright."

"I mean to secure her future, and my own," Ambrose replied. His tone was smooth, but his eyes gave away the iron beneath his threat. He tapped the edge of the leather logbook between them. "Or else London learns your true name, and your daughter will have no future at all—No husband, no dowry, and no standing in society."

The silence between them lengthened until Wrenwood finally reached for the decanter and poured two glasses as if the act alone could steady his hand. "You'll have your contract," he said at last.

Ambrose took the glass and raised it in a toast to his would-be father-in-law. "Pleasure doing business, my lord."

***

The breakfast room held the kind of stillness that did not come from peace, but from long habit. A breeze stirred the curtains, but the silverware lay undisturbed. The fire had burned to embers.

Beatrix entered quietly. Her father was already seated at the head of the table. He looked up at the sound of her steps and offered a small, weary smile.

"Good morning, Bea."

She returned the smile with a hint of suspicion. Her father rarely used her nickname, especially since her mother had died. It was the name only her closest relatives used, and most of them were now long gone.

He gestured to the place set for her. "You are just in time."

She sat and poured herself tea. "You sent for me."

"I did." He set his cup down and leaned back in his chair. He laced his fingers together. "There is something we must discuss. It cannot wait."

Beatrix did not answer. She stirred her tea once, twice, and then set the spoon aside.

"I have accepted a marriage proposal on your behalf."

She blinked and let the words settle, unsure that she had heard them correctly. "You accepted what?"

He met her eyes. "You will marry Ambrose Drake."

Beatrix stared at her father as if he had just announced her betrothal to Satan in the flesh. "Ambrose Drake? The bastard son of Lord Falmouth? The one who, if rumor speaks true, spends his time among smugglers, gambling dens, and women whose reputations are as tattered as his own? *That* Ambrose Drake?"

"Beatrix!" His voice cracked like a whip. "Such language does not become you."

She lifted her chin. "Nor does such company become me, Father, yet you would see me wed to the rake."

Lord Wrenwood sighed. He looked as if he had rehearsed this moment many times. "You may disapprove of his company, but Ambrose Drake is a man of influence. His ships reach ports that few others dare, and his alliances are...formidable. In time, you will see the advantage of such a union. Your life will be comfortable, and your future will be secure."

She narrowed her eyes at him. "Why? I could agree to marry Lord Ashcombe and be a duchess before the year is out. Any number of rich and titled gentlemen could give me a future beyond question. I might even find a husband I could learn to love. Why should I settle for being Mrs. Drake?"

Lord Wrenwood's gaze hardened. "Because the Drakes are not a family to be crossed. Love will not keep you safe, Beatrix. A duchess's coronet will not shield you from the reach of a man like him. Better to have such power at your side than staring down the barrel of it."

She faltered at the chill in his tone. "What has he got over you, Father?" she asked quietly.

He did not look away. "Nothing that needs to trouble you, except to know this: Ambrose Drake is a man who gets what he wants, and he wants *you.* I will see you protected, even if you do not understand the shape that protection must take."

Her brows knit. "Protection?" she echoed. "From what, Father? Or should I ask, from whom?"

Lord Wrenwood's gaze hardened, but his voice softened into the calm tone he used when she was small and stubborn. "From a world that will gladly devour you, Beatrix. You may not see it now, but Ambrose Drake is a shield as much as he is a sword. He is clever, capable, and utterly without fear. These are qualities that will keep you safe when titles and pretty words cannot. You'll curse me for it now, perhaps, but one day you will thank me."

"I'll thank you," she said tightly, "the day I believe safety is worth a lifetime in the company of a man I neither love nor respect."

His jaw locked. "You will marry Ambrose Drake," he said. Each word struck like a gavel. "That is the end of it."

***

The withdrawing room carried the faint scent of starch and rosewater from where the maids had recently washed and ironed the heavy curtains that framed the windows. Sunlight fell between them, scattering light across bolts of fabric arranged in careful order. The sheen of silk caught the light in soft, undulating waves.

Beatrix stood on a raised platform in her shift and stays while the modiste circled her. The older woman paused occasionally to record measurements in a small leather-bound book.

"You have your mother's frame," the dressmaker remarked as she smoothed a length of fabric over Beatrix's shoulder. "Straight-backed and narrow through the waist. We will add a touch of padding at the hips so the skirt holds its line."

Beatrix remained still. The dressmaker, Mrs. Thatcher, had already dismissed cream and pale lavender as unsuited to her complexion. Now she held up a bolt of robin's egg blue, overlayed with ivory lace so fine that it appeared almost translucent. The fabric caught the afternoon light and shimmered softly. It was delicate in texture, but held an undeniable clarity of color.

"This shade would suit you well," Mrs. Thatcher continued. "It brings out the purity of your skin. With your red hair arranged up, perhaps with a few curls left to soften the face, it will create a classic portrait of youth."

Beatrix nodded once, offering a response no deeper than politeness required.

The woman pinned the lace at Beatrix's shoulder and stepped back to admire the effect. "Your mother chose mulberry, if I recall correctly. It suited her. This color tells a softer story."

Beatrix regarded her reflection in the nearby mirror, though she did not really see it. Thoughts unrelated to the wedding dress clouded her mind.

"Does it?" she asked.

The seamstress mistook her comment as approval and smiled. She moved to record additional notes. When the fitting concluded, Beatrix stepped behind the folding screen and redressed with measured efficiency. Her hands moved automatically, but her thoughts were caught in the hush of rising doubt. *Mrs. Drake…* the name sounded like it belonged more to a milkmaid or a housekeeper, but certainly not to Lady Beatrix Wrenwood.

When she emerged from behind the dressing screen, the room stood empty once more. The dressmaker had departed to retrieve pattern samples. On the windowsill, where there had been nothing a moment before, sat a small wooden box.

It bore no seal, no note of delivery, and no markings beyond a strip of ribbon, which was faded to the color of aged ivory. Beatrix lifted the lid with care.

Inside rested a silver locket, nestled in a bed of red velvet. It was oval in shape and softly tarnished by age, but instantly familiar. She had seen it before, though not in many years. On its face was an engraved symbol of two intertwined rings. She picked it up and, beneath it, placed gently on top of the red velvet, lay a folded slip of parchment.

She opened it slowly, already suspecting what she would find. The first lines confirmed it.

The wind may lie, the stars may turn,
But blood will find its line…

Her breath snagged in her throat. The rhythm of the words was instantly familiar. She had heard them as a child, whispered into her hair as she dozed in the garden, tucked into the crook of her mother's arm while the nanny pretended not to notice. It had been a lullaby then, lilting and low. The melody was just complex enough to settle deep in the mind and stay. Now it was something else. She read to the end.

The compass breaks when touched by gold,
The sea forgets the shore,

Yet two shall hold what none can fold,
And open nevermore—
Unless the tune the sea once knew
Be hummed by kin of mine.

Her mother's handwriting was unmistakable. It was angular, deliberate, and without flourish. The message was not affectionate or sentimental—it was only a song.

She lifted the locket from its case and turned it in her hands. It was attached to a long chain. Beatrix looked for a way to open it but found none. There was no hinge or clasp readily visible. *It must hold a secret*, she thought.

She remembered her cousin, Aria, wearing the locket before she had disappeared into thin air. Beatrix had not seen it in nearly a decade.

She folded the parchment and placed it back in the box, then she looped the locket around her neck. It swung low on her chest, so she wound the chain around her neck once so the locket would hang delicately at her throat. Despite its cold metal, the silver felt warm against her skin, as if it had readied itself for her.

***

After the dressmaker's departure, Beatrix did not return to her rooms. She slipped through the western garden gate and followed the path that led toward the sea. The afternoon was still and warm for late spring. Beneath the hedgerows, the ground held a dampness from the morning's rain, but the sky was dry, and the gulls rode the thermals above with ease.

She reached the cliffs within minutes. The wind came gently from the south, carrying the scent of seawater and honeysuckle. Below, the sea breathed against the rocks in long, rhythmic sighs.

She paused at the edge of the path, where pale blooms of yarrow and wild parsley brushed her hem. The locket hung at her throat. Its weight felt steady there. She rested her hand against it and felt the pulse of her own warmth in the silver.

Her mind returned to another spring along these same cliffs. She had been six years old. Her cousin Ariadne—who everyone called Aria—was nearly eighteen then. She was already lovely in her soft features and golden blonde hair. Althea, Beatrix's mother, had brought them to walk along the sea path. She had called it a tradition. Arabella, Aria's mother, had been Althea's older sister, but she had been lost at sea long ago. Her death left Aria to live at Brackwater Hall under Lord Wrenwood's protection.

The sky that day had been nearly this exact shade of blue. The breeze had tangled their skirts around their legs. Together, they had gathered columbine, yarrow, and sprigs of early heather. Beatrix remembered dropping a handful of blossoms into the basket and receiving a warm pat on the head from Althea for her efforts.

Aria had been humming a tune. Althea had joined in, then taken over the melody. She had sung it often, but this was the first time Beatrix remembered hearing the words clearly. It had been a lullaby then. Its sound was gentle and strange.

The wind may lie, the stars may turn,
But blood will find its line.

Aria had asked what it meant. Althea had smiled, but she did not answer.

Now, standing once more on that same path, Beatrix closed her eyes and hummed the verse under her breath. The locket grew warmer against her skin.

She opened her eyes. The tide was rising, and the sky had begun to dim. It was time to make her way back home to dress for dinner.

She turned from the cliff's edge and walked back toward Brackwater Hall. The song lingered with her, as if the cliffs played its somber tune.

***

The halls of Brackwater had grown quiet by dusk. The servants had retreated to the kitchens, and shadows shrouded the hardwood floors. Beatrix, still in her walking gown, made her way up the west staircase toward her chamber. The locket was once again warm against her collarbone.

She did not know she was still humming until the sound left her mouth. The melody was faint but rose from her throat without effort.

The wind may lie, the stars may turn…

She turned the corner and nearly collided with her father.

Lord Wrenwood stood frozen on the landing with one hand braced against the carved newel post. His expression, though quickly masked, betrayed something close to dread.

Beatrix stopped, startled. "Father?"

He studied her closely, then gestured to the locket. "Where did you learn that song?"

Her fingers lifted to the chain at her throat. "Mother used to sing it."

"She did," he said. "But only when no one else was listening."

"She left this locket for me," Beatrix replied. "It was on my windowsill today. Did you put it there?"

"No. I haven't seen that in years."

"Oh. It was in a wooden box, with a couple of lines of the song written in her hand. I thought maybe you had left it for me."

His expression was tense. "No, and I'm not sure you should be wearing it openly."

"I thought it was mine."

Lord Wrenwood gave a quiet breath through his nose, then looked away. "You should dress. We have a guest this evening."

"A guest?"

"Ambrose Drake has joined us for supper."

Her hand stilled on the banister. "He is here?"

"He is punctual," her father said. "Unlike some."

Beatrix did not move. "Tell me what the song means."

His eyes returned to hers. "It means what it always meant: trouble. Your mother left you many things, Beatrix, but that melody was not meant to be sung out loud."

"Why not?"

"Because it calls attention," he said. "And not all attention is welcome."

He turned and descended the stairs, leaving her staring in his wake.

***

The dining room flickered with firelight and candle glow. Though the fire warmed the room, a chill traced Beatrix's spine.

Ambrose Drake stood near the hearth. His dark blond hair was tied neatly. His sapphire coat was tailored to project elegance, but the fit was just a shade too exacting, as if he had chosen his need to impress over his need for comfort. The black opal at his cravat seemed to drink in the fire and candlelight, only to exhale it again in eerie, shifting colors that made the shadows writhe across the walls. His bearing suggested a man accustomed to being observed and intent on controlling the impression he left.

"Lady Beatrix," he said, offering the faintest bow. "I trust you will not keep your future husband waiting."

Beatrix met his eyes. "Patience, Mr. Drake. You may have a contract, but you do not yet have me.

His smile did not falter. "On the contrary, my lady, I always claim what is promised to me."

They had crossed paths often enough over the years—at dinners in neighboring estates, on the occasional hunt, and in a dance or two at county assemblies—but never with the slightest warmth. Ten years earlier, he had turned his attentions to her cousin Aria, and Beatrix had learned then that Ambrose Drake's charm was a blade honed for conquest, not affection. Since Aria's disappearance, his visits to Brackwater had been rare, each leaving her with the uneasy sense of being studied like a puzzle he meant to solve.

Her father cleared his throat, breaking Beatrix from the memory. He gestured to the table. "Shall we sit?"

They took their places. A footman poured the wine in silence and withdrew.

"I find I've grown fond of the countryside," Ambrose said, adjusting his cuff. "After Paris, even country life feels orderly."

The situation in Paris had turned grim earlier in the year when the French executed their king and declared war on Great Britain. Ambrose owned a small fleet of merchantmen, financed by his father, the Earl of Falmouth. His opportunistic nature had no doubt drawn him into the turmoil in pursuit of profit.

Beatrix kept her tone light. "You were in Paris?"

"Only briefly. It no longer suits men with names, let alone the ones without." He smiled faintly. "I left before the fleur-de-lis gave way to the guillotine."

Her father sighed. "The revolution is a fever. It cannot last."

"It never does," Ambrose said. "But it reminds us of what happens when men are denied what they believe they deserve."

He turned his attention back to Beatrix. "Fortunately, England holds to her traditional customs. When we are married, I think we shall keep our estate well out of reach of such nonsense."

"You speak with remarkable certainty," Beatrix quipped, meeting his steely gaze.

"I find certainty useful," he countered.

"I find it presumptuous." She looked down at her plate, realizing she hadn't yet taken a bite. She picked up her fork and started pushing her food around her plate.

He sipped his wine. His gaze never left hers. "We danced, once."

"I was being polite," she replied as she set her fork down with deliberate care.

His mouth curved, though the look in his eyes cut deeper than the smile. "Polite? No...you pitied me."

"Perhaps I did," she said softly, lifting her gaze to meet his.

Ambrose's smile lingered, but his tone turned to steel. "As my wife, you will find pity a far more dangerous indulgence."

"As my husband, you will learn my fortune is no easy theft," Her voice was a silken dare edged in superiority.

Ambrose's smile deepened, but it had lost all warmth. "You mistake me, Lady Beatrix. It is not your fortune I'm after."

Her eyes thinned to slits of disdain. "Then what, pray, compels you to chain yourself to me?"

He leaned back in his chair and studied her as though the candlelight had made her transparent. "A prize far rarer than gold, and far more dangerous to possess."

Her lips curved in something that was not a smile. "Then you will find me well-armed, Mr. Drake."

"Enough," Lord Wrenwood interjected, slamming his fork against the table. "This is not a fencing hall. You might try civility while we dine."

Ambrose smiled faintly as he turned to Wrenwood.

"My apologies, my lord. I was merely recalling how charming Lady Beatrix's cousin Aria could be in conversation. She, at least, had a gentler hand with her barbs."

"She never barbed anyone," Beatrix said sharply. "Aria was too sweet—and too well-mannered—to say anything you deserved."

A shadow flickered in his expression before he masked it with a faint lift of his brow. "That was a long time ago, Lady Beatrix. I was barely more than a boy."

"And I was barely more than a girl when I knew I would rather marry a fishmonger than a pompous, over-reaching bastard like you."

Her father's voice grew sharp. "That is enough!"

Beatrix stood and turned toward the door. As she passed, Ambrose stepped forward and seized her arm.

His voice dropped to a whisper.

"You will marry me in three days, bastard or not." He leaned slightly closer. "Silver burns, Beatrix, and *blood will find its line*. Even you must know that much."

Her eyes widened. *He knows the song,* she thought. Before she could reply, her father's voice cut through the room.

"Beatrix! You will retire now. That language was beneath you."

She turned slowly to her father. "Then you should not have invited someone who drags the whole house down to the gutters."

He stepped back from the table. "Enough. Leave us."

She looked once more at Ambrose, then slipped from his grip with icy composure.

She left the room without another word. The silver locket rested once again warm against her throat.

CHAPTER 2

Beatrix remained in her chamber the next day. She ignored the servant's knock at the door with her breakfast tray, and she did not bother to dress for the day. She did not want to speak to anyone.

She sat cross-legged on her bed with *Gulliver's Travels* open across her lap. She had read the same paragraph three times without truly seeing the words. At last, she focused on the image before her: poor Gulliver, pinned to the sand by a thousand delicate ropes, each strand too fine to hold him on its own, yet together they were strong enough to keep him helpless. She traced the illustration with her fingertip and almost smiled. Marriage to Ambrose Drake would be just that—a thousand tight little bonds, all leading to her damnation.

She had not removed the locket. It hung against her collarbone like a weight. She turned it in her fingers and pressed along the edges, tracing the silver filigree that curled across its surface.

The wind may lie, the stars may turn…
But blood will find its line.

The lyrics returned to her mind without invitation. Her mother's voice hummed sweet and half-forgotten just beneath them.

A soft knock came near midday. A servant entered with eyes lowered and placed two items on the side table: a folded letter and a small white parcel wrapped in cloth and sealed with green wax.

The letter was in her father's hand.

There are choices I regret,
but not the one to keep you safe.
I ask only that you try to understand.
—Father

She read it once, then again.

It was not a command. It was not even an apology. It was love, and it made her hesitate. For a moment, she wondered if her fury was too sharp. Was her judgment too quick? Her father had never raised his voice to her. He had never denied her a kindness. Yet here she sat, in a cage of silence, cloaked in uncertainty about her future.

She opened the parcel.

Inside lay a single velvet box. The note beneath it was written in a different hand.

Three days, Beatrix.
—A.D.

She did not touch the box. She could see enough of its contents through the slit in the velvet. It was a large emerald brooch. A gift meant to impress…or to mark her.

That evening, as the sky darkened, she stepped to the window and looked down toward the garden walk.

Ambrose Drake was standing just inside the iron gate. His arms were folded, and his eyes were fixed on the house. He wore his riding coat unbuttoned and showed no signs of discomfort, though the mist had thickened into a sea-born drizzle.

He did not move at all. He just stared.

Finally, he lifted his head to look at her window. As his dark eyes met hers, she jumped back as if burned. When she peeked cautiously from behind the curtain, she saw him mount his horse and ride off slowly. His posture was relaxed, and his pace was deliberate. He was not finished.

***

The next morning, Beatrix sat cross-legged on the window seat with her arms folded over the closed book on her lap. She had ignored the first knock at her door, but the second was too loud to disregard. Annie, the housekeeper, was the only one who would dare disturb her.

"My lady," she said cautiously, "Mrs. Thatcher's here with the gown."

Beatrix turned her face toward the window. "I don't care."

"She came all the way from the village," Annie pressed insistently. "In the rain. Please, my lady, just try it on. You don't have to speak to anyone."

Beatrix ground her teeth. "I don't want to wear it."

"But it's nearly finished," Annie whispered. "You might want to see it before it's too late to change your mind."

That gave Beatrix pause. She had very few choices of her own left to make. This may be the last one. She stood slowly, pulled on a robe, and brushed past the housekeeper without a word. She descended the stairs like a woman condemned.

In the drawing room, Mrs. Thatcher stood by the hearth. Her arms were folded across a wide chest. Her apprentice was already laying out layers of fabric. The modiste turned as Beatrix entered. Her expression was as practical as ever.

"Well," she said, "you've not lost your coloring, at least. That's something."

Beatrix gave a tight nod and stepped into position before the mirror.

The gown was robin's egg blue. Its silk bodice was trimmed in delicate, hand-tatted lace. The sleeves tapered delicately at the wrist. As the apprentice fastened the back, Mrs. Thatcher stepped around to examine the drape.

"I used this trim once before," she said softly. "For your cousin Aria. I remember because she requested it specially. It was unusual for her to take an interest in fabric, but she was—well, let's say, *particular* about that gown."

Beatrix's throat tightened. "When was this?"

"A few days before she vanished. She said it was for a portrait, but I suspected otherwise. She brought no maid with her and paid in coin. She wore a locket just like the one you're wearing now." The seamstress pointed to the silver oval that glinted at Beatrix's throat.

"This one?" Beatrix asked carefully.

Mrs. Thatcher peered closer. "Yes, I believe so." Beatrix pressed her hand against it.

"She hummed a tune too, while I pinned the hem," the dressmaker added. "It was an odd little thing, with words about the sea and blood and something breaking. I thought it was strange for a young lady, but she said her mother taught it to her."

Beatrix said nothing. Her pulse had begun to thrum.

"Do you know it?" Mrs. Thatcher asked.

Beatrix shook her head. She wasn't sure why she lied. The modiste held her gaze a moment longer, then stood back with a nod. "Well, the dress fits."

Beatrix stepped down from the stool and looked at herself in the mirror. The gown was lovely, and it fit her form perfectly. Her fingers absentmindedly rubbed the lace. How had it looked on Aria? Why had she never seen the dress? She was young when Aria disappeared, but spent at least part of each day with her. She would have noticed such a fine dress.

The seamstress helped Beatrix out of the wedding dress and into a day dress. With a few flicks of a needle and thread, the dress was finished.

***

The seamstress's words lingered after she left—a dress for a wedding, stitched with lace so fine it could catch the light like morning frost. Beatrix told herself it was nonsense to care, yet her feet carried her down the familiar corridor, past the portraits that watched with silent judgment, toward a room she had not dared enter in years.

Beatrix turned the door handle and let the door swing wide. Aria's room was untouched by time. The maids still kept the room dusted and the bed made, just in case its mistress reappeared unexpectedly. A faint trace of lavender lingered in the air. Beatrix stepped across the threshold warily as a strange sense of trespass chilled her bones.

Aria had disappeared nearly ten years prior. There was no tragic tale to tell; she simply vanished. She was twelve years Beatrix's senior, and just four and twenty years old the last time Beatrix saw her.

Beatrix began her search for the silver dress in Aria's wardrobe. Two gowns hung stiffly within; their colors had long faded. Neither was silver with delicate lace. She checked behind them, then crouched to examine the wardrobe's base. Nothing.

Beatrix then searched the trunk at the foot of Aria's bed. She sat on the floor in front of it and unpacked its contents: several shawls in varying colors, two pairs of long, yellowed gloves, and a broken fan. She placed the items back into the trunk and sighed heavily. What could have happened to the dress?

Her eyes scanned the room. Everything was as Aria left it, but then she noticed something strange. A section of the floorboard beside the wardrobe showed a thin, unnatural gap between two planks. She tapped it. It was hollow.

She pried at the edge with her fingertips, and the board lifted with a reluctant creak. Beneath it lay a wooden box, barely wider than a book.

She drew it out slowly, as if pulling something sacred from a tomb. The box was unmarked and held closed by a grey ribbon that had likely been blue at one time. Beatrix untied it gently and held her breath as she opened the box.

Inside the box were folded pages with edges that were softened by time. The ink was still dark, and the hand was fluid and precise. Beatrix began to read.

The sea waits for no name and no legacy; just for me and you. I've made arrangements—quiet ones. I will let you know when all is ready. Bring only what you cannot bear to leave.
—A.

She turned to the next.

Father will not relent. I would rather live in poverty and honesty than be rich without you. Hold fast, my love. I will send for you soon.

—A.

Beatrix's hands trembled. The final letter chilled her.

Come to the cove at midnight. The ship is ready. I have the license and enough gold to carry us to the New World. We'll marry before the sun breaks and start a life with our own names and our own rules. No more shadows. No more silence. I want my future and family with you, Aria.

Come hell or high water, I will be your husband.

—A.

She sat back on the floorboards with the box of letters in her lap.

To her family, Aria had vanished. The only sign of her was a hair comb that washed ashore with no explanation. Everyone assumed she had slipped along the cliffs and drowned in the sea.

The letters were filled with devotion, urgency, and certainty. Whoever this "A" had been, he had intended to build a life with Aria. What happened? Did she refuse to go? Did he get angry and push her into the sea when she refused him?

Beatrix closed the box and held it to her chest.

The initials were too damning to ignore; the letters had to be from Ambrose. She had to confront him. He claimed to have loved Aria…didn't he? Or did he just want her name and fortune?

Was she her cousin's replacement? No. She would not allow it.

She secured the box in its hiding place but kept the last letter. She was determined to use it to get out of her marriage arrangement. As she left Aria's room, she felt something pulling her forward. She could hear her mother humming softly in her mind. It was a haunted memory reminding her that if anyone had known any part of Aria's secrets, it was Althea.

***

Aria's room had felt like a life paused. A shawl was draped across the bed, books were left on the shelves, and a half-filled journal was tucked beneath a cushion. Each item lent warmth to the space, as though Aria might return at any moment. Althea's room was completely different.

When Beatrix opened the door, she was met with a chill that raised the hairs on her neck. Every surface was veiled in muslin. The curtains had long been drawn shut, and the hearth stood cold and lifeless. Even the mirror above the dressing table had been covered so as not to reflect what little light peaked from the cracks where the curtains didn't quite meet. Althea's room was less a chamber and more a tomb.

Beatrix's footsteps were muffled by the thick carpet. She paused beside the wardrobe and peeled back the muslin cover. Inside hung a small number of gowns, each wrapped carefully in tissue and tied with faded silk ribbons. They were not meant to be worn again, but no one quite knew what to do with them.

Beatrix moved next to the window seat, where a cedar chest rested beneath the glass. It contained a few mementos: a bonnet, a child's slipper, and a ribbon her mother once wore in her hair.

Still, something in her resisted leaving. If Aria was hiding letters under the floorboards, where could her mother have hidden her secrets? Beatrix lifted the thick carpet, but all of the boards beneath it were nailed tightly, allowing for little more than the occasional creak.

She turned her inspection next toward the hearth. She brushed her hands along the paneling near the floor. Near the left corner, her fingers found a seam that didn't match the one on the right. She pressed gently, and with a faint click, a narrow panel gave way.

Inside, nestled in shadow, was a small bundle wrapped in oilcloth. Beatrix stifled a small gasp.

With slow, deliberate hands, she pulled the bundle free and laid it on the floor. The fabric unfolded to reveal a boy's sailing clothes: breeches, a white linen shirt, a weatherworn waistcoat, and a dark cravat. Beneath them lay a pair of scuffed boots that were small but well-made. The entire bundle had been carefully arranged.

She picked up each garment and felt for hidden pockets or something sewn within the seams. When she lifted the breeches to investigate their secrets, a parchment scroll fell out of one of the legs and landed on the floor in front of her.

She untied the ribbon holding the scroll together and discovered its contents: a map.

On it were scattered islands. Some were marked with names she recognized, and others were marked with names she had never heard spoken. Lines traced narrow channels and dangerous crossings. Between a string of islands was a symbol: two interlocking rings—just like those engraved on the locket. Beneath the symbol was a single word:

Calverique.

Beatrix stared at it, then traced the inked lines with her fingertips. Was this where Aria had planned to flee with Ambrose? If so, had her mother found the map and not told anyone? The handwriting was not her mother's. Had Althea had it prepared for another purpose entirely?

As she lifted the map, a second paper slipped from beneath it. She caught it before it touched the floor. It was a note, written in Althea's hand.

Beatrix,

There are truths buried deep. Not all are meant to be revealed, but some must be. You cannot trust him, Beatrix. He will never be content with the life he has been given. He will take more than you can give.

This path is not without danger, but it is yours now. Go now, before it is too late. Make your way to Calverique, and trust no one who knows your blood.

What we hid was never meant for men like him. It is your birthright—yours and Aria's.

Beatrix read it twice, and then a third time. The words pulsed in her ears. She folded the letter with trembling hands. Her mother had left her one last message, and that message was to run. *You cannot trust him, Beatrix.* Althea had to have known something was going to happen with Ambrose. It was the only explanation.

Beatrix rolled up the map with the letter inside. She held the map against her chest and closed her eyes, willing the answers to come to her.

The silver locket grew warmer at her throat. It felt alive, as though it recognized her longing. A subtle glow shimmered across its surface and vanished.

The air seized in her lungs. She had no explanation; only a sudden certainty that the map, the locket, and the questions that haunted this house were bound by a thread stronger than chance.

Staying meant surrendering all hope of learning the truth. Her father refused to tell her the secret that meant she had to marry Ambrose, and there was no way Ambrose was going to tell her anything at all.

She rolled the sailor's clothes back in their oilcloth bundle and headed to her own room to pack. By morning, she would be gone.

CHAPTER 3

Greenbank Tavern, Falmouth

The tavern reeked of sweat, smoke, and spilled ale. Its narrow windows were fogged with grime. Beatrix paused outside its crooked door, fingers brushing the tricorn hat that she had pilfered from the head of a slumped drunk just outside the harbor gate. The man hadn't stirred when she took it, though she doubted he'd miss it in his condition.

Her stomach turned as she stepped inside. The place was dim and crowded. Its low ceiling was thick with tobacco haze. The stink of unwashed men met her nostrils as she fought the urge to spill whatever was left in her empty stomach.

A barmaid weaved between tables with a tray of mugs, sloshing froth onto the floor. At one table, a sailor sang bawdy lyrics off-key while others jeered, joined in, or ignored him entirely.

She kept her shoulders squared as she moved through the haze. Her linen shirt itched beneath the waistcoat, and her cravat scratched at her throat. Her copper hair, now roughly cut just below her shoulders and tied back in a low, boyish ponytail, sat awkwardly against the nape of her neck. She touched it once and reminded herself that men don't girlishly twirl their hair, then quickly lowered her hand.

The barkeep, a thick man with graying sideburns, looked up from wiping the bar. He barely glanced at her.

"S'cuse me," she said, pitching her voice deeper than usual. The barkeep scooped something into a bowl and slid it her way.

"You look hungry, lad," He spoke. She was grateful for the sustenance, even though the smell of the fish stew was pungent. The walk from Brackwater to the docks was longer than she had thought, and she had left in too much of a hurry to think about packing food for her journey.

"Thank you. I'm looking to sail—for work, I mean."

He snorted. "Aren't we all." Then he nodded across the room. "Talk to O'Malley. Back table. Stripe in his coat."

She thanked him, finished her stew, and left a coin on the bar. She hoped it was enough; she'd never paid for anything herself, except the occasional trinket at the village market.

O'Malley sat alone at a table in the far corner with a battered ledger open in front of him. He, too, was struggling to swallow the fish stew. He gulped as he swallowed, then immediately took a long swig of his ale to cover the taste.

She approached.

"You're late," he said before she reached him.

"I—?" She didn't know what to say. He must have mistaken her for someone else.

He gave her a long, measured stare. "You've the look of someone running. It always shows in the eyes."

She stiffened. "I'm not running," she lied. Did it really show in her eyes?

"No?" His brow arched. "Then what sends a green slip of a thing into this place asking for work?"

She hesitated, then lifted her chin. "A wedding."

That made him break into a full belly laugh. "Aye, that'll do it."

He leaned back and studied the would-be crewmate. His gaze swept over her boots, the stolen hat, and then her nervous fingers working against her waistcoat. She almost gave him a turn so he could see the backside of her outfit too but thought better of it.

"You've guts, at least. Name?" Oh, right, she needed a name. "Lady Beatrix Wrenwood" would hardly suit a deck hand.

"T-T-Trix," She stumbled.

"Well, 'Trix,' if you can keep your mouth shut and your hands busy, we've room on *The Tempest*. We're merchants, of a sort. Be at the lower quay in one hour. If I catch you lyin', you'll have to swim back to port, sharks and all."

"I understand." She fought to hide the tremble boiling in her chest. Everything about her was a lie. She questioned her sanity and wondered if she'd be better off with Ambrose. No, she'd come this far. She was determined to follow her mother's instructions to run to Calverique…wherever that was.

O'Malley tapped two fingers on the table, then returned to his ledger. She was dismissed.

Beatrix turned and moved through the tavern without meeting any eyes and stepped into the sunlit chaos of the quay beyond it.

Unseen from the shadowed alcove behind O'Malley, a man sat staring into his tankard. His face was obscured by the wide brim of a weather-beaten tricorn. He said nothing. He only watched.

***

The war with France had opened a coveted door: letters of marque, which dispensed authority to gentlemen eager to bleed French commerce under the guise of patriotism. *The Tempest's* captain had sailed to London to secure just such papers, which blurred the line between piracy and privateering. The ink was scarcely dry, but their contents granted a veneer of law to the merchant vessel's ventures that smelled more of gunpowder and smoke than honest trade.

Now, the captain sat with his back to the wall; one boot was propped on the empty chair opposite him, and a mug of ale sat untouched at his elbow. He had chosen the darkest corner of Greenbank Tavern for precisely this purpose: to watch without being watched. His coat, sun-bleached and salt-worn, blended into the shadows, and the brim of his tricorn concealed the sharp line of his jaw.

He had not intended to come this close to his ancestral home, but the message delivered to him in London had been too pointed to ignore. Outside of another tavern with some seedy name—The King's Wench? The Queen's Chamber Pot? Who could remember—an old school chum from Eaton had caught him by the shoulder and whispered in disbelief, "Alverdon? Gus? Is it really you?"

Gus had smiled genuinely at his old friend. After a few rounds of ale and reminiscences of their misspent youth, their conversation inevitably turned to the night everything had gone wrong.

"The rumors swirled. Some said you were killed in a duel. Others said your old man threw you out, and you went to live with your aunt in Ireland. I assumed that girl of yours broke your heart, but then I learned she disappeared too."

Gus's breath stilled at the thought of her. "I guess you could say it was all a little bit true."

His friend, Lord George Calerton, sipped his ale as he contemplated. After a moment, he let out a great sigh. "Well, I think I have something that you might want, but it's not here—it's back in Cornwall."

"I don't plan to ever go back there." Gus's gaze dropped to the table. His father's estate was in Cornwall. He had no intention of going anywhere near the man again.

"For this, you might…" His friend's voice trailed for a moment. "You see, you aren't the only lord to take to 'sailing.' A few years ago, I happened upon the site of an old shipwreck. It was on an unmarked, unnamed island deep in the West Indies. Not much was left. There was a broken mast, and bits of cabin furniture."

Gus could picture the scene. In his years at sea, he had seen his share of voyages gone wrong. "What else did you find?"

"There was a trunk full of rotting ladies' things. My crew dumped it out, looking for jewels or anything else that might be valuable. They found a pearl necklace and a leather journal."

"I assume it's not the necklace you put aside for me."

George snorted back a laugh. "No, it's the journal. If you dock in Falmouth on your way out to sea, I will see that it's delivered to you." George looked at Gus imploringly, not wanting to tell him to whom the journal belonged, but wanting him to have it all the same.

"Was it…" Gus couldn't say her name.

George sighed. There was no keeping the journal's owner from him. "No, but I'm pretty sure it was her mother's."

So, to Falmouth they had sailed. His first mate and quartermaster were both relieved. Cornwall was the perfect place to recruit, as most of its inhabitants had an instinctive connection to the sea.

When they arrived, a man was waiting at the docks just outside this seedy tavern. He pressed a parcel into Gus's hand with a quickly nodded "My lord," and vanished before Gus could respond. The parcel now sat heavy in his satchel.

The leather journal bore a familiar emblem pressed into its cover: two interlocking rings. The mark stirred something old in his chest—something better left buried.

Across the tavern, O'Malley's voice cut through the din. A youth stood before him. The lad was slim and stiff in posture, but the tilt of his chin was pure defiance. The tricorn on his head sat low to shadow his features, but Gus could see enough. The lad was too young, too clean, and trying too hard to appear otherwise.

Still, he admired boldness in his crew. It often burned out quickly, but it flared brightly while it lasted.

He returned to his thoughts. The sea waited, and with it, distance. There were ports to restock, accounts to settle, and waters wide enough to forget this dreadful place.

The journal sat beside him, reminding him of the life he left long ago. He had not spoken his title in years. He left it all behind when he took to the sea. Here in Cornwall, it clung to him like the seasalt he could not scrub off his skin.

He was August Drake, Viscount Alverdon, heir to the 9th Earl of Falmouth…or what was left of him.

***

The Tempest, two days later

The morning sun filtered through a thick veil of mist, casting the sea in hues of pearl and gray. The ship rocked with a steady rhythm. Its sails straining gently under the breeze as *The Tempest* cut through the Channel toward open water.

Gus stood at the expansive windows in the chartroom with arms folded behind his back and eyes locked on the horizon. He had not moved in some time.

Behind him, his first mate, Callahan, cleared his throat. "The wind's good, and it looks like the crew's settled. I caught one lad asleep on watch last night, but he's got bruises enough to remember it."

Gus did not reply.

Callahan shifted his weight. "We've made better time than expected. We could reach Madeira a day early, provided the wind holds."

Still nothing.

"You're thinking about it again," Callahan said, glancing at the desk. "That damned journal."

Gus clenched his teeth. "It is none of your concern."

"Not unless it gets us sunk or cursed."

Gus turned. His eyes were bloodshot from a night without sleep. He crossed the room, opened a drawer, and dropped the leather-bound book inside with finality. "There, now you can mind the crew and the ship instead of prying into my affairs."

Callahan raised a hand in surrender. His tone softened. "Aye, Gus. No prying. I'm just trying to keep my captain from brooding himself into the sea."

Before another word could be said, a shout rang out from the deck.

"Idiot boy—he snapped the pully!"

"I'll toss him overboard if he touches one more line!"

"He just cut the stay—"

Gus and Callahan were out the door before the next voice finished.

On deck, a knot of sailors had formed near the mainmast. A length of rigging swung wildly, while one of its fastenings cracked at the base. Beatrix stood at the center of the commotion. Her coat was soaked from a bucket of seawater, and her hat was knocked askew. One older sailor had her by the collar, and another stood nearby with fists clenched.

"I said I was sorry," she snapped, twisting out of the man's grip. "It was frayed. I tried to fix it."

"You tried to fix it?" the older sailor roared. "You nearly cracked the boom loose!"

Her head lifted in defiance. "Then maybe you should teach me how to do more than swab the bloody deck."

A gasp went up around them.

Callahan stepped in fast, pushing two crewmen back. "What's this?"

The older man pointed. "Boy's green as pond scum and just cut the main boom stay with the dullest blade I've ever seen. He's no sailor."

Gus approached. The crew stepped aside. Their murmurs died on the wind. Beatrix straightened. Her face was smeared with ocean water and embarrassment.

He studied her—no, him, as they still believed. While the boy's chin jutted up in rebelliousness, his hands trembled faintly.

Gus looked to Callahan. "Fix it."

"We'll need the spare line. It'll hold," Callahan replied.

Gus returned his gaze to Beatrix. "Name?"

She hesitated, then said, "Trix."

"Got a surname?"

A longer pause. She hadn't thought that far. She noticed the old sailor's whistle tied around his neck and proclaimed, "Whistle."

Muffled laughter broke across the crew.

Gus's expression didn't change. "Mr. Whistle, if you break another inch of my ship, I shall tie you to the mast until the sun cooks your brain to mush."

Beatrix did not flinch. "Then teach me something worth not breaking."

Callahan let out a low whistle of his own. "He's got nerve, I'll give him that."

Gus turned and walked away without another word. He didn't have the time, or the stomach, for squabbling among his crew.

Callahan lingered just long enough to add, "You've been reassigned, Mr. Whistle. Report to the galley. Cook needs a pair of hands that won't snap the rigging in half."

The crew dispersed. Beatrix adjusted her stolen hat and glared after the captain's retreating form. She yelled after him, "I'd rather peel potatoes all day than be ignored. Aye, Captain!"

From the quarterdeck, Gus caught the words.

He didn't smile, but the corner of his mouth lifted just slightly.

***

The light from the oil lamps in Gus's cabin cast flickering shadows across the dark paneled walls. He sat at the table, staring at the closed leather journal in front of him.

A knock sounded at the door. It was not Callahan's usual rhythm.

"Enter," he called.

The door creaked open. Beatrix stepped inside with a steaming tray in her hands. She set it carefully on the table as her eyes flicked around the room. It was neater than she had expected. The furnishings were simple, well-made, and worn by use, not style. It was a captain's quarters, not a nobleman's salon, though nothing about the man sitting across from her fit either world.

"Your supper, sir."

He looked up from the table, eyeing her without expression. He had no appetite for dinner. "Galley sent you?"

"Cook sent me. Apparently, I hum when I'm peeling potatoes, and he needed a break."

Gus gave a noncommittal grunt. He lifted the lid to reveal stew, bread, and roasted apples. He poured himself a finger of rum and gestured for her to go.

Her eyes had landed on the journal. She tilted her head, reading the cover in the dim light. "Ubi sanguis cadit, veritas surgit."

Gus froze mid-sip.

Her bright green eyes met his grey ones. "Where blood falls, truth rises."

His brow arched. "You read Latin?"

She hesitated. "Some."

"That's not common in the slums of Cornwall."

She drew a slow breath, then gave a sheepish smile. "I didn't grow up in the slums."

"Clearly." His eyes looked her over from her boots to her copper curls, which she had tied back neatly with a slip of rope.

"I was a tutor's apprentice for a time. He was strict about classical studies." Her voice was steady, but she did not meet his eyes.

Gus stepped closer, studying her. "And you left that behind to swab decks and serve gruel to men who would toss you overboard for a misplaced knot?"

Beatrix shrugged. "It's better than the future I had."

"What future was that?"

"A wedding," she replied, a bit too quickly.

Something unreadable flickered across his face.

"Ah," he said at last, returning to the table. "Well, at least the sea is honest work. Brutal, but honest."

Beatrix nodded once. "And it keeps moving." He didn't argue with that.

She started to turn, then paused. The journal had the same symbol engraved on it as the locket she had hidden beneath her linen shirt. "That symbol on the journal… the interlocked rings. I've seen it before."

Gus looked up sharply. "Where?"

She caught herself. "I mean…in books, mostly. Old heraldry. It's probably nothing."

He said nothing, but his gaze lingered long after she had closed the door behind her. What a strange lad.

***

The journal's salt-warped leather cover was stiff, and its pages were bloated from exposure. The cover bore no title, save the Latin phrase and the simple symbol—two interlocking rings.

Below the rings, in gold now dulled by sea air, was a name etched in fading script: *Arabella Loraine.*

Arabella had died at sea nearly twenty years ago. Her ship had gone down somewhere near the West Indies. It was a miracle that this book, this intimate, waterlogged journal, now sat on his desk.

The pages clung together in places, but he pried them apart with care. Some ink had run, blurred by brine and time, but the entries were legible. The voice that emerged was unmistakably that of a clever, observant woman. They were reflective, wistful, and guarded.

Aria hums the tune more often now. I never taught it to her, but she picked it up from Althea, who still sings it when she thinks no one is listening. The melody lingers in the house like old perfume—familiar, but a little haunting. I tell myself it is harmless, a lullaby, but I know better. Some things are carried in blood. Some songs remember.

Gus paused. His fingers curled over the edge of the page. He could hear it dancing across his memory. There was Aria, humming that same melody beneath her breath as she braided her hair, or while lying beside him on a sun-warmed stretch of grass. It had been their secret refrain, and now he realized it had not been theirs at all.

I wonder if she'll ever ask what it means. I pray she doesn't. Not until I'm ready to give her an answer.

He turned a few more pages. The ink grew faint. The script was looser and more hurried. A date caught his eye, just weeks before Arabella's ship had vanished.

There is one island I have not marked. I do not trust myself to name it, even here. The symbol must suffice. If the worst happens, and this falls into the wrong hands… may the sea swallow what we could not burn.

At the very back of the journal, between two pages nearly fused with saltwater, he found a map, or rather, the remnants of one.

The ink had faded. The edges were torn, and the layout was smudged and broken. There were islands—some named, some not—and a string of curved lines that looked like a trade route or a path traced by memory. The corner of the parchment bore the same symbol as the cover: two rings linked together.

Gus stared at it for a long while. He did not know the whole meaning of what he held, but he knew this journal had crossed time and tide to reach him. That meant something. It had to.

He closed the book and ran a hand through his hair.

"Gus?" came Callahan's voice outside the door, followed by a quick knock. "You eating that stew or feeding it to the waves?"

Gus set the journal aside. "I'll eat," he called back, but his gaze lingered on the map a moment longer. He knew he was meant to find something here, but he wasn't sure what.

CHAPTER 4

Falmouth, Cornwall
The Day After Beatrix Fled Brackwater Hall

Ambrose Drake stood at the bar of Greenbank Tavern, still wearing the riding coat he had donned before sunrise. The barkeep eyed him warily. "I haven't seen you in these parts before." Obviously, he recognized Ambrose; everyone in Falmouth knew of Ambrose. His father's title even bore the name of their fair city: Earl of Falmouth. Ambrose even called himself "Ambrose of Falmouth" in more elegant circles—at least those that tolerated it.

Ambrose laid a silver coin on the bar. "I'm looking for a boy; slight build, red hair, may have signed on a ship in the past day."

Recognition flickered behind the man's eyes. He nodded toward the harbor window. "That'd be the lad in the oversized tricorn. Looked jumpy. He signed on with *The Tempest.* They left yesterday morning, just after tide break."

Ambrose's fingers curled around the edge of the bar. "Destination?"

"South, I'd wager. Ship flies English colors but they don't talk like navy boys. They claim to be merchants. Their captain—Gus, they called him—wasn't keen to linger."

"Gus," Ambrose repeated. His held his voice flat. "Did you hear a surname?"

"His crew just called him "captain," but a man came in here looking for him to deliver a parcel. I can't quite remember the name he was asking…"

Ambrose sighed and dropped another silver coin on the bar.

"Oh yes, Alverdon…Lord Alverdon, though why a lord would waste time in our port, I couldn't tell you."

Ambrose ground his teeth in consternation. Of course. Of all the ships she could have boarded, she'd chosen *his*.

He said nothing further. The barkeep, sensing something dangerous, stepped back without asking for more coin.

Ambrose stepped outside into the salt-laced wind and exhaled slowly, fitting the pieces together.

Beatrix had cut her hair and stolen a hat. The groom had seen a red-headed boy slip through the garden around midnight. No doubt she thought her disguise clever. She sought to vanish, but she hadn't gone into hiding. She'd gone to sea.

If she meant to escape him, she would head as far from British shores as possible.

He knew he would not catch *The Tempest* in Madeira. She had a full day's lead. But Santiago… yes. If he sailed hard, he could reach Cape Verde ahead of them.

He turned toward the docks. He already had ships; his small fleet were sleek, fast vessels once meant for importing goods from France and the Mediterranean. One of them would do nicely. He would bring just a single ship. He needed speed, not spectacle.

And when he reached Santiago, he would be waiting.

Waiting for his bride.

Waiting for his brother.

Ambrose smiled, though it did not reach his eyes. Let them think they could outrun him. He would show them just how far he was willing to go to take back what was his.

CHAPTER 5

Beatrix had not anticipated the stench. It was something between spoiled milk, rotten fish, and the unwashed sweat of fifty crewmen with dubious bathing rituals. It clung to the damp wood of the ship and settled sour in the back of her throat. She longed for the lavender sachets that the maids tucked into every drawer in Brackwater Hall.

She had no proper bed. She had been assigned a cramped hammock wedged between two grizzled sailors who both snored like oxen. Her borrowed name, "Trix," had already been stretched and slurred into half a dozen crude variations, some more imaginative than others.

The first night, she tried sleeping upright on a coil of rope beside the galley. That earned her a boot to the ribs from a cook's mate who mistook her for a lazy cabin boy. The second night, she gave in and claimed her hammock. The third, she accepted that her privacy was gone altogether.

The problem of the chamber pot had become its own war. She had managed to claim it at night and steal away behind a stack of sacks near the supply hold. The men noticed how long she took, and how carefully she guarded her back. One of them had begun calling her "Princess Pisspot." She nearly broke his nose with the handle of a wooden ladle before O'Malley dragged her out by the collar and told her she'd be scrubbing the galley floor until it shone "like a saint's halo."

It did not help that the captain—that sun-bleached, self-important brute—was rarely seen except when issuing orders or stalking silently through the ship like a ghost. His eyes were the only quiet thing about him; they were sharp and watchful beneath the brim of his weathered hat. She'd brought him his supper once. He hadn't thanked her; he had just stared. Then there was the journal; it sat there on the desk beside him, as if it had more right to the room than she did.

She couldn't stop thinking about it. The cover was leather, but battered by time and seawater. The symbol—two interlocking rings—had glimmered as the lanternlight passed over it. The same symbol was etched into the locket around her neck and drawn carefully on the map her mother had left for her.

He had looked offended when she read the Latin aloud. "Where blood falls, truth rises." She had seen his knuckles tighten around his fork.

She swept the galley floor now in slow, methodical circles. Pots bubble and sailors complain around her, but her mind wandered. Was it all a coincidence? Or had the captain come to Cornwall for the same reason she had fled it?

If he had the journal, and she had the map…what, exactly, were they both sailing toward?

She knelt to scrub a stubborn streak of grime near the stove and narrowed her eyes. The captain might not be the fool she hoped he was, but she was no fool either.

***

Beatrix carried the captain's tray down the corridor with careful hands and a steady gait. This had become a nightly routine. She delivered his dinner just past seven bells. He gave a nod of acknowledgment, then she made a quick exit.

Each evening, she lingered a second longer. Sometimes she asked a question. Sometimes she simply backed out of the room slowly enough to get a glimpse of what he was reading in the journal while he ignored her with practiced precision.

At first, he'd left the journal open in plain view. He read it slowly, as though weighing each word against some private memory. Then, he noticed her trying to catch a glimpse of it over his shoulder and started closing it when she entered the room.

Tonight, he had left it open again. Was it an accident, or a test?

Beatrix hesitated outside the door with the tray balanced on her hip. She knocked, and his voice called, "Enter."

He sat at the table, as always. Tonight, a single lantern lit the cabin in soft gold. The scent of the sea mingled with leather and the aroma of burning lamp oil.

She set the tray down on the table in front of him. The journal lay open beside his hand.

"Roasted cod," she said. "Cook swears it's fresh. I have my doubts."

The captain didn't smile, but something shifted in his expression. Perhaps it was the edge of tolerance, or perhaps even amusement.

She lingered. "You always eat alone."

He looked up. "You saying you'd like to join me?"

"No," she said quickly. "Just an observation."

His eyes drifted back to the page, and she followed his gaze. A line of spidery script caught her eye:

The cove is quiet now. She hums the tune more often. I think she dreams of it too.

Beatrix's throat went dry. Aria used to hum it constantly: *The Compass Waltz.* The lyrics still drifted through her memory in an endless loop of haunted melody. Her mother had sung it. Aria had sung it. And now this man—this captain—read about it in a journal he clearly guarded with his life.

She leaned forward slightly. "Is that a ship's log?"

He didn't answer.

"Who wrote it?" she asked.

He snapped the journal shut.

"Trix," he said evenly, "you're my crew, not my confessor."

She straightened. "I didn't mean to snoop."

"You've been snooping for five nights."

He stood and walked to a drawer, locked the journal inside with an old iron key, then turned to face her.

"You're clever—too clever. You ask far more questions than a deckhand, even an educated one, should."

Air fled her lungs in a sharp rush. She'd grown more confident since boarding, and apparently, more careless. She couldn't afford for anyone, much less her captain, to notice how much she didn't fit in with the crew.

"I learn quickly," she said.

"Or you're hiding something." It was a statement, not a question. He moved to the table and uncovered the fish, took a forkful, and said nothing more. Beatrix turned to go.

"Wait," he said, just as she reached the door.

"You said something about a wedding," he remembered. "When I asked why you joined my crew, you said you were running from a wedding."

She kept her back to him. "I did."

"Was it yours?" He sipped his ale.

She hesitated. "It was meant to be."

He didn't press further. After a beat, he said, "Tell Cook the cod was fresh after all."

She nodded and left. Her pulse thudded in her ears.

***

Beatrix plunged her hands into a bucket of cold, greasy water and began scrubbing the pans from supper. The skin on her knuckles was raw from days of scrubbing floors and peeling potatoes. A knot of tension had rooted between her shoulders since she'd left the captain's cabin. What she had read looped in her mind unceasingly.

The cove is quiet now…she hums the tune more often…

Could it really be that cove—The one in Aria's letter? She scoured harder.

"Easy, pup," said a sailor behind her. "You'll take the bottom off."

Beatrix didn't turn. It was Melvin. He was tall and wiry, with the look of a man who smiled at storms. He'd taken to teasing her during galley duty. He was always nearby, watching.

Another sailor laughed. "He's sweet on the new cabin pup."

"Only if he cleans up nice," said a third. "Maybe we should give him a proper rinse."

Beatrix stiffened but kept her eyes down. The captain had warned her once already that if she caused another stir, she'd be cast off the ship at the next port, if not thrown overboard.

Still, their words needled her, not because they were cruel, but because she knew they suspected something. She was too clean, too quiet, and too strange.

"Oi, Trix." Melvin leaned over the barrel beside her. "Where'd you learn to speak so fine, eh? Steal a tutor's coat when you ran off?"

"I read the labels on the whiskey bottles," she muttered.

Laughter rolled around the galley. Even Cook chuckled from his chopping block.

"You've got spirit," Melvin said as he clapped her shoulder. "That's why we like you."

She ducked away from his hand and dumped another pan into the rinse water.

What she really wanted was to be alone so she could think about the journal and her next steps. She tried to recall every word she'd seen and recount every detail from the pages the captain had forgotten to close.

Instead, she scrubbed.

After the galley was cleaned, she slipped into the shadows behind the storage barrels and took her locket out of its hiding place beneath her linen shirt. The silver felt warm against her palm, and the etching at its edge had become familiar, almost dear.

Her thoughts returned to the cove.

The journal had spoken of humming…and of Aria. She had to get back into that cabin somehow. She had to read more. Maybe her key to getting to Calverique lay in the journal. She knew she would eventually need to get off this ship and make her journey on her own, but she had no idea how.

She sighed and turned her thoughts back to the captain. He was not the simple merchant sailor he pretended to be. His silence, the private meals, and the careful way he'd shut the journal the moment her eyes wandered—none of it fit.

That journal shouldn't even exist. Arabella Loraine had died at sea. Beatrix had heard the stories her whole life: Arabella, her husband, and their entire crew died in a shipwreck. There were no survivors. There was nothing but wreckage on the tide.

So how did this man have her journal?

She stared at the locket resting in her palm. The locket, the map, the song, the letters in Aria's room, and now this journal—they were all leading her towards *something.*

Beatrix made a silent plan. When they reached the next harbor, she would stay on the ship while the crew took their shore leave. Then, she would sneak into the captain's cabin and read the journal.

***

The Tempest rocked gently in Madeira's harbor. Beatrix crept across the deck cautiously, veiled in shadows. Most of the crew had left the ship to seek the port's pleasures. She had waited, watched, and gambled on the chance that the captain had gone with them. She hadn't seen him since they arrived in port.

She reached the captain's door and hesitated. Her heart pounded. The handle was stiff, but it gave; he had left his cabin unlocked. The door hinges groaned softly as she slipped inside and shut the door quietly behind her.

The room smelled of him: a mix of leather, saltwater, and a musky aroma all his own. A lantern burned low on the table, casting golden light over its cluttered surface. Charts, quills, and a rolled length of canvas covered most of the table, but in the center lay the journal.

Beatrix crossed the floor silently. She walked on her tiptoes to keep her footfalls light. She ran her fingers over the cracked leather cover. The interlocking rings pressed into its surface were unmistakable.

She opened the journal.

The first page bore a name, written with careful elegance: *Arabella Loraine.*

The air in her lungs vanished in a sharp gasp. The following few pages were dated, but the ink had run where it had mixed with saltwater. The edges of the pages were warped, as though the journal had once been soaked and then left to dry in the sun. She turned to a passage mid-way through:

Aria sings it still. The tune haunts her, though she cannot know its meaning yet. I hum it too, sometimes, when the night is warm and the wind carries the scent of lilies. Has Althea taught it to her daughter? If the lockets are ever found again, it will be up to them.

The words blurred. She turned to the back cover of the book, where pages were stuck together. A crude map was scrawled hastily. It was hand-drawn and faded; the coastlines were smudged. The symbol of the interlocked rings remained in one corner. On her mother's map, this symbol had been written above the name of the island, Calverique. This map resembled an earlier, more primitive version of the same map.

She leaned closer, squinting in the darkness.

"You've taken quite an interest in my belongings."

The voice sent a shiver down her spine. Beatrix snapped upright and turned. The captain stood inside the doorway with one hand still resting on the latch.

His coat hung from his shoulders, his collar was undone, and his face was shadowed beneath the brim of his hat. The smell of whiskey clung to him, betraying his former whereabouts.

He stepped forward and shut the door behind him.

"Well?" he said, quietly. "Care to explain?"

"I—I didn't touch anything," she stammered.

"No?" He crossed to the table and closed the journal with one hand. "Then I suppose it opened itself."

Beatrix said nothing.

The captain studied her. For the first time, she caught the steel beneath the calm in his grey eyes. "You read Latin fluently. You speak like a boy who's never seen the inside of a shipyard but could quote Cicero."

"I listen," she said quickly. "I pick things up."

"Where did you learn to read like that?"

"My father was a clerk."

"A clerk," he repeated, unimpressed. "A clerk who paid for elocution lessons…or was that the tutor you apprenticed?"

She tensed.

"You've been on this ship for nearly a fortnight," he said. "You scrub well, you keep your head down, but you don't move like the rest. You're educated...almost noble. You think I wouldn't notice?"

He leaned forward slightly, voice lowering. "What are you really running from, boy? It can't be a simple wedding. You are clever enough to have found another way out without running to the shipyards."

Beatrix swallowed.

He studied her a moment longer. Something unreadable crossed his face. Then he stepped back and slid the journal into a drawer.

"You're lucky I don't toss you into the harbor for trespassing."

"I just wanted to see," she said. "You always look at it like it's the most interesting thing you've ever seen."

"That's none of your concern," he said flatly.

She nodded.

"Get out," he said, and turned his back.

Beatrix slipped through the door without another word. Her pulse hammered in her ears.

***

The door clicked shut behind her, and Beatrix pressed her back to the wall of the corridor. Her heart pounded in her chest like the beat of distant war drums.

She should have been caught in the act, thrown overboard, dismissed at this seedy port, or worse, but he had let her go. It wasn't mercy, she was certain. Rather, it was because he did not yet know what to make of her.

Neither did she.

She crept back to the crew quarters. They were empty, so she climbed into her hammock and folded her arms. She stared at the ship's ceiling as though answers might rise from the planks' grain.

Arabella Loraine—the journal's owner—was her aunt and Aria's mother. She could barely remember Arabella; she had been a very young child when Arabella had died. Why did the captain treasure the journal so much? Why did he keep it so close? Was he a collector of lost treasures, looking for her lost ship's cargo, or was it more than that?

She wrapped her arms around her knees and rested her chin atop them. He had called her educated. He noticed her speech. He had questioned her, but let her go. She would have to be more careful now.

She thought again about the journal's cover. That Latin phrase still echoed in her mind—Where blood falls, truth rises. The truth had to be in that journal. Did Arabella know where to find Calverique?

He knew more than he admitted. She had seen it in his steely grey eyes, behind the questions he fired at her; he was looking for answers too.

She clenched her hands into fists. If he would not let her read the journal, then she would have to take it…without getting caught.

At the next port, she would find a way off this ship. She would disappear into the streets—she would hide in a barrel if she must—and then she would find a merchant vessel bound for anywhere near those islands on her mother's map. She could figure it out; she had made it this far.

She would be gone before the captain even noticed.

CHAPTER 6

The door clicked shut, but Gus didn't move. He stood in the center of his quarters. The journal still rested on the table, its corners were damp from where she'd left her fingers. The flickering lamplight cast soft shadows across the room as always, but his thoughts stirred far darker ones.

The boy, Trix, had nerve...and skill. He had crept into a locked room and had nearly made off with the journal. It had survived fire, submersion in seawater, and time...and now this.

He lowered himself slowly into the chair and rubbed his temple. The lad had quoted Latin, not hesitantly, not phonetically, but with perfect pronunciation. The phrase had slipped from his lips with ease, as if he had been raised among books and classical tutors. Gus had known men born to high towers with less fluency.

So, who was he?

He glanced again at the journal. The symbol of the intertwined rings glinted faintly in the lamplight. He had read the inscription a dozen times. He had felt the familiar pain settle low in his chest as he traced Arabella's words with a finger hardened by rope and sun. She had died at sea, swallowed by the same depths that had nearly taken him on countless occasions. Yet the journal had surfaced and passed into his hands through impossible luck...or fate.

Suspicion twisted in Gus's gut.

Trix. It was too neat a name, and too convenient. The boy's hands were delicate but callused. He was soft-spoken, but clever. He had slipped past three doors, two guards, and the ship's most private threshold. No green sailor learned that overnight.

He tapped the journal's cover with his brow furrowed. "Who sent you?" he murmured aloud.

Was it his father?

Gus scowled. He hadn't seen the old man in years, but this—this would be just the sort of intrigue the Earl of Falmouth might orchestrate. Maybe it was a quiet prod to test the boundaries, to see if the heir was worthy once more. It wouldn't be the first time a servant had come wrapped in borrowed clothing and vague purpose, but this one was different. This one knew something. Maybe he didn't know everything. Perhaps he didn't know enough to be dangerous…yet.

Gus rose and crossed the room. He opened the drawer where he kept the journal. His fingers hovered over it for a breath too long. Then, carefully, he locked the drawer and added the key to the belt at his waist. He would not be caught off guard again.

Whoever Trix was—boy or spy or runaway noble—he was aboard *The Tempest* now. Gus would see what shook loose when the sea took hold of him.

***

Beatrix worked from dawn to dusk in a perpetual rhythm of scrubbing, hauling, and enduring crude remarks she dared not challenge. Her fingers were raw and her temper was frayed, but her purpose—to steal the journal and get off this ship—held her focused.

Each evening, she balanced a tray and climbed the narrow steps to the captain's quarters with his supper, and each evening, he greeted her with less civility than the night before.

"Try not to spit in it," he'd muttered once without looking up.

Tonight, he merely narrowed his eyes and took the tray from her hands. He had studied her face a little too long before shutting the door.

Beatrix clenched her jaw as she descended the steps. He suspects her of something, but of what, she wasn't entirely sure. She hadn't dared another peek at the journal since Madeira. The memory made her cheeks burn with equal parts shame and fury.

She returned to her duties, dodging elbows and jeers. Her ruse held—for now, but it would not forever. The crew had begun muttering about her soft hands and strange manners. One sailor had tried to trip her; another had tried worse. She had fought him off with a fire iron and earned a black eye for her trouble.

She'd need to leave when they reached Santiago. That much was certain. She would take the journal, disappear in the crowd, and find the truth on her own.

A week passed in that endless rhythm: wind, work, whispers and watchfulness.

Then came the morning the bell rang in two sharp, fast clangs. Shouts echoed from the upper deck. Beatrix abandoned her half-peeled potatoes and scrambled to investigate the commotion. The lookout pointed toward the horizon. "Dead ahead, Captain!" He called. She shielded her eyes from the sun's glare and struggled to make out a dark shape cutting across the glittering sea.

It was a ship—a big ship. She could tell it was a much bigger ship than *The Tempest.* The crew burst into motion.

She turned to see the captain standing at the helm. He was as calm as fate itself; untouchable, as if the Fates had already cut his enemies' thread. His voice rang clear through the storm of panic, as sharp as a blade drawn in judgment.

"Run out the guns and prepare for boarding."

The first mate, Callahan, faltered for only a heartbeat. "Captain, she's flying no colors."

"She has no need," the captain replied. His gaze was unflinching. "We will fly ours first."

"Aye, captain," Callahan answered, signaling to the crew to strike their colors.

The crew around Beatrix went still. Slowly, the Union Flag slid down the mast and was replaced by a length of black cloth that snapped open in the wind. A red flag followed; its color bled menacingly against the sky. The men stiffened. Callahan's voice rang out hard and certain. "No quarter! No mercy!"

Beatrix felt the blood drain from her face.

Pirates.

They were *pirates.*

She had fled one prison only to find herself trapped aboard a ship of thieves and killers. She staggered back a step and nearly collided with the mast. The locket around her neck felt suddenly heavy. Her thoughts scattered in every direction.

She turned again and caught sight of the captain—Gus, as Callahan sometimes called him. The name felt far too small for the man at the helm. He stood as if sculpted from marble. His dark coat snapped in the wind. His gaze fixed on the horizon with the calm certainty of one chosen by the gods. Disciplined, waiting fury lived in his bones. It was a fire that called to mind Ares himself: handsome, commanding, and terrible in his stillness. A hand clapped her shoulder and she nearly leaped from her skin. It was Callahan.

"Eyes wide now, boy," he said, grinning like a wolf. "Best stay low. It's about to get exciting."

***

The enemy ship loomed larger now. She carried thirty guns to *The Tempest's* twenty, but she rode heavy and sluggish. That would be her downfall.

Gus stood at the helm with eyes fixed on the horizon. He had traded his coat for a leather vest. His sleeves were rolled high, and his sword hung ready at his side. The salt wind lashed strands of golden, sun-bleached hair from its tie, and the burn of anticipation flickered behind his calm expression.

"They're aiming high," Callahan called from the gundeck. He watched the enemy through his spyglass. "They're trying to clip our sails."

"Let them try." Gus waited with his hand steady on the wheel. He calculated the wind, the angle, and the arrogance of a vessel that thought it could outmatch him.

A cry went up from the rigging. "Shots fired!"

The first volley hit just short. Splinters exploded from the railings.

"Return fire!" Gus's voice rang out clear and strong. It held both steadfast calm and unmistakable urgency. "Starboard side—aim for their helm!"

The Tempest's gunners roared to life. Six-pounders thundered across the waves. Beatrix, crouched near a coil of rope, flinched at the crack of cannon fire and the acrid cloud of gunpowder.

"Brace!" someone shouted.

Another blast rocked the ship as iron tore through the air. The captain did not so much as flinch. Beatrix stared at him, transfixed. Until now, she had seen only the shadowed, brooding man who haunted his own decks. But here, in the fire and thunder of battle, he was transformed. The threat of death did not shake him—it awakened him.

The enemy vessel closed in. Its timbers groaned as its hull scraped perilously near. Shapes massed along the other deck. Silhouettes bristled with steel. Every man coiled like a predator about to spring.

"Grapples!" shouted Callahan. "They mean to board!"

"Let them," Gus said steadily as he drew his sword in one quick, clean motion. "Ready arms!"

The clash was immediate; the enemy's lines flew, and their hooks landed. The ships rocked as they collided, hull to hull. Wood bit into wood. The men screamed their battle cries and their pistols fired. They came swinging over the rails with their faces masked and their blades drawn.

Gus was the first to meet them. His sword split air and flesh with brutal efficiency. He moved like a man possessed; his actions were controlled, precise, and utterly without mercy. One attacker lunged, but Gus parried with a twist and drove his blade up under the man's ribs. Another charged, with a pistol raised. Gus ducked, grabbed the man's coat, and slammed him against the mast. Blood slicked the deck, and still he fought on.

Beatrix watched from the shadows, paralyzed. She had seen death before, when her mother struggled for breath and then finally struggled no more. Death for her was peace. It was nothing like this. Gun smoke, severed body parts, and blood spilled as far as her eyes could see.

A hand grabbed her arm. "Get below, fool!" It was Callahan. His brow was bloodied, but she couldn't tell if it was his blood or someone else's that stained it. He shoved her toward the galley hatch, then turned to fire his pistol into the gut of a boarding pirate.

She ran.

Once she was down the stairs, the noise from the battle dulled into a low roar. The ship rocked with every crashing wave and every body that fell. Beatrix slid against the wall and pressed her back to it. Her heart was pounding. The locket around her neck burned against her chest.

Above decks, the battle raged. Gus drove the enemy captain to the quarterdeck and met him blade for blade. They were equally matched in strength, but not in resolve. Gus fought with the rage of the betrayed and the bitterness of a noble son turned outlaw. With a final strike, he wrenched the enemy's sword aside and plunged his own blade clean through the enemy's gullet. The body crumpled.

Silence followed. The deck was littered with the wounded and the dead. Gus stood amidst the ruin with his chest heaving and his face streaked with blood. None of it was his. The black flag flapped overhead, indifferent to victory.

Callahan emerged and wiped his blade. "What shall we do with the ship, captain?"

"Scuttle it," Gus said coldly. "Take anything worth selling, then send her down."

He turned and looked toward the stairs where the new cabin boy had vanished. *That one's hiding something*, he thought. *And I will find out what.*

***

Beatrix crouched behind a row of barrels in the dim galley with her arms wrapped tightly around her knees. Her palms were slick with sweat, and the pounding of her heart threatened to echo louder than the gun fire that finally seemed to have ceased.

It had been a slaughter.

She had seen it in the captain's eyes—a glint of something cold and untouchable. He was no merchant. He was a pirate, and she was trapped on a ship full of them.

A loud creak snapped her from her thoughts. She froze. Someone else was down there.

She heard a scuffling sound, followed by footsteps on the wood. It wasn't coming from the deck above, and it definitely wasn't from one of *The Tempest's* crew. Whoever it was hadn't come down through the hatch. He had hidden himself, like she had, and now he knew she was there.

"Who's skulking?" came a voice that was low, ragged, and unfamiliar. It wasn't Irish, like most of the crew, nor any other accent she knew. "Come out, boy, or I'll find you with my blade."

She didn't move.

A knife flashed between the barrels. He had found the gap.

In one swift motion, she scrambled out, only to be caught by the front of her shirt. The man was tall and gaunt. Blood was smeared across his temple, and one of his eyes was swollen nearly shut.

"I knew I saw a rat scurry," he sneered. "You'll do fine."

"Let go," she rasped as she struggled against his grip.

He slammed her into the wall and pressed his cutlass against her throat. "Not a word. You're going to earn me safe passage at the next port, or you'll bleed out right here."

Her knees buckled. Above them, the sound of the crew cheering in victory filtered down through the deck.

"You think they'll trade for a cabin boy?" She managed to get out and instantly regretted it. What logic was it to make herself disposable?

He hissed, "They will if he's pretty."

He yanked her forward and dragged her toward the ladder. She kicked at the steps and clawed for a handhold, but his grip only tightened.

On deck, the sun burned too bright. The crew turned with mild curiosity until they saw the bloodied man holding a knife to Beatrix's chest.

"Back off!" he shouted. His eyes were wide and manic. "I want safe passage! Let me off at the next port or this one dies!"

Callahan drew his pistol. Others followed suit.

Gus emerged from the quarterdeck like a shadow slipping from the rigging. His sword was still in his hand.

The pirate pressed the blade harshly against Beatrix's shirt.

"I'll do it!" he yelled. "Don't test me!"

In a single, panicked moment, her captor's cutlass sliced downward. The fabric of her shirt gave way with a tear that sounded far too loud. Beatrix gasped.

The locket slipped into view, and so did the band of linen she'd used to bind her chest. It was now severed and hanging precariously open.

There was silence, then a murmur.

Gus's eyes fixed on his enemy with a searing stare. His hand tightened on the hilt of his sword. His voice came commanding and deadly. "Let. Him. Go."

The man blinked, confused. Then he looked again. "Her, you mean?"

A fist cracked against the pirate's skull before he could say more. Callahan stepped forward and yanked him backward by the collar and dragged him to the deck as Beatrix stumbled away. Her arms crossed protectively over her torn shirt.

Someone tossed a cloak around her. She couldn't see who.

Gus stood frozen with his steely grey eyes fixed, not on her face, but on the locket that now gleamed in the sunlight.

Beatrix clutched the edges of the cloak and fled below deck.

***

Gus had not moved.

The crew murmured restlessly as they awaited his order, but he only stared at the boy—no, not a boy—huddled beneath the brown cloak.

How did she have that locket? It swung as she fled, catching the sunlight in a brief, traitorous glint.

He knew it instantly. It was the same locket Aria had worn every day he knew her. She had pressed it into his palm as her life's blood drained from her body.

"Take it," she had whispered. Then she had sung the song—*The Compass Waltz*—the one she had hummed to herself day in and day out. Her voice had cracked in pain as she gasped the words. She needed him to hear the lyrics, but he could only hold her in his arms and beg her to live.

He had worn it around his neck for years when grief still ruled him. Now, it sat hidden in the chest beneath his bunk...or so he thought. Had this girl stolen the locket that night in Madeira when he found her in his cabin?

Callahan's voice came through the haze. "Captain? What do we do with the prisoner?"

The bloodied sailor lay groaning on the deck. Gus did not answer. Instead, he turned and walked away.

Each step felt leaden, as though the weight of memory had wrapped chains around his ankles.

In his quarters, he shut the door with more force than necessary. He went straight to the chest that held the locket, expecting to find it missing. To his surprise and relief, the locket was waiting in its place, with Aria's letters, and a bundle of dried flowers she had picked on one of their walks many years ago.

He turned the locket in his hand. It was a perfect match for the one around Trix's (was her name still Trix?) neck.

A dozen possibilities stormed his mind. Where did she get it? Had she stolen it? Had it been passed down from one of her relatives? Was she kin to Aria? Or had she merely stumbled into something far older and far more profound than she understood?

The girl had lied to him, but not well enough.

***

Gus's boots pounded the deck as he stormed to the galley. His shirt was soaked with sweat and blood, and a cut along his shoulder seared, but not nearly as hot as his temper. His palm burned where the silver locket pressed into his skin.

He found her in the galley, still clutching her torn shirt closed. She looked small, stunned, and cornered, but not afraid. That infuriated him.

"Strip," he ordered.

She backed away, clutching the brown cloak around her protectively.

He crossed the space between them and grabbed the locket around her neck. "I'm not here for games. I've seen this before."

Her eyes widened.

"Someone died," he said, his voice thick with fury. "She died in my arms, and before she did, she gave me this." He opened his other hand. An identical silver locket rested there, tarnished and caked with dirt. A startled breath escaped her lips.

He stepped closer. His rage simmered just beneath the surface. "Now tell me, who are you really?"

"I was a maid at Brackwater. My mistress, Althea, died. She gave me the locket. I didn't know it had any sort of meaning."

"You didn't know?" His voice was a whip crack. "You wear a noblewoman's silver locket while scrubbing dishes in my galley, and you didn't think that meant anything?"

She hesitated.

"Why are you running?" he demanded.

She stiffened, straightening. "I was meant to be married to a man three times my age. I'd rather drown than be his wife."

He stopped inches from her. The heat rolled off his body. She could smell the blood and sweat on his skin, the brine in his unwashed shirt, and the iron of the blade still at his side. His breath came hard through his nose, and for one harrowing second, she thought he might reach out and shake the truth out of her.

Instead, he leaned in, with a voice low and dangerous.

"Do you know what this is?" He held up Arabella's journal. "There's a map at the back—one that someone died protecting. Do you know anything about that?"

"No," she said too quickly. "I've never seen it."

He studied her. Her cheeks were flushed, and her green eyes were sharp despite the lies.

He didn't know whether he wanted to throttle her or pin her to the nearest wall, but one thing was certain. "You're off this ship at the next port," he growled. "I don't care who you really are."

He turned toward the door, then paused. "Until then, you can rot in the brig."

He grabbed her arm, none too gently, and hauled her after him. He shoved open the heavy door and pushed her inside. The iron bars clanged behind her.

She landed hard on the floor, right beside the unconscious pirate who'd tried to take her hostage moments earlier.

"Get comfortable," Gus said. "You've earned your stay."

He locked the door and walked away without a second glance.

***

Gus slammed the door to his cabin. The chaos of battle still echoed through his bones, and the girl's—no, the boy's—no, whatever she was—face would not leave his thoughts.

He tossed the silver locket and journal onto the table. Both shimmered smugly in the lantern light. Trophies. Ghosts.

He tore off his bloodied shirt and tossed it across the room. His shoulder burned where a blade had skimmed him in the fray, but he barely felt it. His boots followed, then the rest of the grime-soaked remnants of battle, until he stood bare before the wash basin.

The tin basin had been filled by someone earlier. It steamed faintly. He plunged his hands in, then splashed the water over his chest and face. It ran pink, then red…a swirling mess of carnage.

He had worn sweat and blood before, but not like this. Her scent was tangled in it. Her voice echoed in his mind as sharp and bright as cut glass.

She was lying, but not well. Her hands had trembled, just slightly, when he mentioned the map. And that locket…it was too perfect a match to be a coincidence.

He scrubbed harder.

There had been a time when he would have smiled at a secret kept in a corset or a clever lie on the lips of a woman, but this wasn't that. This was something different.

A knock at the cabin door dragged him out of his thoughts.

"What?" he barked.

Callahan entered anyway. His shirt was torn, and he bore a fresh bruise above one brow, but otherwise looked unbothered by the fact that they'd nearly lost the main mast and half their crew earlier that day.

"She's no sailor," Callahan said plainly.

Gus ran a hand through his wet hair. Water dripped from his jaw. "You don't say."

"But she's got grit." He leaned against the wall. "She held her own with you in the galley, and you can't discount that she stood up to an enemy's blade. She didn't scream; she didn't even beg."

"She's a liar," Gus muttered.

Callahan's mouth twitched. "Most of us are."

Gus turned away and reached for a towel. "She's hiding something."

Callahan nodded slowly. "Aye. You think she's here for you?"

"I don't know." The captain's voice was quiet. "I don't like what I don't know."

Callahan glanced toward the table where the locket and journal sat. He didn't ask. He never did.

"I could press her," he offered. "Friendly-like. Or not."

Gus shook his head. "No. Not yet. She will slip up soon enough."

Callahan hesitated at the door. "And if she doesn't?"

Gus stared at the journal. "Then we reach Santiago, and she walks."

"You sure you want her walking off?"

Gus didn't answer.

Callahan let the silence stretch before he shrugged. "Dinner's in the galley if you want it."

"I'll eat here.

"Thought you might." Callahan paused. "You missed a spot."

Then he was gone, leaving Gus in the dim light with wash water drying on his skin. The echoes of a girl—who used to be a boy—sunk sharp hooks into his thoughts.

CHAPTER 7

In the brig, Beatrix sat on a rough bench with her knees tucked beneath her. Her shirt, now hastily tied, still clung damply to her chest. She had not slept. Between the roll of the ship, the ache in her back, and the slow throb of fear in her belly, rest had proven impossible. But the worst of it—worse than the cold, worse than the damp—had been the locket.

The captain had seen it. He had one of his own. She traced her thumb over hers. The key to all of these secrets was in that journal. She knew it. He planned to cast her out at the next port, so how would she get to the journal while locked in the brig?

Above her, heavy boots approached, and then the brig door opened. Callahan stood in front of her, holding a ring of keys. "On your feet, Trix. You're being let out."

She narrowed her eyes. "Why?"

He shrugged. "Captain's orders."

"Changed his mind?"

Callahan scratched his jaw. "He didn't say that exactly, but you're not doing anyone any good locked up. The galley's got dishes to wash, and the sails need mending. We've no space aboard for idle hands nor idle grudges."

She rose cautiously, smoothing her trousers and lifting her chin. "He's still going to throw me off at Santiago."

"Likely." Callahan stepped back as the cell creaked open. "But I wouldn't make it easy for him."

Beatrix followed him up to the deck. She blinked as the morning light struck her face. She hadn't seen the sky since before the battle. It looked deceptively peaceful now: blue, endless, and empty.

Two men stepped into the brig as she and Callahan left. They emerged moments later, carrying the unconscious pirate who had held her hostage. They threw him over the rail without ceremony. She barely heard a splash, but there was no mistaking that he was gone.

When she stepped into the galley, sailors paused their duties just long enough to watch her pass. She didn't meet their eyes. She found a mop and started scrubbing. She pushed her sleeves back and set her jaw. Let them watch. Let them whisper. She was still here.

***

In his cabin, Gus stood at the porthole. His tea cooled beside him, untouched. The ship had steadied, but he had not.

He had not slept either. Every time he closed his eyes, he saw the flash of the blade, the silver locket catching the light, and the way her lips had parted when he'd cornered her and demanded answers she hadn't been ready to give. She had lied, but she had not begged.

Callahan knocked once before entering. "She's working," he said. Gus nodded.

"Still think she's here for your father?"

"I don't know." Gus picked up the locket again—his locket—and turned it over in his palm. "But she has something to do with this. I feel it."

"And if she does?"

Gus's eyes flicked to the journal on the table. "Then I'll find out, one way or another."

Callahan hesitated. "She's not what I expected, that's all."

"She's not what any of us expected," Gus muttered.

Callahan left, and Gus returned to the window. Somewhere below deck, the girl with the silver locket was scrubbing blood from the floorboards.

***

The mop slapped against the planks. It soaked up dirt, blood, and soap in equal measure. Beatrix worked steadily, keeping her eyes down and her ears open. Sailors passed behind her, muttering, joking, and barking orders. None of them bothered her anymore; not openly, at least.

She was wringing out the mop a final time when Callahan's boots appeared beside her. He crossed his arms and waited until she looked up.

"You've been summoned," he said.

Beatrix narrowed her eyes. "Summoned?"

"For dinner...with the captain."

She blinked. "Why?"

"Do I look like a man who asks questions when he's getting his way?" He smirked, then added, "It's not a request, Trix. Clean yourself up. You've got about an hour."

She straightened. Her heart quickened. "In what, precisely? I only have one shirt, and it's cut wide open."

He tilted his head. "Lucky you, then. Turns out our late visitors were transporting some...exotic goods. We found a crate of silk gowns. They're a bit rumpled, but should be your size or close enough. You can have the lot of them."

He gestured over his shoulder. "They're in storage aft. Pick what you like."

She stared at him, suspicious. "Why are you being so nice to me?"

"I'm not," he said mildly. "I'm giving you orders, and so is the captain. You can wear rags to dinner if you like, but I don't recommend it."

She pressed her lips together. "May I ask what this is about?"

"I'd guess he's trying to figure out whether to strangle you, thank you, or toss you into the sea."

"Charming."

"Captains don't like puzzles they can't solve," he said. "And you, Trix, are the strangest puzzle we've had aboard in years."

***

Beatrix's heart thudded as she stood outside the captain's cabin door. She had chosen an amber colored gown that was embroidered with gold thread that shimmered faintly in the dim light. It had been made for someone taller, but it suited her well enough. She had managed to sweep her too-short-to-be-fashionable copper hair into an elegant twist.

She raised her hand to knock, hesitated, then drew a steadying breath and rapped lightly at the door.

"Enter," came the voice from within.

The door creaked open. The captain sat at the table with a half-filled goblet of wine in his hand and the journal lying closed beside him. His shirt was unlaced just enough to reveal the hollow of his throat, and his golden hair was still damp from washing. He looked at her—really looked—and said nothing for several long seconds.

"You clean up well," he said at last.

"And you are…clean," she replied as she stepped inside. "A rare condition, I gather."

That earned a faint twitch of amusement. He gestured toward the chair opposite him. "Sit. Eat."

Dinner was already waiting. They supped on roasted meat, crusty bread, soft cheese, and a bowl of sliced fruit that must have been bartered at port or pilfered from aboard yesterday's enemy ship. The wine was dark and heady, and most likely stolen as well.

They ate mostly in silence, with the rhythm of cutlery and wind against sails being the only sounds between them. Once, their eyes met across the table. Neither smiled.

After a time, he leaned back in his chair and drank deeply.

"You're a liar," he said.

She set her goblet down. "You're a pirate."

The corner of his mouth curved. "Fair point."

"I didn't know," she said. "Not until the black flags were raised. I assumed you were merchants or maybe smugglers, but not…whatever that was."

"And yet you signed on."

"O'Malley never mentioned you raided other ships."

His gaze sharpened. "So, you didn't intend to be on my ship."

She said nothing, which was answer enough.

"I have a crew of fifty men, most of whom will slit your throat if they begin to think you are a curse…or worse, drag you to their bunks."

She clenched her teeth, but she held his gaze.

"I can't keep you in the brig," he continued. "Not if we're to reach Santiago without bloodshed. I don't have a second mate, so there are officers' quarters standing empty.

She blinked.

He stood, walked to the far side of the room, and opened a second door. "They're small, but private. Callahan's cabin is on the other side. You'll sleep here. No one else is to enter. If anyone asks, you've been promoted."

"To what?" she asked dryly.

"Something slightly less expendable. Captain's secretary, perhaps?"

She stepped inside the room. There was a small bed, a chest, and a small desk. It was cleaner than the galley floor and far more dignified than the brig.

He remained in the doorway, watching her. "I've ordered a bath to be brought for you."

She turned, one brow raised. "How generous."

His voice dropped. "If I meant to be generous, I'd join you."

Her lungs locked tight as she realized his meaning, but she said nothing.

He lingered for one heartbeat more, then turned and walked away.

***

Gus shut the cabin door with more force than necessary. He stood for a moment in the quiet. He stared at nothing with his jaw clenched and his blood still running too hot. *That damned gown*, he thought.

She had no right to wear it like that. She had no right to look like a high-born duchess one moment and a storm-swept stowaway the next. Her hair had gleamed like polished copper in the lanternlight. Her posture was proud despite the filth she'd scrubbed these last few weeks.

He tossed his coat across the chair, poured another measure of wine, and drank half of it before setting the goblet down again.

She had lied, of course, about her name, her origins, and even the wedding she fled. He didn't believe a word of the lady's maid's story. Her hands were soft in the wrong places, and her words were too refined. She was far too quick with her tongue to have come up through the servant ranks. None of that mattered tonight. What mattered was the crew.

He had seen how they looked at her after the battle: half with suspicion, and half with hunger. Women were considered bad luck aboard most vessels, and while his crew was more seasoned than superstitious, long voyages bred trouble. Even now, men were joking in the shadows and murmuring in corners. It would not take much—just one drunken challenge or one snide remark—and she would become a target too tempting to ignore. Gus would not have it.

If he meant to keep her alive, he would have to make his claim known. He would not make a public declaration; that would only fan the fire. He had to create a silent understanding that she belonged to him.

He rolled the word across his tongue: *Mine.*

It thrilled him more than it should have. It wasn't just protection. There was something else; it was the way she had faced him earlier, standing in his doorway like a storm in silk, and the way she had held her ground even after he saw the locket.

It was a cursed, gleaming twin to the one Aria had pressed into his hand before she died. There were too many questions and not enough answers.

One thing was sure: If he wanted to keep her safe, she would need to be under his protection. He would keep her close and find out what secrets she carried.

CHAPTER 8

The next morning brought calmer seas, clearer skies, and a fresh round of work. Beatrix quickly realized her duties had shifted. Callahan had met her just after dawn with a crooked smile and a towel over one shoulder.

"You're off galley duty," he said. "Cook says you scrub floors like a poet. Couldn't stomach watchin' you at it anymore."

"I suppose you have something more dignified in mind?"

"Of course not," Callahan grinned. "But I've got an eye for wasted talent. You'll assist with stores and inventory midship. It's still quiet work, but with fewer pots thrown at your head."

She accepted the change with a grateful nod. Her knuckles were still raw from scrubbing, and her pride had taken enough bruising for one voyage.

Now that her secret was out, the men no longer looked at her like a mystery to be solved. Instead, they offered smirks, sidelong glances, and muttered comments when they thought she wasn't listening. She ignored them all. She still wore a dagger in her boot.

She had begun dressing like a woman again, sort of. All she had were the silk gowns stolen from another ship and none had been made with modesty in mind. There were no corsets aboard, no stays, and no chemises. There were only silk gowns that clung too easily to her body and teased scandal every time the wind lifted the hem, which meant she stayed below deck most of the day, tending stores and taking inventory in the cramped hold while Callahan kept watch topside.

That evening, as always, she delivered the captain's meal. Her hands no longer trembled on the tray. He no longer barked at her when she entered. They had settled into a strange, private rhythm.

She knocked once, and his voice called from within. "Enter."

He sat at the table with his jacket discarded and shirtsleeves rolled. The journal was tucked out of sight. His gaze tracked her as she crossed the cabin.

"You weren't on deck today," he said as she poured his wine.

She hesitated. Her back was to him, but she knew his eyes hadn't left her.

"No," she said, measuring her words. "I stayed below. The wind was… difficult."

"Difficult?"

Her cheeks were warm when she faced him. "There were no undergarments in the crate of dresses your men so proudly stole. I wore silk today. *Just* silk."

A beat passed. He didn't speak. He didn't breathe.

He reached for his wine, slowly and deliberately. His gaze was unreadable.

"I see," he said, though his voice had gone a shade deeper.

She sat across from him and focused intensely on her plate. She tried to pretend she hadn't just admitted that nothing but stolen silk lay between her and decency, and that the wind might reveal everything if it dared.

She caught him staring, just briefly, before he looked away.

"I'll have Callahan see what can be done," he said.

"I'm not asking for your pity."

"Pity isn't the word I'd use."

Their eyes met again. The air between them tightened like sailcloth in a storm.

He stood, slowly, as if testing his own control.

She didn't move. She held her breath as he came around the table and stopped just in front of her.

"I should tell you to leave," he murmured. "I should send you to the far end of the ship and never speak to you again."

She tilted her chin up, refusing to cower. "Then why don't you?"

His hand lifted hesitantly at first, then he boldly brushed a strand of her copper hair back from her cheek. His knuckles lingered against her jaw.

Beatrix swallowed.

"You wore blue," he said softly. "The color of storms and secrets."

"I wore what was available."

His thumb grazed the corner of her mouth with just a breath of a touch. She felt it like fire beneath her skin.

"I would not have chosen silk for you," he added, "but now I find I cannot imagine you in anything else."

She stepped back then, not far, but enough. "I'll see to your tray."

He let his hand fall. The contact was broken, but the heat of it clung to her skin.

She gathered the dishes with trembling fingers, all too aware of his gaze. As she turned to leave, his voice stopped her again.

"Your quarters still suit you?"

"Yes."

"Good," he said. "Because if any man looks at you in your half-naked state, I will cut out his eyes."

Beatrix's breath hitched.

She left without another word, but the silk dress made slight swooshing sounds as she exited the room.

Behind her, Gus poured another glass of wine with shaking hands and cursed every god who ever tempted a man with a fire he could not touch.

***

Beatrix slipped into her quarters and closed the door softly behind her. The candle on the table flickered in the draft from the corridor. She did not bother to relight it. The moonlight through the small porthole was enough to guide her steps. She let the silk gown fall from her shoulders and stepped carefully out of it. She folded it across the chair before sitting on the edge of her narrow bed, completely unclad. She would sleep in what was left of her linen shirt.

Her skin still tingled where his hand had touched her.

It had been a simple gesture, if anything about the captain could ever be called simple. She relived in her mind the brush of his knuckle and the warmth of his palm against her jaw. She thought about the way he looked at her afterward…as though he could set her aflame with nothing but the weight of his gaze.

He wanted her…and she was not immune.

Her fingers grazed the silver locket that never left her throat. Her thoughts tangled like storm-tossed rope. She should feel repulsed. He was a pirate—a man who flew black flags and ruled over murderers and thieves. He threatened, he brooded, and he wielded power like a blade. Yet, he had been gentle as he touched her.

Beatrix leaned her head back against the wall and closed her eyes.

Could she use that desire? Could she get closer to the journal, and closer to the truth she sought, without compromising what remained of her virtue? That thought twisted through her like cold water. She had fled a marriage built on coercion only to find herself ensnared by a gaze that promised ruin and wonder in equal measure.

She was a lady, after all. She was trained in decorum and schooled in poise. Her mother had told her once that a woman's best defense was not her silence, but her sense. She would need both if she were to survive this voyage.

And yet her lips still burned from the memory of his thumb brushing the corner of her mouth. She opened her eyes. She could not afford a distraction, but it was already far too late.

***

Beatrix stepped onto the deck at dawn. The sea was still silver as the sun's rays began to break the darkness. She gasped as a salty breeze lifted the hem of her white silk day dress. She gathered the folds quickly with one hand in an attempt to keep the wind from exposing all of her secrets. She exhaled slowly and moved toward the portside rail.

She thought about the journal, the map, and her mohter's instructions to go to Calverique. She thought about Gus—no, the captain. She had to keep her distance. She had seen the way his eyes lingered and the hunger he tried to mask beneath his commands. Desire was a dangerous currency, but one she might yet learn to wield.

She ran her fingers along the railing. It was cool and wet with dew. If she could play this game carefully, perhaps she could get another look at the journal. Perhaps she could even hold it in her hands long enough to—

"On deck rather early, aren't you?"

Beatrix spun, clutching her skirts to her knees.

The captain stood barefoot on the opposite side of the deck with his sleeves rolled to the elbow, and his white linen shirt clinging to the shape of his torso. Damp curls framed his face, and his eyes—unmistakably silver in the early light—scanned her with quiet intensity. He held a coil of rope in one hand, and the other rested at his hip.

She opened her mouth, but words failed her.

He took a step forward, then another, and then the ship pitched hard to starboard. A rogue wave sent a spray of seawater across the bow. Beatrix staggered, and her fingers slipped from the rail.

In an instant, he caught her by the waist. His hands were firm and steady; one splayed across her back and the other braced her shoulder. Her chest collided with his, and she gasped as she felt the heat of his body, his breath, and his unmistakable desire pressing against her through the wet linen of his breeches.

Her breath hitched. So did his.

The fabric of her dress had gone nearly transparent in the spray. She followed his gaze down and flushed scarlet.

He muttered a curse and turned his face away. "You should not be up here like this."

"I didn't expect—"

"That anyone would see?" His voice was rough now with a husky edge of restraint clear in every syllable. "Neither did I."

She moved to step back, but he didn't let her go. Their eyes met, and the moment hung. Then he let her go.

"Go below," he said through clenched teeth. "Before the crew wakes and sees more than they should."

She hesitated. "And if they already have?"

"Then they'll be answering to me."

She caught her breath again. There was more threat in his tone than tenderness, but not enough to hide the way he looked at her.

He turned back to the ropes. His voice was quieter now. "I'll see you at dinner."

She nodded and fled to her quarters, though he did not look up at her again.

***

Gus exhaled slowly and shakily as he ran a hand through his wet hair. *Hell*, he thought.

He gripped the nearest rope and braced himself against the rail. He steadied his breath and willed the tension in his gut to dissipate. It didn't. His eyes were still fixed on the hatch where she'd disappeared. The memory of her clung to him. He could still feel her startled gasp against his chest, burning hotter than the rising sun.

He was not a man easily undone, but there was something about this girl that rattled his reason. She was not meant to be on this ship. She was not meant to be in his cabin, reading journals that weren't hers. She was not meant to be under his protection, let alone pressed against him, flushed and trembling, with her scent tangled with salt water and something wholly feminine.

He swore under his breath. This wasn't a game anymore. She was becoming dangerous—not to the ship or its crew—but to him.

He forced his thoughts toward the day's duties. There were sails to check, charts to review, and the rudder to inspect. He had things to do. He had no time to chase silk-clad stowaways with secrets in their eyes.

As he walked the length of the deck, barking orders and overseeing the morning work, his mind stayed fixed on her. He couldn't shake the flash of her skin beneath white muslin, the heat of her breath against his chest, and the way she had looked at him, not with fear, but with challenge.

She didn't want to be on this ship? Fine. But the longer she stayed, the harder it became to imagine letting her go.

CHAPTER 9

With no proper undergarments to shield her modesty beneath the thin silk dresses, Beatrix kept to the shaded hold and the storerooms. She occupied herself with whatever tasks Callahan could dream up to keep her out of trouble—and off the deck.

She had mended sails until her fingers were raw. She matched thread to canvas and wove repairs with the precision of a lady whose most remarkable talent was needlework. She had taken inventory of the ship's cargo: smuggled spirits, rare spices, crates of sugar, and a mysterious set of boxes marked only with an unfamiliar crest. She had even assisted O'Malley with balancing the ledgers, though the old Irishman's eyes rarely lifted from her neckline long enough to count. Still, she endured it. She had a purpose.

Each evening she returned to the captain's quarters to deliver his supper, and each evening he studied her with more intensity. The captain had not spoken a word about the locket since the night of the battle, but she had seen the way his gaze lingered.

He was watching her and testing her. She, in turn, was watching him.

The journal still lay on the captain's table. He often left it open or half-shut. Its salt-stained pages fluttered when the wind passed through the porthole. The symbol of the intertwined rings on its cover seemed to pulse whenever she passed. She had to see more of what lay inside. She had to understand how it had come into his possession.

She wondered, more than once, if there were dozens of lockets like hers in the world. Maybe the captain's had belonged to someone else entirely. Maybe his connection to the journal had nothing to do with her family at all.

Her questions would go unanswered unless she played her part well. Temptation, she had decided, was a weapon like any other, and she would wield it.

***

The dress was indecent. It was also perfect.

Beatrix had chosen the deepest red silk she could find in the crate in the cargo hold. The bodice had built-in boning that clung scandalously to her figure, and it was held aloft by delicate gold-stitched. The skirts shimmered like swirling flame as she moved.

She had let her hair down for the first time since arriving on the ship. It curled in soft waves that framed her face and fell like fire across her shoulders. Even though it was shorter than she would have liked, it was still unmistakably feminine. The overall effect of her outfit was arresting. That was the point.

She knocked twice, firmly.

"Enter," came the voice from within.

The captain sat at the table, freshly shaven. His golden blond hair was still damp from a recent rinse. His linen shirt was unlaced at the collar, revealing just enough chest to suggest leisure, but his grey eyes were far from relaxed. They flicked over her slowly before he leaned back in his chair.

"You're overdressed for dinner."

Beatrix gave a half-smile and stepped inside. "Would you rather I returned to mending sails and smelling of pitch?"

He arched a brow but said nothing.

She placed the tray on the table and poured the wine herself, deliberately brushing the edge of his goblet with hers as she passed it. "To civility," she said softly.

He watched her. "I doubt you came here for civility."

They ate in silence for a time. The journal sat on the far corner of the table, closed, but present. Its worn leather binding caught the lanternlight like an invitation. She couldn't help but stare at it.

"You read Latin," he said suddenly; it was not quite a question.

She dabbed the corner of her mouth with her napkin. "You knew that."

"And you recognized the name inside the front cover."

"Arabella Loraine," she said. "My mistress's sister."

He studied her. "You read more than the cover."

"I've seen a few passages." She lifted her goblet again. "Enough to know she had secrets. I saw the map, the islands, and some cryptic messages."

He set his fork down with care. "Why are you really here?"

Beatrix met his gaze. "Because I ran from a life I didn't want. Because I was desperate enough to climb aboard a pirate ship dressed as a boy. Because I was curious."

"About the journal? Is that why you're on my ship? How did you even know I had it?"

She gave a slight shrug. "I didn't know you had it when I boarded your ship. I must say, though, sea life is boring. I've read stories about pirates having daring, swashbuckling adventures, but the truth is, other than one battle that lasted a single morning, your pirate's life is quite boring. The journal is the most interesting thing on this vessel. It's like a mystery novel."

His expression darkened. "It's not a story."

"It's someone's story," she said softly. "And it survived; that means something. Shouldn't we read it and try to solve the puzzles?"

"Not everything that survives should have."

Silence fell between them. The wine sat warm in her stomach. He was watching her too closely now. His elbows were on the table, and his hands steepled in front of his mouth, as if she were the puzzle in need of solving. She didn't let herself look away.

"I don't like being played," he said at last.

"I don't like being lied to," she countered.

"You lied first."

"So did you," she said. "You never told me you were a pirate."

He laughed—low and humorless. "Maybe I'm not."

There was a pause, and then his tone shifted and became rougher and more intimate.

"You read too well for a deckhand, or even a lady's maid. You speak too cleanly for the daughter of some clerk, and you wear that dress like you've been breaking hearts since the cradle."

Beatrix swallowed. "Perhaps I've had to adapt quickly."

He leaned forward. "And perhaps I ought to toss you off this ship before you poison my crew with whatever game you're playing."

The heat between them thickened. She rose slowly from her chair and walked to the journal. She stood behind him and leaned over his arm to reach it. The heat of her almost-touch stirred him as her hand hovered over the journal.

"I don't want to play a game," she whispered hotly, ever so close to his ear. "I want to know what happened to Arabella. I want to understand why this—" she met his steely gaze "—means so much to you."

He stood and moved behind her in a single breath.

"You're lying," he said.

She felt the heat of his body at her back, not quite touching her, but close enough that her skin tingled. "So are you."

His hand reached past her. His fingers brushed her arm as he took the journal and snapped it shut.

"Then we're even," he said darkly.

She turned to face him.

Their eyes locked. His breath was shallow. Her pulse thundered.

He was close—too close—and not moving away. His gaze dipped briefly to her lips, then lower. Her chest rose with the effort of keeping her composure.

Then his hand cupped her chin. His rough, calloused fingers felt hot against her jaw as he lifted her face just a fraction.

"Careful," he murmured. "You don't want to tempt me."

Beatrix didn't blink. "Don't I?"

He couldn't stand it anymore. His lips found hers, and he kissed her with all of the desire he had been hiding for the past two weeks since the rogue pirate slit open her shirt and revealed her as a girl. No, a woman. She was a grown woman in a silk dress with no undergarments. He groaned at that idea, entirely lost in the taste of her. His tongue parted her soft, delicate lips and found hers. She yielded to his every move as he deepened the kiss and let his passion free.

His hands tangled in her hair as she gripped his shirt like a lifeline. It took him several moments to remember himself. When they parted, breathless, the air between them vibrated. Neither moved.

Then he stepped back. His breathing was ragged.

"You should go," he said. "Before I forget all the reasons I shouldn't keep you."

Beatrix gathered what remained of her composure. She picked up the wineglass and took a long, deliberate sip.

"I'll see you at dinner tomorrow." Her voice was little more than a whisper as she left his cabin and closed the door quietly behind her.

She left him standing there, haunted, guilty, and starving for more.

***

The following sunrise rose gloriously over the sea. It spread rays of orange, gold, and purple across *The Tempest.* Gus stood at the helm for a long while. His hands rested on the worn wood, but his mind was not on the horizon. He could still taste her.

The kiss haunted him. His mind was filled with its softness, its urgency, and the way her lips had trembled before opening beneath his. It had been a mistake, and yet he would make it again if she so much as looked at him that way once more. He cursed under his breath and left the deck.

Below, the belly of the ship smelled of salt, fish, and old wood, and the dim lanterns barely lit the passageways. Most of the crew were busy above. Their boots stomped along the planks, as they made their preparations for the port ahead. He moved toward the aft section, where spare canvas and rope were stored. He didn't expect to find her there.

She sat cross-legged on the floor with a length of torn sail in her lap. She mended it with neat, careful stitches. Her hair had fallen from its pins, and a long curl brushed her collarbone each time she shifted. She was humming quietly, almost absently, but the tune struck him cold: *The Compass Waltz.*

She didn't see him at first. He watched, rooted to the spot, as something in his chest tightened with each note. That song belonged to Aria. Or rather, it had belonged to them both. She had sung it on every outing, from walks along the cliffs to lazy days lying in the grass while the waves crashed against the rocks beneath the cliffs. She had hummed it with her head in his lap, and finally, she had sung its lyrics as she bled out in his arms, with her voice faltering with each final breath.

Now Beatrix was humming it naturally, as if it lived in her bones. He stepped into the light.

She startled. "Captain," she said. Her voice caught as she set down the needle and sat up straighter. "I didn't hear you."

"No one's told you to stop working," he said, though his tone lacked its usual bite.

She nodded and reached again for the sail. He watched her hands for a moment. They were small, but strong and capable. This wasn't some nobleman's daughter flitting about in silks. She was surviving and doing so with more grace than he would have expected.

He exhaled, and the tension between them shifted into something unfamiliar: compassion.

"I'll be reading tonight," he said at last. "From the journal."

She looked up sharply.

"I'll allow you to join me, if you'd like."

The needle paused midair. "You'd let me?"

"I'd rather not read alone." His voice was soft now, and the corner of his mouth tugged into something almost resembling a smile. "But don't think this means I trust you."

"Of course not," she said. A ghost of a smile played at her lips as well.

He turned to go. "Wear something that doesn't make me regret the invitation."

***

The captain's quarters were dimly lit by a single lantern. Gus stood near the table with the journal in his hand. His linen shirt was rolled at the sleeves and slightly unbuttoned at the collar. Tonight, he wore his locket. It rested in the middle of his chest. The chain caught the lamplight as he turned.

Beatrix stepped into the room without knocking. Her presence was soft but confident. She wore a deep blue dress that glowed faintly in the warm light. Her hair was pinned again with care, though one loose strand curled near her cheek, almost as though it had escaped just to tempt him.

"You said you might read to me tonight," she said. Her voice was soft but unwavering.

Gus cleared his throat and gestured toward the bench near the desk. "I did, and I will, but we'll keep it to just that." His tone was firm. His grey eyes were cool and unreadable.

Beatrix tilted her head. Her eyes drifted to the locket that hung against his chest. "You're wearing it tonight," she said.

His gaze followed hers before lifting to meet hers again. "Thought it fitting," he replied. "The journal and the locket seem tied together."

He opened the book carefully. The salt-stained pages were timeworn and fragile in some places. He flipped to a passage he had marked earlier and began to read aloud:

The map is not the end. It is the beginning. The key is the song. Two rings—one voice. I left a copy in the cove, hidden beneath the old stones. If Aria follows it, she will find the rest.

He paused, watching her reaction. She said nothing, but he saw her pulse quicken at her throat. She leaned forward slightly, caught in the mystery that hovered between them like a dense fog.

"Arabella wrote that?" she asked.

He nodded. "It's her hand, I'm almost certain."

Beatrix rose slowly and crossed the room to stand beside him. "Do you think it was meant for Aria?"

"I don't know what I think," he muttered.

She lifted her hand to touch the page, but he caught her wrist gently. Their eyes locked. Thick silence swelled between them. He was determined to keep his distance, but she was not.

Her free hand rose, light as a breeze, and brushed against his chest, just above the locket. "Why are you trying so hard not to want me?" she asked. Her voice was barely above a whisper.

His restraint snapped. He pulled her toward him with a force that surprised them both. His mouth found hers in a kiss that was all-consuming. The lockets pressed between them as their bodies collided. Her hands wound around his shoulders. His mouth slanted over hers again and again, and when her tongue found his, he groaned with something near agony.

His hand slid down her spine and found the curve of her waist as he pulled her tight against him. She gasped, and he kissed her again, silencing any sound but the soft moan that escaped between them. His other hand trailed down her hip, and his fingers pressed into the silk and the heat beneath.

They broke apart only when the kiss became too dangerous. He rested his forehead against hers. His breath was shallow, and his hands trembled. "We reach Santiago tomorrow," he said. His voice was hoarse. "And then this madness can end. You should go."

***

Beatrix stood motionless in her borrowed room. She pressed one hand to her lips as if it might keep the taste of him from fading. Her chest rose and fell in quick, shallow breaths; her skin still tingled from his touch. The kiss had rattled her; no, it had ruined her mind, body, and resolve.

He had said they would reach Santiago tomorrow, and this madness would end. She did not want it to end…not like this, with half-truths and a parting kiss that left her whole body aching.

She crossed the floor and placed a hand on the wall to steady herself. Her fingers brushed the fabric of the silk gown. It whispered against her bare skin, and she flushed at the memory of his hands gripping her waist. There had been hunger in him, but also restraint. She had felt him hold himself back. She hadn't wanted him to. She turned toward the door.

Just as her hand reached for the latch, it moved beneath her fingers. She startled back as her heart slammed in her chest.

He stood there.

Gus.

Not the captain; not the pirate; not the man who had called her a liar, nor the one who had threatened to toss her overboard.

He was just *Gus.* His eyes were dark, and his breath was unsteady. His shirt was untucked, and its collar was open.

They stared at each other. She didn't speak. Neither did he. Everything between them screamed louder than words.

If he entered her quarters, there would be no pretense left; no decency, and no restraint. They would cross a line neither could uncross.

Still, she stepped aside. Slowly, deliberately, he passed through the door and closed it behind him. The click of the latch echoed like thunder.

She stood by the window, barely breathing. He crossed to her in two strides.

"I shouldn't be here," he said. His voice was rough.

"Then go."

She didn't mean it...not even a little.

He reached for her, cupping her cheek. "Say no, Trix." It was not a demand, but a plea.

She didn't.

He kissed her again, but it wasn't like before. This wasn't desperate or hurried; this was slow and certain.

She melted into him. Her fingers slipped beneath the open collar of his shirt, tracing the taut muscle along his shoulders and chest. His hands moved over her back, her waist and her hips; his touch possessive and reverent. When his mouth found the hollow of her throat, she gasped and arched into him.

They stumbled toward the bed. Their lips never parted. Their breath quickened between kisses. He pressed her down onto the mattress and followed her there. Their bodies tangled in silk and linen. Her fingers fumbled with the ties of his shirt, hungry to feel more of him.

He touched her thighs and her sides. Every part of her seemed made to be held, and he intended to memorize her, inch by inch. He kissed her neck, her shoulder, and the place just beneath her ear that made her shiver. She whimpered as his hand moved to the back of her dress.

His breath was hot against her cheek. "I need to see you," he murmured as his fingers found the fastenings of her bodice. "I need—"

"Wait," she whispered.

He paused, hovering above her. His eyes were wild and dark with desire. "What is it?"

She hesitated, then met his gaze. "I've never done this before."

He stilled. His hand remained at her bodice, unmoving. "You're…untouched?"

She gave a single, breathless nod.

He cursed under his breath and leaned his forehead against hers. "Damn it," he said softly. "You've no idea what you're doing to me."

Her hands were still on him, pulling him back and urging him closer. "Then teach me," she whispered.

He groaned and kissed her hard, deeply, letting his passion pour into her. But when his hand returned to her laces, he stopped again. "Not like this," he said. "Not tonight. You deserve something better than a stolen moment in the night."

She touched his cheek. "You're not what I expected."

His lips curled faintly. "Neither are you."

Instead of unlacing her dress, he gathered her into his arms, wrapping her in the safety of his body and the chaos of his longing.

They lay there, limbs entwined, mouths still brushing, hands exploring, but only went as far as his sense of honor (or what was left of it) would allow.

Sleep came slow and tangled, and though no clothes were shed, everything had changed.

CHAPTER 10

The harbor of Santiago, with its sleepy collection of merchant vessels and craggy coastline, promised freedom—but Gus felt only the slow, inexorable pull of something slipping from his grasp.

He stood at the rail in silence. His hands gripped the weather-worn wood as *The Tempest* eased toward the docks. The breeze tugged at his linen shirt, and the scent of salt and spice drifted up from the distant port.

Callahan approached without a word. He leaned beside his captain, surveying the coming land. "You've been quiet all morning."

"I'm thinking," Gus replied.

"Dangerous habit, that," Callahan said with a crooked smile. When Gus didn't return it, he added more gently, "She's leaving, then?"

Gus didn't answer right away. His gaze followed the slow shift of the sails as the rigging creaked above their heads. "That was always the plan."

Callahan lifted a brow. "Whose plan? Hers or yours?"

Gus exhaled. "Both, I suppose."

They watched the crew make ready. Ropes were cast and tied. Sails were drawn and furled. Below them, the dockhands shouted in Creole as they prepared for the ship's arrival.

"She'll vanish the moment her feet touch land," Callahan said. He folded his arms. "So, are you going to stop her?"

Gus gave him a sideways glance. "What should I say exactly? Stay aboard my pirate ship, be my…what? Mistress? Captive?"

Callahan shrugged. "A woman like that doesn't seem content to be kept."

"No," Gus murmured. "She wouldn't be."

He turned away from the rail and began to pace the length of the quarterdeck. The tension in his shoulders coiled tighter with every step. "I've offered women anything they wanted—jewels, gowns, a place in my bed—but this one..."

"She wants something you can't give."

Gus stopped. "What's that?"

Callahan tilted his head. "Truth...Everything."

The words struck harder than they should have. Gus rubbed the back of his neck. "What if I offered her something real? A place here, as crew, or something more."

Callahan didn't scoff or laugh. He merely watched his captain. "Then you'd better tell her before we dock."

Gus nodded once and strode toward the cabins. His boots echoed across the deck as his heart pounded in a rhythm far too fast for a man who faced down cannon fire without flinching.

He knocked once, then opened the door to her quarters. They were empty.

The room was spotless. The bed where they'd held each other just hours earlier was neatly made; the rumpled sheets had been smoothed clean. Her pack was already slung over her shoulder. She was standing by the door, waiting.

She looked up at him with her bright green eyes and gave him a small smile. She didn't look shy or regretful but resolved.

"I'm ready," she said.

He opened his mouth, but the words tangled on his tongue. She was already moving past him. The skirt of her silk dress brushed his hand.

The moment passed. He didn't stop her.

***

She stepped off the gangplank like a woman walking toward her fate. Gus watched her go. Her figure grew smaller with each step across the sunlit wharf. Sailors unloaded crates and shouted greetings in broken Portuguese, but all he could see was the set of her shoulders beneath her silk dress and the fire-colored braid tucked tight at the nape of her neck.

He should have stopped her. He should have said something. He gripped the rail until his knuckles turned white. Below, Callahan barked orders to the men securing the ship. He cast a knowing glance at Gus but offered no counsel. None would help now.

Gus turned from the railing. What more could he do?

"Help!" A scream shattered the air. He recognized her voice instantly.

Gus turned sharply. His body reacted before his mind caught up. He was down the plank, cutting through the noisy throng of dockworkers and merchants. His sword was already halfway drawn.

"Trix!" He called for her. His mind willed her to make another sound, so he'd know which way to go.

Another scream rang through the crowd; it was closer. Through a narrow cut between weather-stained buildings, he caught a flash of pale skirts and copper hair. A man was dragging her backward into the shadows. His gloved hand was clenched tightly around her arm.

Gus pushed through the final crowd and drew his sword in one fluid motion. "Let go of her," he barked. His voice was thunderous and echoed through the alley.

The attacker turned slowly, and Gus stopped cold.

Ambrose.

His brother.

He was dressed in a fine traveling coat, and his pristine boots were dusted with the streets of Santiago. A familiar sneer curled the corner of his mouth.

"Well," Ambrose said. He released Beatrix with insulting ease. "Look at you."

Gus stepped forward, placing himself between Trix and the man who had once been his closest friend before he became his bitterest rival. "What the hell are you doing here?"

Ambrose dusted off his glove. "Fetching what's mine."

"She is not yours." Gus's voice betrayed his possessiveness.

"Is that so?" Ambrose's gaze flicked toward Trix, who Gus protectively held behind him. "She was promised to me. Her father signed the marriage contract. I have the special license."

Gus narrowed his eyes. "You're lying."

Ambrose gave a cold laugh. "Am I? Look at the evidence! She's run off, hasn't she? Disguised herself, stowed away on some ghastly ship. She's quite the little fugitive. Unfortunately for her, I have eyes everywhere."

Gus's fingers tightened on the hilt of his sword. "She's under my protection."

Ambrose raised a brow and took a slow step forward. "And what exactly does that mean, *Captain*?"

Gus said nothing.

Ambrose let his eyes drift over Beatrix. "Has she told you who she is?"

"Her name is Trix," Gus said. He lowered his sword, but did not look away from his brother.

"Trix," Ambrose echoed. "Funny, I could have sworn her father called her 'Bea.'"

He stepped closer, and with an exaggerated flourish, proclaimed, "May I be the first to present to you, Lady Beatrix Wrenwood, soon to be Mrs. Drake."

Gus's breath hitched, and he nearly dropped his sword.

Ambrose smiled. "There it is."

The two men stood with eyes locked; the space between them was suddenly too small for everything that had just shifted.

Beatrix Wrenwood…Aria's little cousin. How old was she when he last saw her? Ten? Twelve? Aria had doted on her, but she was too small to do more than play in the gardens and walk along the cliffs with her governess. He had paid no attention to her back then. He hadn't recognized her, but had she recognized him? They had spent mere moments in each other's company, and she had been just a child.

"You really didn't know," Ambrose said. "Of course you didn't."

Gus turned his head slightly, just enough to glance at her over his shoulder.

She stood frozen and trembling. Her lies were unraveling too quickly. She had to know more about the journal than she let on. She was Arabella's niece, after all.

Ambrose's voice turned cutting. "You've been sleeping on the same ship as my betrothed—likely in the same bed—and you didn't even know her name. That's rich indeed."

"I'm not your anything," she snapped, finally finding her voice.

Ambrose didn't even flinch. "Yes, you most certainly are. I have a license and a contract that allows me to make you my wife at any church, anywhere, no matter where you run. You *will* be my wife."

"Like hell she will," Gus growled.

Ambrose stepped back, smiling like a man who had already won. "Well. Now that we've had our introductions… I suggest you keep her close, because I will be coming for her."

Ambrose turned and vanished into the street.

Gus turned slowly, meeting her wide, horrified gaze.

"Beatrix?" he asked, voice thick with disbelief.

She opened her mouth to speak, but nothing came out. Gus didn't wait for her to find the words.

"We're leaving. Now."

***

Gus didn't let go of her hand, not when she stumbled behind him through the crowd, and not when they reached the gangplank. He pulled her behind him and never looked back at her.

"Callahan," he barked, "ready the ship. We sail within the hour. Faster if you can manage it."

"The cargo—" Callahan started.

"Damn the cargo. Do as I say."

The look on Gus's face brooked no argument. Callahan's mouth snapped shut, and he turned on his heel. He began shouting for the crew to haul anchor.

Gus dragged Beatrix across the deck and into his cabin, slamming the door behind them. Only then did he release her.

"Sit," He barked.

She didn't.

"I said *sit*." He enunciated each word through his clenched teeth. Trembling, she sat.

He paced once across the room, then turned to her. "Now, talk. Tell me everything, from the beginning, and don't lie to me again."

Beatrix's throat tightened. She folded her hands in her lap and tried to keep them from trembling. "It started with my father," she said softly. "He told me I was to marry Ambrose. He said it was for protection, but I'm not sure if he thought it was for mine or his."

Gus didn't speak. His jaw clenched tighter.

"He wouldn't say why we needed protection, only that we were in danger if I refused." She lifted her chin slightly. "I never agreed to the marriage. My father and Ambrose made it seem like I had no choice. The seamstress came and she made my wedding dress. It's probably still hanging in my room at Brackwater Hall. While she was there, I found a package from my mother containing the locket—the one that's just like yours."

Gus's gaze never left her. His expression was tense, but unreadable.

She swallowed. "The seamstress told me how the lace she was using on my wedding dress was the same as the lace she used on Aria's. I never knew Aria planned to marry, so I went looking for the dress.

"I snuck into Aria's room. It's been completely preserved for her, just in case she reappears one day. I looked through her wardrobe and in her storage chest, but I didn't find the dress."

Gus closed his eyes. He knew the dress. It was silver and trimmed with the most delicate lace he had ever seen.

Unsure if he was still listening, Beatrix kept telling her story. "Then I found Aria's letters; they were hidden beneath a loose floorboard. They were beautiful, love-filled letters; all of them were signed only with an 'A.' He swore he would be her husband, despite his father's disapproval. I don't know what happened to her after that…she vanished."

He opened his eyes, but his expression didn't change. His stillness made her nervous.

"My mother left a note," she continued. "A warning. That's when I realized that Ambrose had tried this before, with Aria. He was 'A.' His letters were just a manipulation, and he wanted to use her blood for something...but I'm not sure what, exactly. My mother didn't want the same thing to happen to me, and her note told me to run."

She breathed, finishing her story. "So, I ran. I dressed in the boy's clothes my mother had hidden behind her hearth, and I ran."

Gus never moved. He only blinked from time to time as she told her story. She didn't think he believed her.

"I have proof," she said hesitantly, then reached into the folds of her dress and withdrew a weathered letter. "This was the last letter Ambrose wrote to Aria before she vanished. I meant to confront Ambrose about it, but ended up running away before I had a chance."

She held the letter out to him with trembling fingers. Gus took it.

He opened it with a reverence that startled her. The paper was creased, but the ink remained dark. The lines were written in a hand that he had not expected to see again.

He read it once, then twice, then he folded it carefully and placed it on the table.

"No, Beatrix," he said, his voice barely more than a whisper. "Ambrose didn't write this."

Beatrix blinked. "How do you know?"

His eyes met hers.

"Because I did."

She didn't breathe. She barely blinked.

He looked down at the letter, then back up at her. "It was mine, every word. I wrote it the day Aria and I were to leave and start our life together. We didn't get the chance."

"You? But…" she started.

"Yes. I am August Drake, Ambrose's older brother, Viscount Alverdon. I am 'A.'"

***

Before either of them could speak again, the ship lurched hard to the side. The sound of splintering wood was followed by shouting on deck.

Then *boom*. It was the unmistakable thunder of cannon fire.

Gus's eyes snapped toward the door. "What the hell—?"

Another cannonball struck, closer this time. It rocked the ship with enough force to knock Beatrix against the table.

Gus was already moving. He flung open the cabin door and barked, "Callahan! Who's firing on us?"

Callahan's voice rang through the chaos. "Starboard—fast-moving schooner, Captain! Flying no colors!"

Gus's face darkened. He turned back to Beatrix, who was still bracing herself against the cabin wall.

"Stay here," he growled. He was gone before she could answer. His boots pounded across the deck towards the battle.

Beatrix clutched the locket with one hand and steadied herself with the other. She dragged in a jagged breath. There was no mistaking what this was.

Ambrose had followed them.

Part II: The Map of the Forgotten

CHAPTER 11

Gus had spent a decade distancing himself from his family. Today, at the edge of Santiago's harbor, he remembered why. As his boots hit the deck, he locked eyes with his first mate, who was steadily calling orders to his scrambling crew.

"It's Ambrose," Gus confirmed, not needing the spyglass Callahan offered him. "The bastard didn't even wait until we cleared the harbor."

Beatrix had ignored his order to stay in his cabin, though she couldn't venture far. Men scurried around the deck, readying ropes and weapons.

Gus roared, "Get us angled, hard to starboard. Ready port guns."

"Aye, Captain!"

The schooner was so close that she could see Ambrose's figure on the quarterdeck. He stood with perfect posture amidst the noise. His ship was sleeker and faster but lacked the armaments of *The Tempest.*

"Fire!" Gus bellowed to his crew. The whole ship lurched as the cannonball flew towards the schooner. Ambrose's ship rocked as the ball met its mast.

Gus drew his sword. His eyes were cold and focused. They bore no resemblance to the warmth and gentleness she'd seen in them the night before. This was not the man who had kissed her with passionate abandon; this was Captain Drake, the ruthless, merciless, unassailable pirate lord. She almost felt sorry for Ambrose…she saw in that moment that he had started a war he could not win. Gus would not relent now that he had been provoked.

"Boarding hooks!" someone yelled. "They plan to come aboard!"

The ships locked as grapples caught *The Tempest's* rails. A dozen figures leaped across the narrowing gap between the ships with blades drawn. They didn't stand a chance. Immediately, *The Tempest's* crew met them in a crash of metal and flesh.

Beatrix lost sight of Gus; there was too much smoke and chaos for her to see more than a few feet in front of her. She knew she should duck back into the captain's cabin. She was about to do just that, but then the wind shifted, and the gun smoke cleared just enough for her to see them.

Ambrose had boarded the ship and was now facing Gus, sword-to-sword. Ambrose's blade gleamed, already red, but she couldn't see if it was Gus that was struck by it, or some other crewman.

"You've made a habit of taking what's mine," Ambrose snarled. His voice carried above the madness of clashing blades and pistol fire.

Gus circled him with his sword raised. "You've made a habit of assuming everything is yours. You're entitled to nothing, brother."

Ambrose lunged. Their swords clashed with a resounding sound that rang through the chaos. Gus parried but did not strike.

"She is mine, August. Just give her to me, and we can stop this bloodshed. You can go back to skulking about the sea, and I can get on with claiming my rightful place in the world." Ambrose tried to sound reasonable, but his cocky visage just angered Gus further.

"You have no rightful place. You were born a bastard, and you will always be a bastard." Gus continued to circle; his eyes never blinked. He knew all too well that his brother would attack as soon as he let down his guard. They had practiced their swords together daily in their youth. They each knew the other's vulnerabilities.

"You shouldn't have shot wide when you had the chance to end me, then. This could have all been prevented, but you were a sentimental fool." Ambrose was goading Gus now. Beatrix knew it, even if she didn't know what he meant.

"I won't make the mistake again!" Gus roared as he lunged, slashing his brother's arm. Ambrose held back the bleeding with his opposite hand as the two fell into their inevitable battle.

"You never understood what she was worth," Ambrose shouted. "You were going to throw away your whole life to what? Become a farmer on some remote island somewhere? I would have given her the world."

"Aria chose me," Gus spat. "She didn't want the world. She didn't even want my title; all she wanted was to be my wife."

"Then she died for her shortsightedness, didn't she?" Ambrose meant it as cruelly as it sounded. Gus struck in unbridled fury. His blade punctured Ambrose's flesh before Ambrose even knew what had happened.

Air fled her lungs in a sharp rush. For the last ten years. Beatrix and the rest of her family had held out hope that Aria was alive somewhere and would return one day to let them know what had happened. Even though it seemed impossible, even though they never spoke aloud their assumption that she might be gone forever, they held hope. Now Beatrix knew the truth: Her cousin was dead.

***

"Callahan!" Gus shouted. His brother's blood still dripped from his sword. "Get her below, NOW."

Callahan didn't hesitate. He moved from the helm and crossed the deck in an instant. When he grabbed Beatrix's arm, she immediately recoiled.

"Now, damn it!" he roared again.

Callahan yanked her toward the stairs just as a second wave of Ambrose's men stormed over the rails. Gus turned back to the fight. He had lost sight of his brother, but he knew Ambrose was significantly wounded, maybe even fatally.

"Hold the port rail!" Gus shouted to O'Malley, who had taken the helm from Callahan. "Don't let them take the quarterdeck!"

"Aye, Captain!" The old sailor may have been assigned to ledgers and logs these days, but he was a seasoned warrior. Ambrose's men did not stand a chance against the Irishman.

Ambrose had fired on them, knowing Beatrix was aboard. He held no regard for her safety—he only wanted to possess her, at any cost. The bastard always took what he couldn't earn.

A blade slashed toward his ribs. Gus ducked, twisted, and drove his sword through the attacker's gut.

He looked to see Ambrose clutching his side. Blood soaked his fancy shirt from the wound and dripped from his arm onto his well-polished boots. He was as white as a sheet. His voice was barely audible as he called for retreat, but his remaining men followed him back to the schooner.

Coward. Gus thought about following him and finishing the job, but decided to leave Ambrose to his fate. He wouldn't be pursuing Beatrix again any time soon, and with any luck, his wound would fester, and he'd meet his demise without Gus's help.

"Break the grapples! Ready to disengage!" O'Malley was shouting the orders now. Crew scrambled to obey. The ropes were hacked away, one after another, until the ships drifted apart. As the final hook splashed into the sea, Gus watched his brother's schooner pull back toward the edge of the harbor.

Callahan approached. His shirt was soaked through at the collar, and his expression was grim.

"That was no ordinary skirmish," the first mate said, lowering his voice. "That was personal."

Gus didn't answer. He stared after the disappearing sails of his brother's ship. The murmurs began behind them. Crewmen shouted, grumbled, and dragged the wounded off the main deck while casting pointed glances toward the captain.

"She's the reason we were fired upon!"

Gus turned slowly to face them.

A young sailor, barely more than a boy, stepped forward. His hands trembled. "We have no quarrel with Spanish fleets or frogs—but this? This was a man with a vendetta over a woman—Your woman."

The word struck like a challenge. The deck fell silent.

"She is my responsibility," Gus said evenly, voice cold as steel. "This ship is mine. If you don't like my command, you're welcome to swim back to Santiago."

Gus glared at his crew, daring them to push the matter further.

Callahan stepped closer to him. "If you want to keep your crew, you'd better give them more than that," he said under his breath. "If you're going to ask men to die for you, you have to give them a reason."

Gus realized the wisdom in his first mate's counsel. He thought a moment and addressed his crew.

"The ship that fired on us belonged to my bastard brother," he said with eyes sharp and his voice level. "He's been hunting her."

A ripple passed through the crowd.

"She was his betrothed, but now she is mine," Gus lied with the confidence of a man who needed no second opinion. "She fled him for her own safety and sought passage on my ship. She now sails under our protection. That is the end of it."

Callahan gave a half-smirk. "That ought to do it."

The men stilled. One spat over the rails, while another adjusted his grip on a bloodied bandage. No one spoke; no one dared.

Gus didn't stay to gloat. He turned on his heel and strode belowdecks.

He had sought to find Beatrix, but instead he found the ship's surgeon elbow-deep in wounded sailors. Luckily, he had not lost any of his crew in the skirmish, but a large number had been injured in the fray.

Gus rolled up his sleeves and set to work binding wounds and bracing limbs; then he saw her.

In the far corner of the infirmary, Beatrix sat beside a wounded boy with a shredded arm. Her hands were delicate but sure as she worked a needle and thread through the ravaged skin as if she were mending a fine cushion in a stylish drawing room. Blood stained her silk skirt. A lock of her copper hair had slipped free of its knot and clung to her cheek.

She didn't see him at first. She was bent over her work, whispering something to the boy in a low, comforting tone. Only when she tied off the last stitch and leaned back did her eyes meet his.

He didn't speak; he just moved to the next cot and knelt beside her.

For the rest of the night, they worked silently in tandem. She sewed while he steadied. He dressed wounds while she washed. Through blood and exhaustion, they never strayed more than a few feet from one another.

Neither of them spoke a word about Ambrose, Aria, or the weight of loss they both carried now.

CHAPTER 12

Gus stood at the railing, watching the sunrise over the ocean, as had been his respite for countless mornings at sea. Callahan joined him and scratched at a healing wound near his temple.

"We've got good wind," Callahan's voice was hoarse with fatigue. He hadn't slept either. "It held steady through the night."

Gus nodded absently; his gaze still followed the rising sun.

Callahan cleared his throat. "The sails need mending, and the starboard cannon's listing in its mount. Then there's the rather large hole in the side helm there. It's above the waterline, but we should repair it sooner rather than later."

"And Ambrose?"

"No sign of his schooner. Maybe he bled out on the way back to Santiago," He shrugged." More likely, he's licking his wounds and falling back to reload."

Gus grunted. "He won't give up now. He'll bribe every dockhand in Santiago to learn our trek. I doubt many of them know much, but some have probably figured out which ports we frequent."

Callahan exhaled. "So, what's our heading, then? We can't go back to Santiago for repairs; he'll be waiting."

A long silence stretched between them. *The Tempest* creaked as the waves slapped her hull. Gus leaned over the railing and spotted the hole in the side of his ship. One rough wave and they'd take on water. It wasn't likely they could make it to Barbados or Martinique.

Finally, Gus spoke. "How far to Dakar?"

Callahan narrowed his eyes at the sea. Dakar was a desperate choice.

"A day, maybe two if the wind shifts." He paused. "It's off the usual shipping routes, which is good for vanishing, but not always good for supplies. It's rougher folk than in Santiago."

"Good," Gus said curtly. "I'm not looking for civility. Let's get the ship fixed."

Callahan tilted his head. "You're not worried about the girl in a place like that?"

Gus's gaze locked on the sea. "If Ambrose catches her, Dakar will look like a garden party by comparison." The thought of his brother touching Beatrix made his blood boil.

Callahan nodded. "Then Dakar it is."

***

Portholes provided the only daylight in the make-shift sick bay. Beatrix sat on a barrel below decks with a bloodstained rag in her lap. Across from her, a young sailor whimpered in his sleep. His leg was bound in a splint she had helped tie.

She had worked through the night, stitching gashes and changing dressings. She did what she could, but in truth, she had no medical knowledge. Her sheltered life at Brackwater hadn't afforded many opportunities for tending injuries.

Gus had helped where he could, too. Obviously, his life of piracy provided him with numerous opportunities to witness human carnage. He had barely spoken as they worked, but his presence had steadied her more than she wanted to admit.

At dawn, he had left to do whatever pirate captains do after a battle. The quiet should have comforted her, but her thoughts drifted to all she had learned in the last day.

Aria.

She remembered her cousin smiling at her as they made flower crowns in the garden. They giggled when the cat knocked their flower basket off the stone wall.

Gus was "A."

Her mind still hadn't fully comprehended this fact. The letters had been his. Those haunting words, tender and determined, were not the product of Ambrose's manipulation. They had been from Gus's heart.

"Come hell or high water, I will be your husband." He had loved Aria deeply. She must have loved him too—enough to buy a secret dress for their runaway wedding.

She paused her stitching and stared at the locket around her neck. Just a few weeks ago, it had gleamed in its box. Now, it was grimy with sea salt, sweat, and dirt, but then, so was she. She thought about Gus wearing Aria's locket in his grief.

A lump rose in her throat. She swallowed it back.

She had wanted to hate him. He was a brutish pirate, but there was much more she had come to know about him. He was steady in a crisis. He was passionate, yet tender in private. He was well educated, titled, and even hailed from her home county. In different circumstances, he would have made a perfect match for her…or Aria.

The image of Aria in that final moment haunted her. Had she truly died in Gus's arms? Had she sung to him as the light faded from her eyes?

Beatrix wiped her hands and sighed. She didn't know how to discuss any of this with him. She didn't know what words could bridge his grief; he had carried it for so long, alone. She wasn't sure she should even try.

The ship creaked around her. Someone coughed, snapping her back to the job at hand. An older sailor had already burst his stitches, and she had a steadier hand at sewing than the ship's surgeon.

***

Beatrix stood outside his cabin door with a dinner tray balanced carefully in her hands. When she finally raised her knuckles to knock, he opened the door at once, as if he'd had his hand on the door handle, waiting for her to appear.

Gus stood in the doorway in his shirtsleeves. His eyes met hers, but they were unreadable in the lantern light.

"I wasn't sure you'd come tonight," he said. "I know you haven't slept."

"I know you haven't slept either," she answered. "I wanted to make sure you had a proper dinner after the turmoil of the last two days."

He stepped aside, and she entered, setting the tray on the table. He poured the wine. She uncovered the food. They sat and ate in silence. The food was good, but neither of them tasted it. Gus watched her across the table. She recognized that she must look a fright after a sea battle and a night and day without sleep. She also realized that the last time she had slept was in his arms.

"I heard what your brother said during the fight," she said quietly, setting her fork on the table.

His eyes flicked to hers.

"I stayed back," she went on, "but I heard it."

Gus had stopped chewing. He took a long sip of his wine.

"What did you hear?" He asked.

"I heard that Ambrose wanted Aria; I had guessed that much. But then I heard him say she died for her shortsightedness. I didn't know she was dead…not really."

Gus stared at his plate. He knew he would have to tell Beatrix about the night Aria died. He didn't know if he had the strength.

"I used to wonder if she'd come back," Beatrix said. "I dreamed she'd just walk through the door one day and laugh about how silly we all were to think she was gone forever."

Gus couldn't look her in the eyes. He struggled to find any words at all.

"She died in my arms," he whispered.

Beatrix's throat tightened.

"I'm sorry," she said. "I didn't know what she meant to you."

"She meant *everything.*"

His words hung in the air. She had been gone ten years, yet his wound seemed as fresh as if she had last breathed yesterday.

Beatrix studied him; his eyes were closed. His face showed the turmoil of a man wrecked with grief. She realized that she could not compete with her cousin's ghost—not to this man.

"I understand why you want me off this ship," she said; her voice was barely more than a breath. She didn't want to face Ambrose alone, and she had no idea how to follow her mother's instructions to get to Calverique. What she did know was that she didn't want to torture Gus with her presence any longer than necessary.

Gus looked up sharply. "That's not—"

"I'm not Aria," she interrupted. "I could never replace her for you. I just need you to know I'm not here to hurt you; I never was."

He held her gaze. A long pause stretched between them.

"You wear the same locket, and you sing the same song," he said at last. "But you're nothing like her."

Beatrix tilted her head, uncertain.

"That's not an insult," he added. "Aria was like a gentle breeze. When she walked, her feet barely touched the ground. She swept through life with her head in the clouds, humming as she daydreamed. She was everything I needed. She was the complete opposite of everything I had ever known." He smiled sadly at her memory.

"I remember her that way, too. She was sad sometimes, and I know she missed her parents, but she was a gentle soul who never had an unkind word for anyone, not even when they deserved it." Beatrix realized just how much she missed Aria. She had lost a friend, not just a cousin.

"But Beatrix, you're all fire."

A smile touched her lips. She tried not to blush. She raised an eyebrow. "Is that what I am? A fire?"

Gus leaned back in his chair; his demeanor had changed. He knew he would eventually have to tell her about the duel, but it wasn't tonight. Right now, he just wanted to think about her. He thought about the night, less than 48 hours ago, when he had kissed her fiercely. Her passion had met his, driving him closer and closer to losing his senses completely and ravishing her, maid or no.

"Sometimes I think you'll burn me alive." He smiled a wicked grin back at her.

They both laughed, but she knew he meant it—she was passionate, demanding, and unrelenting—a fire if there ever was one. For a moment, the tension between them loosened its grip. They finished the meal in silence, but it was different this time.

They smiled when they met each other's glances and both realized that they were beginning to understand each other, at least a little.

When they had finished their dinner, he cleared the plates, set the tray outside his cabin door, and motioned for a deckhand to take it to the galley. When he shut the door, he could see that Beatrix was still concerned about something. She stared down at her hands in her lap, lost in thought.

"What else is on your mind, Trix?"

"You don't have to call me that," she said. "I made it up when I joined your crew."

"I think it suits you. You always surprise me. It's like you always have another trick, even when I think I've figured them all out." His smile was teasing now. She blushed.

"Tomorrow," she said, "we'll reach Dakar."

He nodded.

"Then what happens?" she asked.

Gus paused, not quite understanding her meaning. She had meant to leave in Santiago, before Ambrose grabbed her and Gus dragged her back to his ship. Did she still mean to leave? Where would she even go?

"That depends," he answered, "On whether you're done running."

Beatrix wrapped her hands around her goblet and stared into the dark liquid.

"I don't know if I'll ever stop running," she said quietly. "Not with Ambrose hunting me. He won't stop until he gets what he wants."

Gus's mouth drew a hard line. He could only imagine what Ambrose would do to her. He had a marriage license and a marriage contract, so if he could get Beatrix to a church, she wouldn't have much recourse to refuse him. The thought of Ambrose's hands on her made him want to hit something.

"Then we don't let him get it," Ambrose said with finality.

She lifted her gaze to his. He thought she might cry with worry, but her eyes were dry. "How do we do that?"

His answer came without hesitation. "We protect you. I protect you."

Something in his voice settled her chest for the first time since her father had announced her betrothal. She believed him.

CHAPTER 13

The Port of Dakar

The Tempest limped into the port of Dakar with one sail patched hastily. Her rigging was frayed but intact. Thankfully, the seas had stayed calm, so the gaping hole in the hull had not taken on water.

From the forecastle, Gus surveyed the shoreline. Dakar was a much less organized port than the ones where he usually landed. It wasn't exactly a welcoming port, but it would do for a place to hide and regroup. It was the kind of place where no one asked too many questions.

Callahan joined him with a ledger in one hand and a deep frown etched across his face. "We'll need at least three days. The main boom's still holding, but she's splintered. I'll need fresh tar for the seams if we want to keep from taking on water halfway to the Indies. Of course, there's the matter of the hole in our hull…"

Gus nodded. "Do what you have to, but keep the crew quiet. Don't draw any sort of unnecessary attention."

Callahan's gaze flicked to the pier where locals were already eyeing the vessel. "This place isn't exactly known for subtlety."

"We don't need subtlety; we need supplies, repairs, and undergarments."

Callahan turned sharply. "I beg your pardon?"

"For Trix," Gus said, as if it were the most obvious thing in the world. "Don't act like you haven't noticed. She doesn't have on a stitch beneath those thin silk gowns. That's why she mostly stays below decks—so I don't have to gouge out another man's eyes for staring at her nether regions when the wind blows a certain way.

Callahan blinked. "Ah, right. Of course. Wouldn't want gouging."

"I'm starting to think that crate of gowns you pilfered from that attack ship was meant for a brothel somewhere. That purple one was cut almost clear to her navel."

Callahan gave a low chuckle and made a note in his book. "I'll see what I can scavenge from the market."

Gus's eyes lingered on the gangway as it was lowered to the dock. He rarely had the chance to go ashore anywhere, and when he did, he usually ended up in the back of a tavern, alone. "I'll take her myself."

Callahan raised a brow. "To shop for underthings?"

"Yes. I think she'll do a better job picking them out than you or me, don't you?" Gus quipped.

"Aye, my experience has more to do with taking them off than putting them on, if you get my meaning," Callahan couldn't hide his smile. Neither could Gus. It felt good to have a little levity after so much tension.

"I owe her a day without looking over her shoulder," Gus said. They both needed a day where they didn't have to worry about judgmental glances from his crew or his bastard brother popping out of the shadows.

"You sure that's wise?" Callahan asked. "A woman like her, dressed like that? She'll turn heads."

"Let them look." He left Callahan on deck and headed below to find her.

***

Africa's heat pressed down on them like a heavy blanket. The sun reflected brightly against the little port's bleached stone and packed dirt. Gus led Beatrix through the narrow streets, past rows of stalls shaded by woven awnings in various states of disrepair.

Women dressed in vivid patterned wraps sold baskets of dried fish and glossy red peppers. French traders haggled loudly over baskets of fruits and casks of wine.

Beatrix had never seen anything like this port. She's only had a moment in Santiago before Ambrose grabbed her, so she didn't even have anything to compare. She kept close to Gus.

Her blue silk skirt brushed against baskets of cassava root and strings of scarlet peppers. Beatrix felt the sweat at the small of her back as the sun beat down on her exposed skin. Her dress clung to her legs uncomfortably, making it difficult to keep walking.

Gus glanced at her flushed cheeks and muttered, "You are roasting in that. It's only going to get hotter when we go back out to sea. We should find you something made for this heat."

She opened her mouth to retort, but he was already steering her toward a stall where lengths of pale linen hung in the shade.

The merchant was a short, dark-skinned man whose years in the sun were revealed in deep wrinkles on his face and hands. He looked her over with a shrewd smile. She was quite a sight in her clingy dress, now soaked in sweat, with her lack of undergarments putting her body's secrets on full display.

"Zees is good cloth," he said in English tinged by his heavy French accent as he ran his hands over the fabric. "It will keep you cool in zee sun."

Beatrix brushed the linen between her fingers; it was soft and airy. "Yes," she said, already imagining the relief of moving without wet silk clinging to her limbs. She chose a few pieces: several loose, white and pastel blouses, a grey skirt, an indigo-dyed dress, several linen dresses that exposed her shoulders, and a long sash that could be tied for modesty or loosened in the heat. Without her having to ask, the merchant added a couple of shifts and petticoats to her collection. As she reached for her pouch to pay, Gus took her hand.

"I will handle it," he said, and gave the merchant three gold coins. The merchant's eyes lit up as he smiled; it was obvious Gus had just paid him a small fortune.

"Merci, monsieur. Please remember me next time you are in port." The merchant's joy was contagious. Neither she nor Gus could stop smiling as they crossed the way to a cobbler's booth.

Soft-soled leather slippers were arranged in tidy rows. Gus pressed a pair into her hands. "For the deck," he said simply. The thought of walking the deck's hot planks in comfort was too tempting for her to refuse.

Next, he bought her a broad-brimmed straw hat from a laughing Senegalese woman. Her stall overflowed with dyed fabrics and carved wooden bangles. Anything she admired, Gus simply bought for her with his seemingly endless stash of gold coins.

The last market stall was a narrow table stacked with brass trinkets, compasses, and sailors' charms. The merchant greeted them warmly, but when his eyes caught the silver locket at Beatrix's throat, his smile faltered. He leaned forward and spoke quietly; his voice carried a heavy French accent. "Your necklace…I have seen one like it. It means something, if you know where to look."

Beatrix felt Gus's gaze shift to her, defensively. "And where would that be?" Gus asked, placing his arm protectively at her waist and gripping the hilt of his sword with the other.

The man only shrugged, undeterred by Gus's show of apprehension. "The sea has many doors, monsieur. The right key opens the right one." He looked between them, then smiled again, too easily. "For you, monsieur, a fine price on this spyglass."

He held the glass up for Gus to inspect. Gus didn't buy it; instead, he steered Beatrix toward the wharf. He swung the bundle of purchases over his shoulder.

"What do you think he meant?" She asked.

"I don't know. We'll come back tomorrow," he murmured. "People talk more when they've seen your face twice."

***

Heat was already rising from the port's stone streets, even though the sun had barely risen over the horizon. Under Callahan's supervision, *The Tempest's* crew worked on repairs for the second day. Gus found himself once again walking beside Beatrix through the jumble of market stalls.

She was dressed in the linen garments they had purchased the day before. The loose, pale dress was clearly meant for comfort at sea rather than elegance, but he could tell by the way she moved that she felt lighter and happy to be rid of her clingy silk gowns. Her hair was pinned back to keep the wind from catching it, even though a stray curl had already escaped. She tucked it behind her ear, unaware that he was studying her attractiveness.

Callahan had sent them out with a list of provisions: ropes, tools, and spare sailcloth. They were all things that would help keep them in motion once they left port. Gus found himself watching the ease with which she bargained with the merchants. Today, she was all smiles as the sun caught the silver of her locket whenever she leaned forward.

She was haggling over a tin of sewing needles when he caught the eye of a man across the way. The merchant was tall and lean, with skin darkened by the sun, almost unnaturally. He was arranging bolts of faded sailcloth when Gus caught him staring at Beatrix. The man's gaze dipped briefly to her chest, where the locket rested against her shirt.

Gus felt the shift immediately.

The merchant abandoned his cloth, crossed the narrow lane, and stopped in front of them. He offered no greeting and spoke quickly in English. "You carry a key, mademoiselle. Do you know what it opens?"

Before Gus could speak, Beatrix answered warily, "A key?"

The man's eyes flicked between them. "Some call it a key. Some call it a curse. It depends on who is telling the tale." His gaze lingered on Beatrix. Gus's shoulders stiffened in subtle warning.

"What tale?" Gus asked evenly.

The merchant looked around them, studying the crowd. "I cannot tell you here. There are eyes everywhere. Come tomorrow, just after dawn. There is a warehouse located near the northern pier, marked by a blue door. Ask for Lemoine. Bring the key and you will learn the rest."

Beatrix's fingers twitched near her locket. She glanced at Gus, and he saw the unspoken question in her eyes: *How much did this man know?*

"Why us?" Gus asked, his voice low.

The merchant only shrugged, then stepped back. "No one else has come with the key in many years. I grow weary of waiting."

Without another word, the man melted into the crowd, vanishing between stalls.

For a moment, they stood silent. The sounds of the market pressed around them: the cries of fishmongers, the haggling fishwives, and the murmur of foreign tongues.

"You know something," Beatrix said quietly; her eyes fixed on Gus.

"I don't know...maybe." Gus adjusted the strap of the bag on his shoulder. "We will see what the man has to say tomorrow."

The muscles in her jaw flexed, but she said nothing more. Instead, she turned toward the next stall. Her steps were brisk, but he could see the questions gathering behind her composed expression.

They spent the remainder of the day buying what they needed, but the merchant's words lingered between them.

***

Neither of them said much after the encounter at the market. They ate dinner quickly that night, but both of them were contemplating what the following day would bring. Finally, Beatrix could take the silence no more and spoke.

"This morning, in the market, you looked like you knew the locket was a key. How did you know?"

Gus studied her for a long moment before speaking. "Because someone once told me it was."

She felt her chest tighten. "Aria."

His jaw shifted, and he gave the slightest nod. "We were readying to run away, and I was trying to figure out where to go. She said she knew of a place—an island deep in the Caribbean."

"*Calverique*," Beatrix whispered without thinking.

He breathed in sharply. He had only heard that word from Aria.

"Yes." He confirmed. "I wasn't completely sure it was even a real place, but Aria told me the locket was the key to getting there. I thought it was one of her daydreams—a made-up fairyland—but then I saw this."

From inside his coat, he drew Arabella's leather-bound journal. He opened it carefully and turned to a page where the ink had faded to a soft, brown hue. He angled the book toward her. The script was precise but delicate:

The lockets are the beginning. In the right hands, they will turn the way to Calverique. Guard them, for they are the keys and the curse.

Beatrix read the words aloud. Gus watched as she mouthed them a second time.

"Aria believed her locket was meant for something important, but I wonder if it leads to something dangerous," he said ominously.

Beatrix looked down at the silver chain around her own neck. The locket was warm from resting against her skin. She wanted to ask what else Aria had told him, but his expression, guarded and shadowed, told her it wasn't the time. They would learn more on the marrow.

"We will speak of it again," she said softly, and he inclined his head as if sealing a quiet pact.

***

The street was eerily empty at the far edge of the quay. The warehouse had sat unused for what seemed like a very long time. Its door had once been painted a deep blue, but now it was badly sun-faded. The paint was chipped throughout, revealing the layers that had come before it.

Gus glanced once over his shoulder. "No one followed us," he muttered, but his hand still rested on his sword. He reached for the locket at Beatrix's chest; he had left his on the ship. "Are you certain you want to do this? We could go back to the ship. The repairs are almost done, so we could sail with the evening tide."

She held his gaze. "Yes. I want to know."

Gus stepped forward and knocked on the door. No one answered.

"Hello! Bonjour!" He called, knocking again. A small man in Monk's robes opened the door.

"Bonjour, Monsieur," he answered.

"Are you Lemoine?" Gus asked.

"Oui. Are you the couple with the necklace? May I see it?"

Beatrix held the locket out to Lemoine. He took it in his hand, inspecting it thoroughly. Finally, he looked up at her and smiled. "Come with me."

Lemoine led them inside the warehouse. The air inside was thick with heat and disuse. The building was completely empty, except for a single sea trunk in the center. It was bound with iron and covered with dust.

"What do we do?" Gus asked. The logistics of opening a sea trunk with a locket perplexed him. To his amazement, the locket around Beatrix's neck began to glow. She moved—no, floated—towards the chest.

His heart thumped as Beatrix knelt and set the locket against the chest's lock. Its glow brightened, illuminating her face, but the woman he saw was not Beatrix. Her eyes were fixed straight ahead; her gaze was absent. It was as if she were no longer in control of her movements. He stepped towards her, but a muted click sounded, and the lock on the chest dropped, followed by the irons it held. The chest opened with a creak; its hinges were stiff from their abandonment.

Inside the chest, on a lining of decayed velvet, lay a single gold ring. Its surface was worked into the shape of two bands. They entwined so seamlessly that Gus could not see the point where one began and the other ended.

Beatrix reached for the ring, but her face showed no expression. In her trance, her fingers closed around the metal. The moment her skin met the metal, her locket's glow faded.

Gus's eyes adjusted to the warehouse's darkness. He saw Beatrix slide the ring onto her left hand's fourth finger without hesitation. Gus reached for her, setting his hand gently on her shoulder.

"Beatrix?" He studied her expression. Her eyes were unfocused; her breathing was slow. It was as if she were listening to something far away.

She looked up at him, and the moment had passed. She was back with him. Relief swept his body.

"It belongs to me," she said simply.

"That," Gus replied, his voice lower than before, "is what I am beginning to fear. Whatever this is," He held up her locket. "It is older and stranger than we know."

Her lips parted, but no answer came. She had no idea what to say.

Gus turned to demand answers from Lemoine, but the man had vanished. They were completely alone.

***

The Tempest's crew lingered on the deck as they arrived. It was obvious that repairs were complete. The hole in the hull had been repaired, they had restocked their supplies, and it was time to leave Dakar.

The sun caught on the rather large gold ring Beatrix now wore on her left hand. A whistle rang out from the crew.

"Didn't hear the bells," one muttered.

"Bells?" the other replied.

"For the captain's wedding." A grin. "Looks like he didn't invite the crew."

Beatrix ignored them, but her cheeks warmed. She should have moved the ring to the chain around her neck, she realized.

"That's enough," Gus said to them, "Get ready to get underway. We sail with the tide."

While Gus, Callahan, and the crew prepared to leave port, Beatrix headed to the galley to see what was to be done about dinner.

***

Gus was not in his cabin when she arrived with the dinner tray. She opened the door anyway and sat at the table. Within a few minutes, he entered and sat across from her.

"You should know," he said quietly, "half my crew now believes you are my wife."

"I did not start that rumor," she replied. Her cheeks flushed. She hadn't contemplated what it would be like to be his wife. It seemed impossible. He may be a titled lord, but he was also a pirate captain. What kind of domestic life could they build? It's not like she could retrofit his ship to host balls and tea parties.

"No," he agreed, his eyes flicking to the ring. "But you've done nothing to stop it."

She folded her hands before her, and the ring caught the light. "Neither have you," she said simply.

He studied her for a moment longer, then leaned in and took her hand. He held it close to his face, examining the ring. He tried to remove it from her finger, but it wouldn't move.

"That ring came from a locked chest in a forgotten warehouse. It was opened by a locket that has not left your neck since I met you. I am not a superstitious man, but you cannot expect me to ignore the…weight of the situation."

She glanced away. "You speak as if you think it means something."

"I do," he said. "Do you remember what happened in the warehouse?"

Beatrix furrowed her brow. She remembered walking with Gus to the warehouse. She remembered walking back from the warehouse. "I—"

"You don't," He declared. "That's because you weren't there."

"What do you mean? I have the ring…"

"When we entered the warehouse, your face went blank. The locket began to glow. There was a chest bound in irons. You kneeled before it, but never so much as looked at it. The locket opened the chest in a flash of light, and inside was that ring. You took it, put it on your finger, and didn't so much as look at me until it was all over and the locket stopped glowing."

She searched his face, looking for some sign that he was joking. She didn't remember any of that.

"And I think you know more than you've told me," he continued. "What is Calverique, really?"

"I don't really know." She said. It was the truth. He opened Arabella's journal to a map at the back and pointed to the symbol of the two entwined rings.

"That ring appears on the cover of this journal, and it's engraved on both of our lockets. Then, there's this map; it has that ring drawn right here. The map is faded, and it doesn't fit with any map on this ship, and I have collected hundreds." He searched her eyes, imploring her to tell him anything to make it all make sense.

Beatrix's pulse quickened. Without a word, she turned and walked briskly toward her quarters. Gus watched her go with confusion flickering across his face. A minute later, she returned with a rolled length of parchment in her hands. She set it on the table and unbound the aged ribbon.

"This," she said, "was my mother's."

He recognized the map immediately. It had the main trade routes from Cornwall to South America marked, with solid lines indicating those used primarily by merchants and various European Navies, and dotted lines showing routes that were particularly hazardous and belonged mostly to pirates and select privateers.

Three locations were marked in red; the one nearest to their current location was at the edge of Dakar's harbor. The others were in the West Indies. In the open sweep of sea between the coasts was a small symbol drawn with a steady hand: two rings, intertwined.

Gus leaned forward, his breath catching. "Where did you get this?"

"I found it hidden in my mother's room at Brackwater Hall. This note was included with it." She handed him her mother's letter. His eyes scanned the words:

There are truths buried deep. Not all are meant to be revealed, but some must be. You cannot trust him, Beatrix. He will never be content with the life he has been given.

This path is not without danger, but it is yours now. Go now, before it is too late. Make your way to Calverique. Trust no one who knows your blood.

What we hid was never meant for men like him. It is your birthright—yours and Aria's.

"So, you read this and ran to board a ship." He thought out loud. "You aren't going to the 'new world.' You are looking for Calverique."

"Yes, though I have no idea how to get there. Did Aria?"

"I don't know. She died before we could leave. She said she had a map…maybe it was this one. Even if it was, the map isn't exactly clear. I have passed by that area at least 20 times in the past 10 years. I don't remember seeing anything there." He realized, of course, that he hadn't been looking.

He pointed at the first red mark. "The first place marked on the map is Dakar. People recognized the locket almost immediately, and we found the ring."

"So…if we go to the other two marks on the map, maybe we will find more clues?" She asked, realizing that he wasn't just wandering the sea. He had a job to do, selling his current cargo and…pillaging and plundering?

"Well, neither of these points is particularly off our course. But Beatrix, what I saw today was disturbing—if not dangerous. We don't know what we'll find."

"There's another problem…" She started.

"Ambrose." He finished.

"Yes, my mother knew he was after something, and he needed me to find it. What if he is after Calverique, too?"

"If he is, he must think there's some sort of treasure there. Neither of our maps shows anything about a treasure. I haven't been able to make out every word in Arabella's journal, but there's no mention of treasure anywhere so far. He might be misinformed." Gus had heard Ambrose talk of "making his fortune" throughout their youth. If he thought there was some incredible treasure trove in the middle of the sea, he would indeed search for it.

"I don't know what, if anything, we will find, but I want to go, Gus. Will you take me?" She hoped he would just say "yes" and they could be on their way, but she knew better. She could tell he had doubts. He stared at the map while his fingers traced the routes.

"I will take you on one condition," he said after careful contemplation.

She gulped. "What's that?"

"You take that damned ring off your finger."

CHAPTER 14

The days at sea after they left Dakar blurred into a steady rhythm of chartroom study and monotony. Each night, Beatrix and Gus pored over Arabella's journal. They spread her mother's map beside it, then bent their heads close under the lamplight. They traced lines, compared distances, and argued over what the faint marks might signify.

When her eyes grew tired, she would absently touch the chain around her neck. The silver locket was now nestled beside the gold ring from Dakar. They were cool against her skin. Gus's gaze would follow the movement every time.

On the sixth evening, the monotony finally broke.

Just before sunset, Beatrix heard a cheer on deck. When Beatrix emerged from her cabin, she found the crew stringing lanterns between the masts. A grimy deckhand had found a battered fiddle. Another had a tin whistle, and already a deep, stomping rhythm was rising from the deck beneath their boots.

Callahan was at the center of revelry, grinning broadly. He was already well into drinking from the mug of rum in his hand. From the looks of him, it wasn't his first.

"It's St. Elmo's Day, my lady," he called, sweeping her an inebriated bow. "He's the patron of sailors. We honor him, and he keeps the lightning from striking our mast…or so the old yarns say. Come, join the fun."

She hesitated, but Callahan pressed a tankard into her hand. Against her better judgment, she took a long swig. The rum was strong and burned her throat, but it loosened something in her chest. She smiled—truly smiled—for the first time in days.

The sailors stomped their feet as the music quickened. Before she could protest, Callahan caught her hand and pulled her into the whirl of a reel. She held her head back and laughed. The sea wind tossed her hair as Callahan spun her around wildly. She couldn't remember the last time she'd had a moment of pure fun. She closed her eyes and let herself go. She was dizzy from the motion and the rum, but she loved every second.

As she came out of a big spin, she saw Gus leaning against the rail. He had a mug in his hand, and his eyes were fixed on her. He didn't smile. His face held only that steady, unreadable gaze that made her breath catch. Callahan spun her once more, then stepped back with a mock bow. Before she could breathe, Gus was there, taking her hand.

"You're mine to dance with tonight," he said. His voice was low enough for her alone. Like Callahan, Gus had lost count of how many mugs of rum he had drunk so far.

His words shivered through her. He drew her to him. His palm was firm at her waist, guiding her with an almost unnerving control. The music shifted, and the fiddler drew long, sweet notes. Gus was a masterful dancer, and their steps matched without effort. Her soft, blue linen skirt brushed against his legs. His breath warmed her temple.

"You've been drinking," she murmured.

"So have you," he countered, his lips curving faintly. "You wear it well."

She laughed softly, but the sound was swallowed by the music. His thumb brushed her side, lingering just long enough to send a rush of heat to her cheeks.

The ring and locket at her throat shifted as they danced, reflecting the lantern light. His eyes flickered to it, and his hand at her waist tightened almost imperceptibly. "The ring suits you better there," he mumbled.

She was going to retort with something witty about his fear of what the ring symbolized, but her reply caught in her throat. She could smell the salt on his skin and the faint spice of rum on his breath. The world beyond the circle of their dance seemed to fall away. The music was growing distant and blurred. She was intensely aware of every place their bodies touched.

When the tune ended, the crew roared their approval. Gus did not release her. His intense, unblinking gaze held hers until the clamor faded. Finally, he took a step back. His hand lingered on hers before he let her go.

"Happy St. Elmo's Day, Beatrix," he said quietly.

Her pulse thundered in her ears. She told herself it was the rum, the dancing, or the heat of the lanterns, but deep down, she knew better.

***

The celebration wound down slowly, as the moon cast its shadowy glow on the deck and the last of the lanterns burned out. One by one, the crew had retired to their bunks or drunkenly drifted to sleep on the deck, leaving only the occasional creak of the rigging in the night wind.

Beatrix lingered at the rail. The last sip of rum warmed her stomach. Her cheeks were still flushed from the dancing. She closed her eyes to steady her head. Her hand touched the chain at her throat without thinking. Tonight, the locket was cool, but the gold ring was warm from her skin.

"You're not sleeping yet."

She turned to find Gus a few paces away. His vest was long forgotten, and his shirt collar was open, baring the taut muscles of his upper chest. The breeze lifted the damp strands of hair at his temple. His voice was quieter, roughened by drink.

"I'm not tired," she said.

He came to stand beside her and rested one hand on the rail. "Neither am I."

For a moment, they simply listened to the water, the wind, and the faint snore from a passed-out sailor. His closeness was different now than it had been during the dance. There was no audience and no music to hide behind. There was nothing but the slow thud of her heart.

"You surprised me tonight," he said at last.

"How?"

"You laughed." His gaze slid to her. "You don't do that often enough."

She smiled faintly with her eyes fixed on the water. "You don't make it easy."

His answering smile was small. "No, I don't."

They stood in silence for another breath before he reached out and touched the chain at her throat. His fingers brushed her skin as they traced the line of it to the locket and ring. Both gleamed faintly in the moonlight. "I keep thinking about what happened in that warehouse," he said.

She swallowed. "So do I."

His eyes lifted to hers, and for a long moment, she thought he might kiss her. The night air seemed to thicken between them as the deck shifted gently underfoot. He let the chain fall against her skin. His hand lingered at her collarbone. Something in his expression darkened. She could see a flicker of his want and decision. He closed the space between them in a single step.

His lips found hers with a heat that startled them both. She could taste the spicy rum on his breath, mixed with the salty sea air. She braced her hands against his chest before curling them into his open shirt. The world seemed to narrow to the press of his mouth, the sure weight of his hands at her waist, and the way the ship's slow roll pushed them even closer.

When he drew back, his breath was unsteady. "You're trouble, Beatrix Wrenwood," he murmured as his forehead brushed hers.

She let out the faintest laugh. "So are you, captain."

For a moment, they stayed in that position, with their arms around each other and their foreheads touching tenderly.

"You should sleep," he said softly.

"You're the captain," she replied, her voice low, "not my keeper."

Something unreadable passed across his face. It wasn't quite a smile, nor was it quite surrender. He turned and left her with the sea and the memory of his kiss.

***

The days after St. Elmo's Day sank into the familiar monotony. The crew spoke in shorter sentences as they conserved their energy against the heavy, sweltering air.

Neither Gus nor Beatrix spoke of their St. Elmo's day encounter on the deck, but neither could stop thinking about it. They filled their days with reading the journal and poring through maps in the chartroom. Their conversations stuck to their ideas about various clues that didn't seem to be leading anywhere, and the night's dinner contents (fish, fish, and more fish). Both replayed the memory of rum-flushed laughter and the press of their bodies locked in a slow dance or enflamed by a kiss.

On the fourth evening after St. Elmo's Day, Gus sat with Callahan in the chartroom. They shut the door against the noise of the sea wind and unfurled a map of the West Indies. Callahan leaned over it with one rough hand braced on the edge of the table.

"Eventually, you have to give me a clue where we're heading." He pointed at a chain of islands on the map. "It looks to me like we're headed to Martinique. I don't recall seeing a pickup or drop-off there on our manifest."

"You've a good sense for direction," Gus replied evenly.

"I've a good sense for more than that," Callahan said. "Martinique takes us several days off course, and you've been spending more hours in that journal than in your own bed."

Gus's mouth curved, but there was no warmth on his face. "Perhaps I've taken a liking to read."

"Perhaps you're after something," Callahan pressed, his eyes narrowing. "And I'll wager it's not sugar or rum."

Gus set down the journal in his hand. "If I told you the truth, would it quiet your curiosity?"

"Depends on the truth."

"The journal tells of a place somewhere in the open sea. It's shrouded in mystery. In some places, it's said to be a curse. In others, it talks about something hidden."

Callahan's brows lifted. "Sounds like a ghost story."

"Maybe it is," Gus began rolling the maps. "But considering the ghost, it's worth following." He opened the journal and showed Callahan the name engraved inside. Recognition instantly flashed across his face.

"Wasn't she one of the…" Gus cut him off immediately.

"Shhh…no one knows about all that, and it may not even be true. What I do know is this *place* is where Trix has been trying to go all along. Arabella was her aunt."

Callahan studied him for a long moment, then grunted. "You're not going to tell me more."

"Not tonight."

His first mate gave a short, humorless laugh. "Then I'll be watching, Captain. I'll know if you steer us toward folly."

They doused the lanterns, sinking the chartroom into darkness. Gus stepped out onto the deck. The night was still, and he lifted his head to the sky to admire the thick blanket of stars. The ship moved gently beneath him; its ropes creaked gently in the warm breeze.

He started for his cabin, then caught sight of it. It was a light—not moonlight—but a pulsing golden glow spilling from beneath Beatrix's door.

His pulse quickened. *Fire.*

He strode to her cabin and rapped hard. "Beatrix?"

No answer.

"Beatrix!"

Still nothing.

He swore under his breath and set his shoulder to the door. It opened with a loud crack. He froze at the sight before him.

The small cabin was drenched in gold, as though a hundred candles blazed. The locket and the ring lay on the bedside table. They were glowing with a heatless light that shimmered against the walls. Beatrix stood before them with her hands resting lightly on the wood. Her eyes were half-lidded and fixed on an unseen object. Her lips were moving, and a low, lilting song spilled from them. The notes were rich and peculiar.

He knew them instantly: *The Compass Waltz*. Aria's haunting lullaby.

Unlike Aria's unearthly humming, Beatrix sang the words with unearthly precision. Her voice was both beautiful and chilling:

The wind may lie, the stars may turn,
But blood will find its line.
A ring of flame, a silver burn,
A vow in brine and pine.

The compass breaks when touched by gold,
The sea forgets the shore,
Yet two shall hold what none can fold,
And open nevermore—

Unless the tune the sea once knew
Be hummed by kin of mine.

She sang it again, slower, with each note enunciated with ethereal meaning.

"Beatrix," Gus said quietly.

She did not turn her head.

He stepped closer to her, and the glow from the locket and ring warmed his skin. He could feel the vibration of the unheard music pulsating from them as he drew closer to Beatrix.

"Beatrix," he tried again, this time laying a hand on her arm. The instant he touched her, the light flared blindingly, and the song stopped.

Her eyes focused on him as though she had just woken from a dream. She blinked rapidly. The golden glow faded from her pupils as though the sunrise-lit sea retreated within them. The locket and ring dimmed to their usual dull silver and gold; their strange radiance was gone as if it had never existed.

She swayed. Gus caught her before she could fall. His hands closed firmly around her waist.

"What happened?" she whispered, her voice thin.

"That," he said in a low, hoarse voice, "is what I was hoping you could tell me."

Her brow furrowed. "I don't…remember."

He searched her face; his own expression was shadowed. "You were singing Aria's song."

She blinked again as her confusion deepened. "I was… what?"

"You knew every word," he said. "Clear as day. And your locket—" He broke off, glancing at the table. "It was glowing, Beatrix. Its glow was so bright that I thought your cabin was on fire."

Her gaze fell to the locket lying motionless beside the ring. It looked as harmless now as any other trinket. She lifted it slowly, letting the chain pool in her palm. "I don't remember touching it," she murmured. "I only remember going to bed."

"That's twice now," Gus said; his voice was quiet but edged. "Twice I've watched your mind vanish from your eyes while the locket shot light across a dark room. You're telling me you don't remember either time?"

"I'm telling you the truth," she said, meeting his gaze with steady defiance, but he could see the faint tremor in her fingers and the slight quiver in her breath.

He still hadn't released her. One hand remained firm at her waist, while the other brushed against her back as though steadying her.

The ship groaned gently around them. In the close space of her cabin, the scent of her hair and the warmth of her body seemed to draw him nearer. His eyes dropped briefly to her mouth before flicking back up to meet her gaze.

"Whatever this is, it's not a game anymore," he said softly. "If that locket is leading you somewhere, I need to know. If it's leading you into danger…" His jaw hardened. "I need to be there when it happens."

Something in his tone was protective, possessive, and laced with something far more dangerous. It sent a shiver through her.

She swallowed. "You already are."

The shadow in his expression deepened as a flicker of emotion passed across his face. Was it fear, perhaps, or longing? He leaned in before she could think to move. His lips brushed hers in a slow, deliberate kiss that left no room for doubt.

The contact was brief, but the air between them seemed to pulse with heat when he drew back. His hand lingered at her waist a moment longer, then he released her and stepped away.

"Lock the door," he murmured, his voice rougher than before. "And don't sing for anyone but me."

Without waiting for an answer, he left her standing there. The ring and locket gleaming faintly, illuminated now only by the lamplight.

***

On the third night after Gus had found her singing in that strange, golden glow, something shifted. The sea was unnervingly calm, like smooth black glass. Its reflection was undisturbed by moonlight, as last night's moon had waned the last light of its cycle.

After dinner, Gus had gone topside for the midnight watch. She drifted in a dream.

It began with a low hum that was so faint she could barely hear it, even in the night's stillness. Slowly, it grew richer and more melodic. It danced and twirled, luring her into a state of deep, languid calm.

The hum became a voice, weaving through the darkness. She held her breath. Was it her mother's? Aria's? She could not tell. It wrapped around her heart like a silken tether, drawing her upright in her bed.

The locket against her breast began to glow. Its silver frame threw pale light beneath her shift. It pulsed; each glow was a heartbeat urging her onward. She followed it.

She was back on the high cliffs of Cornwall, down the path from Brackwater Hall. The wind combed through her hair, and she could hear the waves crashing far below her. Starlight spilled over the water, and a gleaming path appeared leading straight up the cliffside.

The locket's light grew stronger. She walked toward the path. Her steps were sure and soundless; she could feel that she was meant to follow the glittering trail down to the sea to meet the unseen songstress. The melody swelled as at last she met the edge of the path. She lifted her foot to make the great leap of faith…

"Beatrix!"

A strong hand seized her arm, wrenching her back. She stumbled into a hard chest. The breath was snatched from her lungs as her mind's haze shattered like glass. Gus's arms closed around her, holding her fast. His breath was hot against her ear, harsh with alarm.

"What in Hades' name are you doing?" His voice was low but fierce.

She blinked up at him, confused. The night air was suddenly cold against her damp skin. "I… I don't know," she stammered. "I was dreaming. Someone was calling me—"

"You weren't dreaming," he cut in. "You were walking straight for the rail. Another step and you'd have been in the sea." His grip tightened for a heartbeat before he eased it, searching her face for any sign of deceit. "You are wearing the locket."

Her gaze dropped to it where it lay against her collarbone, silver and innocent in the moonlight. "It was warm," she whispered. "And there was…music."

Gus's jaw clenched; its muscles started ticking. He held her a moment longer, as if making certain she wouldn't slip away again. Then he made his decision.

"That's it," he said, his voice leaving no room for argument. "You're sleeping in my quarters from now on."

Her chest constricted, refusing her breath. "Gus—"

"This is not up for debate," he said, already steering her toward the companionway. "I'm not leaving you alone on this deck again in the middle of the night. If that thing calls to you again, I intend to be there to stop it."

She opened her mouth to protest, but the hard set of his jaw told her it was pointless. She had long learned that arguing with Gus when he was determined was a losing game.

Besides, though she would never admit it out loud, the thought of sleeping in the same cabin as Gus Drake sent a warm, treacherous flutter through her chest.

***

Gus's grip on her arm hadn't loosened. He glanced toward the bow where O'Malley stood staring out to sea.

"O'Malley!" The older sailor turned at once, catching sight of Gus standing holding Beatrix's arm. She was dressed in nothing but her shift. He raised his eyebrows. "Aye, Captain?"

"Take my post for the rest of the watch. I've got something that requires my attention." Gus's voice was even, but the look in his eyes allowed for no questions.

"Aye, sir," O'Malley replied. A smile split his face as he moved toward the forward rail.

Without another word, Gus guided Beatrix to his cabin. He had let go of her arm, but his hand was warm and unyielding at the small of her back. They reached his quarters, he pushed the door open, and then stepped aside to let her pass.

"You'll take the bunk," he said, closing the door firmly behind them.

"And where will you sleep?" In all the times she had been in his cabin, she had never noticed a second bunk or even so much as a hammock.

"In the chair." He gestured towards one of the chairs they so often used for dining.

She frowned at him. "This is ridiculous. I can go back to my own—"

"Beatrix, you nearly walked into the sea," he said flatly. "You'll sleep here; end of discussion."

Her lips pressed into a thin line, but she crossed to the bunk. She was suddenly uncomfortably aware that she was not properly dressed for being in his quarters. Her linen shift moved against her skin as she slid beneath the blanket. *His* blanket. It smelled like him—almost clean, but somehow musky from the warm nights at sea.

Gus, for his part, had discarded his boots and rolled his sleeves up to the elbows. He wore only an open-necked shirt and his trousers. The shirt's loose fit did nothing to disguise the breadth of his chest or the strong line of his forearms. With his shirt undone, she could see that he was wearing Aria's locket. She wondered when he had started wearing it again and if it was a symbol of his grief or something related to the puzzle they were trying to solve.

He dragged the chair nearer to the bunk and sat, stretching his legs out in front of him. His eyes never quite left her.

For a long moment, the only sound was the creak of the timbers and the soft rush of the sea outside.

"You're staring," she murmured.

"I'm making sure you don't vanish into thin air," he replied. "Forgive me for keeping watch."

Her pulse beat unsteadily at his words. She pulled the blanket higher, as though it could shield her from the weight of his gaze. "If I fall asleep?"

"Then I'll still be here."

Something in his tone was so sure that it sent a shiver along her skin. She turned on her side to face the wall, but she could still feel him there. His presence filled the cabin. Every small movement seemed magnified in the silence.

The ship rolled gently, and in the quiet sway, she wondered if he could hear the way her heart quickened.

***

The ship rocked gently in the darkness. Four nights had passed since Gus had moved her into his quarters, and neither of them had truly slept. He took the chair by the window and braced his boots against the door. She lay in the narrow bunk, staring into the shadows above her.

The nearness, the heat, and the constant awareness of him were utterly unbearable. Every breath she took seemed too loud in the stillness. She could feel his gaze even when his eyes were closed.

"This is ridiculous," she whispered into the dark. "We slept in the same bed the night before Santiago, and I see no reason why you can't join me in your bed right now."

There was a pause. She heard the faint creak of leather as he shifted in the chair. "That was before I knew who you really were."

She sat up. Her copper hair tumbled loose around her shoulders. "Why does that matter?"

His voice was roughened by exhaustion. "Because you're a lady, and despite my best efforts, I am still a lord. If we make it through this voyage without being forced to marry, it will be nothing short of a miracle."

Her pulse quickened. She thought about all of the impropriety of the past weeks at sea: dining alone with the captain every night, the stolen touches of his hands on her waist, and the savage kisses that spoke of a hunger neither of them dared to name. There was no saving her reputation now—not without a wedding ring.

"Would marriage be a curse?" She asked quietly.

Silence stretched between them, as thick as the humid night air.

"Being married to me would most assuredly be a curse for you," he said slowly. Then, after a beat, his voice dropped to something dark and raw. "For me, being married to you would mean I finally had the right to strip that scrap of clothing from your body and make you writhe in pleasure until you forgot your own name and could only call mine."

Her lungs forgot how to draw the next breath. She should have been outraged. She should have ordered him to take back every word. Instead, her skin prickled with heat. She gripped the blanket tighter around herself as if it could shield her from the image his words painted.

In the dim light, he leaned back in the chair. He stared at her dark silhouette as though daring her to speak again.

CHAPTER 15

Fort-La-Republique, Martinique

The next morning, Fort-de-France stirred awake with the creak of mooring lines and the sharp calls of sailors bargaining for dock space. The scent of sea salt and sugar cane mingled in the sweltering air.

Beatrix stood at the rail as *The Tempest* glided toward the wharf. Her skirts clung lightly to her legs in the humid warmth. Beyond the bustling waterfront, the town rose in a patchwork of whitewashed stone, red-tiled roofs, and bright awnings. It was the closest thing to civilization she had seen since she left Cornwall with this band of pirates.

The sounds of the island reached her as the ship docked. She could hear merchants speaking French as they called their wares. It was a far cry from Paris—at least, the Paris she remembered visiting as a teenager, before the revolution had started—but it felt less like a desperate trade port and more like a place where people lived their lives quietly. She could even hear laughter from children darting through the market stalls.

Gus came to stand beside her. He was close enough that she could feel the heat as his arm brushed hers. "Martinique," he said, as though the name itself was a lure and a warning. "This is their capital city, Fort-de-France. I heard you speak some French to the merchants in Dakar. How fluent is your French?"

"Assez bien pour demander tout ce que je désire…et comprendre la réponse, aussi scandaleuse soit-elle," She answered. The lift of his eyebrow told her his French was excellent as well.

"Good enough to ask for anything you desire, and to understand the answer, no matter how scandalous…" He translated back to her. "Très bien. Keep your eyes open. People here make a living off secrets."

Her gaze flicked to him. "Then perhaps they'll know something of ours." His eyes turned watchful as they disembarked.

***

The streets pressed close around them. Narrow lanes were shadowed by balconies draped in bright pink bougainvillea. As they neared the market, the scent of the sea was replaced with the smell of fresh bread. It was a welcome change after weeks at sea. Oh, was that coffee? It had been weeks since she'd had a proper cup of tea.

Men in loose shirts lounged in doorways, smoking cigars and pipes. Their eyes followed Beatrix in a way that made Gus adjust his pace to keep her just ahead of him. They passed dark taverns with scandalous names (The Coquette's Purse, The Dandy's Wand) and inviting inns as they made their way towards the market.

The market was alive with vendors and townsfolk; all engaged in the back-and-forth bartering dance that set the cadence for life on the island. Each vendor had something practical and something luxurious—literally something for everybody. Crude pottery mugs sat in a stall next to fine bone china teacups. A jewelry vendor displayed rings and bracelets made of copper and tin next to those made of gold.

Beatrix wore her locket openly over her linen blouse, hoping someone would recognize it and lead them to the next clue. She couldn't tell if Gus was wearing Aria's locket, but she suspected he probably was. The locket caught glances, but no one approached them.

Beatrix stopped to question a merchant with a collection of maps and books. She held up the small sketch of the entwined rings from Arabella's journal. He frowned in confusion and offered her a book of French poetry.

Next, she showed the gold ring on her chain to a jewelry merchant and asked if he knew anything about it. He waved her away.

She asked a watch merchant if he knew how her locket opened, but he glanced over his shoulder and returned to his repair work, rudely ignoring her question.

A man and woman stared at Beatrix as she walked to the next stall. Their heads turned as she passed, as if they recognized her.

"That's twice now," Gus whispered. His breath brushed her ear. "They know something; they just won't say it."

She felt the faintest shiver at the proximity of his voice. Her heart warmed at the steady way his hand lingered at her back as they moved through the market. The memory of his scandalous words—*make you writhe in pleasure until you forgot your name and could only call mine*—still rang in her ears. Every glance and every touch carried their weight.

They turned down a shaded street and the noise of the market faded behind them. "We're not going to get answers out here," Gus said at last. "There's someone I need you to meet."

"What if your someone won't talk either?" she asked.

His eyes flicked to hers. They were dark with something unreadable. "He'll speak to me. And if he doesn't…" He let the thought trail off, but the edge in his voice was sharper than the sword at his hip.

***

François Moreau lived above a narrow tavern called Le Plaisir Caché (The Hidden Pleasure). The shutters were half-closed against the glare of the midday sun. The interior was cool and dim, and the thick scent of pipe smoke burned Beatrix's throat. She was pretty sure the lady in the bright orange dress leaning against the bar was a prostitute, but she couldn't be sure. Gus walked past the bar scene, pulling Beatrix up the stairs to François's rooms.

Gus rapped once on the upstairs door before pushing it open. François rose from a chair beside a small desk. He was shorter than Gus, and his skin was a sun-warmed tan shade. His linen shirt was open at the throat, and a single gold hoop glinted in his left ear. His eyes lit in recognition.

"Capitaine Drake," he said warmly, slipping into French before switching to English. "I did not expect to see you so soon. And with a…guest." His gaze lingered on Beatrix in a way that made her pulse beat a little faster, though she wasn't sure if it was caution or irritation.

"This is Beatrix," Gus said. "She's here because of this." He unfolded Arabella's sketch of the entwined rings and set it on the desk.

François bent over it. His brows lifted. "Mon dieu. I have not seen this in many years."

"You've seen it?" Beatrix asked quickly.

He looked from her to Gus, then back to the paper. "Not the drawing, no. But the symbol, yes."

Gus exchanged glances with Beatrix. She lifted the chain around her neck and held out the gold ring and locket.

"The gold ring matches the symbol. It was left for me in Dakar. Something is supposed to be left for me here, too. Do you have any idea what it could be?" She asked. He took the locket and ring in his hand and inspected them.

"I am not sure if something has been left for you, but I have seen the symbol that matches this ring."

"Where?" Gus asked.

"There was a plantation, north of Saint-Pierre. Sugar cane as far as the eye could see. They say the owner had a fondness for riddles and…dangerous things."

"Dangerous how?" Gus did not want to lead Beatrix into any more danger…this journey had been dangerous enough already.

"Dangerous in the way that he is dead now, and no one really knows why. After the hurricane and the fire, his house was abandoned." François's voice was ominous.

"Where did you see the symbol?" Beatrix was undeterred. Her mother had told her to go to Calverique. She could feel that there was something there waiting for her.

"The mark was carved into the stone above the study fireplace. It looked just like your drawing: two rings, entwined."

The line of Gus's jaw sharpened. "When did you see it?"

François shrugged. "Fifteen years ago, maybe more. The house still stands, though it is not a place locals care to visit. They say it is cursed."

Beatrix's mind shifted once again to Gus's words that night in the darkness—*For you, marriage would be a curse. For me, I would finally have the right to strip that scrap of fabric from your body…*

She swallowed, forcing her focus back to François. "How would we get there?"

"A cart, if you want to be comfortable. A horse, if you want to be quick." His eyes flicked again between them. "But if you are wise, you will not go at all."

Gus straightened. His expression was unreadable. He looked at Beatrix, sensing her determination and knowing there was no way they were leaving this bloody island without finding their clue. "We'll take our chances."

François exhaled sharply through his nose, as though he'd expected no other answer. "Then you'll want to leave now, before the sun sets." He scribbled an address on a scrap of paper and slid it across the desk. "The road is not safe after dark."

When they stepped back into the blinding heat of the street, Beatrix adjusted her skirts to keep pace with him.

His hand lingered at the small of her back as they descended toward the harbor. The contact was brief, but enough to remind her that every step toward this mysterious plantation was also a step deeper into whatever tangled thing lay between them.

***

The road to the plantation was little more than a rutted path through tangled greenery. Late afternoon light filtered through broad banana leaves and the towering stalks of overgrown sugarcane. This far from town, the only sound was the hum of insect wings.

"Gus?" She asked, making conversation on the long walk.

"Yes, Beatrix?"

"Would you tell me what happened the night Aria died? Maybe there's a clue there…something we haven't thought of yet." He stopped suddenly. His jaw clenched, and his eyes closed. She took his hand in hers, willing him to speak.

"You're right; You should know," he said. He started walking again, but did not let go of her hand.

"Go slow. Tell me the story, and I won't ask questions until you're through."

Gus took a long breath, and the words spilled out as they walked.

"Aria and I had been courting for months. I met her in the village when I returned home from Oxford. She was buying ribbons from a merchant, and I could not take my eyes off her. She smiled when she saw me staring, and we were inseparable after that. We met every day. We walked along the sea cliffs. She packed picnics and we lay together in the tall grass. She would hum that tune of hers and hold my hand, just like you're doing right now."

She looked down at their entwined hands. She could picture Aria walking with him, humming and swinging his hand as they strolled.

"When I realized that I couldn't picture my life without her, I asked her to marry me. It was the most natural thing in the world. She said yes without the slightest hesitation. She ordered the silver dress with the delicate lace, while I asked your father's permission to marry her. He agreed and seemed genuinely happy for us." He paused a moment, then exhaled sharply.

"My father was not so happy. Apparently, there are things I didn't know about your family. I still don't, to be honest. My father forbade me from marrying Aria and threatened to disinherit me. Of course, I am his one and only heir, so he really had no way to do that." Gus's voice trailed. He sighed and stared up at the clear blue sky. Then he continued.

"So, behind my back, my father and Ambrose came up with a plan. Ambrose would marry Aria. Since he was illegitimate, my father didn't really care who he married. Your cousin had a sizable dowry, which would set Ambrose up for life. He loved this idea, so he pursued her.

"In the meantime, Aria and I had come up with our own plan. We would leave Cornwall and start our own life together, somewhere far away. Everything fell apart. Ambrose proposed to Aria; her refusal enraged him. She told him about our plans to leave together. He swore it would never happen, and that she would be his."

"Sounds familiar," Beatrix murmured under her breath. Gus looked down at her.

"Indeed. So, Ambrose decided he was offended by her refusal. He came home to Merthwaite, where I was packing to leave, and challenged me to a duel. It was completely illogical but being young and reckless, I agreed. We chose pistols and set a time that evening to meet in the field behind the house. The only witnesses were our grooms.

"When I didn't arrive at the cove that night where I was supposed to meet Aria, she came looking for me. She found me and Ambrose in the field just as we were about to take our shots. I had no intention of shooting Ambrose. He was my brother—my friend—and I loved him. I knew his rage was all our father's doing. So, I shot wide. Ambrose aimed straight at my chest. Aria stepped in front of me, and his shot tore through her gut." He breathed in sharply and exhaled with slow deliberateness. When Beatrix looked up at him, she could see that hot tears stung his eyes, but he did not let them spill.

"I tried to stop the bleeding, but there was no way to save her. I sat on the cold ground and held her in my arms, willing her to live. I bargained with God and the fates. I begged them to take me instead, but there was nothing I could do. Ambrose knelt beside us as she pressed the locket into my hands. Her eyes bore into mine as she sang the lyrics to that song. She was teaching it to me, urging me to find something.

"When she fell limp in my arms, I dropped into a fit of tears and fury. Ambrose kept apologizing, saying he didn't mean for her to die. He sent his groom to the house to get our father, who took over the entire situation. He told me to leave immediately—to go to my aunt's estate in Ireland. He put me in a carriage, and in my grief and shock, I just left. All I had was Aria's locket and the clothes on my back. I never made it to my aunt's house. I met Callahan in a tavern in Dublin on the way there—he was running from the cassock, of all things—we went to sea and never looked back."

"Callahan was meant to be a priest?" She asked incredulously. She had kept her promise not to ask questions until his story was finished.

"Oh, aye. Don't let him fool you—he's the second son of the Viscount of Kilbride. He's nearly as noble as you…or me, I suppose."

She smiled as she tried to picture Callahan in a priest's robes. Then, she turned her attention back to Gus's tragic tale. "Have you spoken to your father since that night?" She asked, quietly.

"No," he answered. "I don't know what I would say to him. I don't even know where he buried Aria."

"I think he must have buried her at sea," Beatrix thought out loud. "Her hair comb—the silver one with the sapphires—washed in on the tide a few days after she disappeared."

Gus nodded. "That would make sense for my father. He would have had to hide her body to keep his sons from being arrested for dueling. Ambrose could have hung for murder."

They walked in silence for a while. Their hands stayed entwined. Beatrix was beginning to understand the depths of his grief and why he chose this life away from the luxury of their gilded homes in Cornwall.

They reached the plantation ruins just as the sun dipped low. It cast the charred edges of the great house with molten light. What remained of the façade was streaked with soot and strangled in creeping vines. Shattered shutters hung from rusted hinges; their faded green paint flaked under her fingertips as she followed Gus inside.

The interior was hushed but not silent. There was a faint rustle as lizards scurried across the once opulent walls. She heard the cry of a bright green tropical bird that landed on what was once a windowsill. The bird tilted its head, studying her as her feet met the marble floors that were cracked and veined with weeds. The scent of damp stone and ash lingered even after years of neglect.

Gus stepped to the doorway and scanned the overgrown grounds as the sun began fading over the horizon. "We're not making it back to the ship tonight. The road is too dangerous after dark."

Her pulse stumbled. "So we…?"

"We stay here," he said simply.

They explored what was left of the house in the dark, looking for somewhere to sleep. The upstairs parlor was the least ruined room they found. It was a long, narrow space with faded blue wallpaper that was curling at the seams. Its tall windows were draped in cobwebbed lace. Against one wall stood a sofa covered in canvas. Gus pulled back the covering. Dust flew into the air, and Beatrix coughed and fanned the air in front of her. The dust cloud dissipated, revealing a once-elegant sofa. Its upholstery was threadbare, but miraculously intact.

"You'll take the sofa," Gus said in a tone that left no room for argument. She might have bristled, but she was too aware of the sinking dark outside and the desolate hush of the plantation.

"Where will you sleep?" She asked. Her eyes searched for another piece of furniture in the ever-darkening room.

He tossed his coat over a broken chair and loosened the collar of his shirt. "The floor by the door, in case we have visitors."

The idea that anyone would come here, to this forgotten ruin, in the pitch-black dark made her shiver. She sat on the sofa and drew her knees up; the cushions sank under her weight. On the floor across the room, Gus stretched out with one arm behind his head and rested the other over the pistol at his side.

Silence settled between them. She could still hear insects humming and frogs ribbiting, but the loudest sound was in her mind. She recounted Gus's story of the day Aria died, but the sins of the past were constantly interrupted by her memory of last night in his cabin. She could hear his rough, tense voice: *For me, being married to you would mean I finally had the right to strip that scrap of clothing from your body and make you writhe in pleasure until you forgot your own name and could only call mine.*

Her skin prickled with heat. She shifted on the sofa, trying to push the memory away, but her eyes found him in the darkness. His white shirt was open at the throat, revealing the hard lines of his chest.

As if he felt her gaze, he turned his head. "Can't sleep?"

She hesitated. "It's too hot."

"Is it?" One corner of his mouth lifted. "You're thinking about it, aren't you?"

She swallowed. "About what?"

"You know." The statement held something dangerous…he dared her to speak her wicked thoughts out loud.

"I suppose you're used to better accommodations," he said. His velvet voice was gruff with exhaustion.

She gave a quiet, incredulous laugh. "Is that what you think keeps me awake?"

He pushed himself up onto one elbow and studied her across the narrow stretch of floor. "Then what does?"

"You know very well." The memory of his words burned in her mind with humiliating clarity. She could feel the heat rise in her cheeks.

The air between them tightened. He rose from the floor with the slow, deliberate grace of a cougar. He stood beside the sofa. She could feel his warmth and smell the faint scent of musk and sea salt on his skin.

"Tell me," he insisted softly.

She shook her head, but her defiance was weak.

He leaned over her with one hand braced on the back of the sofa. His body was large and teasing as he loomed over her. "I could make you," he murmured, and there was no mistaking the truth in his tone. He could coax it from her, wring it from her, until she said anything he wanted.

Her pulse thundered. "And what then?"

His gaze dropped to her mouth, then lower, and when his answer came, it was little more than a growl. "Then I stop pretending I don't think about it every damned night."

She should have pulled away. Instead, she rose toward him, drawn by something she could no longer deny. Their lips were so close that her breath mingled with his. Then, just as she thought he might close the distance, he pushed away, leaving her aching with the absence of him.

He returned to the floor, his voice unsteady. "Sleep, Beatrix. If you can."

But she did not sleep, and neither, she suspected, did he.

***

The morning light crept through the ruined plantation's shutters in thin, dusty beams. Gus sat on the floor with his back braced against the cold stone wall. He listened to the slow, even rhythm of her breathing.

Beatrix lay curled on the faded sofa with her copper hair spilling loose over the pillow. One arm rested above her head, and the blanket slipped just enough to bare the pale line of her shoulder. She looked impossibly soft in the harsh morning light.

He should not have been watching her. He should have been thinking of the task ahead: Calverique and the clue they hoped to find. Instead, his gaze kept tracing the gentle rise and fall of her chest and the curve of her mouth as she dreamed.

Every tender or torrid thought he had of her felt like betrayal. The ghost of his love for Aria still clung to him. Even now, it was fierce and unrelenting. He had promised himself he would never replace her.

Telling Beatrix about the night of the duel had been difficult. In all of the years since Aria had been passed, he hadn't spoken the entire story out loud to anyone. Callahan knew the basic idea—Aria's name, that she died the day before they met, that he blamed himself for her loss—but that was the closest he'd come to talking about it.

Saying the words aloud as Beatrix held his hand felt freeing in a way. His confession lifted something from his chest. But still, it felt wrong to have feelings for another woman, even if she was the most alluring woman he had ever met.

He closed his eyes and pictured Aria. Her long, pale hair spilled down her back like a cloud kissed by the sun, part gold and part silver. Her crystal blue eyes held only warmth when she looked up at him and smiled. He could hear her humming softly, as if her inner world was enchanted by an opus that no one could hear but her.

His love for her felt pure and light. In his dark underworld of seedy taverns, deadly weapons, and brutal battles, he clung to her memory to remind himself that there was good and kindness in the world, even if her soft light had been extinguished all too soon.

Beatrix was a whole different kind of light. She was a burning flame that ignited his senses in a way he didn't know was possible. Where Aria had been all gentleness, Beatrix was all passion—burning, all-consuming passion that made him forget himself, and even Aria. That felt like betrayal.

But Aria was gone. Beatrix was here.

In the quiet of that morning, surrounded by dust, decay, and the harsh Caribbean sun, it struck him with sudden, brutal clarity: He could no longer stand not touching her—not for one more moment. She had to be his.

He closed his eyes one more time, and he remembered Aria on the cliffside. Her hair was filled with the flowers she had picked along their walk, and she skipped along in front of him joyfully, humming her tune. *I love you, Aria,* he thought. *But I have to let you go now.* She kept skipping along, but this time, he didn't follow.

He opened his eyes and took a long breath. He rose from the floor quietly and crossed to the sofa. For a moment, he simply stood there, relishing the sight of her. His emotions were torn between the tenderness of wanting to cradle her sleeping body against him protectively and the carnal temptation of wanting to possess her body and soul.

Her lashes fluttered, and she stirred. "What time is it?" she mumbled, her voice still heavy with sleep.

"Late enough," he said, though he barely knew the hour.

She stretched and shifted to rise, but he stepped forward. He braced one hand on the back of the sofa, caging her in without quite touching her.

"You're in my way," she said. A faint flush crept into her cheeks.

"Am I?" His voice was soft. Something was different about him this morning, but she couldn't tell what.

He reached down and brushed a strand of hair from her face, letting his fingers linger longer than they should.

"I see you finally fell asleep. You look as though you dreamed well," he said; his voice was gruff with desire.

"I suppose I did." She whispered. His closeness was intoxicating.

"Did you dream of me?" He asked. She couldn't tell if he was teasing her or tempting her. His expression was different from what she had ever seen. It was heated yet somehow resolved.

Air seemed too fragile to draw. "Do you really want to know?"

His gaze deepened. "What did you dream, Trix?" He raised an eyebrow, compelling her to tell him some wild, hidden desire.

She didn't answer, but her hands came up to rest against his chest. He could not stop himself from closing the distance. He sat beside her on the sofa and pulled her into his arms. He kissed the soft hollow of her throat gently.

"Did you dream of this?" He asked, his voice muffled against her skin. His kiss moved higher to the space just below her earlobe. His breath was hot, and her entire body shuddered in surrender to his touch.

"How about this? Did you dream of me taking your earlobe into my mouth?" He demonstrated his dream-worthy ministrations, sucking gently on her earlobe. He took it into his mouth and flicked his tongue around it. She melted against him, pulling him tighter, completely lost in his touch.

His mouth released her earlobe as her breath stilled in protest. He wasted no time capturing her lips. He kissed her lightly at first, almost as if testing her resolve, but the kiss quickly became something hungrier. His hands explored her back, feeling her womanly curves through her soft linen dress.

If he didn't stop now, there would be no stopping at all. He wanted all of her. He wanted her to be his—only his—right now, and forever.

"Beatrix," he said against her mouth. His breath was unsteady, almost a pant, filled with longing. "Say the word, right now, and I'll find a priest right here in Martinique. Today. This hour."

She stared up at him, wide-eyed in shock. Her eyes searched his, and he could feel her rejection looming in the words she couldn't find. Her silence burned through him more than any answer could have.

Reluctantly, he forced himself to let go of her. He closed his eyes to hide his disappointment. He couldn't meet her gaze, not now. He had gone too far. What was he thinking?

"We'd best find the next clue," he said, though his voice was rougher than he intended.

He turned away and walked towards the door. He knew the image of her in that morning light and the feel of her in his arms would haunt him long after they left Martinique.

***

Her breath caught against his mouth. His words—*say the word right now, and I'll find a priest here in Martinique*—still rang in her ears, as vivid as his hungry, earth-shaking kiss.

Had her pirate lord just proposed to her?

He pulled away before she could speak. He turned his back to her as if he had not just threatened to make her his wife before sundown. She sat there on the sofa. Her heart pounded in wild, uneven beats as she stared at the broad line of his shoulders.

Did he mean it? Or was it just the heat of the moment—the inevitable byproduct of too many nights spent in close quarters?

He crossed the room to gather his coat. He never looked back at her. She was left stunned as he opened the door and stepped into the dilapidated hallway. The moment had passed, but she was pretty sure what her answer would have been if he had given her just another moment to gather her thoughts.

***

The house was a skeleton of its former glory. Columns crumbled under the grip of climbing vines as the jungle sought to reclaim its borrowed space. Gus led the way with his sure stride. His boots crunched over broken tiles and rotting timbers.

They found the study on the bottom floor. The ceiling and roof above had burned in the fire, leaving the room exposed to the elements. Faded portraits hung crooked on the soot-stained walls. The previous occupant's faces were blurred by mildew, grime, and ashes.

Gus ran a hand along the edge of a massive desk. Its mahogany was blackened with age and disuse. "This place must have belonged to someone with deep pockets," he said.

Beatrix moved toward the oversized hearth. Her eyes roved over its ornate carvings of vines and serpents. "It's beautiful," she whispered, brushing her fingers across the soot-dark stone. "I wonder what happened to them. Why would they let it all fall like this?"

Gus crouched beside her, squinting at the symbols etched deep into the hearthstone. What he thought were vines from a distance weren't vines at all; they were precise, repeating shapes.

"Look closer at these," he beckoned her. He took her hand and guided it to the vine-like shapes.

"It's the interlocking rings," she gasped. Her hand flew to the gold ring on the chain around her neck. The shapes on the hearth matched it exactly.

"I think we're in the right place," he said.

Before she could respond, the locket against her breast flared to life, casting a golden light over the soot and dust. He turned to see that her expression had gone blank. She looked into the hearth unblinking, and then stepped inside the dark, giant hole, as though pulled by an invisible tether.

"Beatrix—" Gus reached for her but stopped when warmth bloomed against his own chest. His locket—Aria's locket—was glowing too. It pulsed in rhythm with Beatrix's. The pull was sudden, fierce, and impossible to resist.

Together, they pressed their lockets into a carving on the back wall of the fireplace. It gave a deep, grinding groan in response, as their lockets fell back against their chests, still glowing.

A hidden panel slid open, revealing a small iron box. Gus lifted it free. He brushed a thick layer of ash from its lid and then raised it open. Inside the box, nestled in charred and rotting velvet, lay a brass compass. It was beautiful, ornate—and entirely wrong.

The needle spun lazily but never settled. It didn't point north. In fact, it didn't point at anything.

Beatrix's vacant eyes fixed on it, but didn't focus. It was as if she were staring into an unseen horizon. Her lips parted, and a faint hum escaped her. The haunting *Compass Waltz* melody echoed through what was left of the room.

Their lockets pulsed in unison, spilling light over the room. Then Gus heard it: a voice, soft and distant. It threaded through the air like a ribbon of light. It wove into his thoughts, coaxing him to surrender to the golden haze penetrating his mind. For a breath, he lingered.

The faint sway of Beatrix's body in front of him cut through the spell. He caught her arm and held her steady until the glow dimmed and the air cleared. She blinked at him, as if waking from a dream.

Between them, the box from the hearth sat open, revealing the compass. It was unlike any compass he had ever seen, and he had seen many during his years at sea. Its needle still spun without settling, but Gus noticed a small indentation at its center in the shape of a ring.

Without a word, Beatrix lifted the chain from her neck. The gold ring they had found in Dakar slid into her palm. She passed it to him, and their fingers brushed. Gus fit the ring into the indentation in the compass. At once the needle stilled, then swung to a fixed bearing with an almost imperceptible tremor, as if it were eager to be followed.

"It wants me," Gus said quietly. The pull of the compass's direction settled deep in his bones. "It wants me to take it there."

Beatrix's lips parted, but no words came. She had been certain this journey was about her mother's legacy. She thought it was her path to unraveling all of the secrets that seemed to follow her: Aria's, her mother's, and even Arabella's. Yet in that moment, watching the compass answer to Gus and not her, she felt an unsettling shift, as if the journey no longer belonged to her at all.

Still, she managed a small nod. "Then we follow it," she said, trying to sound sure and confident. The words felt heavier than she expected.

***

They left the ruined plantation with the compass tucked safely inside Gus's coat. The air outside was thick with the scent of approaching rain.

They hadn't spoken a word since they left the study. Beatrix thought about how the compass had immediately responded to Gus. *Maybe this was never my journey at all*, she thought.

When she really thought about it, Gus had started this journey a full decade before she even knew it existed. He and Aria had planned to follow this path together. How far would they have gotten with only one locket?

Maybe he understood the song's lyrics? She certainly didn't. They seemed nonsensical, like a lot of children's lullabies.

The song was certainly a clue they had not investigated…not yet anyway. She wondered why. It was *right there*, all the time, never-ending. The tune played unceasingly in her mind and since they found the ring in Dakar.

The compass breaks when touched by gold—Didn't they just use a gold ring with a broken compass? How had they just known that the ring would fit inside it?

She resolved to ask him about it later. Something was obviously occupying his mind as they walked back to the harbor. His stride was so swift that she had trouble keeping up with him.

As they descended the overgrown path toward the harbor road, the rustling of cicadas gave way to the low murmur of village life. Halfway down the hill, an old woman sat in the doorway of a weathered shop shelling peas into a chipped bowl. Her eyes followed them without blinking.

"Best leave the sea's business to the sea," she called after them as they passed. Her voice creaked like an old wooden door. "She doesn't take kindly to those who pry into her secrets."

Beatrix faltered. She turned to look at the woman; did she know something? Gus gave the woman a short nod. His expression was blank. He put his hand on Beatrix's waist and guided her on without a word.

A few more silent moments passed between them as they reached the main street. It was quieter than the day before. Women were hanging laundry out to dry in the warm afternoon sun while looking up at the clouds to see if rain would keep them from completing their chore. Just ahead, a whitewashed church rose above the rooftops. A simple cross hung above its door.

Their pace slowed as they drew closer to the church, as if an invisible force was making the walk more difficult. It was like walking uphill against a harsh wind. The wide wooden doors stood open, inviting entry.

Beatrix's gaze lingered on the threshold. She thought of the words he had spoken that morning—*I'll find a preacher right here in Martinique.* A shiver of memory traced her spine. Their pace had come to a stop at the edge of the street.

"Do you want to go in?" she asked softly.

He didn't look at her. "Do you?" His voice was barely more than a whisper. She studied him. His eyes were fixed on the church's open doors, but something brewed behind them. He wouldn't look at her.

She thought for a moment about what it would mean to be his wife. His life was spent wandering the sea. Would he expect her to wander with him, or would he take her back to Cornwall and stick her in an estate somewhere to wait for him?

Lord and Lady Alverdon. She could picture herself on his arm, being announced as they entered fine ballrooms in London. *Lady Beatrix Drake, the Right Honorable Viscountess of Alverdon.* That would be her title, a name entwined with his forevermore. Well, at least until he inherited his father's earldom and they took on a grander title.

But no, that wouldn't be their life at all. He was a pirate: a lord, a captain, but still a pirate. She would be called simply, *The Captain's Wife.*

When she thought about this morning, and how he had teasingly kissed her throat, her neck, and her lips…well, they could call her whatever they wanted so long as they called her *his.*

Still, something wasn't right. His posture was rigid. He wouldn't even look at her. Had he changed his mind?

They lingered a moment longer; the open church door beckoned like a question neither dared to answer.

At last, he made a long sigh and stepped back onto the cobbled street. "We've a tide to catch," he said. She followed, reluctantly. She secretly wished he'd turn around, take her hand, and lead her to the altar.

Tears formed in her eyes over their missed opportunity, but he didn't notice. His eyes were fixed on the path in front of them, pushing them toward *The Tempest* and away from their private moments in Martinique.

***

By the time they reached *The Tempest*, the sun had set. Callahan was waiting near the gangplank with his arms folded across his chest.

"I was about to send out a search party," he chided. They had been gone two whole days without checking in. "Find what you were looking for?" he asked.

"Found enough," Gus replied shortly. "The final mark on the map points to Saint Lucia. Let the men have their fun tonight, and we'll set sail in the morning."

Callahan gave a slow nod, then busied himself with the night watch. Most of the crew were off enjoying their shore leave, so it would be a quiet night.

Beatrix lingered at the rail, looking back at the village. She could hear distant laughter and the muffled thump of music. Village life seemed filled with simple pleasures, like outdoor dinners with family and shared dances with friends in the square.

"Hungry?" Gus asked, his voice low beside her.

"I could be persuaded," she said with a smile. They hadn't had a proper meal all day.

Below decks, the galley was quiet save for the soft crackle of the stove. The cook was long gone, likely enjoying a night at a tavern somewhere. Gus ladled them a simple meal of salt fish and bread, then placed it before her at a small table in the galley.

They ate without hurry. After a few minutes, the conversation turned naturally to the compass and the gold ring. Gus laid both on the table between them.

When the meal was nearly gone, Beatrix spoke. "When the lockets glowed in the study, you heard it too, didn't you?"

Gus's eyes lifted to hers, cautiously. "I did."

"The Compass Waltz?" She asked, clarifying they had heard the same thing.

He exhaled slowly, leaning back. "What I heard today wasn't just a song. It felt like—" He broke off. He struggled to find the right words. "Like something meant to *hold* me there."

Beatrix nodded. "It's always been that way for me. Even as a child, when my mother sang it to me, it felt like more than music. First, it's relaxing—just like a lullaby, but then it starts to feel alive…like it wants something."

"Wants?" he echoed.

She looked down at the locket resting against her bodice. "Like it wants to be found…or to lead. I'm not sure which."

Gus thought about Aria humming the song as they walked together when they were courting. Back then, it calmed him. He thought he was soothed by his love's sweet voice, but maybe it was something more.

"Have you thought about the song's lyrics? I mean, I'm sure you've thought about them, but what do you think they mean?" She asked.

"I don't know. For years, I tried not to think about them. It was too painful. When Aria was alive, she didn't sing the lyrics…she only hummed. I didn't hear them until the night she sang them to me as she lay dying." This time, when he spoke of Aria, he sounded clearer and less haunted. She couldn't put her finger on it, but something had changed.

"My mother used to sing the lyrics when we were alone in the garden or when I couldn't sleep during a thunderstorm. I just thought it was a child's song. It didn't seem special, especially with Aria humming it through the house all day." She thought about her mother. She had been more attentive than most mothers of the upper class. She took walks with Beatrix almost every day, and they would spend hours in the gardens playing cards and making up games.

"Ok, then let's think about the words, line-by-line."

"Yes, I'll start: *The wind may lie, the stars may turn,*

But blood will find its line," She spoke the words, one by one, without the tune to cloud them.

"Hmm...maybe it just means that no matter what weird thing happens, you can trust your blood—maybe your kin?" The beginning sounded like a riddle to him. He pictured a nonsense poem spoken by children.

"Maybe...next it's: *A ring of flame, a silver burn, A vow in brine and pine.* When the lockets glow, they look like flame...so much so that you thought my cabin was on fire that night you found me singing."

"Yes—and they're both oval, kind of like a ring, so this line must be about the lockets. The vow, though, I'm not sure about that one. *'Brine and pine'* could mean a ship. *The Tempest* is always soaking in a seawater brine, and while her outer hull is English Oak, the deck is pine."

"That's definitely something," She nodded. "I think we solved the next line today: "The compass breaks when touched by gold."

"Ah, yes, that is precisely what happened. The compass spins until the gold ring is placed in its slot, then it 'breaks' by pointing to what it wants rather than to true north." He smiled broadly. It felt great to be getting somewhere with this riddle.

"But the next line doesn't make sense: "*The sea forgets the shore,"* She furrowed her brow. "How can the sea forget the shore? Isn't the sea always touching the shore?"

"I've actually heard of a phenomenon where the sea left the shore. Sailors from the Far East talk about how sometimes the sea will disappear, then reappear in a huge wave, whipping out entire villages in a moment." Gus made waving motions with his hands, pantomiming how the sea would smack a village.

"That's terrifying." Her eyes grew wide as he made the motion.

"Yes, but it's not something I've seen, and I've been at sea for nearly a decade. It might not be what the song means." He tried to reassure her. "What are the last lines?"

"*Yet two shall hold what none can fold, and open nevermore, unless the tune the sea once knew, Be hummed by kin of mine.*" She recited.

"*Two shall hold*...well, we have two lockets, and I don't see a way to fold them, but then, maps can be held by two people, and we have two of those..."

"The last line is about the song, and clearly, I have to sing it...or hum it?" She thought out loud.

"Well, one or both of us have heard the song both times we found a clue. When we reach the big secret, it sounds like you have to sing it back to...whatever is there." He summed for her. He picked up the compass on the table absentmindedly.

"The compass listens to you," Beatrix observed. "Not to me."

"Perhaps," Gus said, as he picked up the gold ring and slipped it onto his pinkie finger. The compass needle steadied instantly, as if in recognition. "But it seems we both have a part to play."

Her eyes lingered on his hand before meeting his gaze again. There was a weight between them now that went further than just the mystery of Calverique.

He cleared his throat as he slipped the compass back into his pocket. "Let's get some rest. We have a long day ahead."

***

They lay in silence for a long time. She lay in his bunk, staring up at the ceiling, while he scrunched down in his chair with his feet propped on the table. Both were thinking about the last two days in Martinique.

Beatrix had stopped trying to solve the riddles of Calverique at least an hour ago. Her mind focused instead on a bigger enigma: August Drake.

What in God's name had happened today? One moment, he looked at her like a man starved, and the next, he kept his distance, as though a single touch might destroy them both. He had hardly spoken on their way back to town, and then stared at the church door as if stepping through it would damn him to hell.

At last, she found the nerve to speak. Rather, she couldn't stand not knowing where she stood with him any longer.

"Would you have done it?" Her voice was quiet, but the question was sharp.

His eyes found hers in the dim light. "Done what?" The low rasp in his voice made her stomach twist.

"Married me today," she said quickly, before courage could desert her.

He did not answer at once. She could hear the slow draw of his breath. His gaze was fixed on her.

He was silent long enough that she could hear her own heartbeat hammer in her ears. Finally, he spoke, slowly and deliberately. "If I had walked you into that church, it would have been because I wanted the right to keep you in my arms, in my life, and in my bed—and God help the man who would try to take you from me."

For a heartbeat, she could only stare at him. Shock rolled through her, followed by a rush of heat, longing, and something tender she couldn't quite name yet. In that moment, the riddles of Calverique, and everything they knew and had yet to know, ceased to matter.

He was it for her. He was the only man she wanted—the only man she had *ever* wanted. Even if she never found Calverique and never understood her family's secrets, she would not care, so long as she had *him*.

The blanket slid from her shoulders. She swung her legs over the bunk and crossed the small space. Her pulse thrummed in her ears. His gaze tracked her every step.

When she reached his chair, she braced her hands on the arms and leaned in, close enough to feel the warmth of his breath.

"Then keep me," she whispered, giving him the right he'd thrice confessed he wanted. This time, he would not mistake that she wanted him too.

His chair scraped back as he stood, pulling her to him. His mouth claimed hers. His kiss was rough and hungry, and she answered in kind. When he broke away for breath, his eyes searched hers.

"I'll ruin you," he rasped.

"You already have," she said, and this time, there was no fear in her voice, only certainty.

His eyes narrowed and searched hers for a long, charged moment. "Do you know what that means?"

She swallowed but held his gaze. "Tell me."

"It means," he said slowly to make sure she understood every word, "I would make you mine in ways you can never take back. You would think of me when you wake and when you sleep. You would feel me in every touch and every breath, until you couldn't remember a time before me.

"And just so we are very clear," His voice turned serious, "if another man so much as looked at you, I would make sure he understood you were not his to want."

Her pulse pounded in her ears. The raw possession in his tone sent a shiver down her spine.

He leaned forward, pressing his forehead to hers. "If I ruin you, Beatrix, it won't be by mistake. It will be because I've decided you belong to me, and even more, you've decided you *want* to belong to me."

Her breath stilled at the nearness of him, the heat of his skin, and the quiet command in his words. She should have been outraged. She should have told him she belonged to no one, but deep inside, something unfurled. It was an ache born of every stolen glance, every near-touch, and every night they had spent in this small cabin with the air between them electric and weighty.

Finally, she found her voice and answered, "And if I did decide that?"

His gaze held hers, intense and unwavering. "Then nothing—not my brother, not your father, not my crew, not even the fates would take you from me."

The pounding of her heart grew almost unbearable. The truth of it hit her all at once: she wanted that. The rest of the world could burn, and she would still want him.

Her voice was a whisper, but it trembled with conviction. "Then let me be yours, Gus."

He held his breath, playing her words in his mind over again to make sure he heard them correctly. His hands came to her waist, pulling her flush against him as if the tiny space between them had become unbearable.

"God help me," he whispered in surrender, the words brushing her lips.

He kissed her, harder this time, unrestrained. Her fingers curled into the front of his shirt, clutching the fabric as though she might anchor herself against the wave of heat rolling between them.

His mouth left hers only long enough to trail along her jaw, down the line of her throat. His stubble grazed her skin. She shivered, and his hands moved up her back until his thumbs brushed the curve of her shoulders. He caught the straps of her shift and eased them down.

The thin fabric pooled on the floor, baring her body to his gaze. He held his breath, and for a moment, he simply looked at her, as if memorizing every line of her curves.

"You are the most beautiful woman I have ever seen," he declared to her, then his hands framed her face again. His thumbs caressed her cheekbones as his mouth claimed hers once more. Each kiss was deeper and hungrier, telling her wordlessly what it meant to belong to him.

She remembered his words about tearing off the scrap of fabric and making her writhe in pleasure. The fabric now lay in a pool at her feet, and she began to wonder about what pleasures he might have in store for her.

She gasped softly as his hands slid from her face down the line of her throat, over her collarbone, and lower still, until they cupped the soft rise of her décolletage. His thumbs brushed their peaks and teased until they hardened beneath his touch.

She let out a little gasp, and he smiled against her lips. His expression was both wicked and knowing. He bent his head to her chest and his mouth closed over one taut peak, drawing it into the heat of his mouth. A rush of sensation shot through her, and she clutched his shoulders for balance.

"Gus…" she whispered, uncertain whether it was a plea or a warning.

"Yes, call my name," he murmured against her skin before lavishing her with the same slow, deliberate attention on the other swell of her chest. His hands roamed lower and skimmed over the curve of her waist and hips, until his fingers brushed the bare skin of her thighs.

Her knees weakened under the heat of his touch. He guided her backwards until she felt the edge of the bunk behind her legs. His mouth found hers again, and his tongue stroked hers as his fingers slipped higher between her thighs and coaxed her legs apart.

The sensation made her gasp, and her head fell back against the mattress.

"Gus?" Her voice was questioning this time. She wanted to push him away and pull him closer at the same time.

His lips traced the column of her throat while his fingers explored her folds with confident, patient strokes, circling, pressing, until she was trembling and clutching at him. Her slickness beckoned him.

"You are ready for me," he said against her ear, his voice low and rough with desire. "Do you have any idea what you do to me?"

She could only shake her head. Her breath was coming fast, and her body arched into his touch.

He eased her further onto the bunk, bracing himself so that his weight didn't crush her. Her hands went to his shirt, fumbling at the ties until she could push the linen aside and lay her palms against the hot, hard plane of his chest. He slid the garment off his body and threw it carelessly to the floor, taking her hand in his and pressing it against his chest.

"Do you feel that?" He asked her. His heart raced beneath her touch. "That's what you do to me, but that's not all."

He undid his breeches and discarded them to join her shift on the floor. She gasped at the sight of him. Every line of his muscled body was taut, and his manhood jutted forth in hard readiness. He let her look at him a moment.

"If I take you now," he said, taking a moment to catch his breath so he did not hurt her with his raw desire, "there is no going back. You'll be mine."

"I already am," she whispered. Boldly, she took his hardness in her hand and stroked it tenderly, circling the tip with her finger curiously. He moaned in ecstasy. He was a man undone.

With a groan, he kissed her again and entered her slowly, carefully, until he was seated fully within her. She gasped as she felt her body stretch to accommodate his unfamiliar fullness, but the heat in his gaze held her there, grounding her in his touch.

He began to move, slowly at first, giving her time to adjust. His lips brushed hers between ragged breaths. Their rhythm built gradually. Each thrust drew soft sounds from her that only spurred him on. Her nails dug into his back, and her body rose to meet his in perfect, desperate sync.

When the crest broke, it was like a wave crashing over them both. Her cry—*Gus*—was swallowed by his kiss. His body shuddered as he spilled into her, and he held her tight as though he would never let go.

For a long time, they stayed tangled together, with the sounds of the ship and the sea fading into the background. Only when her breathing steadied did he shift. He drew her against his chest and tucked the blanket around them.

"So," he asked teasingly, "Do you remember your name?"

Her lips curved against his chest. "No… Perhaps you ought to remind me again."

His laugh was low and wicked. "Careful, sweetheart. I'm quite happy to spend the rest of the night doing just that."

She tipped her head back, and her copper hair spilled over the pillow. The playfulness in her eyes stole the last of his resolve. Something inside him settled with a finality he could neither fight nor name. He had spent weeks holding her at a distance, convincing himself he could keep her there. Tonight, that lie was shattered.

He brushed a loose copper strand from her cheek. She was his now, not just in body, but in every way. Even more, he was hers, whether he liked it or not.

Without another word, he pulled her close. Her body fit against him as though they had always been meant to sleep this way. He kissed her forehead and closed his eyes. There was no going back now.

CHAPTER 16

The sun had barely risen when Gus strode down the narrow street toward the heart of Fort-La-Republique. Martinique's capital city had, up until the start of La Révolution, been called Fort-Royal, and most of the locals still used the old name. This morning, political upheaval was the furthest thing from Gus's mind. He moved through the bustle of morning vendors and fishermen carting baskets of the day's catch. His thoughts fixed on the pealing church bells breaking with the dawn.

Her scent still lingered on his skin. He could feel the warmth of her hands, the softness of her mouth, and the way she had pulled him into her as though she had always known that she was meant for him and him alone. She had looked at him in the darkness with such fierce trust and wanting that he could barely breathe for the memory of it.

He had risen before first light and untangled himself from her embrace without waking her. He had paused long enough to look back and study the way the dim lantern light still edged her shoulders where the sheet had fallen away. She had never looked more beautiful, peaceful, powerful, and absolutely his.

On his way out, he had stopped beside Callahan on the railing, where his first mate was watching for their crew to stumble their way back to the ship after a night of drinking and debauchery. He hadn't offered an explanation, but made a quiet, firm announcement.

"We won't be sailing to Saint Lucia today."

Callahan had blinked, but kept staring straight ahead. "No?"

"No." Gus's mouth had twitched into something close to a smile. "Today, I'm getting married."

Now, every step brought him closer to the church and the future he had tried so long not to imagine.

His mother's ring rested in his pocket. Suddenly, its small weight felt enormous. He had kept it with him all of this time, since the day he took it out of her jewelry box to place it on Aria's finger some ten years ago. He had carried it from port to port like an anchor to a life that was no longer his. Now, he knew exactly where it belonged. He could not wait to see it take its rightful place on Beatrix's finger.

They had taken the step no respectable man could ignore, and though he doubted he had ever been respectable, he would not leave her to the ruin the world would heap upon her name.

He paused outside the whitewashed church where they had stood the day before. The priest was not yet in sight, but he would be. Gus was not leaving Martinique without finding him. Today, she would become his wife.

***

Beatrix woke slowly. Her body was languid and warm beneath the linen sheets. Her bare skin still tingled from his touch. Her body ached in places she had never noticed before; not unpleasantly, but deeply, as though he had left his mark on every inch of her.

She shifted leisurely, and the sheet brushed over her thighs. Memory washed over her in a rush: his mouth on her collarbone and the low, wicked sound he'd made when she gasped his name.

A flush crept up her neck before her eyes even opened. She smiled against the pillow, biting her bottom lip. She expected the warmth of him beside her, but when she reached across the mattress, she found only the soft hollow where he had lain.

Her eyes opened. The bed was empty, and the room was quiet…and then she saw it.

At the foot of the bed, carefully laid over Gus's worn sea chest, was a dress unlike anything she had ever owned. It was soft dove-gray silk with pearl-threaded embroidery along the bodice. It was as light as air; its fabric rippled faintly in the morning breeze blowing in from the open cabin window. The sleeves were sheer and elegant, and the neckline dipped just low enough to whisper at what lay beneath. It was regal, exquisite, and daring.

A note lay atop it, held in place with a frangipani blossom. She picked up the blossom and inhaled its lush scent, then she lifted the paper with trembling fingers.

I will send for you when everything is ready. Wear this today. I can't wait to take it off of you later when we celebrate our wedding night.

—Gus

Beatrix let out a breath she hadn't realized she was holding. Her knees weakened, and her heart pounded. She sat back on the edge of the bed, holding the note and the flower. He had chosen this. He had thought of her, touched this fabric, imagined her wearing it, and then imagined her bare again beneath his hands.

The memory of his voice in the dark whispered through her. *"You would think of me when you wake and when you sleep. You would feel me in every touch and every breath, until you couldn't remember a time before me."* He was right; now that he had claimed her as his, all she could think about was him.

She pressed the frangipani to her lips, then let it fall onto the bed as she stood to dress.

***

The church was quiet when Gus stepped inside. A few candles flickered near the altar. Compared to his family chapel in Merthwaite—the place he always thought he would marry, before his father forbade him to wed Aria—this church was plain, with little more than a few embellished candlesticks at the end of the aisle and a single brass crucifix hanging above the altar to speak of religious pageantry.

The priest sat in a chair near the altar, languishing over an open Bible. He was dressed for morning mass in fine white robes that were embroidered with gold thread. He blinked up at Gus, surprised to see a foreigner so early in the morning.

"May I help you, monsieur?" He asked in his native French.

"I need to be married," Gus said without hesitation. "Today."

The priest gave a soft, incredulous laugh. "Today?"

"Yes." Gus's jaw was set. "Now, if you're willing."

"Do you know where you are, monsieur?" The priest folded his hands. "This is a Catholic parish. We do not perform hasty ceremonies for strangers who walk in off the street."

"I'm not a stranger. My name is August Drake. My bride and I are from Cornwall, and we have no family here. We have no parish to proclaim the banns, but I will not leave this island until she is my wife."

"Cornish?" The priest's brows drew together as he switched to English, "Then you are Protestant."

"Yes," Gus said plainly, matching the priest's language swap. "But I was baptized, and I can say the vows. So can she. We don't need witnesses, or anything special—just your blessing."

Father Renaud sighed, already shaking his head. "Monsieur Drake—" Gus could hear a "no" coming. He knew he needed to play all of his cards to make this wedding happen.

"That's Lord Alverdon." He interrupted. His voice was commanding with the weight of his ancestral title.

"My Lord Alverdon, I cannot marry a couple without first reading the banns. It is canon law. There are forms, records, and procedures. This is not how things are done."

Gus stepped forward, drew a small pouch from his coat, and placed it carefully on the rail between them. It landed with a soft, unmistakable clink.

The priest hesitated.

Gus held his gaze. "No one will know but us. She is waiting. I am asking for mercy, not spectacle. There is no time to lose."

Father Renaud looked at the pouch, then at Gus. He let out a long breath and crossed himself slowly. "You are certain?"

"I've never been more certain of anything in my life."

Another moment passed, then the priest reached for the pouch and nodded once. "Very well. I will perform the ceremony, but it will be quiet and quick. No choir, no pageantry."

"I don't want pageantry," Gus said. "I want her."

The priest gave a weary sigh and turned toward the altar to begin his preparations.

Gus moved to a narrow table near the side aisle, where a quill and inkpot stood beside the parish register. He tore a scrap of paper from the corner of a hymn leaflet and wrote in a firm hand:

Callahan,

Bring her now. Tell her I'll be waiting at the altar. Come alone; we don't want to make a spectacle.

—A.D.

He folded the note once, then looked up to see a boy in a red cassock lighting the tapers near the side nave.

"You there," Gus said quietly.

The boy turned, startled. "Monsieur?"

"Take this to the harbor. There's a ship in dock called *The Tempest.* Find a man called Callahan—he has broad shoulders and a red beard. He's likely pacing. Put this note in his hand. Can you do that?"

The boy nodded, eyes wide. "Oui, monsieur."

Gus slipped a coin into the boy's palm, then pressed the note into his fingers. "Go. Now."

As the child slipped out the door, a few townspeople began filing into the church, murmuring to each other as they took their places for morning mass. A woman dipped her fingers in holy water while an old man genuflected at the end of a pew.

None of them knew the man in the dark coat standing alone by the altar rail with his heart pounding, and his eyes fixed on the door.

***

Beatrix heard Callahan's boots on the deck. He climbed the steps two at a time and paused in the doorway. He cleared his throat and then knocked.

She opened the door, already dressed in the gown Gus had chosen. The silk clung to her in all the right ways. It made a faint "swoosh" as she moved. She had left her hair unbound, and it spilled in soft curls over her shoulders in a way that felt daring and exactly right. Tucked just above her ear was the frangipani blossom. Its pale petals stood out brightly against her copper curls.

Callahan gave her a look that was part admiration, part disbelief. "You're sure you're ready for this?"

She smiled, faintly. "Yes."

He offered his arm. "Then let's get you to the altar before he explodes."

They descended the gangplank into the sun-warmed streets, winding past vendors and shopkeepers who had begun packing away their morning wares. Children darted between stalls, chasing one another with ribbons.

They walked in silence for a while. The church bells had long since stilled. Mass was over.

Callahan cleared his throat again. "He's a good man," he said with eyes fixed ahead. "He's stubborn, and prideful as hell…but he's got more heart than he lets on. He would bleed himself dry to keep someone he loves safe."

Beatrix glanced up at him.

"He doesn't say much," Callahan went on, "but I've known him a long time. I've never seen him look at anyone the way he looks at you."

She swallowed. The frangipani's scent rose as the sun warmed into midday. "We've never spoken of love."

Callahan gave a quiet snort. "Maybe not, but if you don't love him now, you will. Just…be kind to him. He needs that more than he'll ever admit."

Beatrix nodded, and a sudden ache bloomed in her chest. She hadn't said the words; neither had he, but she felt them now, fierce and clear.

She *did* love him.

The church stood just ahead of them. She could see its whitewashed walls catching the sun. She stepped forward, and her silk skirt brushed the stone steps as she climbed.

The doors opened, and there he was: standing at the altar with his back straight, coat brushed clean, and his hands folded loosely in front of him. His grey eyes found hers at once. He smiled.

***

Gus turned as the doors opened, and for a breathless instant, he couldn't move.

She stood at the threshold, bathed in light. The silk dress clung to her like morning mist. Her copper hair was unbound and wild around her shoulders. The frangipani bloom he had left for her glowed pale behind her ear. She looked like something conjured—part angel, part warrior, and somehow still more than both.

She was *his*.

She walked toward him with slow, measured steps, while Callahan beamed at her side. She held her head high, with her green eyes fixed on Gus—not the altar, not the priest, not even Callahan—only him.

Every heartbeat echoed like cannon fire in his chest.

When they reached the altar, Callahan turned to her with a gentleness that surprised even Gus. He took her hand, lifted it carefully, and placed it into Gus's.

"She's yours now," he said quietly. "See that you deserve her."

Then Callahan stepped to Gus's right and folded his arms. His shoulders squared and his jaw set. He would stand witness; he would guard the moment.

Gus looked down at Beatrix as his fingers closed around hers. Her hand was warm and steady with the same impossible certainty he felt thrumming in his bones.

He raised his eyes to the priest and gave a single nod.

The priest opened his book and began the ceremony in measured, solemn tones. Latin lilted at the edges of the French, and Gus caught only fragments of it. He'd stood at many altars in his life, but never like this—never with a heart that knew its answer before the question was asked.

He barely heard his own voice as he spoke the vows. Each word bound something inside him that had been unraveled for far too long.

"I, August Leander Drake, take thee, Beatrix Althea Wrenwood, to be my lawful wife. To have and to hold from this day forward…"

Her voice followed his, but hers was soft, steady, and radiant as a sunrise. When she said his name, *August Leander Drake*, the world tilted.

They stood with hands clasped together, sharing even breaths between them. The priest raised his eyes and turned the page. This was it—in mere seconds, the priest would proclaim her his, forevermore. Gus held his breath in anticipation.

"If any man here present knows of a reason why this union should not lawfully proceed," he said, "let him speak now or forever hold his—"

The door slammed open. Wood cracked against stone, and a shout echoed through the nave.

"STOP!"

The shout cracked through the air, loud enough that the candles flickered in response. In the stillness of the sanctuary, the sound felt profane.

Gus turned; his heart was already racing. His hand flew to his waist to brandish…a weapon he hadn't brought. He cursed under his breath. Of course, he hadn't; even a dedicated sinner knew bringing weapons into a church was sacrilege.

He glanced at Callahan, who stood tense beside him. His first mate's face had gone grim. He, a devout Irish Catholic once meant for the priesthood, was empty-handed as well.

Ambrose stepped into the aisle, framed by the light from the doorway behind him. Despite his haggard appearance, he bore no sign of the wound Gus had inflicted upon him just a few weeks prior. Dust clung to his boots and coat. His cravat was loose, and the black opal he kept there hung to one side. His dark blonde hair was wind mussed and dripping with sweat.

Gus felt all of the air leave his lungs as he saw the pistol slung openly at his brother's side. It was clear and visible in a house of God.

Ambrose's gaze never touched the priest, or Gus, or Callahan. It went straight to Beatrix…and he smiled.

"Drop the weapon," the priest said sharply, stepping forward. His voice shook with restrained fury. "You bring a gun into a sanctified church?"

Ambrose offered a theatrical glance around the nave. "Sanctity is a matter of perspective, Father. I'm here to uphold a contract made in the eyes of God."

He reached into his coat and removed two documents, folded and creased.

"These," he said, laying the documents with slow precision on the altar rail, "are a marriage contract and a license filed in Cornwall. The woman here is my betrothed, and the documents are signed by her father, Lord Wrenwood."

He met the priest's eyes now. "You are officiating a ceremony in direct violation of both."

Beatrix's voice cut through the silence. "I never consented to marry him."

The words were clear. Her chin lifted, even as her hand trembled in Gus's.

Ambrose didn't even look at her. "Your father did."

"That doesn't make it binding." She countered.

"It does under English law," Ambrose said coldly, his eyes met hers in callous fury. "Under the terms of the contract, you are mine by right."

Gus stepped forward, placing himself fully between them.

"She's not yours," he said, his voice firm and threatening. "She was never yours."

He looked at Ambrose without blinking.

"She chose *me*, and I swear to God and every man in this room that I'll burn the whole damned world to the ground before I let you take her."

Gus kept Beatrix behind him, with one hand still wrapped protectively around hers. With the other, he flexed two fingers down at his side—barely a motion, hidden by the fall of his coat.

Callahan caught it instantly. The sailor shifted his weight, just enough to position himself near the edge of the aisle, between Beatrix and the nearest side door.

It wasn't much, but it was something…Callahan would grab her and get her out as soon as a chance presented itself. Beatrix, sensing the change in the air, tightened her grip on Gus's hand. Gus didn't turn or speak, but he squeezed her hand. She knew immediately what he meant. *Be ready.*

Ambrose's smile thinned, but he didn't rise to Gus's threat. Instead, he turned back to the priest and gestured sharply to the documents.

"Read them." The command was curt, but insistent. He didn't even look at Gus. "Let the good father see for himself what was promised. Let us all see what she is—" his voice sharpened on the words, "—bound to."

His gaze slid back to Gus, cold and cruel. "You may have her favor now. But I have the law. I'll see her wed properly before the day is out."

The priest reached for the papers. He opened the contract first, traced the ink with a fingertip, and then he moved on to the license. He took his time. His lips moved silently as he read.

"This is an Anglican document," he said finally, his voice firm with decision. "It was filed in Cornwall. This—" he tapped the contract, "—is a private agreement. It names the bride's father but not her consent. Neither document is valid here in Martinique and certainly not in this church."

Ambrose's gaze struck like lightning in shadow. "The law—"

"The law of this island," the priest said, eyes flashing, "requires a woman's consent at the altar. You have no legal claim here."

The sound she made was half-breath, half-cry. For a heartbeat, she thought it might be over. Then she heard the thunder of boots, falling hard on the cobblestones outside.

Gus heard them first. He turned toward the doors just in time to see a dozen men step inside. All were armed. One carried a musket slung across his chest. Two more had pistols drawn. Others had swords and pistols strapped to their waists. The last, a tall man with a knife strapped to his belt, closed the doors behind them with a soft, echoing thud.

There was no escape.

Callahan swore under his breath, then immediately apologized, "Sorry, Father."

Ambrose didn't bother to look back. He simply smiled.

"I'm not interested in the Church's opinion, Father," Ambrose said. He was entirely sure of himself. "I'm here for what I was promised."

The priest stood his ground with his shoulders drawn back in the shadow of the altar.

"This is sacred ground," he said. "You bring weapons into the house of God, and you speak of promises made in dark corners with broken ink. What you are owed," he said, his voice rising with each word, "is not greater than what *she* is owed. She has not given you her consent. She has, however, given her consent before God to him. I see no reason why their marriage cannot be declared, and we all move on with our day."

Ambrose's gaze frosted over.

"She's a daughter," he said, "not a sovereign. Her father signed her future into my hands. That's all the consent I need."

Gus stepped forward again, just half a step, but it was enough.

"She gave her future to me," he growled. "She is *my* wife, not yours."

One of the men near the doors shifted. The sound of a musket butt tapping the floor echoed through the nave. The altar boy looked as though he might faint.

Ambrose let out a breath through his nose; it was almost a sigh of disappointment.

"I had hoped this would be clean and simple," he said. "But if we're going to dig our heels into righteousness—"

He drew the pistol slowly from his belt. The polished barrel caught the light from the altar candles. He didn't raise it yet, but the threat was enough to draw another sharp inhale from Callahan.

Gus shifted again, one arm instinctively braced across Beatrix's waist, keeping her behind him.

Ambrose's voice boomed as he lost what little control he had on his anger. "I've come too far," he said. "I've paid too much. I will not give her up to you, brother. Not this time."

He turned his head just slightly and gave a single nod to the man closest to the door. His hired men moved as one, closing in and cutting off every possible exit.

Beatrix pressed a hand to Gus's back.

Callahan didn't move, but his eyes never stopped calculating. He could take one, maybe two, but not twelve.

Gus turned to the priest, begging his case. "Please, father, finish the ceremony and declare her my wife. She's said the vows, and I have sworn myself to her. All that's left is for you to declare that we are married, before God and man."

The priest looked to Beatrix then—his face pale, drawn tight with grief and powerlessness.

"Mademoiselle," he said quietly, "I can do nothing without your consent. What is it you want to do?"

Ambrose snapped his fingers, and two of his men moved forward. One seized Gus by the arm, and the other blocked his path, shoving him hard enough that the pew groaned under the impact.

"Get your hands off me," Gus growled, struggling against their hold.

Ambrose's tone was almost lazy, but his eyes glittered with satisfaction. "Hold him. I want him to see every moment."

The preacher looked stricken. "Sir… this—"

"This, father, is justice, pure and true. This man is a *pirate.* He cannot be a husband to this well-born lady. He belongs on the gallows with the rest of his kind." Ambrose spat.

"Is this true, sir?" The priest looked at Gus and then at Callahan. Suddenly, the danger in the room was heightened. One word from the priest, and Gus's entire crew could be arrested and hung.

"No," he protested, "I am an English lord, a merchant, and yes, a privateer, but nothing more, and this woman is my lady—that's all that matters." Callahan nodded in solidarity. It was only a half-lie; they did have letters of marque, but it certainly didn't cover all of their business dealings, and it gave them permission to pillage French ships, which wouldn't help their case in Martinique.

Ambrose snorted. "You think yourself her savior, August, but you're nothing more than a thief stealing a woman already promised to another."

Gus was fighting like a man possessed. His muscles strained against the two men's grip. Fury burned in his eyes, locked on her, as though his sheer force of will could shatter the scene unfolding before them.

Ambrose stepped closer to her, lowering his voice so that only she could hear. "When he's gone and the sea swallows him whole, you'll be mine entirely."

Her heart pounded. "You'll never have me," she whispered.

"Oh, but I will," Ambrose replied, his smile thin and cruel. "In every way that matters."

He grabbed her hand and forced her back towards the altar. Callahan moved forward to grab her, but Ambrose's men stepped in front of him, forcing him to back away.

"Father, if you please, start the ceremony."

"No!" She screamed. The priest stared on incredulously, unsure what to do. This was not the quiet morning he had planned.

Ambrose's smile vanished. The black barrel of his well-polished pistol caught the candlelight as he leveled it—not at her, but at Gus.

The preacher stumbled back a step.

"Yes," Ambrose said, his voice perilously quiet, "is the word you are searching for, Beatrix."

"You wouldn't—"

His thumb pulled back the hammer with a crisp, metallic click. "Do you truly wish to test me? Because I assure you, the instant I squeeze this trigger, the great August Drake will lie bleeding at your feet."

"Beatrix—don't." Gus's voice was hushed, strained with urgency. "I'd rather die than see you chained to him."

Ambrose's gaze never wavered. "And I'd rather you live just long enough to watch me take what's mine."

The pistol did not move. The men holding Gus tightened their grip as they dragged him half a step forward. She saw the vein in his neck stand out as he strained against them.

She could not breathe, nor could she think over the roaring in her head.

"Say it," Ambrose demanded, his words dripping like poison. "Say you will marry me, and your pirate lord walks out of here alive."

Her hands trembled at her sides. The church felt smaller by the second. The air was thick and stifling. Ambrose's pistol remained fixed on Gus's heart.

She looked at him—really looked at him. His shirt was torn from the scuffle. His golden hair fell into his eyes. Even now, in this impossible moment, his grey eyes were only for her. His gaze was desperate, pleading with her and the heavens…anything to end this hell.

Tears blurred her vision. She could not lose him. Not here, not like this.

Her throat burned as she forced the words out. "I...agree." The sound of her own voice broke something inside her.

Ambrose smiled again, slowly and with satisfaction. He lowered the pistol just enough to ease the tension in the room. The men restraining Gus did not release him, though; if anything, they tightened their grip.

"No," Gus said sharply, his voice breaking through the ringing in her ears. "Beatrix—"

"Enough," Ambrose snapped, turning just enough to glare at him. "She's made her choice. Priest, do your work."

The priest hesitated, but ultimately, he knew nothing would stop the scene before him other than marrying this poor lady to one of these brothers.

Beatrix's tears spilled freely now, tracing hot lines down her cheeks. She kept her gaze fixed on the floor. She was afraid that if she met Gus's eyes again, she would shatter completely.

Part III: The Threads of Fate

CHAPTER 17

The preacher's voice wavered as he pressed onward, each word falling like a stone into the silence. Beatrix barely heard him. Her heart pounded too loudly. She felt the weight of Ambrose's hand on hers as he slid the gaudiest ring she had ever seen onto her finger.

"Repeat after me," the preacher said with a heavy sigh.

Her lips moved, but the vows were empty sounds. The words came in meaningless syllables that she recited only to keep the pistol from firing. She did not dare look at Gus, but she felt him. His presence thrummed behind her like a cord stretched to breaking, powerless, yet still aching to reach her. He could not move. He could not save her. But she felt him fighting with every breath not to scream.

When the final words came, *I now pronounce you husband and wife,* Ambrose turned to her and claimed a kiss that was all possession and no tenderness. She flinched; her stomach twisted, but she did not resist.

Gus surged forward instinctively, a raw, guttural sound tore from his throat, half protest and half agony.

The men holding him tightened their grip and yanked him back. His boots scraped across the stone floor. He didn't feel it. He could see nothing but her. He'd seen men take blows in battle with less pain than what carved itself across his face now…and Ambrose knew it.

He lifted his head from the kiss and looked straight at Gus. He smirked like he'd just won some child's game, and Gus was the loser over whom he claimed victory.

Ambrose nodded to his men. "Get him out of here."

Two of the crew shoved Gus forward, dragging him toward the doors. Callahan fought against his own captors, swearing under his breath, until the cold press of steel at his back made him still.

Outside, the sun seemed too bright. The air was too sharp. Ambrose strode out after them with the pistol still in his hand. He pulled Beatrix behind him, dragging her by her sleeve like a dog on a leash.

"Take them back to their ship," he ordered his men. He then turned to Callahan. "You'll set sail immediately, or I'll see every man aboard your ship hanging for piracy before the week is out. I've already sent word to the port authority."

Gus straightened, meeting his brother's eyes without a flicker of fear. "Do it," he growled. "I'll not leave her."

Ambrose's mouth curled. "You don't have a choice."

Callahan stepped forward, placing a firm hand on Gus's shoulder. His voice was rough with restraint.

"Captain…think of the crew."

He waited a beat, but kept his eyes locked with Gus's.

"We have fifty men. Most of them have wives and children. Think of the mothers who'd never hear their voices again."

He swallowed.

"Don't make them martyrs for a fight you can't win."

Callahan's words hit hard and more brutally than any blow could have. Gus's fists clenched at his sides as rage tightened every muscle. His jaw twitched, but he said nothing. He didn't have to. The silence said it all.

Ambrose smiled again with his poisonous curl of triumph.

"There's the good captain. Sail away, brother. She'll be in my bed before nightfall. Think on that—no one will be there to play her hero this time…not even the great Lord August Drake."

The men hauled Gus and Callahan toward the gangway. He twisted once in their grip, fighting for a final glimpse of her. His gaze locked with Beatrix's. Tears had formed in her eyes, but she did not let them fall. The torture in his eyes told her everything he could not say aloud: *I will come for you.*

The crowd closed around them, and he was gone.

***

Gus stood at the rail like a man shackled; his hands clenched so hard that they shone white against the wood. The harbor of Fort-La-République blurred before him, but he could see the church spire rising above the rooftops. He had been *right there.*

Behind him, no one spoke. The crew waited in tight silence. The ship rocked gently beneath them.

Callahan came up to him cautiously, as if approaching a wounded animal. "We can't stay here," he said.

Gus didn't move.

"If we linger, Ambrose will have us boarded and arrested by nightfall."

Still nothing.

Callahan's voice hardened. "You think he won't spot our sails? He's watching and waiting for you to do something stupid so he can finish what he started."

Gus turned to face him. His eyes were wild with grief. "I'm not leaving her."

Callahan didn't flinch. "She's already gone, Gus. We both saw it."

Gus lunged forward, grabbing the front of Callahan's coat. "Don't you say that."

The crew tensed, but Callahan didn't raise a hand; he just looked Gus straight in the eye.

"You want to die here? Fine, but you'll take fifty men with you. They didn't get a say in your vendetta. These are men with families that expect them to come home."

The words landed like fists. Gus faltered. Callahan gently peeled Gus's hands from his coat.

"We're sailing to Portsmouth. It's British waters and a safer harbor; no one will question our motives there. We can regroup and plan. We don't die today."

Gus swayed. His grief overtook his fury. His voice was hoarse.

"She was right there. She'd said the words. She was mine."

Callahan placed a steady hand on his shoulder. "Then we make damned sure we are ready to take her back."

He turned to the crew and gave the order.

"Raise anchor. Set for Dominica. Full sail."

The men jumped to action, and slowly, with the wind catching the canvas, the ship turned away from Martinique. Gus stood at the stern, watching the island disappear behind them.

***

Beatrix stood in the middle of the cobblestone street in front of the church, frozen. She wasn't sure she was still breathing. Gus was gone. She was on her own.

The streets of Fort-La-République had returned to their usual rhythm, with vendors shouting over their carts, soldiers laughing near the square, and bells clanging faintly from ships in the harbor. It was all just noise to her now. She didn't hear any of it. All she could hear was Gus's tortured cries as she said the words that made her his brother's wife.

Lady Beatrix, Mrs. Ambrose Drake. It was the correct surname, but everything else about it was wrong.

Ambrose stood beside her. He beamed in victory as he holstered his pistol. When she didn't move, he leaned in and whispered with breath that was too warm against her ear.

"I've imagined our wedding night a thousand times," his voice held the same refined country accent as Gus's, but with a higher timbre that made her skin crawl. "I can't wait to untie that dress, one ribbon at a time, and then take you into my bed where I will finally prove that even a wild thing like you can be tamed by the right master."

She stiffened, but he grabbed her arm and began pulling her toward the docks.

"I used to wonder what your skin would taste like after a summer rain," he continued. He kept his voice low. His words were meant only for her. "I dreamed about the sound you'd make when I kissed the inside of your wrist."

He demonstrated, pulling her wrist to his mouth and placing a kiss as he described, then he stuck out his tongue to taste her skin. She shivered and pulled her wrist away.

"Funny, isn't it?" He drawled, unfazed by her reaction. "How some dreams finally come true."

Her silk skirt dragged in the dust as he continued pulling her along.

The two rings now on her fingers felt suddenly heavy. Gus's mother's ring was on her right hand now; she had moved it before Ambrose shoved his ring on her wedding ring finger. Gus's was a delicate, perfect ruby which caught the sun's light in a quiet promise of another life. Ambrose's ring was a big, gaudy gold band with a giant emerald surrounded by small yellow stones. She was certain it could be seen by the ships looming on the horizon, miles out at sea. She curled her fingers in, but the metal still burned.

"Tonight, Beatrix," he said, his voice thick with self-satisfaction. "I want you to be soft, quiet, and ready to yield to my touch. You'll lie back and let me learn every inch of what's mine. In time, I think you'll even thank me."

She said nothing.

"Don't worry," he added as they neared the docks. "I'll be gentle, at first. I will take your maidenhead patiently. I can't wait to feel your hot virgin blood dripping from my…well, you'll see."

Well, at least he would be wrong about that, she thought. She closed her eyes as the memory of Gus's hands on her body overtook her senses. At least she would have those memories to cling to as she resigned herself to her fate.

Ambrose's schooner, *The Resolute*, waited at the end of the pier. He had repaired most of the damage from the sea battle with *The Tempest.* Two of his hired men stepped aside as they boarded. They didn't make eye contact with either her or Ambrose.

He led her below deck without another word. He opened the door to a small, windowless cabin. It was hot and barely furnished, with just a small cot beside a single chair and a tiny table.

He gestured her inside with a mock flourish.

"Rest. I want you ready when I come to take you tonight."

She turned toward him, jaw tight. "Do as you please, but I will never be yours."

Ambrose smiled at her, sure of his triumph.

"You already are. No one is coming to save you, Beatrix. Look around—your pirate has abandoned you. His crew is even now rushing out with the tide. It's just you and me now, and I will show you that you are, most definitely, mine."

He did not wait for her to reply. The door shut with a solid, final click.

She stood alone in the hot, dim room. She clutched the locket at her throat, then dropped to the tiny cot and sobbed quietly. She could not hold back her grief any longer, but she would not give Ambrose the satisfaction of witnessing it.

***

Ambrose had pulled out all the stops for his wedding night. His cabin had been thoroughly cleaned. A white linen tablecloth covered the small table, and crystal wine glasses caught the flicker of candlelight. A silver tray held roast duck, tropical fruits, and a bottle of wine that sweated in the heat.

Beatrix sat at the table with her hands folded in her lap and her face blank.

Ambrose sat opposite her, watching her with unsettling patience. He'd dressed for the occasion in a dark coat, crisp cravat, and a signet ring gleaming on his right pinky finger. Beatrix noticed that the black opal he normally pinned to his cravat was missing.

She still wore her wedding dress—the dove grey silk that Gus had picked out for her. It was now stuck to her skin, but she didn't have anything else to wear.

"You haven't touched your food."

Beatrix looked at the roasted duck. The scent turned her stomach.

"I'm not hungry."

He poured her wine anyway. The red liquid sloshed into her glass.

"You should eat. We've a long night ahead."

She didn't move.

Ambrose leaned back in his chair. His eyes never left hers. He reached for a slice of pineapple and bit into it, letting the juice run down his fingers.

"I used to wonder if you were as proud in private as you are in public," he said quietly. "But I think I've always known the answer. You pretend at defiance, but you want to be taken."

She stared into his eyes coldly. "I want you dead."

Ambrose smiled.

"You don't mean that. Not really. Think about it—you have a husband now. You have a purpose to fulfill, beyond your great family secrets. You will give me heirs. You will be the vessel that carries my legacy into the next generation. Think about all the fun we're going to have making a houseful of children."

He gestured to the tray, and a hired steward stepped inside to clear it.

"Come, Beatrix, let's get started." He stood and reached his hand out to her. Beatrix rose, stiffly, as if she might walk straight to his bed in surrender.

Instead, she moved to the shelf near the wall. Her fingers found what she had been eyeing since the moment he brought her to his cabin: a tall, brass candlestick. It was heavy and cold in her hand.

"Beatrix." His voice was a warning, but she didn't heed it.

She turned, and the candlelight caught her eyes. They were ice.

"Don't," he said, quietly, realizing she wouldn't respond to demands. "I want this to be—"

She swung.

The candlestick connected with the side of Ambrose's face with a sickening crack. Ambrose's eyes widened, and he dropped to the floor without a sound.

For a moment, she stood there with her heart pounding, unable to breathe.

Then, she left the room and found her way back to the stifling cabin he had locked her inside earlier in the day. Beatrix bolted the door behind her and slumped to the floor. Her hands trembled as she wiped blood—his, not hers—from the brass candlestick with a rag that had been left on the floor.

The room was stifling. There was barely enough space to pace, let alone breathe. Had she killed him? She hadn't stayed long enough to check that he was still breathing. What would she do if he were dead? Would his crew hang her?

She wedged the chair under the door handle, then collapsed onto the narrow cot and curled around the ache in her chest. Her pulse refused to slow. She didn't sleep. She didn't dare. All she could do was wait.

***

Hours passed, and somewhere in the night, Beatrix had drifted off. She still clutched the candlestick in her slumber.

The bolt jerked. She shot upright. The chair scraped, then the lock gave, and the door slammed open with a force that rattled the hinges.

Ambrose stood in the doorway, eyes blazing. His hair was matted with blood on the side of his head that she had struck. A deep black bruise was blooming on the side of his face. His cravat was gone. His coat hung askew. He looked like a storm borne in hell itself.

Beatrix backed away instinctively, but she had nowhere to go. He stepped inside.

She held up the brass candlestick again, but he batted it aside. She gave a small squeal as it clanked against the floorboards.

"Enough."

She struck him with her fists—once, twice—but he caught her wrists and shoved her hard against the wall.

"You will not hit me again."

She struggled, kicking, twisting, and spitting her fury. "Get off me!"

He held her there. His chest heaved. His face was only a breath away from hers.

"I should take you right here, right now," he growled. "I've waited long enough."

Her green eyes burned. "Then do it. Prove you're the brute everyone says you are. I don't care anymore."

Ambrose didn't move. His fingers clenched around her wrists.

"No," he said, his voice quieter now. "You'll yield. I can see it in your eyes."

He stared at her, as if trying to will it into being. She didn't look away.

"You'll die waiting," she hissed.

He shoved away from her with a ragged breath. Fury and desire twisted together in his expression.

"You will give yourself to me, Beatrix, one way or another. It's only a matter of time."

He turned and slammed the door behind him. This time, he didn't lock it.

***

The captain's cabin was stifling in the midday heat. The linen-draped table stood between them, set for two with polished silver and crystal goblets. A roasted fish sat untouched between platters of mango, pickled vegetables, and sugared figs. Beatrix had not lifted her fork.

She sat stiffly with her shoulders drawn back. Ambrose reclined with unhurried ease across from her. He had cleaned the blood from his head and hair, but he could do little to hide the bruise that was now coloring half of his face. He had rolled his sleeves to his forearm, and the opal was pinned to his cravat once more. He watched her carefully, unsure if she would strike again or relent and become his dessert.

"You've scarcely touched your food," he said softly. "Do you not find it to your liking?"

She didn't answer.

"I asked the cook for something light but indulgent. I thought today warranted it."

Her eyes flicked toward him; her disgust was barely concealed.

"We are not celebrating."

"No?" His smile deepened. "Then let us call it fortification. You'll need your strength. There are discoveries ahead of us, my dear."

He pushed her wineglass closer to her.

"At least drink something. The heat must be making you thirsty. I brought a cask of lovely French wine."

She hesitated, but her throat was dry. The heat, the nerves, and the ache behind her eyes all conspired to make the wine tempting. She lifted the glass and drank. The wine slid cool and smooth down her throat. She had swallowed more than half the glass by the time she set it down.

"I know about Calverique," Ambrose said abruptly.

Her gaze snapped to him.

"Aria wrote about it to August," he went on. "I intercepted one of her letters one morning when he was in town. The letter was full of nonsense; it read like a riddle with words of love and vague references to their plans. It contained this opal, which I kept as a memento." He touched the fiery black stone. "One thing was for certain: Their destination was Calverique."

Beatrix's fingers tightened against the edge of the table.

"She was going to run away with him," Beatrix said before she remembered she was giving Ambrose the silent treatment.

"Yes," he said, leaning forward. "I'm well aware." He took the letter out of his coat pocket and unfolded it. There was no mistaking Aria's flourished handwriting. The letter was yellowed with age, and its creases were deep—as if it had been read hundreds of times…or more.

Ambrose pointed at a line in the letter.

"They were going to stop in Saint Lucia on their way. Why?"

Her mind raced. St. Lucia was the last mark on her mother's map. She and Gus planned to head there next to retrieve the last clue.

"I don't know," she lied.

Ambrose tilted his head, studying her. "You're wearing the locket—Aria always wore that locket. I watched her press it into August's hand as she lay dying. Did he give it to you?"

"No. It's my mother's."

His expression didn't change, but something colder flickered behind his eyes.

"I think you've spent your life running from your family's secrets. It's time to stop running and face them, Beatrix."

She took another long sip of the wine. Her hand felt oddly heavy as she set the glass down. The room tilted slightly.

"You seem flushed," he said gently. His voice curled around her. "Perhaps the heat is too much for you."

Beatrix tried to stand, but her knees buckled beneath the table. She grasped the armrest instead, breathing shallowly as her pulse fluttered erratically.

Ambrose moved to her side with practiced ease and crouched beside her chair. His hand grazed her wrist, then he lifted one to her chin and guided it gently until she faced him.

"You are a beautiful puzzle, Beatrix," he whispered.

"You won't touch me," she hissed, but it lacked force.

He smiled. "Not yet. Not until you want me to. Do you want me to?"

Her vision swam. She tried to blink him away. She tried to force her thoughts into order. The wine was too strong.

"Did you put something in the wine?" She slurred her words.

"It's nothing—just something to help you relax."

He brushed his lips gently against hers. She didn't fight him. When his tongue seductively parted her lips, she let him. His mouth was warm and possessive, but the kiss stayed gentle. Despite herself, she leaned into it, drunkenly. Slowly, he ended the kiss and pulled back from her.

"Rest," he said, brushing her hair from her forehead. "You'll want to be sharp when we reach Saint Lucia."

He rose without another word, leaving her alone in his cabin with the room spinning slowly around her.

***

Beatrix lay curled beneath a thin linen sheet. Her gown was a wrinkled mess, and her limbs felt too heavy to lift. She had not moved in hours. Her thoughts drifted in and out of clarity, as though she floated just beneath the surface of herself, unable to break free.

The cabin door creaked open. She did not startle. The sound felt distant and muffled, like it belonged to a dream.

Bootsteps crossed the room. She heard a quiet voice in the darkness.

"You're awake."

Her eyelids fluttered, but she could barely focus on the figure approaching her bedside. A smile touched her lips. She reached out, but her fingers trembled with the effort.

"You came back," she said. Her own voice felt far away, like it was her speaking, but from someplace else.

"I told you I would." His voice answered. *Gus*, she thought, his voice was blurred by the fog in her mind. Her heart melted at the simple thought of his name.

He exhaled softly, "You forgive me, then."

She reached for him blindly. Her hand found the open collar of his shirt and stroked the warmth of his skin beneath it.

"Don't leave me again…"

He breathed in sharply and sat beside her on the edge of the narrow bed. His hand slid around her waist.

"Never," he whispered, bending to kiss her.

It was gentle, at first—worshipful. Her lips parted beneath his, soft and yielding. One of his hands tangled in her hair. The other traced the line of her shoulder, slipping the neckline of her dress aside with aching care.

He trailed kisses along her throat and over her shoulders as his fingers worked behind her back to undo the ties on her dress. The first one fell away, and he kissed the now exposed flesh worshipfully. Her hands stroked his hair absently, as she lost herself in his touch and the warm lull of the wine that still lingered in her head.

She sighed against him. Her eyes were still closed.

"Gus…" she whispered. The sound of his name on her lips was like a whispered prayer.

Ambrose pulled back abruptly. His hand froze on her collarbone. Her lips were still parted, but her expression was dream-drunk. She was completely unaware of what she had said or even where she was.

"What did you call me?" His voice was quiet, but deadly.

Her lashes lifted slowly. Her pupils were unfocused, but her smile remained.

"Gus…"

Ambrose's eyes darkened. His hands closed around her throat, and for a moment, he thought he might end her right then and there.

"You thought I was him."

A beat of silence passed. She blinked slowly, and the fog in her mind began to lift. Her mouth opened, but no words came.

Ambrose let out a bitter laugh. "You'd have given yourself to him, wouldn't you?" He tightened his grip on her throat. Her eyes were wide with fear. He studied her for a moment as her face turned red with the lack of air. Then it dawned on him.

"You already have!" He roared. Her hands flew to his now, as she tried to pull them off her throat. He let go abruptly.

He paced once toward the door, then back again.

"Even drugged—even half-mad—you dream of *him*."

Beatrix tried to sit up. Her arms gave way beneath her.

"Ambrose—"

"Don't," he said, voice sharp. "Don't say my name in the same breath you said his."

He stepped forward again, looming over her. His chest rose and fell in ragged motion.

"You were going to let me touch you," he sneered. "You let me kiss you. You let me untie your dress! All along, you were just playing my brother's whore."

His words stung as if he'd slapped her.

"Yes—I said it—*whore.* You don't deserve my patience. You don't deserve any sort of tenderness." He was filled with rage. He grabbed her wrists and pressed her against the bed. "Spread your legs and welcome me the way you welcomed him!"

"You're not him," she said, forcing the words out. Hot tears filled her eyes. "You could never be him!"

His mouth twisted. "You're right, *whore.* I am *not* my brother."

Then, without another word, he let her go and left the room, slamming the door behind him. She heard the lock click into place.

Beatrix slumped back against the pillow. Her breath was ragged. His violent outburst had rendered her momentarily sober, but now the drunken haze threatened to consume her once more. Beneath it, cold, clear terror reverberated in her mind.

***

The masts groaned overhead as *The Resolute* eased into the harbor at Castries. Sailors shouted from the rigging, and ropes slapped the deck, but Ambrose heard none of it. He stood at the rail and watched the green hills of Saint Lucia rise like a promise he no longer believed.

Even though the tropical heat caused his face to sweat, he felt a cold shiver pulse through his body.

She had whispered *his* name.

Curled in his bed, half-naked and yielding, she had looked up with heavy-lidded eyes and reached for him, not as a wife, not as a bride, but as a woman burning for another man.

"Gus..."

It played over and over in his mind. *I should have strangled her*, he thought. Now she continued to breathe below decks. Her presence incensed him with every passing moment.

He had thought she was clever, defiant, and well worth the effort. He had even allowed himself to believe that once she bore his name, she might come to value what he could offer her: protection, passion, and power.

It had never been about passion for her…and not for Aria either. Not for anyone. They had all wanted August Drake.

The golden son. The chosen one. The one who stood taller, spoke silkier, and carried every ounce of the name Ambrose had been born denied.

His hands curled into fists again.

He'd seen it in her eyes when she thought he was August. It wasn't blind passion…it was love. He thought about how she had looked at his brother in the church, like he was her only salvation. She had sacrificed herself easily for him when she thought Ambrose would shoot him.

Worse, he knew now that August had lain with her—and she gave herself to him willingly. That much was obvious now.

Even in Ambrose's triumph, August had managed to mark his wife first.

Whore.

Ambrose turned from the railing. His coat whipped behind him as he strode across the deck. Sailors parted quickly to give him space, but he did not see them. All he saw was the door to his cabin—the one where he'd left her dreaming not of her husband, but of his brother.

Once again, August had taken what was his, but not again. She would open the next door—the door to Calverique—and it would all belong to Ambrose. Then he would dispose of her.

CHAPTER 18

Casteries, Saint Lucia

The door opened with a sharp crack against the cabin wall. "Get a move on," Ambrose said. His voice was cold and angry. "We're here."

Beatrix stirred from his bed, blinking against the morning glare that spilled through the cabin windows. Her limbs ached. Her mouth was dry. The gauzy remains of yesterday's wine-induced haze still lingered at the edges of her mind.

She swung her legs over the side of the bed, and the satin skirts of her wedding gown crumpled beneath her. Ambrose's eyes raked over her.

"You look like hell," he muttered ironically. His face still bore the black and blue bruise from Beatrix's candlestick attack. "We'll find something for you to wear in town. Don't dawdle."

He dragged her down the gangplank moments later. The harbor bustled with fishermen and French soldiers on patrol. None seemed to take notice of the badly bruised Englishman pulling along a woman with tangled red hair dressed in a wrinkled, filthy silken gown.

Beatrix kept pace beside Ambrose. He walked with one hand on her back. His grip was never enough to bruise, but never far enough for her to forget that she was his captive bride.

They reached a small row of market stalls where bolts of fabric hung from rafters and rough-spun dresses fluttered in the breeze. A woman with dark skin and watchful eyes raised a brow in greeting. Beatrix pointed silently to a simple cotton dress with short sleeves and a gathered waist.

"That one," she said softly.

Ambrose grunted his assent and stepped forward to negotiate the price. As he spoke to the vendor, a hand brushed lightly against Beatrix's elbow.

She turned, and a small-framed woman with sharp eyes stood beside her, seemingly browsing a collection of linen shifts. Her lips barely moved.

"You're the heir."

Beatrix froze. The woman's gaze flicked toward the street, then toward a narrow alley beyond the market stalls.

"Come," she whispered. "Quickly, before he notices." Beatrix's heart thudded in her chest.

Behind her, Ambrose counted coins into the vendor's hand.

"Now," the woman mouthed, and then she turned and slipped away into the crowd.

Beatrix followed the woman through a narrow passage that wound behind the market. The path was choked with vines that Beatrix had to keep swatting so they wouldn't smack her face. Behind her, she could hear Ambrose's boots clapping against the ground steadily. He carried the folded blue dress she'd chosen moments ago in one hand and held the other firmly over the pistol at his waist.

The woman stopped beside an ancient wall. It was half-covered in bright pink bougainvillea. Her eyes darted once toward Ambrose, then back to Beatrix. Without a word, she knelt and pushed aside a stone at the base of the wall. From within, she drew out a small, lacquered wooden box, no larger than a man's palm. It was black with silver inlay. The delicate image of intertwined rings was carved into the lid.

She placed it in Beatrix's hands and whispered, "For the heir." Then she was gone. She vanished into the alley before Ambrose could reach for her.

Beatrix stared down at the box. It was cold from its shaded hiding place and heavy for its size. There was no latch and no hinge, but it had an oval depression at its center.

Ambrose came beside her, a scowl twisting his features. "What is it? What did she give you?"

Beatrix didn't answer. She was already moving, as if her body knew what to do before her mind could catch up.

Her fingers found the chain around her throat and drew out the silver locket. As she brought it close, the surface of the box began to shimmer faintly, like moonlight rippling on dark water. A soft hum filled the air. It was so quiet that she felt it in her ribs more than she heard it.

The locket glowed with its warm golden glow; it swirled around her like a cocoon. The hum grew louder, and her vision slipped sideways. She could not tell whether she was dreaming or awake, standing or drifting. A wash of sensation enveloped her. She felt salty wind against her skin. She could hear distant music. Then, she felt a sudden, piercing awareness.

Gus.

She felt him, not as memory but as presence. She didn't question how or why. She reached through the feeling, and with all her will, sent him one word:

Calverique.

Then the trance shattered.

She blinked and looked down to see the box open in her hands. Inside sat a single object: a silver watch, old but beautifully perfect, resting on a velvet lining.

Its glass face shimmered in the glow of her locket. Where numbers should be, faint constellations were etched into the surface of the watch. The glow from her locket revealed new stars, etched so faintly that they vanished as the glow receded. A single watch hand floated just off-center. It ticked toward a star she did not recognize.

Carved along the inner rim in curling script were the words: *To chart the unfindable isle, follow the stars that do not belong.*

Ambrose reached over her shoulder and snatched the watch from the box.

"What is this?"

Beatrix swallowed. Her voice was soft. "It's how we find Calverique."

He turned the watch in his hands. The strange stars had already begun to vanish. He pressed the face, shook it gently, and turned to her with fresh anger.

"Make it do it again."

"I can't," she said. "The locket only glows on its own. I don't control it."

"You're lying." His look was cold and accusatory.

"I'm not."

He seized her wrist. "Then you'd best learn to control it."

She wrenched away, fire in her eyes. "You can threaten me all you like, but it won't change the fact that we can't see the stars."

Ambrose held her gaze for a long, tense beat. Then he tucked the watch into his coat and stepped back.

"Let's get back to the ship, *whore*. We sail with the tide."

***

Gus sat alone in his cabin aboard *The Tempest*. Charts were piled everywhere, but he paid them no attention. Arabella's journal sat open with Beatrix's notes about potential clues scattered beside it. He'd read them all over and over again, but it was no use. He took a long drink of the rum in his tankard.

His thoughts ran in circles. Portsmouth was quiet…too quiet. He couldn't figure out how to find her. Ambrose could have taken her just about anywhere. He had won…they were married. Days had passed since that horrible day in Martinique.

By now, Ambrose had likely consummated the marriage. He thought about his brother's hands on her and his fists clenched in rage. He took another long drink.

If Ambrose had consummated the marriage—and why wouldn't he?—she could never be Gus's wife. That thought stung, but not as much as living without her. He would live in sin with her for the rest of his life, and he would be content just to have her beside him.

"Damn it!" he roared. He hoped the drink would quiet his racing mind, but its warm burn only fueled his spiraling thoughts.

Then the locket on his chest grew warm.

It happened without warning. One moment, everything was still; then the next moment, light burst from beneath his shirt. He stood as his heart pounded in his ears and pulled the chain from around his neck.

The silver locket glowed.

A low hum filled the room, pulsing through the air in time with his racing heart. Gus staggered back as the walls of the cabin blurred and swayed. He closed his eyes, and the trance overtook him.

He felt her. It wasn't a memory or even a thought. It was *her*.

"Beatrix?" He called for her through the blinding golden light that had surrounded him.

Then, as clear as if she had whispered in his ear, he heard her single word: *Calverique.*

His eyes flew open, and the light faded. The hum vanished, but his heartbeat thundered like cannon fire.

He reached into his pocket and pulled out the broken compass. He picked it up and stared at its dial, the one that spun oddly and refused to follow north. He pulled the golden ring from Dakar out of his pocket and slid it onto his pinky. The dial immediately stilled and pointed towards something.

He understood it now. It had always been pointing to Calverique.

Wherever she was now, that's where they were heading. Somehow, Ambrose had figured out where to find the hidden island, and he was taking Beatrix there.

Gus didn't know where Calverique was or how long it would take to get there, but he knew its direction. He swung his cabin door open and didn't stop to close it.

"Callahan!" He shouted. His first mate sat watching the horizon. His expression was serious. He turned quickly at Gus's urgency.

"I know where she is. At least, I know where she's going." Callahan looked him up and down, clearly believing he was drunk or deranged.

"Gus…"

"I know, I know, but believe me, I know where she's going," Gus implored his first mate. Callahan had run the ship alone since they'd left Martinique. He knew Gus was driving himself mad with grief and worried he might have finally cracked.

"Alright, tell me what you think you know," Callahan said with a sigh.

***

Ambrose had raised anchor and left Saint Lucia the moment they were back on board. He didn't speak another word to her.

She waited until nightfall, when the ship fell quiet under the hush of the open sea. Beatrix sat on the bunk in the tiny dark cabin with the watch in her lap and her locket clutched in her hand. It looked cold and ordinary.

She thought of Gus, his locket, and his compass. She thought about her mother wearing the locket and singing to her in the garden. She thought about walking through the wildflowers as Aria hummed.

Her voice shook as she began to hum it quietly to herself. It was a tune passed through blood and memory. As she hummed, the locket warmed against her palm. She closed her eyes and let the melody wrap around her.

The locket began to glow. Its hum began to join with hers, pulling her mind toward the glow. She surrendered to the warmth of the light swirling around her. She let it wash over her as it lulled her into its every note.

Slowly, she opened her eyes and stilled her mind to stay in the trance. The constellation watch, still cradled in her lap, glowed in response to the locket. Its false stars flickered to life, bright and impossible.

They aren't random. They are pointing somewhere. Just as the thought took root, the cabin door slammed open behind her.

Ambrose leaned in the doorway with his arms crossed over his chest. He watched her like a viper sizing its prey. His coat hung open. His cravat was gone, and the bruise on his face was fading from blue to a brownish hue. Rage radiated off him in silent waves.

"Stop stalling," he snapped. "I know you've figured it out. Don't pretend your little light show's just for spectacle."

Beatrix's trance broke, but she didn't look up. Her eyes tracked the faint star patterns, aligning what she could recall from her mother's map with what shimmered here.

"I'm not stalling," she said softly.

"No?" He stepped forward, kicking the lone chair out of his way. "Then you're hiding it from me purposefully. You're obviously good at that."

She flinched but kept her eyes on the watch.

Ambrose's lip curled. "Don't act like you don't know what I mean."

Still, she said nothing.

"I should have killed him in that church and made you watch. I would have if I'd known what a whore fool you really were."

When she still didn't speak, he continued his mocking tirade.

"How filthy a whore do you have to be to open your legs to your betrothed's brother? Was it just him? Or were you open to the entire crew?"

She spun around to look at him. His words were simple cruelty, but they still stung. She loved Gus…their act of love was beautiful, and she did not regret it—not for one moment. She would take Ambrose's chiding for that with her head held high.

Accusing her of prostituting herself to *The Tempest*'s crew was another matter. She slapped him, square in the jaw. Her hand hit with a stinging crack.

His hand flew to catch her retreating wrist, holding it in the air with a crushing grip. She squealed in pain. His glare bored into her; he was furious.

"Once Calverique is mine, you can rot. There's nothing left in you I want."

"Then let's bloody well get there," she spat at him. A long silence passed, and then Ambrose let her go.

She sat back on the bunk and held the watch in her hand. She hummed *The Compass Waltz* quietly as her locket began to glow. This time, not wanting to leave herself vulnerable to Ambrose, she fought its pull, but the locket's light illuminated the watch.

Beatrix lifted the watch higher. She turned it slowly, studying the unfamiliar constellations.

"They aren't real," she murmured.

Ambrose snorted. "Clearly."

"No," she said more firmly. "They don't belong to any known chart—believe me, I've spent weeks on *The Tempest* studying charts. That's the point. They're not from the stars. They're meant to form something."

He moved closer again. He put his anger aside to understand the puzzle before him. He took a rolled scroll out of his pocket and unfurled it in front of her, revealing a map of known islands in their near vicinity.

Beatrix rotated the watch to angle the constellations against the sea map. Her hands trembled, but not from fear but from certainty. Slowly, a pattern emerged. The shapes formed not a sky, but a coastline—one that didn't match any known land.

"Here," she whispered, pointing to a crescent arc on the watch face. "That's the northern reef they say doesn't exist. And this—this is the inlet."

Ambrose inhaled sharply. He studied her through a taut, simmering stare.

"You know where it is?" he asked.

Beatrix met his gaze at last. Her voice was calm, cool, and unafraid. "I do."

He straightened and was silent for a beat; then he turned away.

"Good," he said. "You'll tell the helmsman at dawn." Without another word, he left her alone in the dark.

***

Several days out from Portsmouth, nearing the edge of any known chart

The sea had turned a strange shade of deep ink blue. Overhead, the stars no longer aligned with anything familiar.

Gus stood at the helm. The compass rested beside the wheel. Its needle pulsed with faint light, always pointing toward a place no one could find on any of the numerous charts he had collected in his time at sea.

He had not slept; he barely ate. The wind lashed at his coat and salt stung his skin, but still he stood there, with his gaze fixed westward, like a man possessed.

Below decks, Althea's map lay spread across the navigation table. Its corners were pinned with bits of flint and coral to keep it from curling. He'd memorized every mark, every cryptic curve, and every faded annotation.

Calverique.

It called to him now. His locket glowed, and he could hear its hum just below the thoughts in his head. He could feel Beatrix when he let himself fall into the humming. She was somewhere out there, heading to the same place his compass was guiding them.

Callahan climbed the steps and stopped beside him, casting a glance at the red-rimmed exhaustion in Gus's eyes.

"Let me take the helm for a few hours," he said. Gus didn't move.

"The compass won't work for you," he said. His voice was strained with exhaustion. "It only points when I touch it."

Callahan looked down at the object, noting how its light dimmed slightly when Gus pulled his hand away, then brightened again when he returned it.

He exhaled. "Damn unnatural, that thing."

Gus nodded once. "So is she."

The two men stood in silence as *The Tempest* pressed further into unfamiliar waters.

***

Several days west of Saint Lucia

The cabin swayed with the rhythm of the sea, but Beatrix had long stopped noticing. The sky outside remained a blanket of gray. It had rained steadily for the past two days. She sat curled in the corner of the narrow bunk, with the watch and locket clutched in her hands like lifelines.

They hadn't spoken much since Saint Lucia. Ambrose had stopped pretending that he cared about her.

A slam against the door jolted her upright. A moment later, it burst open.

He filled the doorway, soaked to the bone. His coat hung open, his shirt was half-unlaced, and his boots left wet, dirty streaks across the floor. He looked more like a pirate now than Gus ever did. His countenance was feral and unhinged.

"We've been sailing blind for days," he growled, stepping inside. "I am quickly losing patience."

She stood slowly, refusing to cower. "I've told you, I don't know exactly where it is."

"You knew how to make that locket glow. You knew how to open the box that held that damned haunted watch." He jabbed a finger at her. "So don't lie to me again."

"I'm not lying," she said, her voice steady despite the pounding in her chest. "Navigating this way is not an exact science. I can't just draw you a map to Calverique."

He stalked toward her; his dark brown eyes were wild with fury. "If we don't find Calverique by tomorrow, by Tartarus, Beatrix, I'll cast you overboard and let the abyss drag your secrets down where no soul returns."

She flinched. Not at his words, but at the way he said them. His voice was cold and final.

"I mean it," he whispered, stopping inches from her. "Don't think that ring on your finger makes you safe."

The locket's light pulsed once, but Ambrose didn't see it. Beatrix stared into his face, no longer afraid of the threats. She took the gaudy ring off her finger and thrust it in his hand.

"Then cast me to Charon, Ambrose. I'd sooner pay the ferryman and ride the Styx straight into Hades than spend my life chained to you." She meant it. "But you'll never find Calverique without me."

For a moment, the rage in his expression wavered—just enough to reveal the desperation underneath. He turned without another word and slammed the door behind him, taking the hideous ring with him.

Her breath was shaking as she sank back onto the bunk. The locket warmed against her palm. They were close.

She said a silent prayer to whoever was listening—God, Poseidon, or even Hades himself—*let Gus get there in time.*

***

Gus's eyes squinted against the salt spray as the dark silhouette of Calverique rose from the morning mist. He could see jagged cliffs, a dense green interior, and a crescent-shaped bay.

He gripped the wheel tighter. The compass's needle no longer glowed. It had dimmed the moment land came into view, confirming what he already knew. They were here. He had found it.

Callahan joined him, squinting toward the shoreline. "God help us. She's real."

"Drop the sails," Gus ordered. "We'll wait offshore, beyond the bluff."

Callahan looked at him sideways. "We're not landing?"

"Not yet. We don't know what's waiting, and I'd rather not meet Ambrose's canons unawares."

"It's good I restocked our ammunition in Portsmouth," His first mate remarked. Gus smiled for the first time in days. He knew he was lucky to have a first mate who was always watching his back, even in his darkest moments.

They steered *The Tempest* behind the rocky edge of the island. The view from the sea was now cloaked by a line of high cliffs and dense foliage. From there, they would spot any ship entering before it reached land.

Gus stood unmoving as the crew lowered anchor and the ship came to rest in the shadow of the island. He turned the compass over in his hand. Its needle was lifeless now. He put it in his pocket. The locket rested against his chest, constantly warm now. Its light pulsed with the beat of his heart.

He knew she was close. He could feel it. He breathed deeply, forcing down the ache in his chest.

"Let them come," he declared with eyes fixed on the open water. "This ends here."

***

"There," one of the crewmen shouted. "Off the starboard bow!"

Beatrix forced herself to rise from the cot where she had spent the night curled in tension. Her legs trembled as she crossed the narrow cabin and stepped onto the deck. She shielded her eyes from the blazing sun. The ocean spread in endless deep blue ripples—until it didn't.

The island loomed in a mist. Dense green hills rose out of the sea. It was wilder than she had imagined. It looked perfect and completely untouched.

She felt the locket stir against her chest. It began pulsing gently. Its rhythm quickened as the ship drew closer to the island.

Ambrose appeared beside her without warning. He reeked of sweat and impatience. His sleeves were rolled, and the lines around his eyes were carved deeper from days of fury and suspicion.

"That's it, isn't it?" he said with more accusation than question.

Beatrix didn't answer. Her throat was dry, and her mind was fogged with exhaustion and the sickening dread that had lived in her stomach since they left Martinique. Still, she met his eyes.

"Get ready," he said sharply. "We go ashore the moment we anchor."

She stiffened. "Just us?"

Ambrose's smile was bitter. "You think I'd let my men have a chance at whatever's hidden there? No. It's just you and me. We'll find whatever treasure lies here, and then you can burn in Tartarus for all I care."

Since the night he'd realized she'd already been claimed by his brother, Ambrose had thought of a hundred ways to dispose of her. He wasn't sure which method he'd use, but he was sure she wasn't leaving this island…not alive anyway. He stalked off, barking orders at the crew to lower the sails.

Beatrix stayed where she was, watching the island grow closer as the locket continued to pulse. She knew, somehow, that he was already here. Gus had made it first.

She closed her eyes and pressed her fingers over the locket. *Please*, she begged silently. *Please find me before it's too late.*

***

"They're here," Callahan said, lowering the spyglass.

Gus didn't answer. He was already striding hastily to the rail. On the horizon, *The Resolute* sliced through the waves like an arrow. The wind had picked up, and she was coming in fast.

Gus felt the compass in his pocket shake. He pulled it forward and saw it point to the cove. "They'll make for the cove," he called to Callahan.

His first mate stepped beside him, his face grim. "Then we've got to be faster."

Gus turned sharply. "Lower the longboat. You and I are going ahead."

"What about the crew?"

He looked to O'Malley, who stood waiting for orders near the helm. "Bring *The Tempest* around and land close to the eastern ridge. I want the full crew ready, armed, and behind us within the hour. If we don't come out, sink that ship and burn the cove."

O'Malley nodded once, then turned to shout commands.

Callahan was already pulling two pistols from the weapons chest and slinging his musket over his shoulder. "We'll have one hell of a fight waiting for us."

Gus checked the load on his own weapons and strapped his sword to his side. "I'm counting on it."

The longboat splashed down into the waves. The ropes creaked and the oars clattered as they climbed in. Behind them, *The Tempest* began to maneuver. Her sails angled to follow the coastline.

Ahead, the jungle-covered island loomed. Ambrose's ship drew ever closer to the mouth of the hidden cove. The race had begun, and this time, Gus wasn't just fighting for love; he wanted blood.

***

The ship rode the swells swiftly, closing the distance to the island's cove. Finally, she saw it, sailing forward from behind the island—*The Tempest.*

Ambrose noticed too. "August." He muttered the name like a curse. He shouted orders, and his crew sprang into motion. They tightened lines and angled the bow just enough to block *The Tempest* from the narrow inlet ahead.

Wave by wave, the gap closed. The two ships drove hard toward the same strip of sand. Their crews shouted, and their sails strained, but she couldn't see Gus anywhere among the chaos.

And then—almost at the same moment—both ships' hulls cut into the cove's shelter. The wind fell still in the lee of the cliffs. The clouds overhead broke open and sunlight slanted in molten gold across the water.

Inside the crescent of pristine, untouched beach was the dark mouth of a cave at the base of a cliff. *That's it,* she thought. *But where is Gus?*

CHAPTER 19

The cove's sand was as white as eggshells. Ambrose's long strides pulled Beatrix in his wake. His cruel grip bruised her arm.

On the far side of the beach, Gus vaulted from the longboat, pistol in one hand, sword in the other. Callahan was close behind. Gus's eyes found her instantly, and he breathed deeply. She was alive and whole but bound in Ambrose's grip. Relief flared in his chest before rage quickly smothered it.

They converged at the same time at the cave's gaping mouth. Inside, the air was damp, and the sound of the tide echoed in its dark expanse. The walls glistened faintly with salt crystals.

In the very center, half-buried in sand and rock, stood a low stone plinth. Upon it, carved into the surface, was a shallow recess, shaped precisely to hold the two silver lockets.

Beatrix's heart pounded. Her fingers trembled as she pulled the locket from beneath her dress. Ambrose noticed her movement. "Do it," he ordered, shoving her forward so hard that she stumbled.

Across the chamber, Gus sheathed his sword and stepped forward. He pulled Aria's locket from beneath his shirt. The hum from the lockets grew louder as both began to glow. Gus and Beatrix locked eyes for the barest moment before both lockets pulled them to their place in the plinth.

All at once, the golden light from the lockets converged and pulsed bright and brighter, until the light forced both Callahan and Ambrose to cover their eyes. Gus and Beatrix stood before the plinth. His hand reached for hers as they stood back, waiting for the secret that was sure to reveal itself.

The sand at their feet shifted, falling away to reveal...nothing.

The glow faded to nothing more than the ordinary shine of the silver lockets. The plinth was empty. The floor beneath the sand was bare stone. There was no chest, no treasure, no map—nothing.

Ambrose's face darkened. "No. No, no, no. After everything..." His voice cracked into a snarl. He whirled to Beatrix, grabbed her arm and yanked her away from Gus. His eyes blazed. "Do you understand what this has cost me?" He yelled down at her.

Gus saw it—the flash in her eye. She was terrified of Ambrose. What had he done to her? Gus raised his pistol. "Let her go, Ambrose."

Ambrose drew his own weapon in a single, fluid motion, pushing Beatrix to the ground. Her eyes flicked to Gus's, horrified at the scene before her. She knew Ambrose would kill him this time. He'd all but said so.

The two men leveled their pistols across the narrow space between them. The smell of gunpowder hung thick in the air. Callahan, too, leveled his musket at Ambrose.

"Step aside, August," Ambrose said. "You've already lost."

"You'll have to kill me first."

"My pleasure," Ambrose snarled. Before either of them could react, Beatrix leaped toward Gus.

The crack of gunfire shattered the air. For a heartbeat, no one moved. Then she staggered, her blue linen dress blooming crimson where the ball had torn through her side.

Gus's pistol clattered to the stone as he caught her before she could fall. "Beatrix—"

He lowered her to the ground and lifted her into his lap. Her head lolled against his shoulder. Her breath was shallow, and she struggled to keep her eyes open. His chest was heaving, but his voice was steady as he glared up at Ambrose.

"You just made the last mistake of your life."

The cove erupted into chaos. Shouts echoed against the rock walls, and the sharp tang of gunpowder filled the damp air. *The Tempest*'s crew surged forward. When they found their captain bent over his lady, and his brother holding the smoking gun, they stopped dead in their tracks. With no crew to protect him, Ambrose had no choice but to surrender. He held up his hands and threw his pistol to the ground.

"Take him to the brig," Gus ordered, his voice like iron. "I'll deal with him later."

The scuffle moved toward the cove's mouth, leaving only the sound of receding footsteps and the hush of the tide. They were alone.

Beatrix slumped against him. Her dress was now soaked with her blood. Gus pressed his hand desperately against the wound.

"Stay with me," he said, his voice shaking despite his effort to steady it. "Don't you dare leave me, Beatrix."

Her lips were pale, and her eyes were glassy. She reached for him, but her fingers slipped against his until he removed his hand from her wound to catch them. With what strength she had left, she brought his locket into her palm, pressing it to her own locket in their entwined hands. Silver met silver, and the lockets glowed warmly despite her life's blood drenching them.

Her breath came raggedly, but her voice—soft and thin—carried the tune he knew too well.

The wind may lie, the stars may turn,

But blood will find its line.
A ring of flame, a silver burn,
A vow in brine and pine.

The air seemed to shift. The very stone beneath them thrummed faintly with a vibration Gus could feel in his bones.

The compass breaks when touched by gold,
The sea forgets the shore,
Yet two shall hold what none can fold,
And open nevermore—

The plinth began to glow, first dimly, then with a brilliance that forced Gus to close his eyes. She struggled to speak the last words.

Unless the tune the sea once knew
Be hummed by kin of mine.

The sand and stone in the recess dissolved into nothingness, revealing a yawning black beyond, as though the very earth had opened.

Her hand fell limp in his, dropping the lockets. Hers fell against her chest, while his hung around his neck, swaying gently as he gripped her tight against him.

"Beatrix!"

She had lost consciousness. Her head rolled against his chest. The dark passage stretched before him, calling to him, *summoning* him.

"Beatrix!" Gus's voice cracked as he shook her lightly, but her lashes stayed still against her pale cheeks.

The stone glowed brighter, spilling warm golden light across the cave walls, painting her skin in an otherworldly sheen. The dark hollow beyond the plinth seemed to breathe, drawing him toward it.

"Captain!"

Callahan's shout echoed down the narrow path, and Gus struggled to focus his attention away from the opening, feeling its pull growing stronger by the second. A moment later, the ship's surgeon followed Callahan into the cave.

The surgeon dropped to his knees. His hands reached to feel for Beatrix's pulse at her throat. He nodded to Callahan, signaling that she was still alive, then pressed a fresh cloth against her wound. "We need to get her aboard the ship now, captain. She won't last long without proper care."

Gus looked from the surgeon's hands to the dark threshold. The locket around his neck pulsed in time with his own heartbeat. Hers was dark and silent.

She had led him this far. Together they had chased this island, fought Ambrose, and fought each other…and now—now—they stood here. How many people had died to lead them here? Arabella, Althea, Aria…

He could carry her back, trust the surgeon, and pray she survived, or he could take her forward, into the unknown and perhaps find whatever Calverique had hidden for decades.

"Captain!" Callahan's voice was sharp. "We have to go."

Gus's jaw clenched. His gaze fell to Beatrix's face. She looked serene in unconsciousness. Her fingers still curled faintly around his as if she, too, was willing him to decide.

A light in the portal flared, casting golden light across them all. Gus tightened his grip on her as the decision pounded in his skull.

Gus shifted his weight toward the portal; his boots scraped across the stone floor as he stood, clutching Beatrix in his arms.

"Gus—no." Callahan's voice cut sharply through the shimmering hum in the air. He stepped between Gus and the glowing archway, his face set in iron. "If you take her through there, she may never see daylight again. You know nothing about what's on the other side."

"I know what's *here*," Gus said, his tone dangerous. "A slow death…rotting away without her. I've lived that once already, Callahan."

"No, it's not the same. What's here," Callahan shot back, "is a surgeon with the tools to keep her breathing. If you go in there now, you might as well have put the ball in the pistol yourself."

The surgeon tried to follow Gus, staunching the gaping wound in Beatrix's side. "I have to remove the ball. She needs stitches; otherwise she won't make it. I have to stop this bleeding."

Gus's jaw flexed. His eyes moved from Callahan to the surgeon, and then to Beatrix's face. He remembered her voice in the dark of his cabin, calling his name. He remembered her warmth, her fire, and the way she had looked at him just before the shot.

Callahan took a step closer. His voice dropped to a plea. "August, don't make me give the order to haul you out of here. You've got a whole crew out there that will follow you into hell, but only if you've got the sense to lead them back out again."

The golden light from the arch shimmered across Gus's features. For a heartbeat, he looked ready to push past Callahan and vanish into it.

Then his grip on Beatrix tightened, not in resolve toward the portal, but in surrender. "Take her back to the ship," he relinquished at last.

Callahan gave a sharp nod and bent to take Beatrix from him. Gus hesitated. His hands were reluctant to let her go. His fingers curled against the fabric of her blood-stained dress. When her weight left his arms, the absence hit him like a cannonball to the chest.

Callahan and the surgeon started for the mouth of the cave. Gus stood rooted, his chest rising and falling with slow, measured breaths. He stared into the stone archway; its golden light rippled like a sunrise on the open sea.

Calverique.

It was there, just beyond that impossible shimmer. It held the treasure Aria had died for. It was the answer to all of it: the lockets, the map, the compass, and the riddles. The golden light swirled around him now, beckoning him with the soft hum of that haunted tune.

He took a step forward.

From down the beach, Callahan's voice carried back, urgent. "August!"

Gus clenched his fists until his knuckles ached. He had to turn away...

He burned the image into his mind. He memorized every curve of the stone, every flicker of light, and then, before it could pull him in forever, he turned his back on it.

The rocks rumbled back into place as he turned away, closing the gap and sealing whatever lay beyond them. Gus didn't look back at them.

The sea's wind hit him as he stepped out of the cave and into daylight. Waves crashed against the rocks. Ahead, Callahan's broad shoulders were steady beneath Beatrix's small, limp form. The surgeon rushed behind him, gripping his satchel.

Gus caught up to them and fell into stride beside Callahan without a word. Deep inside him, a vow took root. Calverique wasn't finished with him.

The next time he made it back here, nothing—not storm, nor steel, nor blood—would keep him from crossing that threshold.

CHAPTER 20

"Clear me a table!" the surgeon barked. His voice sliced through the rumble of men talking below decks. "Boil water—now! Bring every clean rag you can find."

Crewmen scrambled to obey, shoving charts, tools, and tankards aside until the scarred wooden surface stood bare. Callahan shouldered down the stairs with Beatrix limp in his arms. Her head lolled against his chest as her tangled, copper hair spilled across her face and trailed down Callahan's sturdy arms. Her locket dangled at her chest, drenched in blood.

"Here," the surgeon ordered, pointing to the table.

Gus moved in beside him, and his throat tightened. "Lay her down gently."

Callahan eased her onto the planks. Her skin looked almost translucent, and the rise and fall of her chest was shallow and uneven. Gus's hand found hers instinctively, gripping it as though his sheer will might keep her with him.

The surgeon's knife flashed in the lantern light. With quick, practiced cuts, he sliced through her blood-soaked blue cotton dress. Fabric fell away in damp folds, revealing pale skin and the angry, pulsing wound in her side. Something small and metallic slipped from a hidden pocket in the now ruined dress, tumbling to the floor with a muted clink.

Gus's head snapped toward the sound, but he didn't release her hand. Callahan stooped, and his fingers closed around a silver watch etched with faint constellations. He turned it over once, brows furrowing, then slid it into his own pocket without a word.

"Hold her steady," the surgeon snapped and reached for his instruments.

Gus kneeled next to her. His forehead was nearly touching hers. "Stay with me, Trix," he whispered, his voice breaking. "Don't leave me."

The surgeon pressed a clean rag against the wound, and it was instantly soaked crimson. "She's losing too much blood," he muttered through clenched teeth. "O'Malley! I need more light—hold the lamp here." The old sailor instantly complied. He shot a worried look towards his captain as he held the light close to the hemorrhaging wound.

The surgeon worked with grim efficiency. His fingers probed for the ball of lead lodged deep in her flesh. Beatrix's head rolled slightly. A low moan escaped her lips before she sank back into unconsciousness.

Gus clenched his teeth. "You're hurting her."

"I'm trying to keep her alive," the surgeon shot back without looking up. "Now hold her still before I lose my grip."

Callahan braced her shoulders, but the locket slipped sideways, and the chain tightened against her throat. He reached to unclasp it, intending to set it aside.

"No." Gus's voice cracked like a whip.

"Gus—"

"It stays," he said, low and unyielding. His eyes never left it. "It ties her to me. I can't explain it, but it stays."

Callahan's gaze flicked to the locket at Gus's own throat; the silver was dulled beneath the smear of Beatrix's blood. Worry passed through his eyes before he looked away. Gus caught it and felt the sharp edge of his own protectiveness rise, though he said nothing.

The surgeon squinted in concentration. Then, with a swift movement, he drew the bullet free and dropped it onto the table. It rolled in a slow, wobbling arc before coming to rest against a knot in the wood.

Without hesitation, he reached for a curved needle and a length of waxed silk thread. "This should hold until we find a real infirmary," he said, glancing briefly at Gus. "Pray we make port before fever sets in."

Each pull of the thread made Gus's stomach twist, but he didn't look away. When the final knot was tied, the surgeon bound the wound tightly in clean linen and stepped back. "That's all I can do here. Keep her still, keep her warm, and get us to civilization before she worsens."

Callahan wiped his hands on his breeches. His shirt was soaked with Beatrix's blood. O'Malley leaned in beside him, keeping his voice low but urgent over the creak of the hull and the clatter of the surgeon's instruments.

"Martinique has the bigger ports," O'Malley said. "Every supply and surgeon you could want."

"And every pair of eyes that saw the scene at that church," Callahan snapped. "We'd be arrested before her wound was cleaned."

"Saint Lucia, then," O'Malley countered. "It's closer than most."

"Also French," Callahan said flatly. "And they'd have us answering questions until she's cold."

"Barbados is safe," O'Malley argued, "but it's a long haul."

Gus's voice cut through the exchange, low but edged with steel. "Then we haul. We'll make Bridgetown if we tear the wind from her sails to do it."

Neither man argued.

O'Malley gave a short nod and turned on his heel. His boots pounded up the companionway to bellow the orders.

Callahan and Gus lifted Beatrix together; both were cautious not to strain the delicate stitches now holding her together. She was frighteningly light. For the first time, she felt frail to Gus.

They carried her through the narrow passageways to Gus's quarters. They laid her gently into his bed. Gus gently cleaned the last of the blood staining her skin, hair, and locket, then found one of her night shifts to pull gently over her head. Callahan tucked the blanket snugly around her shoulders.

Gus lingered a moment longer. His eyes traced every fragile line of her, committing her to memory as if afraid she might vanish between one breath and the next.

"Stay with her," he said finally, the command gruff but steady.

Callahan nodded, settling himself in the chair beside the bed. "Aye, captain."

Gus turned and noticed someone—probably O'Malley—had left Ambrose's things on the table. There was his signet ring, carved with the Drake family crest, a couple of small knives, and the black opal he had used to decorate his cravat. Gus picked them up and dropped them in his coat pocket, unsure what to do with them just now.

He opened the cabin door and left, closing the door softly behind him. The dim lamplight of the passageway caught the hard set of his jaw as he headed for the brig.

***

Ambrose stood with his shoulder braced against the cold iron of the brig wall. His eyes were fixed on the porthole's narrow view. Beyond the rippled glass, *The Resolute* was a diminishing silhouette. Her sails were fat with wind as she cut away from Calverique. The men he had paid, bribed, and threatened into loyalty were now under another's command, leaving him with nothing.

"Faithless curs! Every last one of you will die in some nameless gutter before your ship bleaches to bones at anchor!" He cursed. The manacle at his wrist bit into his skin as the ship rolled in his departing crew's wake. He barely felt it. Rage, bitter and sharp, had long since swallowed his physical discomfort.

The hatch swung open, spilling light into the damp brig. Gus filled the doorway. His shoulders were squared, and his eyes burned like coals stoked to white heat.

Ambrose's smile was a blade in the dark. "Come to gloat, brother?"

Gus stepped inside. The wood under his boots groaned as if straining to hold him back. "Gloat? No. I came to hear your last words before I break you apart with my own hands."

Ambrose laughed. It was a low, mocking sound that scraped along the timbers. "You think you scare me? You've already taken everything from me: Aria, my future, my name, Calverique, and now that whore—"

Gus's hand slammed against the bars so hard the iron shrieked. "Call her that again, and I'll make sure the sharks are gnawing your bones before nightfall."

Ambrose leaned forward. His chains clinked, but his eyes were alight with cruel delight. "She's mine now, brother. She's my wife, with my mark on her skin. No matter if she lives or dies, you'll never wash that from your mind...or from her soul."

Ambrose watched the fury continue to rise in his brother. He knew Gus was going to kill him. He had nothing left to lose anyway.

"She called for you, you know…right before I took her to my bed. '*Gus…*'" He mimicked her voice in mockery. "It was soft and sweet, like a little plea for her stalwart hero—the great pirate lord, Captain August Drake—to swoop in at the last moment with his sword swinging about his head and save her…and you didn't."

The words hit like musket fire. Gus gripped the bars so tightly the rust bit into his palms. He could picture her, helpless, locked below decks in his brother's ship, with his brother's hands on her body as she trembled in fear and resignation. His voice came out low and lethal.

"You are already a dead man, Ambrose. The only reason you still draw breath is that she needs me, and I will not squander what moments I might have left with her scrubbing your blood from my boots. But mark me, brother—I will see the deed done."

Ambrose tilted his head, smiling as though the threat were a rare vintage to be savored. In whatever time remained to him, he meant to relish watching his brother's descent into unbridled fury, making him a far more entertaining figure than the noble hero he had always played.

"Then pray she dies quickly, August. If she lives, she will see precisely what you have become. You, dear brother, are no longer the hero in her tale…You are simply the man who stood by while his brother took her to his bed and then cradled her broken body after he put a ball in her side."

For a moment, Gus said nothing, though his stillness was answer enough. Ambrose's smirk deepened, sensing the strike had landed. The truth in those poisoned words scraped raw against Gus's mind. His hands curled into fists, but he forced himself to turn away. He needed to return to Beatrix more than he needed to cast his brother to the deep—at least for now.

***

Gus came from the brig like a man walking out of hell's fire. His hot fury still clung to him. He pushed into his quarters without knocking. The lantern light caught the sheen of sweat at his temple.

Callahan was exactly where Gus had left him, in the chair beside Beatrix. She looked even paler in the flickering light. The thin rise and fall of her chest were barely visible beneath the blankets.

Callahan's eyes lifted to meet Gus's. "So? What's the plan?"

"I'm going to kill him." Gus's voice was quiet, stripped of heat, but honed to a razor's edge.

Callahan didn't flinch. "Quickly? Or slowly?"

"Slowly," Gus said, his gaze fixed as if he could already see it. "I want him to know from the first moment what's coming, and I want him to dread every heartbeat that follows."

A flicker of unease passed over Callahan's features. "That's a dangerous sort of pleasure. What were you thinking?"

Gus's mouth curved, but showed nothing close to a smile. "I'll take his sight first, then his tongue. I want to watch him stumbling in the dark and choking on the taste of his own blood while he wonders which piece of him I'll take next."

Callahan leaned back a fraction, as though the air between them had grown colder. "Christ, August…"

"No law will touch me," Gus went on, almost as if to himself. "When I'm done, the sea will take what's left."

Callahan studied him for a long moment, then looked away. "Aye… just be sure you're ready to live with it when it's done."

They were quiet for a moment. The only sound in the room was the faint rattle of Beatrix's breath. Gus reached down and brushed her fingers with his own. The fury gripping him wavered for a heartbeat before he pulled back.

"She's not losing another drop of blood," he said, more to himself than to Callahan.

"Then you'd better keep your head clear until we get her safe," Callahan replied, standing. "I'll see to O'Malley—make sure his course to Bridgetown's the swiftest we've got." He moved toward the door, pausing with his hand on the latch. "I'll bring you something to eat when I'm done. You're no good to her starving."

Gus gave a short nod and lowered himself into Callahan's chair. His eyes never left Beatrix as the door shut, sealing them in together.

She lay far too still. Her lips parted just enough for each shallow breath. He took her hand in his and was startled again by the chill of her skin. He began to warm it between his palms.

"Stay with me," he whispered. His voice was raw. "You don't get to leave me now...not when I finally have you back."

The ship rocked gently beneath them, but he barely noticed. His eyes never left her.

"If you live for me, Beatrix," he said, tightening his hold, "I swear Ambrose will never hurt you again. I'll kill him with my own hands, and when he's gone, you'll be free to marry as you choose." His mouth curved bitterly. "Even me, if you'll have me."

He leaned closer, his words a fierce vow. "I'll give up the sea if that's what you want. We'll go back to Cornwall. You can be a proper lady in a grand estate, and I'll be a respectable lord—no more storms, no more battles—just the life you deserve. I'd trade every horizon I've ever chased to see you safe and happy there."

His forehead hovered just above hers, his breath mingling with hers. "But if you let go now...you'll leave me with nothing but a thirst for vengeance. I'll spend every breath I possess making Ambrose suffer in slow, sweet agony, until he begs for the end."

For a moment, he simply held her hand, willing his warmth into her, searching for any sign of strength. "Live, Beatrix," he whispered. "And I'll make good on every word."

A quiet knock came at the door. Gus did not look up from Beatrix's still face. "Yes?"

Callahan slipped inside. The smell of fish stew followed him. He carried a small tray with a battered tin bowl brimming with steaming broth and a tankard of rum sloshing darkly with each step.

"O'Malley's got us on a straight course to Bridgetown," he said, setting the tray on the small table by the bunk. "If the winds hold, three days will see us in port."

Gus only nodded. His thumb brushed over Beatrix's cold knuckles.

"You need to eat," Callahan urged, nudging the tray toward him. "Cook made fish stew. It's still hot. I poured you some rum, though I'd not drink too much if you mean to keep a clear head."

"I'm not leaving her," Gus said, his voice low but firm.

"I didn't expect you would." Callahan studied him a moment, then added, "I'll make sure O'Malley gets us there with all haste."

He stepped back toward the door. He paused with his hand on the latch. "Three days, Captain. Hold on to that."

The door clicked shut, leaving Gus in the dim lanternlight. He looked down at Beatrix. "Three days, sweetheart," he murmured. "Live for me until then…and I'll see you free of him."

***

Gus woke with a start. His neck was stiff and his back ached from the hard, narrow chair. At some point in the night, exhaustion had dragged him under. He still clasped her hand in his. The lantern had dimmed, and pale morning light slanted in through the small stern porthole.

Shouts drifted down from the deck, and he realized what had awakened him. The rhythm of *The Tempest*'s motion had changed. It was off somehow. A deep, splintering groan from the timbers followed, and another cry.

He looked back at Beatrix. She was still…too still. His thumb brushed over her limp fingers. "I'll be right back." The words caught in his throat. It felt like betrayal to let go, but the noise above was growing louder by the second. Whatever was happening could threaten their ability to get her to Bridgetown. He was halfway up the steps before he'd fully decided to go.

On deck, O'Malley and half a dozen men were fighting with a tangle of rigging at the foremast. A block had given way, dropping the spar dangerously off its line. If not repaired, the mainsail would tear in the wind.

"Hold her steady!" Gus barked, striding into the fray. He was already hauling on the nearest line and shouting for a fresh block and belaying pin. Men moved faster at the sound of his voice, and within minutes, the spar was lashed back into place. The damage was temporary. It was stable enough to keep them on course for Bridgetown.

"Keep an eye on it," Gus ordered, before turning and heading below again at a near run.

The air in his cabin was stifling when he returned. She lay where he'd left her, but her face was sheened with sweat, and her lips moved faintly as though she were speaking to someone in a dream.

"God's blood, no!" He dropped to his knees beside her and pressed his palm to her brow. The heat under his hand made his stomach turn cold.

He bellowed, his voice carrying through the narrow corridors. "Surgeon! Callahan!"

The surgeon burst in moments later with Callahan on his heels. The surgeon's coat was half-buttoned. His hair was sticking out at odd angles from being pulled hastily from his nap below decks. He carried his satchel already open, rummaging through it as he crossed the room.

"What's happened?" he demanded, though one glance at Beatrix told him enough.

"She's burning," Gus said. His voice was strained. "Fever came on fast."

The surgeon set his bag on the table and pulled out a cloth and a small glass bottle. He turned to Callahan. "I need more fresh water, as cold as you can manage. If there's citrus left, bring it."

Callahan nodded once and was gone without a word.

The surgeon dipped the cloth in the water jug on the sideboard and wrung it out before pressing it to Beatrix's forehead. She flinched against the touch.

"Can you keep her still?" the surgeon asked.

Gus shifted to the edge of the bed and braced her gently but firmly.

The surgeon uncorked a bottle and poured a small measure into a cup. "If she can swallow, this will help bring the fever down. But I'll not lie to you—she's weak, and this will take time."

"She hasn't got time," Gus muttered, his jaw tight.

The surgeon glanced at him but said nothing. He focused wholly on his work.

Callahan returned at a near run with a sloshing bucket of seawater in one hand and a netted sack of lemons in the other.

The surgeon dipped fresh cloths into the bucket and wrung them until the water streamed between his fingers. He layered them across Beatrix's throat, arms, and chest. Gus inhaled sharply when the surgeon lifted her locket, and he set it down quickly on top of the cold cloth. "We'll keep changing them as they warm," he said. "Captain, squeeze the juice from two lemons into that mug. The acid will help fight the fever."

Gus obeyed without hesitation. His large hands worked the fruit until the pale rind collapsed.

Callahan stood at the foot of the bed, watching the surgeon work. "What else?"

"Boil water for an infusion," the surgeon replied. "Ginger, if the cook has it. She must drink something that will keep her strength."

Callahan left again to follow the surgeon's orders.

The surgeon turned to Gus. "You'll have to help me keep her cool. Change the cloths. Give her the drink every hour if she can manage it." He fixed Gus with a sharp look, "Speak to her, captain. Keep her here. Give her a reason to fight."

Gus swallowed hard. The lemon's scent lingered sharply on his hands. His voice was roughened by fear. "I'll hold her here if it kills me. She's not slipping from my arms. Not now. Not ever."

The surgeon didn't answer; he only reached for another cloth.

***

Tortured hours passed and night settled heavily over *The Tempest.* Beatrix lay pale and still. Her skin was still damp with fever. Gus sat close with one hand resting gently over hers. The rhythmic rise and fall of the sea outside seemed too calm for the storm inside his chest.

He leaned forward. His voice was barely more than a whisper.

"You're going to open those eyes, Beatrix," he said, his thumb brushing over her fingers. "And when you do, I'll see to it you never have to set foot on another damned ship unless you want to."

A small, humorless smile tugged at his lips. "We'll go to London first. I'll take you to every ball worth attending, and you'll have your pick of gowns in every color. I'll dance with you until dawn, even if I make a fool of myself in front of half the peerage. They'll be shocked to see me—the lost Lord Alverdon. You will be the talk of the ton."

He glanced at her still face, willing her to hear him. "After that, I will take you to Paris. The shops will be yours to command. You can buy lace, silk, jewels…whatever your heart desires. I'll carry every parcel myself. You won't have to lift a finger."

His voice caught, and he tightened his grip on her hand. "Just stay with me, Trix. We've so much left to do."

She stirred in her fever. Her lashes fluttered, and her eyes opened.

"Beatrix?" He called to her, gripping her hand tighter as he reached to move the damp cloth at her forehead.

Her gaze found his, unfocused at first.

"You didn't take me through," she whispered, her voice dry and cracked.

"No, love. I had to save you. You were dying." He spoke to her calmly, but his heart leaped to hear her voice again.

"You left it," she said, the accusation barely louder than the lap of the waves against the hull. "You left Calverique."

"It's ok, it will still be there when you're well again," He assured her.

Her lips trembled. A soft light pulsed gently from the locket against her chest. "But…if we'd gone through—"

"Shhh," he cooed to her. Beads of sweat were forming where the cloth had been. "If we'd gone through, you would have died. I can't lose you."

Suddenly, her expression turned to panic, and the locket's light went out. She gripped his hand tightly. "Ambrose is going to kill you. He told me so."

"Shhhhh…you have to calm down. You have a fever; you have to rest."

"He's going to kill us both," she whispered before her eyes slid closed again and her body fell back into the fever's grip.

Gus placed a fresh cloth on her forehead. His heart ached to know her dreams were clouded with fear and terror, even as she fought for her life. What had Ambrose done to her to make her so terrified, not only for his life, but for hers, too?

Callahan knocked on the door and entered without waiting for an answer. He set a fresh bowl of cold water on the table.

"Any change?" He asked.

"She was just awake. She opened her eyes." Gus's eyes stayed fixed on her face.

"That's a good sign, isn't it?" Callahan's voice held the smallest trace of hope.

"She told me Ambrose was going to kill her. She was terrified. She told me he planned to kill me, too, but that's not exactly news.

Why would Ambrose kill her after forcing her to marry him?" He looked up now, imploring Callahan for any reasonable answer.

"I can't say, Gus. He's a madman."

"He's hurt her, Callahan, and not just with the gunshot." Gus couldn't imagine what she'd been through. "Stay with her. I have questions for my brother."

"Aye, Gus." Callahan sighed but knew it was useless to argue.

***

The brig door slammed against the wall. The iron clang echoed in the small, dank space. Ambrose looked up from where he lounged against the bench. Chains were draped across his lap as he squinted in the darkness and arched a brow.

"My, did the fever take her already?" he drawled.

Gus closed the distance in three strides. His fists curled around the bars. "What did you do to her?"

Ambrose's smile was lazy, almost bored. "Be more specific. I'd hate to answer for the wrong offense."

"I'm not talking about the gunshot—you clearly meant that for me," Gus snapped, his voice edged with steel. "She wakes screaming your name. She's afraid for her life. That's not hatred, Ambrose. That's fear. What did you do?"

The smile widened into something colder. "Fear makes her more...pliable. You'd be surprised what a woman will promise when she thinks her next breath depends on you."

Gus's knuckles whitened on the bars. "If you touched her—"

"Touched her? You'd know all about that, brother." His eyes turned dark. "You may have gotten there first, but I was the one to show her how quickly your claim could be broken. I showed her exactly who holds the power between us."

"That's not power," Gus said, his voice low and dangerous. "That's a coward's trick."

"And yet," Ambrose murmured, leaning forward until the chains clinked, "you're here, demanding answers from me, because the thought of what I might have done is eating you alive."

Gus's hands tightened around the bars until the iron bit into his palms. "Then tell me all of it. I want to know every word you said to her, every threat you made, and everything you did while I wasn't there to stop you."

Ambrose's eyes gleamed with something between amusement and malice. "You want the litany? You want me to paint it for you, stroke by stroke, until you can see it every time you close your eyes?"

"I want the truth," Gus ground out. "Because she's lying in my bed, burning with fever, and even in her half-conscious state, she fears you. Not just hates you—*fears* you. What did you do to make her shrink from you as from the Devil himself?"

Ambrose tilted his head, as though considering whether the truth was worth telling. "I made her see what it was to belong to a man. She fought me, at first; I still have the bruises to prove it. So, I pinned her against the wall and made her rethink her...priorities."

Gus's jaw flexed, a muscle ticked as he fought to keep his voice level. "And you thought that would make her yours?"

"No," Ambrose said, his smile twisting. "It would make her mine *to break*. There's a difference."

"And did you?"

"Break her? Oh yes. With only a single glass of wine, she came to my bed."

Gus lunged for him but was held back by the bars.

"Now, now, brother. You must remember that she might be your whore, but she is my wife, to do with as I please. It's my right to show her what punishments await a wife who fails to please her husband. That's all I did."

The chains rattled as Gus gripped the bars so hard they shook. "If she dies, Ambrose—"

"You'll kill me?" Ambrose cut in, mocking. "I believe you. But you should also believe this: If she lives, you'll never erase what I've put in her head."

Gus's voice dropped low and deadly. "If she lives, I'll still kill you, but not today. Today, every breath I take goes to keeping her alive. When she's safe, when she's healed, and when I know she can stand on her own two feet again…then I'll come for you."

Ambrose only smiled. The chains clinked as he leaned back against the bulkhead. "Then I hope she lasts long enough for you to try."

CHAPTER 21

Bridgetown, Barbados

Three days blurred together into one endless stretch of sea, sweat, and worry. *The Tempest* surged forward under every scrap of sail. Her timbers groaned as O'Malley pushed her to the brink.

Beatrix drifted in and out of fevered dreams. Her skin alternated between burning hot and ghostly cold. The surgeon visited several times a day. The wound refused to close, and he had replaced its stitches once already.

Ambrose remained in the brig. Callahan risked Gus's wrath to bring the prisoner a tray once a day, figuring it was a small mercy for a condemned man.

At dawn on the fourth day, the cry came from the masthead: "Land ho! Bridgetown ahead!"

Bridgetown's harbor opened before them in a sweep of turquoise waters and bustling masts. O'Malley eased *The Tempest* toward the pier. Gus was already shouting orders before the first line hit the bollard.

"Callahan—go. Find the best surgeon in Bridgetown, preferably one with a well-stocked infirmary. Tell him it's urgent and I'll pay whatever he asks."

Callahan didn't waste a second. He vaulted over the rail and onto the pier before the gangplank was even secure. Gus stayed at Beatrix's side as "the best surgeon in Bridgetown" returned with him twenty minutes later. The ship's surgeon met him at the gangplank and filled in the details. The new doctor was a tall, grave-faced man whose manner left no doubt he was accustomed to commanding his own domain.

"This is Dr. Morris," Callahan introduced, "Dr. Morris, this is Lord August Drake, Viscount of Alverdon." Callahan knew that throwing around a title could mean the difference between life and death for Beatrix with this pretentious English doctor, even if Gus would reprimand him for it later.

"And who is the patient?" The doctor asked, looking between the two sea-worn sailors at the fevered woman lying in the bed behind them.

"Lady Beatrix Wrenwood, my betrothed," Gus replied as grandly as possible, failing to mention that she was actually married to his bastard brother. It wouldn't matter. Ambrose would soon be dead, and it would be the truth once again.

"She needs more than I can do aboard," the surgeon said briskly after a single glance. "We'll take her to my infirmary. You'll have to clear the way."

The doctor ordered a high-sided cart brought to the dock. It was padded with folded sailcloth, meant to cushion her on the ride through the rough cobble and dirt streets. Gus laid her into it delicately, as though she were made of glass and even the slightest movement might shatter her into a million pieces. Her head lolled limply against the cushion. Gus straightened her locket, so it sat in the center of her chest, nearest her heart. He climbed up beside her, but the doctor blocked him with a firm hand.

"No visitors until I've stabilized her. You'll do her no good pacing at her bedside."

Gus's muscles tightened visibly, and he opened his mouth to protest, but Callahan gave the slightest shake of his head. With a reluctant step back, Gus watched as the cart rattled away through the narrow streets, every turn carrying her further out of sight. He thought he felt the locket around his neck warm, but he couldn't be sure.

***

Gus stood on the Bridgetown quay. His boots were planted as though the planks beneath him might try to give way. Every creak of a cart's wheel, every snort of a horse, made his head snap up. It was always someone else—merchants, sailors, townsfolk—never word of Beatrix.

Callahan leaned on the bollard beside him with arms folded. "You'll wear a trench in the boards, captain. She's in good hands."

"She's in a stranger's hands," Gus corrected, jaw tight.

"Aye, but not in *his*." Callahan's voice carried a sharp edge, trying to nudge his friend toward the brighter side of it.

Gus's gaze flicked toward *The Tempest* at anchor. Her brig still held a single prisoner in chains. "He still breathes, and that's one mercy too many."

Callahan followed his glance. "Not here. Not in a British port, and not with her fighting for her life a street away. If you kill him now, we'll be in irons alongside him before nightfall."

The muscles in Gus's forearms tightened. "When she is safe, I will see to him. There will not be enough left of him for our father to mourn, let alone bury."

"Yes, see to her first." Callahan's tone left no room for debate. "Let the surgeon do his work. Keep yourself free so you can finish him when the time comes."

Gus forced a slow breath, though the air seemed to scrape his lungs raw. He looked back to the road. The waiting gnawed at him like hunger. "She'll live. She has to."

***

Gus paced like a caged animal. The day crawled past with excruciating monotony. For him, the world had narrowed to one dusty street and the building beyond it.

Callahan brought Gus food he barely touched and rum he barely tasted. Mostly, he stood nearby, watching his captain pace.

By nightfall, a few whale-oil lamps flickered along the main quay. Their glass panes were clouded with soot. Beyond that dim ring of light, the rest of Bridgetown was swallowed in shadow. The salt air cooled enough to raise gooseflesh. Gus waited on the quay with every muscle braced for bad news, because bad news always traveled fastest.

Morning broke in a wash of orange and gold over the harbor. The sun had barely cleared the rooftops when the sound of boots striking the quay caught his ear. A young errand boy darted toward him, panting, with his hair plastered to his forehead.

"My Lord Alverdon?" the boy gasped, feigning a hurried and sloppy bow.

Gus stepped forward. His heart hammered. Callahan stepped to his side, braced for bad news. "Aye?"

"She's awake, sir. Doctor Morris says her ladyship will live."

The words hit him like a cannon broadside. The shock, the disbelief, and then the swell of relief were so fierce it almost took him to his knees.

He didn't think; he ran. The boy scrambled out of his path as Gus tore up the street. His boots pounded the dirt and cobblestones, and his coat snapped behind him. Shouts from vendors and curses from startled passersby blended into a meaningless din. Somewhere behind him, Callahan called his name. His long stride closed the gap, but Gus didn't slow.

He vaulted up the infirmary's steps two at a time and threw the door wide. His chest was heaving, and the pounding of his heart was louder than the creak of the hinges.

"Where is she?"

The surgeon met Gus at the door. The smell of lye and scorched flesh clung to his coat. His face was drawn, and his eyes were heavy from a night without rest.

"She's out of danger," he said without preamble. "The ball punctured a section of her intestine. I've repaired it, but it was touch-and-go. I cauterized the wound to keep the rot from setting in." He rubbed a hand over his weary face. "There will be a scar, but she will heal."

Gus closed his eyes and let relief wash over his body. The knot in his stomach started to untwist, finally.

"There is more," the surgeon said, his voice measured, as though weighing each word. "The damage was grave, my lord. I fear she will never bear children. You should consider what that means before you make any further plans."

For a long moment, Gus only stared, then he shook his head. "I don't care," he said, his voice raw. "I only want her—breathing, alive, and in my arms. Nothing else matters."

The surgeon's expression softened, though his tone remained brisk. "Then see that she rests and keep her from any strain. She's a strong one—most wouldn't have survived the blood loss—but she'll need weeks before she's truly herself again. I will keep her here for a few days before I release her to your ship's surgeon."

"I'll see to it," Gus said, already stepping past the surgeon. Callahan fell into stride beside him, his boots echoing in the narrow hall as they made their way to the infirmary.

Inside, Beatrix lay propped slightly against clean pillows. Her tangled, copper hair was spread loose about her shoulders. Her skin was pale but no longer deathly. Her lashes fluttered, then lifted when he came closer to her.

"Gus?" Her voice was soft and uncertain, as though she feared speaking his name might conjure a dream instead of reality. He reached her in two strides and took her hand gently in both of his.

"Aye, love. I'm here."

Callahan stepped closer to the foot of the bed, his face eased at the sight of her awake. "You've given us a fair scare, lass."

A faint smile curved her lips. "I thought…I didn't know if I'd ever see you again."

"You'll see me every day from now on," Gus vowed, brushing a stray curl from her cheek. "You're safe now. I swear it."

Her fingers tightened around his. "You left Calverique."

"I had to save you." His voice was soft but unyielding. "There's nothing on that island—nothing in this world—worth more to me than your life."

She closed her eyes briefly, a tear slipping free. "I knew you'd come for me."

"I'll always come for you," he whispered, bending to kiss her forehead. "Now, you rest. Doctor's orders."

She gave a soft laugh. It was breathless, but real. Then the light in her eyes dimmed as her thoughts shifted. "Where is he?"

"In the brig," Gus said, his tone sharpening. "In chains."

Her voice dropped to a whisper. "Promise me you'll never let him touch me again."

"I promise," Gus said. Each word was edged in steel.

Callahan's voice joined his with firm certainty. "We'll see to it." He and Gus locked eyes. Callahan's look carried the same vow, though shadowed by a deeper worry that killing Ambrose might cost his captain more than it would save.

***

Gus stayed seated beside her. His thumb brushed slow circles across the back of her hand. They spoke only in fragments with small reassurances and words meant more for the comfort of sound than their meaning.

When her breathing grew heavy and even, he eased his hand from hers and pulled the blanket higher over her shoulder. For a long moment, he just watched her sleep, memorizing the rise and fall of her chest.

"You should go, Captain." The doctor stood in the doorway. His expression was tired, but kind. "She needs the room to be quiet if she's to rest through the night."

Gus glanced once more at Beatrix before rising. "I'll be back in the morning."

"I'll send word if there's any change," the doctor assured him.

Outside, the cooler night air carried the scent of the harbor—day-old fish, smoke from cook stoves, and the ever-present damp salt of the sea. Gus's steps were purposeful as he made his way down to the docks, where *The Tempest* rocked gently at her moorings.

In the brig below, Ambrose sat on the narrow bench. He looked up as Gus descended the steps. He gave a smile that was more a baring of teeth than a warm greeting.

"So, the little whore still breathes," he said, his tone thick with contempt. "Shame. I'd have thought the bullet would have finished her like the last woman you stole from me."

Gus gritted his teeth and stared at him, forcing his silence.

"She deserves what she got, August, and more." Ambrose leaned forward until the light caught the sharp planes of his face. The bruise Beatrix had given him with the candlestick had faded to a sallow tan. Gus noticed it for the first time.

"It looks to me like she gave you a taste of what *you* deserve. What was it? A brick?" Gus's voice dripped with sarcasm, but a flicker of pride curled at the thought. The image of Beatrix smashing something into his brother's face almost brought a smile.

"It was a candlestick, and believe me, she paid for it. Women like her need more than a man's affection. They need fear in their bones and obedience in their blood."

The metal handle of the lantern bit into Gus's palm as his grip tightened. His knuckles turned bone white.

"Did you strike her?" Gus demanded. The question came low and cold, carrying the promise of violence in the answer.

Ambrose's smirk deepened, as though Gus's rage was a reward in itself.

"Oh, I did more than strike her. I made her understand her place. A woman like that needs reminding. She needs to feel the press of a man's hand until she knows who holds the power. When I'm dead and gone, she'll still remember it every time you touch her. She'll always wonder if you'll do the same."

The air in the brig seemed to snap. Gus dropped the lantern onto the floorboards with a clatter, seized the chain binding his brother's wrists, and yanked. Ambrose lurched forward, hitting the bars so hard the breath punched out of him. Gus hauled him close until the iron bit into both their hands. Gus's grip continued to tighten until the chain links screeched.

"One more word," Gus said, his voice like steel drawn from a sheath, "and I'll drag you to the magistrate's steps and tell them exactly what you are: a smuggler—maybe even a pirate—but definitely a coward who shoots unarmed women. They'll hang you in the square before the tide turns, and I'll make certain you swing long enough for the whole island to watch the light leave your eyes."

Ambrose's smirk faltered, but he said nothing.

Before Gus could lunge again, Callahan thrust himself between them, driving Gus back with a stiff forearm to the chest. "Hold, August," he bit out. "Another inch, and I'll see him to the devil myself—but not here, and not this day."

Callahan stopped for a beat to let his words land. Gus didn't say a word. "We're in a British port, under a British flag. You spill his blood here, and they'll string you up beside him before the day is out. Then where does that leave her? She lies grimly wounded in a land that is not her own, thousands of miles from home."

Gus's eyes burned in fury. He shook Callahan's arm off of him and stormed to the deck with Callahan at his heels.

"You're not thinking like a captain!" Callahan's voice was strained and ragged at the edges. He had grown tired of being the only man aboard willing to pull Gus back from the brink. "Every day it's the same: rage first, sense later. I've had my fill of dragging you out of your own fires."

Gus wheeled on him, casting his fury in Callahan's direction. "You think I'm wrong to want him dead?"

"I think you've lost sight of everything else," Callahan shot back. "With him near, you don't think about crew, your ship, or even her. You're letting him steer you straight onto the rocks, and I'm damned if I'll watch you take us all with you."

The words hit hard, but Gus said nothing. He could only glare at Callahan with the cold fury that had taken root in his eyes since the failed wedding in Martinique.

O'Malley had stepped forward; he was afraid he was going to have to break up the battle brewing between the captain and his first mate. Luckily, most of the crew was ashore, unable to witness the mutinous scene.

Callahan exhaled sharply and shook his head. "I'm leaving before I say something I can't take back." He started for the gangway, then paused just long enough to glance over his shoulder. "But mark me, August—if you keep on like this, you'll become the very devil you claim to despise."

Without waiting for a reply, he strode down toward the quay, leaving Gus with O'Malley, his wrath, and the cold sting of truth in his ears.

***

Callahan had not returned by morning. Gus stood at the rail, watching the light creep over the town. The quarrel with Callahan still gnawed at him. The words from last night replayed in his mind with unwanted precision. He had let Ambrose pull him into the muck, and in doing so, he had driven his oldest friend from his side.

He hated admitting it, even to himself, but Callahan had been right. His rage had narrowed his vision until nothing existed beyond the brig. He hadn't thought about the crew or their voyage. They had been off track for weeks, and he had not yet righted his ship.

He thought about Beatrix. He had been granted the greatest blessing—she was back in his life, alive. She deserved more than a man obsessed with blood, and if he meant to be the man she needed, he would have to prove he could master his temper.

He stepped out onto the deck, inhaling deeply. Bridgetown's harbor shimmered in the morning light. Masts swayed gently against the turquoise backdrop. The stench of fish and tar mingled with the sweeter notes of bread baking and coffee roasting from the shore.

He was about to make his way to shore to see her when he heard it—his brother's voice—low at first but singing an unmistakable: *The Compass Waltz*.

The melody curled upward through the ship's belly. Each note was drawn out, slow and taunting. He could hear the words in his mind even though Ambrose replaced the ones he couldn't remember with "la, la, la."

Ambrose was in the brig, chained and caged, yet somehow, he still found ways to poison the air.

Gus's hand twitched toward the companionway that led below. He could already imagine storming down there, grabbing Ambrose by the collar, and forcing the notes back into his throat.

But he didn't. Instead, he turned toward the gangplank. Beatrix was waiting for him, and Ambrose would not win this morning. He had to contain his rage for the good of her and the crew.

Still, as he stepped onto the dock, the last bars of the waltz followed him, lingering like the taste of something bitter that refused to fade.

***

Inside the infirmary, the cool air carried a faint scent of dried herbs and boiled linen. The surgeon greeted him with a nod that carried good news.

"She's stronger today," he said, leading Gus toward the back. "I'll allow her to be out of bed for a short while. She can take a few steps and even sit at the table for her midday meal, but she mustn't push herself. Her body is mending, but it's still fragile."

Gus inclined his head, though his eyes were already searching for her. "I'll see she takes it easy."

He found her propped against her pillows, dressed in a clean shift, with the locket sitting at its rightful place between her breasts. Her skin still held the pallor of illness, but there was a flush of life in her cheeks now, and her eyes brightened when she saw him.

"You're here," she said, her voice soft but steady.

"Of course I'm here." He crossed to her side, taking her hand gently, careful not to disturb her. "The doctor says you're ready for a little walk."

Her lips curved in a small smile. "A grand adventure, then?"

"If you'd like to call it that," he said, helping her swing her legs over the side of the bed. His arm stayed firm around her waist as she stood. Her weight leaned into him. She moved slowly, cautiously, but each step seemed to steady her.

They made it to the small table by the window, where a simple lunch awaited: a bowl of broth, fresh bread, and a cup of weak tea. Gus eased her into the chair, then took the seat beside her.

"I think I might actually eat," she murmured, surprised by her own appetite.

"That's the idea." His gaze softened as he watched her tear off a piece of bread. For the first time in days, he felt the slightest flicker of hope that they might yet leave this port together.

Beatrix dipped the bread into her broth, but her hand slowed halfway to her mouth. The faint smile she had worn moments ago faded. She set the bread back down and stared at the table for a long moment before speaking.

"He tried to strangle me," she said at last, her voice so soft he almost thought he had imagined it.

Gus stilled, his fingers curling loosely around the edge of the table. "When?"

"The day after the wedding. She swallowed, but her eyes remained fixed on the grain of the wooden tabletop. "His hands were around my throat, and he pressed until the room spun. I thought… perhaps it would be easier to let go. At the time, I wished he'd finished it."

Her breath trembled, and she did not wipe away the tears that slipped down her cheeks.

Gus reached across the table, his rough palm cupping her face, guiding her gaze to meet his. "Don't say that. Don't ever say that. He doesn't get to take you from me—not like that."

Her lips parted as if to argue, but the words caught in her throat. She leaned into his touch instead and closed her eyes against the warmth of his hand.

"I'm here," he murmured. "He won't hurt you anymore."

A tear fell onto his thumb, and he brushed it away gently before letting his hand fall back to the table. She took a sip of tea, still quiet, but her shoulders eased just enough for him to believe she'd heard him.

For a moment, the only sounds were the clink of the spoon against the bowl and the soft rustle of the breeze at the window.

***

Once again, Gus left her in the infirmary at the doctor's insistence. His relief at seeing her recover was tempered by the heaviness of her words. He could not shake the image of his brother's hands locked around her delicate throat, her lips parted in panic, and her eyes going dim as the life was choked from her.

It coiled in his gut like a length of cold rope, tightening with every step back toward the harbor.

By the time his boots thudded onto the deck of *The Tempest*, the relief he had felt in the surgeon's ward had hardened into fury once again.

Gus didn't slow. He strode to the brig. His shadow stretched across the narrow passageway until it fell over the man inside. Ambrose sat on the bunk, leaning back against the wall, his expression a lazy mask of boredom—until he caught sight of Gus.

"You've been to see my wife again." Ambrose let the words spill slowly, each one bitten off with disdain. "So, she still breathes? Pity."

Gus stepped up to the bars. His fingers curled around the iron like claws. "You had no right to threaten her life! No death I can imagine will be good enough for you."

Ambrose's mouth curved into a thin and wolfish smile. "Tell me, brother, how do you picture it? My hands were wrapped around her pretty little neck, squeezing the air from her lungs." He raised his bound hands and mimed the motion, a look of cherished remembrance stretching across his face.

"Did she tell you how her nails tore at my skin? Or how about the soft whimper she made when she realized she couldn't break free? Shall I describe the color—how her head turned red, then blue, before the light began to fade from her eyes?"

"I can imagine enough," Gus fought to keep his voice even. He knew he couldn't repeat the violence of the night before.

"Good. Hold onto that image. Let it burn. It'll make it all the sweeter when you finally decide how to do it." Ambrose leaned forward, the chains at his wrists rattling. "So, tell me, how will you kill me? A blade? A bullet? Or will you give me the same gift I almost gave her?"

"Watch and wait, Ambrose."

Ambrose's eyes squinted as he studied him. "You're smiling," he said slowly, almost in disbelief. "You're enjoying this."

Gus didn't deny it. He let the faint curl of his mouth remain as he stepped closer to the bars. "I will end you, brother, make no mistake, but I am going to savor the moment. Sit here and think about all the ways you believe I've wronged you… and then imagine what I might have done had I actually cared enough to wound you on purpose. Then multiply that by all the salt in the sea."

Ambrose's eyebrows lifted in recognition. For the first time, he saw himself in his brother, and the realization seemed to please him.

***

The next morning, Gus arrived at the infirmary with a small parcel under his arm. Beatrix sat propped in a chair by the window. She looked pale but was upright. Her hair was brushed and fell unbound over her shoulders.

"I thought you might like something proper to wear," he said, setting the bundle on the table. "Here's everything you'll need. Even undergarments."

Her brows lifted faintly, and for a moment, there was the ghost of a smile. "You think of everything, Captain."

"Only for you," he said, holding her gaze until she looked away.

The doctor came in and gave Gus a brisk nod. "She's mending well. If she continues to rest and take her broth, she may return to your ship tomorrow morning. She'll still need care, but I trust you can manage that."

"I can," Gus replied without hesitation.

When the doctor left, Beatrix began unfolding the clothes. Her fingers lingered over the soft linen shift and the pale lavender gown. She smiled again, though there was something distant in it, as if part of her stood in some other room at some other time.

"What is it?" he asked quietly.

She shook her head, but the movement was small and guarded. "Nothing."

He didn't believe her. He could see it in the way her shoulders stiffened when his shadow crossed the floor. He knew what it was. Every memory of Ambrose's hands on her, every word and threat, had sunk claws deep inside her mind. She had survived him, but the echo of his touch still clung to her.

Gus's muscles tightened as he watched her fold the last piece and set it aside. It wasn't enough to keep Ambrose chained. It wasn't enough to see him starve or rot.

In his mind, he began to turn over the possibilities, each one crueler than the last. He thought of a dozen ways to strip Ambrose down to nothing and then make him beg before the end. He could almost hear the crack of the whip, the grind of the keel, and the hiss of salt on raw skin.

He'd make him wish he'd never touched her at all.

***

That night, Gus descended into the brig. Ambrose still sat in chains on the bench.

"She's strong enough to come back aboard tomorrow," Gus said flatly. "And when she does, you'll not say a word to her."

Ambrose's mouth curved in a slow, knowing smile. "Did she tell you more today, brother? What images dance in your head now, I wonder."

Gus didn't answer.

Ambrose leaned forward as the chains clinked softly. "Did she tell you about when I untied her wedding dress? You know, the one you so thoughtfully chose for her?"

Gus's grip on the bars tightened.

"Or how I took her wrists and pinned her to the bed," Ambrose went on. His voice lowered like a confession meant for the shadows. "Her skirts bunched around her waist, and I forced her legs open beneath me." He gave a humorless chuckle. "She fought—oh, she fought—but I enjoyed that most of all."

The muscles in Gus's jaw worked, but his voice was calm, deadly. "Enjoy your words, Ambrose. They're all you have left. Every syllable you spit at me will come back to you before I'm done. And I promise you—" he leaned closer, his voice dropping to a whisper that was all steel, "—I'm going to make sure you live long enough to feel every last thing I've planned for you."

Ambrose smirked, but there was the faintest flicker in his eyes.

***

Callahan came aboard just as Gus was leaving the brig. The lantern still swung in his hand. His first mate's boots thudded on the deck boards. His expression was unreadable, but his eyes tracked Gus like a hunter sizing his prey.

"I heard every word," Callahan said quietly.

Gus stopped, the space between them charged. "Then you know why I said them."

"I know what he said," Callahan replied, his tone sharp. "I also know what you said back. You're not just answering him, August—you're meeting him on his level. I've seen men go down that road, and they don't come back."

Gus's eyes blazed dark and dangerous. "He hurt her. Am I supposed to answer that with civility?"

"I think," Callahan said, stepping closer, "that if you keep feeding off his filth, you'll become exactly what she fears, and you damn well know it."

The warning hung heavy between them, thick as the humid night air. Gus didn't answer. His stare was cold, but Callahan saw the flicker of something else beneath it; whether it was doubt or fury, he couldn't tell.

"If you want to kill him, fine," Callahan said, voice dropping low. "But you're supposed to be the captain, and right now, you're losing yourself faster than you're losing him. Pull yourself back, before there's nothing left worth saving."

Callahan didn't wait for a reply. He turned and strode for the gangway once more, leaving Gus standing in the shadows with the echo of his own words in the brig still ringing in his ears.

CHAPTER 22

Gus offered his arm to Beatrix, guiding her slowly along the wharf. Her steps were careful. Her strength was still returning, but he matched her pace without hurry.

The Tempest waited at the end of the pier. Her crew was lined up along the deck, all except her first mate. When Beatrix stepped aboard, a cheer rose from the men. Rough voices softened with relief at the sight of her on her feet again. Gus felt her hand tighten on his arm, and he leaned down. "They've missed you," he murmured, his voice meant only for her.

His cabin had been scrubbed until the wood gleamed. A vase of bright hibiscus and frangipani stood on the table. Their colors were a burst of life against the polished surface. Beside them lay a neat stack of folded linen dresses that Gus had picked out for her in town.

"I wasn't sure what you'd like," he said, watching her eyes take in the room, "so I bought a few."

Her lips curved faintly, though her gaze lingered on the flowers. "They're beautiful."

He stepped behind her and rested his hands lightly at her waist. "You'll sleep here," he said simply, with no hint of question in his tone. "With me. Every night, for the rest of our lives."

She didn't protest. She leaned back into him and tilted her head until it found his shoulder. He closed his eyes for a moment, breathing in the faint scent of her hair, and silently vowed that no harm would touch her again while he drew breath.

***

Beatrix woke from her nap to the muffled creak of timbers and the nearby sounds of the boats in the harbor. The sea breeze slipped in through the open stern windows, carrying the scent of sea salt and jasmine. She pushed herself up slowly, testing her strength.

When Gus returned to check on her, she gave him a small, hopeful smile. "Could I…walk on deck for a while? I want to breathe in the fresh air."

He hesitated only a moment before nodding. "Just for a few minutes." He fetched her shawl and draped it around her shoulders, then offered his arm as they stepped out into the warm sunlight.

The harbor spread before them in a shimmering expanse—bright sails, glinting water, the low hum of life ashore. She let her gaze wander. The motion of the ship beneath her feet felt both strange and familiar after so long on land.

They had just reached the main deck when a voice thundered up from below.

"Beatrix!"

Her steps faltered. The sound came from the brig's iron-barred door beneath the aft grating. Ambrose's voice cut through the warm air like a whip.

"Are you coming to attend me, wife? Or are you too busy lying abed for your pirate captain?"

Air fled her lungs in a sharp rush, and her pace slowed. She turned her face away, refusing to give him the satisfaction of seeing her flinch. Gus stopped, pivoted, and strode for the hatch to the brig.

"Gus—" she called after him, her voice still weak. But he was already thundering down the steps. She hesitated only a moment before clutching her side and slowly following him into the dim, stifling air below.

***

Ambrose's head lifted as Gus came into view, and a slow, knowing grin spread over his face.

"You've got a loud mouth for a man who's chained like a dog," Gus said quietly, almost pleasantly.

Ambrose leaned back against the wall, feigning ease. "You didn't come down here to talk about my mouth. You came to hear what else I might say to her."

Gus's mouth formed a slow and deliberate smile. "No, I came to see how much rope I should give you before I hang you with it."

Ambrose's brow arched. "And here I thought you didn't want me dead quickly. You've got a plan now, have you?"

"Oh, I have more than a plan," Gus said, his tone silken and dangerous. "I intend to make you think about it. Every hour. Every time you close your eyes. I want you to wonder if today's the day I end you, or if I'll wait until you've rotted down here so long that you beg me for it."

Ambrose's chuckle was derisive. "You're learning, brother. It's good to see you playing with your prey before you slit its throat. Hell, it's almost admirable."

Gus leaned one forearm against the bars. His voice dropped to a whisper meant to slide under the skin. Gus's eyes stayed locked on him. "I'm not playing, Ambrose. I'm perfecting the kill."

Ambrose's grin didn't falter, but something colder flickered in his gaze. "Careful, August. You're starting to sound like me."

"Maybe," Gus said, straightening, "but unlike you, I'll keep my word."

He turned and walked away before Ambrose could dig in another word.

Behind Gus, Beatrix stood at the foot of the steps, her shawl pulled tight around her shoulders. She was pale as a sheet once again. She had heard every word.

She did not speak as he led her back toward the companionway. When they reached the main deck, she stopped. "You sounded just like him," she said at last, weakly.

He stilled, his hand still resting lightly at her elbow. "I'm nothing like him."

Her gaze searched his face, as though she were trying to convince herself. "Maybe not yet. But I know the way hatred grows. It doesn't stop. It takes and takes until there's nothing left of you."

Gus exhaled sharply. "You sound like Callahan. If you're asking me to pity him—"

"I'm not," she interrupted, shaking her head. "I'm asking you to remember yourself. I've already seen what Ambrose can do when he loses his soul. I could not bear to watch it happen to you."

The wind stirred her hair across her cheek. For a moment, neither spoke. Then Gus guided her toward the rail, away from the hatch to the brig. "I'm still me, Trix. When this is over, I'll be free of him and so will you."

She nodded faintly, but the faraway look in her eyes told him she didn't believe him. He took her hand in his and led her back to his cabin to rest.

***

By evening, the lanterns in Gus's cabin cast a warm light across the freshly polished table. A simple supper of roasted fish, bread still warm from the galley oven, and stewed vegetables waited between them. He had insisted they eat as they once had, before everything between them had been shaded by Ambrose's shadow.

Beatrix sat opposite him. Though she slept most of the afternoon, she still looked exhausted. The linen of her new dress fell neatly over her lap. The tropical flowers still stood in a vase at the center of the table, and their scent mingled with the steam from the plates.

Gus poured her a measure of watered wine and then his own. "You should eat," he said softly, pushing the bread toward her.

She tore a piece free, but her gaze lingered on him rather than the food. "You've thought of everything," she said; her tone held somewhere between gratitude and hesitation.

"I told you I'd take care of you." He watched her closely. He cherished the way her fingers toyed with the edge of her plate and the way her eyes dipped when he held her gaze for too long.

"I know," she murmured, taking a sip from her cup. "But sometimes, I wonder if you're caring for me…or protecting me from yourself."

He set down his fork. "You think I'd ever hurt you?"

Her eyes lifted to his, clear and steady. "I don't know, but I think you might lose yourself trying to hurt him."

The words hung between them. Gus reached across the narrow space and covered her hand with his own. "I'll keep my promise, Trix. You'll be safe. And when this is over, Ambrose will be nothing but a memory."

She searched his face for a long moment before nodding. "Then I'll hold you to it."

When the plates were cleared and the lanterns dimmed, Gus helped her to the bed with a care that felt almost reverent. She moved slowly, still guarding her side, but she let him guide her beneath the soft linen sheets he'd found for her in port.

He shed his coat and boots, then slipped in beside her. His arm looped gently around her waist. She fit against him affectionately, but there was a stiffness to her posture and a tension in her muscles that had nothing to do with her injury.

"I'll be careful," he whispered, pressing a kiss to her hair. "You're safe here."

She breathed in sharply before she whispered, "Even now, when I close my eyes, I can feel his hands."

Gus's hand stilled against her stomach. She could feel the tension tightening the muscles in his arms around her. "I will never let him touch you again."

Her voice trembled, though her words were steady. "I know. But it doesn't stop the memories." She turned toward him then and rested her cheek against his chest. Her fingers curled into his shirt as if anchoring herself.

He held her closer, careful not to jostle her wound. His palm smoothed over her back in slow, steady circles. "Then I'll hold you through every one of them, as long as it takes, until there's nothing left but us."

She closed her eyes, and her breathing evened out in time with the rhythm of his heart. Gus stayed awake long after she slept, listening to her breath and feeling the faint tremors in her body even in rest.

In the darkness, with her safe in his arms, he vowed again that Ambrose would pay for every ghost that haunted her.

***

The first pale light of morning shone through the stern porthole. Gus had not moved all night, unwilling to disturb her. His arm still curved protectively around her.

Beatrix stirred against him, and for a moment, he thought she was waking easily. Then her breath hitched, and her fingers dug sharply into his shirt.

"No—please, no…" she whispered, the words tumbling from her lips in a dream-laden panic. Her body tensed; every muscle was rigid against him.

"Beatrix," he said to her gently, tilting his head to press his lips near her ear. "Wake up, love. You're with me."

Her eyes fluttered open, but they were glassy, as though some part of her was still trapped in the dream. She swallowed hard, then gave a small, jerky nod. "I'm all right."

"You're not," he said quietly, brushing a damp strand of hair from her temple. "Not yet."

She looked away, her voice barely audible. "I thought I was past it. But every time I close my eyes…" She shook her head. "It's like I'm back there."

Gus's chest burned with the effort of keeping his voice level. "Then I'll keep you here, in my sight, until the day comes when you close your eyes and only see what's ahead of us."

She managed a faint smile that didn't reach her eyes. "You make it sound so simple."

"It is," he said, though they both knew it wasn't. He pressed a kiss to her hair again. "It's just a matter of time, and I'll give you every moment you need."

As she settled back against him, Gus's gaze hardened on the far wall. Time alone would not erase Ambrose's hold on her memories. That would require something more...something final.

***

While Beatrix rested after breakfast, Gus once again gave in to temptation and visited his brother in the brig. The key in his hand felt heavier than it should have, though he had no intention of using it to open the cell. Not yet.

Ambrose sat sprawled on the bench, his shirt half-unbuttoned as though he were lounging in a drawing room instead of rotting in a brig. He looked up at Gus's approach, and a slow, serpentine smile curled across his lips.

"So, how is my bride this morning? Still clinging to you like a child afraid of the dark?"

Gus stopped just outside the bars. "She dreams of you," he said flatly.

"Of course she does," Ambrose drawled, shifting his chains with a faint clink. "I make quite an impression."

"She wakes in a cold sweat, trembling. She thinks she's back there, with your hands around her throat."

"Ah, the memory serves her well, then." Ambrose leaned forward, his voice dropping into a mockery of intimacy. "She looks very pretty that way. Soft, helpless, almost...pliable."

Gus's grip tightened on the bars until the metal groaned faintly. "You've already signed your death warrant."

Ambrose tilted his head, feigning curiosity. "Oh, have you come up with new ways to torture me before you end me? Let me guess: You'll sever my toes with fishing line. Or maybe you'll peel off my fingernails, one by one, with your jackknife. Do you still play the violin? Listening to that would be torment enough to make me want to die. Or have you thought of some other way to make me feel every second of your righteous fury?"

"You'll pray for me to kill you," Gus said evenly. "And I'll make sure your prayers go unanswered for a very, very long time."

Ambrose's smirk faltered for the barest moment, but he recovered quickly, leaning back in mock ease. "I'll look forward to it."

"You should," Gus said, his eyes like ice. "Because when the day comes, you'll wish I'd put a bullet in your head quickly." He turned and left without another word. The sound of the hatch slamming shut behind him echoed in the close air.

O'Malley lingered by the hatch, arms folded, his weathered face lined with worry.

"What, you too?" Gus challenged.

The old sailor only shook his head, as if weighing whether the captain before him was the same man he'd sworn to follow.

"Does Callahan plan to come back before we sail?" Gus asked.

O'Malley's gaze didn't waver. "If he's wise, he'll wait 'til you're done playin' cat and rat with your brother. That game doesn't end without one beast dead…and the other half-eaten."

Gus turned his head slowly toward him. The look in his eyes was enough to make even O'Malley wonder if he'd just stepped too close to insubordination. The sailor cleared his throat, crouched, and became very interested in some loose tar along the deck seams while Gus strode away without another word.

***

For the first time in weeks, Gus and Beatrix walked side by side without urgency. The harbor was alive with the bustle of trade.

Sailors unloaded barrels of molasses, and the scent of roasting coffee was almost too much to resist.

Gus stayed close to her with his hand light against her back as they wove through the market stalls. She was still weak, but she was going stir crazy in her convalescence.

Her eyes lingered over baskets of ripe mangoes, strings of coral beads, and bolts of bright calico cloth that fluttered like pennants in the breeze. Gus bought everything she admired, instructing vendors to have it all delivered to the ship. She smiled more here, though the faraway shadow still crossed her gaze now and again.

They shared a paper cone of sugared almonds from a cheerful woman at a street cart, and Gus found himself watching her enjoy them as though he might never see her smile again. When she paused before a bookshop, he guided her inside, where the scent of ink and paper was strong. He bought her a worn copy of *Robinson Crusoe*; its cover had faded, but the pages were still sound.

At midday, they stopped at a shaded courtyard café. The air was heavy with the perfume of blooming jasmine, and the clink of porcelain cups accompanied the low murmur of conversation from other patrons. Gus ordered grilled fish with lime and fresh bread, and they lingered over the meal, letting the hours slip by like the tide.

By early afternoon, the heat pressed more heavily, and Beatrix's steps slowed. Gus noticed the way she steadied herself with her hand against his arm. "We've walked enough for one day," he murmured.

She didn't protest. Gus led her back to the ship, afraid he would have to carry her if they lingered much longer.

"Was it worth the morning?" he asked.

Her lips curved faintly. "Every step."

He bent, pressing a kiss to her hair. "Tomorrow, we sail."

Her hand found his and held it. Her grip was warm and sure. They stood on the deck and faced the town. "Then let me remember Bridgetown like this." He held her close to him, supporting her weight as she watched the people going about their lives in the hot summer sun.

For a long while, they stood in companionable silence, and the sounds of the harbor drifted up from the streets below.

***

Beatrix had napped through the hottest part of the afternoon. By the time the sun sank into the horizon, Bridgetown's streets glowed with the flicker of oil lamps. The air carried the faint hum of music from a nearby tavern. It mingled with the low lull of the tide against the pilings.

Gus returned to the cabin with a covered basket in hand. The scent of roasted chicken and spiced rice escaped from beneath the cloth. Beatrix was waiting for him, seated near the porthole where the evening breeze drifted in. She had changed into the pale linen dress he'd bought her. The soft fabric was loose enough not to press against her healing side.

"You've been busy," she said as he set the basket down on the small table.

"I thought we deserved better than bread and broth," he replied, pouring wine into two cups. "A proper meal before we're back to the ship's fare."

They ate slowly. The quiet between them was comfortable. He carved the meat for her so she wouldn't strain herself, and she slipped him the crispest pieces of bread from the loaf. Outside, the sounds of the town faded into the steady rhythm of the sea.

When the plates were cleared, Gus drew her gently to the bed, careful as always of her bandaged side. She settled against him with her head on his chest. For the first time in weeks, it felt like the world beyond the room could wait. His arm curled protectively around her.

They drifted into sleep with the small window wide open. The salt wind whispered with the murmur of the harbor below like a distant lullaby.

CHAPTER 23

Morning light crept once more through the porthole. Gus stirred, blinking against the light. Beatrix was still nestled against him with her copper hair spilling across his chest. Her fingers traced idle patterns on the linen of his shirt absentmindedly.

"How will you do it?" she asked at last, her voice soft but unflinching.

He stilled, tightening his arm around her. "Do what?"

Her eyes lifted to his, clear now in the morning light. "Kill him."

A muscle ticked in his jaw, but his voice was deceptively calm. "That's not something you need to trouble yourself with."

"I want to know," she pressed, her tone sharper. "I want to know exactly how you plan to end him."

He studied her for a long moment. She did not look away.

"You're certain you want that picture in your head?"

"I already have worse ones," she whispered.

His expression hardened. "I'll bleed him slowly, so he knows what it is to feel his life drain away. I'll keep him conscious long enough for him to understand exactly why it's happening. I'll strip from him every ounce of dignity and every scrap of control until he begs me to finish him. Then, when I'm finished, there won't be enough left of him to cast a shadow."

She swallowed but did not protest. A shiver ran through her body as she pictured Gus standing over Ambrose in a way that was impossible to tell where one devil began and the other ended.

***

The afternoon sun slanted through the brig's narrow portholes, striping the damp floorboards in pale light. Ambrose watched the scene before him with interest.

Gus stood just outside the bars with a whetstone in his hand, drawing it slowly along the length of his sword. The rasping scrape carried in the stillness. Each pass was deliberate and unhurried, like the sound of time running out.

He didn't speak; he only watched Ambrose through the low, predatory tilt of his head, with eyes fixed as though measuring where to strike first.

"You planning to gut me here?" Ambrose asked at last. His voice was bored, but his gaze was wary.

"Not here," Gus said. The whetstone glided again with an ear-grinding scrape. "I'll choose the place. I'll choose the moment. You'll see it coming, and you won't be able to stop it."

Ambrose's smirk faltered for a fraction of a second, but he forced it back. "You think that frightens me?"

"No," Gus said evenly. "I don't need to frighten you. I just want you to know."

The final scrape of the stone rang louder than the others. Gus sheathed the sword without taking his eyes off his brother, then turned and walked away.

From the shadows of the passage, Beatrix stood frozen, holding her breath. She had only come below to find him, but what she saw instead made something cold settle in her chest. This wasn't the man who had held her so gently the night before. This was someone who looked—and sounded—like Ambrose.

She waited until Gus's footsteps were gone before stepping back from the shadows. The faint rasp of the whetstone still echoed in her ears.

***

On deck, the light was softer, and the harbor breeze lifted strands of her hair. She spotted Callahan striding up the gangway. His expression was carved from stone, and his eyes were set forward as though the ship were an adversary he meant to face down.

"You're back," she said, stepping into his path before he could disappear below.

His gaze softened a fraction when it landed on her.. "Aye. It's good to see you up and about. I hear we sail today."

She hesitated. "Then you haven't heard?"

One brow lifted in wary question.

"Gus," she said, her voice low so only he could hear. "He's...sharpening his sword."

"Is he, now?" He saw the panic behind her eyes and realized she didn't mean he wasn't performing routine maintenance on his blade.

"You look pale," he said, concern edging his voice. "Should you be out of bed?"

"I needed air. But Callahan, I saw him, in the brig with Ambrose."

Callahan let out a long sigh. "Ah, I see."

Her throat tightened. "It wasn't Gus. Not the man I know. He—" She swallowed. "He looked at him like prey. He was sharpening his sword, slowly...and savoring it."

Callahan's jaw shifted. "He's been through hell to keep you alive, lass. It changes a man."

"That's what frightens me," she said, her voice barely more than a whisper. "If he lets this need for revenge eat at him, I don't know what will be left when it's over."

Callahan studied her for a long moment before letting out a slow breath. "I've tried, lass. We quarreled harder than we had in years. I nearly didn't come back aboard, and I may yet leave." His gaze sharpened. "You know as well as I—Gus doesn't forgive, and he doesn't forget. If he's to be stopped, it won't be by me. It'll have to be by you."

She looked frail again, but lifted her head, bolstered by his words. "I'll try."

***

Gus sat at the small table in his cabin with a half-empty glass of rum beside him. His shirt was open at the collar. He looked up when she entered, and his expression softened instantly.

"You should be resting," he said, rising to pull out her chair.

"I will," she replied, though her voice was quieter than usual. She sat and folded her hands in her lap. For a moment, she simply watched him as he poured her a cup of water. The easy gentleness in his hands was entirely at odds with what she had seen in the brig.

"Gus…" She hesitated. "I saw you today…with Ambrose."

He stilled and set the pitcher down. "And?"

"You were sharpening your sword like…like you were hunting him. You had the same look he had when he…" She trailed off, unable to say the words. "It frightened me."

Something flickered in his eyes—hurt, maybe, but he quickly buried it. "I told you, Beatrix. He will pay for what he's done."

"I know, but not like this." Her voice trembled, but she did not look away. "If you become him to destroy him, then he's already won."

His gaze stayed locked on hers. "Do you want me to let him live? What then? He's not the kind of man who disappears quietly."

"Find another way," she urged. "Please. I want the gentleman who holds me tenderly in the night, not the pirate lord who stands over a chained prisoner, savoring how he'll kill him."

For a long moment, he said nothing. Then he exhaled slowly and reached for her hand. "You think I'm lost to him."

"I think you're close," she whispered. "Too close."

He pulled her gently toward him, pressing her hand to his chest. "You won't lose me, love. Now, rest."

When he'd seen her to bed, Gus emerged onto the deck. Callahan stood near the mainmast, checking the lines with O'Malley. Their eyes met across the space.

For a beat, neither man spoke. Then Callahan gave a single, measured nod. Gus returned it, just enough to acknowledge him, before turning toward the helm.

The crew moved with practiced efficiency. Canvas unfurled overhead. *The Tempest* eased from her berth; her prow angled toward open water. Whatever words waited between captain and first mate would have to wait until they were at sea.

***

When they were safely through the harbor, Gus turned his attention once again to his brother. This time, he planned to end their sparring and ready the man for a quick death at sea. He stood outside the bars, arms folded, with his shadow stretching over Ambrose in the dim light.

Ambrose looked up. "Back so soon? I was beginning to think my whore wife had finally tired you out."

Gus's jaw flexed, but he said nothing. He had promised himself—promised her—he would keep his temper.

Ambrose tilted his head. "Tell me, did she wake with that same haunted look in her eyes?"

"Careful," Gus warned, his voice a rough whisper.

"Oh, I'm being careful." Ambrose's smile was slow and poisonous. "Because I know exactly which strings to pluck to make you play, brother. I always have. Remember Eton? Remember how it burned you that Father paraded you like the golden boy while I stood in the shadows, keeping track of every one of your secrets?"

Something in Gus snapped. He stepped closer, gripping the bars so tightly the iron bit into his palms. "You think you know my secrets? You wouldn't recognize the truth if it gutted you. I made my own life—my own fortune—while you clung to Father's coattails and called it ambition."

Ambrose's smile widened. "Yet here you are, threatening me like a dockside thug. Father would be so proud."

"No." Gus's voice dropped to a dangerous calm. "Father would be ashamed that he ever let you carry his name. You've lived your life feeding off *my* family name, and you've never created anything worth keeping. That's the difference between us. When I take something, I keep it. When you take something, you destroy it."

The words hung in the air like a drawn blade. Ambrose's smirk faltered, just for a moment, and Gus saw the wound land.

He stepped back, forcing his hands to unclench from the bars. "Enjoy your chains, brother. We are at sea now. I'll be back when I decide where to cast your body into the deep."

***

Beatrix was waiting near the mainmast when Gus emerged from the companionway. The wind lifted the loose curls around her face. She studied him as he crossed the deck, noting the taut set of his jaw and the darkness simmering in his eyes.

"What did you say to him?" she asked quietly.

"Nothing you need to trouble yourself over," he said, striding past her.

"That's not an answer," she pressed, stepping into his path. "I hear the way you speak to him, Gus. It's not you."

He stopped short. His head snapped toward her. "You think I'm becoming him?" His voice was low and dangerous.

"I think the more you feed on this, the more you let him live in your head, the more—"

"You don't understand!" The words came out like a growl, sharp enough to make her flinch. "You weren't there all those years—"

"Maybe not, but I've felt his cruelty too, Gus," she shot back, her voice trembling. "I can still feel his hands on my throat and his hot breath on my face. Don't tell me I don't understand what he is."

Something in him snapped. He seized her arms and yanked her close with a grip too tight to be protective. "I will end him for it. Do you hear me? I will." His breath scorched her cheek. His eyes blazed with a fury that made him almost unrecognizable.

"Gus, you're hurting me," she whispered, her voice small and shaking.

"Captain!"

Callahan's voice cut through the air like a blade. In an instant, he was there, forcing Gus's hands away and stepping between them. "What in God's name has gotten into you?"

Gus blinked as if waking from a dream. The reality of what he'd done settled into his gut like lead.

Callahan turned to Beatrix, his voice softening. "Come on, lass. Let's get you below." He guided her away, his arm firm around her shoulders, leaving Gus standing in the middle of the deck with the weight of his own rage pressing down on him like a storm cloud.

***

The chartroom door slammed against the bulkhead as Gus shoved it open and strode inside. He shut it behind him with a violent shove. The latch rattled in protest.

He gripped the edge of the table, staring down at the neat spread of charts and navigational tools, but the lines blurred. He didn't see the islands and shipping lines. All he could see was Beatrix's face, her eyes wide with fear, when he grabbed her.

His stomach twisted. He had done that…not Ambrose. It was all him.

He raked a hand through his hair and paced the narrow space. His fury was still there, coiled and hot in his chest, but now it was threaded with something else: shame. He'd meant to protect her. Instead, he had put that same fear in her eyes. The realization burned like salt in an open wound.

He stopped pacing and gripped the hilt of his sword where it rested on the table. The steel caught the light and cast a gleam that seemed to beckon him in the same way the arch had beckoned him back at Calverique.

Ambrose deserved to die, but if he let this rage run loose, he would be no better than the man he meant to destroy.

He braced his hands on the table and bowed his head.

***

Beatrix sat in the cabin, turning the pages of *Robinson Crusoe* but not reading a word. She still felt the ghost of Gus's grip on her arm. It wasn't painful now, but weighed heavily in her thoughts.

Callahan knocked and entered with a mug of watered wine, holding it out without a word. She took it as her fingers brushed his in thanks.

"You all right, lass?" he asked.

She gave the barest nod, then took a sip before answering. "I'm worried for him, Callahan. He's… changing."

"Aye." Callahan glanced toward the closed door of the chartroom. "Ambrose is poisoning him. He's got nothing else to lose, so he's pushing in the way only a brother can."

Her lashes lowered as she set the mug in her lap. "I can't watch it anymore."

Callahan sat across from her at the table with his arms crossed. "He's carried that rage since Calverique. At first, it was grief—raw and bleeding after the wedding. But when Ambrose nearly took your life, something broke in him. You're the only tether left between him and the abyss."

She looked up at him. A flicker of resolve replaced her worry. "Then I'll have to do more than just hold him away from it. I'll have to take it from him entirely."

"How do you mean?"

"I'll convince him to let me choose Ambrose's fate." She spoke the words slowly, testing them as she went. "If the choice is mine, then the blood is on my hands, not his. It will free him from the weight of it."

Callahan studied her for a long moment. "You think he'll agree to that?"

"I think…" She paused, her eyes drifting toward the chartroom. "I think he cares about me enough to try. If I can make him see that holding on to this hatred is exactly what Ambrose wants, he'll listen."

Callahan's mouth curved in the faintest grin. "It's a dangerous game you're playing, lass, but maybe the only one worth playing. I'll back you in it."

"Then we'll do it together," she said, lifting her chin.

***

Gus stood at the table in the chartroom with hands braced on either side. His eyes were fixed on a chart, but he'd long given up trying to choose their next route.

The door creaked open. He looked up sharply to see Beatrix step inside with Callahan at her shoulder.

"What is this?" Gus's voice was edged and defensive.

Beatrix didn't answer immediately. She came closer until she stood across the table from him. "We need to speak to you about Ambrose."

His gaze darkened. "There's nothing to discuss. He's my problem to solve."

Callahan stepped forward and leaned against the doorframe with arms crossed. "That's just it, Gus. The way you're going about it isn't you anymore."

Gus clenched his teeth. Every word strangled before it could form. "What would you have me do? Let him walk free after what he's done?"

"No," Beatrix said softly, but her voice held more steel than she'd shown since Ambrose shot her in Calverique. "I would have you let me choose his fate."

For a moment, he simply stared at her. Then he laughed once. "No."

"It's my right," she pressed, meeting his gaze without flinching. "He wronged me, so the choice belongs to me."

"You don't understand what you're asking," he said, his voice rising. "The man tried to kill you. He—"

"I do understand," she cut in, her tone sharper now. "Better than anyone, which is why I can decide without letting hatred consume me."

Gus shook his head. He moved to the other side of the table to put distance between them. "This is not your burden to bear."

"Yes, it is," she said. "If you carry it for me, it will destroy you, and that's exactly what he wants."

Callahan's voice rumbled from the doorway. "She's right, August. You've been dancing to Ambrose's tune since Calverique, and it's eating you alive."

Gus looked between them. His chest rose and fell in slow, deliberate breaths. "And if I refuse?"

Beatrix's chin lifted. "Then you'll prove Ambrose right; you're no better than he is."

The silence stretched as heavy as the sea in a dead calm. At last, Gus dragged a hand through his golden hair. His expression was caught between fury and defeat.

"Fine," he said at last. "You decide. But understand me—both of you—if you falter, I will end him myself."

Beatrix nodded once. "Then we have an agreement."

The door shut behind them with a finality that made the lantern flame waver. Gus remained where he stood with his palms braced on the chart table, staring down at the curling edges of parchment.

He told himself he had agreed only to keep the peace and to give Beatrix the illusion of control until the moment came. Yet, the image of her standing there, unflinching, declaring that Ambrose's fate was hers to choose, kept cutting through his resolve.

He could still hear Ambrose's voice, mocking him, daring him to strike. He didn't know if he could let her have that choice; not when the thought of Ambrose still breathing made his blood boil.

***

The air in the brig was thick with the stench of a man who had not bathed for more than two weeks. Beatrix paused at the threshold. The lantern on the far wall threw a weak, amber light across the bars, cutting Ambrose's face into sharp planes of shadow.

He looked up at the sound of her footsteps, and the slow smile that spread across his mouth made her skin prickle.

"Well, well," he drawled. His chains clinked as he shifted forward. "The ship's trollop graces me with her presence. Does August know you're here? We could let him watch…"

She forced herself to step closer, even as her heart thudded against her ribs. "I came to tell you something."

Ambrose's eyes glinted. "Oh, do. I could use the entertainment."

"Your life is no longer in Gus's hands," she declared. "It's in mine, so you have no more reason to taunt him. I haven't decided yet whether you live or die."

For a moment, he was still. Then his laugh rolled through the brig. It was coarse and full of disbelief. "Is that so? Little Beatrix *Whore*wood, holding the sword of Damocles over my head? You've grown bold since the last time I had my hands on you."

Her stomach turned, but she did not flinch. "Enjoy your cell, Ambrose. I'll be back when I've made my choice."

He tilted his head. "Make it soon, wife. You might find I'm not so easy to kill."

Beatrix turned before he could see the shiver that ran through her. She walked away with her spine straight, each footstep echoing down the companionway.

***

Gus was still hunched over the chart table when the door slammed open. He looked up sharply, and his eyes blazed the instant he saw her standing there alone.

"Where the hell have you been?" His voice was perilous.

She shut the door behind her. "I went to see your brother."

The silence that followed was thick enough to choke on. Gus straightened slowly. His hands flattened on the table as if to steady himself. "You did what?"

"I told him his life is mine to decide," she said, refusing to step back even as his eyes darkened. "Not yours…mine."

"You went into the brig, *alone*." The way he said the last word was as sharp as his blade. "After everything he's done to you?"

Her chin lifted. "Yes. Because I'm not afraid of him."

His hands curled into fists on the map, crumpling the paper. "You should be. You should be terrified."

"I won't be," she said simply.

He rounded the table in two strides, stopping just short of grabbing her by the shoulders. His voice dropped to a rough whisper. "You think this is a game, Trix? You think walking into his cage doesn't put you back in his power?"

"I'm not in his power, Gus." She searched his face. "I'm in yours, and if you keep following this path of vengeance and fury, I promise you I won't be in that either."

For a moment, it looked like he might say something vicious or final, but instead, he turned away sharply, bracing himself against the edge of the table as if the wood was the only thing keeping him from shattering.

***

The Tempest cut through the darkening waves. The lights of Bridgetown had long since vanished behind them. Gus and Beatrix attempted to have a typical dinner in his cabin, though neither of them had eaten much. They had not spoken any further about Ambrose, but both thought about him.

Gus finally set down his fork and leaned back in his chair. His demanding gaze held hers. "We can't put it off much longer. Before we choose another port, his fate must be decided. Tell me, Beatrix, how do you want it done?"

She folded her hands in her lap. Her eyes drifted briefly toward the small, darkened porthole windows before returning to him. "Is the idea of a pirate's death true, or is it only a story?"

His brow creased slightly. "Which story?"

"The one where they maroon a man on a barren spit of sand with nothing but a pistol," she said quietly. "And only one shot."

A corner of Gus's mouth twitched—not in amusement, but in recognition. "It's no fantasy. It's been done more times than I can count. It's a slow death, unless the man has the courage to take the quick one."

Her voice was calm, almost too calm. "Then that's how I want him to go."

Gus studied her, searching for any flicker of doubt. "It's a cruel choice."

She didn't look away. "Crueler than you would have chosen?" She held his gaze steadily before casting her lashes down at the table. "Besides, it's no crueler than what he did to me."

The lantern light caught the gold flecks in her red hair as the ship rolled, and in that moment, Gus understood—her choice wasn't vengeance for vengeance's sake. It was her reclaiming the power Ambrose had stolen from her.

He reached for his wine, but his hand lingered at the stem of the goblet as his gaze stayed fixed on her. "Then so it shall be."

CHAPTER 24

Callahan traced a finger across the chart spread between them, his knuckles rapping lightly on the parchment. "You want a place where he won't last a week, Captain? I've one in mind."

Gus leaned over the table. "Go on."

"A scrap of sand and rock southeast of here," Callahan said. "No fresh water, no shade. It's barely more than a reef with a spine of land jutting out in the middle. It's not on any chart, but every man who's sailed these waters long enough has heard of it."

Gus narrowed his eyes at the spot Callahan indicated. "Does it have a name?"

"Aye. Dead Man's Cay," Callahan replied. "It's an old habit among the Windward captains. When a pirate's crimes were too much for the whip, but too little for hanging, they'd row him out there with a pistol and a single ball, then let the sea and the sun decide the rest."

Gus studied the distance. "How far is it?"

"With this wind, probably a day and a half…two if the current turns on us."

"No trade ships pass close?" Gus asked.

"Not a one," Callahan said. "It sits well off the main routes. A man left there has no rescue but the mercy of the waves."

Gus's gaze lingered on the lonely speck inked on the chart. "Perfect."

***

Gus found her in his cabin, seated by the stern windows where the sunlight spilled across the polished table. She looked up as he entered, ready for another argument.

"We have a plan," he said without preamble. "Callahan's found a place. Fittingly, it's called Dead Man's Cay. It's a barren spit of rock, a day and a half from here. There's no fresh water, no shade, no chance of rescue, and no chance of survival.

Her fingers tightened on the arm of the chair, but her voice was calm. "Then that is where we will leave him." She rose without hesitation.

"Beatrix—" Gus began, but she was already moving for the door.

"You told me his fate was mine to choose," she said over her shoulder. "I intend to tell him myself."

He caught up to her in the companionway. "You're not going to him alone."

"Then follow me," she said, not slowing.

They descended together. Ambrose's gaze went first to Beatrix, and a slow, poisonous smile curved his mouth.

"Wife, brother—what a nice family reunion," he purred. "Have you come for tea?"

She stepped up to the bars, unflinching. "I came to tell you your fate. Tomorrow, we will set you ashore on Dead Man's Cay. You'll have one pistol and one ball—nothing else. Whether you die by your own hand or let the sun take you is no concern of mine."

Ambrose's smile did not falter, but there was a flicker in his eyes. "So, this is what my dear wife has become: judge, jury, and executioner. I'm almost proud."

Gus's voice was restrained. "I'll be there to watch you walk into the sand, brother, and I'll relish every step you take away from me."

Beatrix did not look at either man as she turned and walked out. Gus remained a moment longer, meeting Ambrose's gaze with an unspoken promise, before following her back toward the upper decks.

***

That night, neither of them found rest. Beatrix lay curled against Gus. Her head rose and fell with the rhythm of his breath. His arm was wrapped securely around her.

"You're not sleeping," she murmured. Her voice was soft against his chest. Her fingers gently traced the outline of his locket that shared the space with her. She could feel his heartbeat against the back of her hand.

"Neither are you," he said as his hand brushed slowly along her back.

"I keep thinking of his face," Gus admitted after a long pause. "The moment he realizes there's no one coming for him…that the sun will be the last thing he sees. I want to watch that." His voice was almost reverent, and it chilled her more than if he had shouted.

"You'll watch it," she said, lifting her head so her eyes met his in the dim light. "But you'll watch it knowing it's what I chose."

His jaw flexed, but he nodded once. "I can live with that."

She settled her head back against him, though sleep still refused to come for either of them.

***

Dawn broke blood-red over the horizon; the sky and sea met in a thin, sharp line beneath the crimson sunrise. *The Tempest* lay at anchor with her sails furled as the longboat rocked gently against her side.

Gus stood in the stern with one hand on the tiller, and the other resting on the hilt of his pistol. Ambrose sat shackled with the iron biting into his wrists and ankles. Even with the chains, he managed to look like a man on the verge of triumph rather than ruin.

Callahan took his place at the opposite Ambrose. A musket was slung across his chest. He pulled a spyglass out of his pocket to scan the water. As he did, Ambrose noticed something familiar. The chain of the constellation watch—the one Beatrix had used to navigate to Calverique—hung loosely from Callahan's pocket.

Beatrix took her place beside Gus. She wore a plain linen dress and no hat. She had pulled her hair back in a low knot at the back of her head. At her belt, the hilt of a small knife glinted in the morning light. Gus had offered it to her without words before they'd left the cabin; she had taken it without hesitation.

"Ah, a family outing," Ambrose drawled as the oars bit into the water. "Tell me, brother, is this the sort where we stroll some gentleman's paradise, or the sort where you paint the sand with my blood to amuse your simpering damsel?"

"Shut your mouth," Gus said. His voice was even but threaded with warning.

Ambrose smiled, leaning forward so the chains clinked. "And if I don't? Will you slit my throat here, before she can watch you play executioner? Or will you save the show for that bit of sand ahead?"

The island grew clearer with every stroke of the oars. It was little more than a spit of land crowned by scrub and a few wind-bent palms. The surf was breaking white against its edges.

"I imagine you've thought about this night after night," Ambrose continued with his eyes fixed on Gus. "About how you'd finally end me. Would you not prefer to drive that blade through my gut slowly so that she can savor every inch vanishing into her husband's flesh?"

"Enough," Callahan snapped. The oars dragged hard in the water.

Ambrose only laughed. He turned his gaze to Beatrix. "How about you, my dear? Do you plan to watch? Or will you be so tenderhearted that you turn away? I'd hate for you to miss the moment your lover kills his own blood for you."

Beatrix met his eyes. Her fingers tightened on the hilt of her knife. "I'll watch," she said, dropping her voice low and cutting. "Every second."

Ambrose's grin faltered for just a breath before returning, sharper than before. "Good girl."

The bow scraped sand a moment later. Gus stepped out into the shallows with his pistol drawn. His gaze never left his brother.

The surf hissed against the sand as Gus and Callahan hauled Ambrose out of the longboat. The chains dragged heavy furrows in the sand behind him. As Callahan bent to adjust his grip, Ambrose's bound hands brushed against the edge of his coat. His fingers moved like a pickpocket's instinct, quick and unseen, slipping the small weight of the constellation watch into his palm before the next wave broke.

The island was silent save for the cries of gulls circling overhead. Their shadows flit over the white sand like restless spirits.

Dead Man's Cay was a cruel scrap of land. There was no sign of fresh water, and no shelter beyond the wind-gnarled palms. When the tide rose, Ambrose would drown slowly, and his body would be washed out to sea.

Gus shoved him forward. "Walk."

Ambrose glanced over his shoulder, smiling as though they were taking a casual stroll along the cliffs of Cornwall. "You've wanted to see me dead for a long time, brother. After Aria, I thought you'd come for me. Then, after Martinique, I felt certain you'd find a way to climb aboard my ship and finish me in my sleep."

"You've earned it a hundred times over," Gus said coldly. "This is where it ends."

They reached the center of the beach and stopped. Callahan dropped a battered pistol into the sand at Ambrose's feet; a single lead ball rested in the chamber.

"A pirate's death," Callahan said flatly. "Though no pirate would count you among his peers."

Ambrose looked at the pistol, and then at Beatrix, who stood just behind Gus. Her hand hovered over the knife at her side. "One shot? That's generous."

"It's more than you deserve," Gus said.

Ambrose bent slowly. The chains clinked as he picked up the pistol. He weighed it in his hands. "Oh, I know how this works. You expect me to save it for myself, to end it clean."

"That's the idea," Callahan muttered.

Ambrose's grin turned feral. "But why would I do that… when I can take you to hades with me?"

He lifted the pistol in a sudden, fluid motion and fired.

The shot rang across the beach and gun smoke curled into the wind. Gus didn't flinch, but the ball whistled past his ear, burying itself in the sand behind him.

For the third time, Ambrose had aimed a loaded pistol at his brother and missed.

Gus took a step closer. His grey eyes were like iron as he met his brother's brown ones. "Now you have nothing: no weapon, no escape, and no way to do anything but die."

Ambrose tilted his head, still smiling, though sweat trickled down his temple. "Ah, but I still have your attention. That's worth something."

"Not for long." Gus turned his back on him. "Let's go."

"What about you, little wife?" He turned his head towards Beatrix. "Won't you plead with your hero to spare his brother? Wouldn't it be noble to save the damned from the blade hanging over his head?"

She stepped forward, just out of his reach, still clutching the blade at her waist. "No. The sword of Damocles has fallen, Ambrose," She made sure to reference his chide from the brig. "There's nothing left to save."

He laughed once, low and bitter. "Then your hero's as damned as I am. When the sea takes me, it will take whatever was left of him...and you'll know you helped finish him."

Before he could say anymore, Callahan shoved Ambrose toward the interior of the island. Ambrose was left alone with his chains, his empty pistol, and the endless stretch of sea.

Gus climbed back into the longboat and reached a hand to help Beatrix in beside him. Callahan gathered the oars and sat facing them. Ambrose continued to yell slurs and curses at them as they rowed towards *The Tempest* and away from his malice.

Gus hadn't looked back once. He sat with his shoulders squared and his eyes locked on the horizon ahead as if the very sight of his brother might pull him back into darkness.

When the cay was gone entirely from sight, Beatrix's voice broke the stillness. "It's really over?"

Gus finally met her eyes, his expression unreadable. "Aye. He's never coming back." Gus shifted to pull her against him. His arm was a solid band around her shoulders.

***

Gus stepped onto the planks first, then reached back to steady Beatrix as she climbed after him. Callahan followed; his boots thudded on the deck.

"O'Malley," Gus called, his voice carrying with the certainty of command. "Get us out of here."

The quartermaster didn't hesitate. He barked orders to the hands, and canvas unfurled. The smell of salt and pitch filled the air as the wind caught in the sails.

Gus turned toward the helm. "What heading?" he asked, glancing over his shoulder at Callahan.

The first mate's answer came without pause. "Anywhere but here."

A faint, grim smile tugged at Gus's mouth. "Aye. Anywhere but here."

The deck tilted underfoot as *The Tempest* turned her prow toward open sea, leaving Dead Man's Cay shrinking into the horizon.

CHAPTER 25

Beatrix was exhausted from the trip to Dead Man's Cay. She made her way to Gus's cabin as the ship began to move. She wasted no time crawling into his bed and pulling the sheets around her. She drifted off to the sound of the sails cracking in the wind as she let the lull of the wake rock her to sleep.

***

Beatrix woke to the low thrum of music, muffled through the cabin walls. For a moment she thought it part of some half-remembered dream, until a roar of laughter rolled across the deck above and jolted her fully awake. The shadows in the cabin told her it was well after sundown. She pushed herself upright and crossed to the washbasin.

Cool water chased the last fog of sleep from her eyes. She smoothed her hair as best she could. The music was louder now. She could hear fiddle strings ringing brightly, accompanied by a pan flute whistling a lively melody, broken only by bursts of shouts and cheers.

Curiosity tugged her to the companionway. When she stepped onto the deck, the night opened around her in a blaze of lantern light and motion. Sailors stamped their boots to the rhythm while rum sloshed in their cups. Laughter and song tangled together in the warm, salt-heavy air.

Beatrix's gaze swept the crowd, searching for the reason behind such revelry. It did not take long to find him.

Gus stood at the center of it all. Lantern light caught the angles of his face and the glint of the tankard in his hand. His coat hung open, and his shirt collar was loose, as if he had shed the last trappings of restraint. He laughed—full-throated and unguarded—while clapping a sailor on the shoulder, and the sound rose above the music.

Men pressed in around him, drinking, dancing, and slinging jests that he returned with a swaggering ease she had rarely seen. He looked every inch the captain: untouchable, magnetic, and impossibly alive. Yet, beneath the bright flare of it, something in his eyes was too sharp and bright, like a flame burning itself out.

A smile tugged at her lips despite herself. It had been too long since she had seen him like this. He was laughing, with his burdens seemingly cast into the sea. Her smile faltered almost as quickly as it came. His manner was too loud and too careless, as if he were trying to drown something in rum and noise.

She moved through the crowd toward him, but before she reached his side, she caught Callahan watching from the shadow of the mainmast. His arms were crossed, and his eyes were fixed on Gus. Beatrix approached him warily.

"Seems the captain is in good spirits," she said lightly, though the words felt wrong in her mouth.

Callahan's eyes flicked to hers. "Aye, *spirits* being the word." His gaze returned to Gus. "That's not the kind of laughter that comes from peace, lass. That's a man whistling loudly to keep the darkness from catching him."

The music swelled again. Gus's voice rang above it in a drunken toast. Beatrix felt the truth of Callahan's words like a cold wind on her back.

Before she could answer Callahan, Gus caught sight of her through the crowd. His face split into a broad, reckless grin, and he shouldered his way toward her with his tankard sloshing in one hand.

"There she is!" he boomed, sweeping an arm around her waist and pulling her into the circle of stomping boots and laughing voices. The sudden movement made the wound at her side flare with pain, but Gus didn't notice.

Gus," she said quietly, leaning closer so only he could hear, "I need to sit down."

For a heartbeat, something flickered in his eyes—concern, or perhaps guilt—but it vanished beneath his grin. "Aye, sit if you must," he said, guiding her toward a coil of rope near the rail. "But you can still drink to our freedom."

Someone thrust a tankard of dark, spiced rum into her hand. The smell was so strong that it burned her nostrils. Gus laughed wildly at her reaction. He clinked his tankard against hers before draining half in one gulp. He turned back to the crew.

"To the wind at our backs, the sea at our bow, and to leaving bastards where they belong—behind us!" His voice carried above the music.

The cheer that followed shook the rigging. Beatrix forced a smile. Her breath still caught from the pull at her wound. Across the deck, she caught Callahan's eye. He didn't cheer. He didn't move. He only watched.

Gus moved back into the throng. He clapped shoulders, laughed too loudly, and drank too deeply. Every motion was big and performative—like a man acting out the role of joy for an audience he needed to convince.

"Never seen him so merry," O'Malley muttered near her, though his tone was uneasy.

Beatrix glanced up at him. Like Callahan, he kept his eyes on Gus, studying him like one might study a powder keg's swelling seam before it bursts.

Across the deck, Gus threw back his head in another roar of laughter. It carried too sharply on the night air, like glass breaking in the middle of a song.

Beatrix set the untouched tankard on the nearest barrel. The music, the laughter, and the heavy scent of rum all pressed too close and too loud. She caught Gus's gaze once more across the crowd; his smile was dazzling, but it didn't quite reach his eyes. She had seen enough.

Without a word, she slipped back to their cabin. He didn't even notice. The sounds of the revelry faded behind her into a dull roar. She sat on the edge of the bed and unlaced her shoes, then crawled back into bed.

She was nearly asleep when the door swung open and struck the wall. Gus stepped in, reeking of rum. His golden hair was a tangled disarray. He grinned as if the whole world had turned in his favor.

"Thought I'd find you hiding down here," he said, crossing the cabin in three unsteady steps. Before she could answer, he caught her hand and tugged her to her feet.

"Gus, I—"

"Dance with me," he interrupted, already pulling her into a clumsy turn. His voice lifted in a half-sung, half-slurred bawdy tune. It was the sort she'd heard below decks when she first joined his ship, but she'd never heard such vulgarity from his lips. His steps were erratic, and the strength of his grip left no space for escape.

"Gus, stop—please." She tried to free her hand, but he only laughed, spinning her once more before pressing his mouth to hers. The kiss was clumsy and firm, but empty. It held none of the warmth or passionate ache she remembered. It had only the taste of rum and the press of a man desperate to feel something.

When he pulled back, she saw nothing of the tenderness she'd once found in his features. Now, there was only the shadow of a smile, and the glint of a man who had chosen revelry over rest.

When he pulled back, she steadied herself against the table. "You're not yourself," she said softly, searching his face as though she might find the man she knew beneath the drink.

His smile lingered, but his eyes were flat. "Oh, I'm exactly myself, sweetheart. This is me when the fight's over and the sea's mine again."

She pulled her hand from his and stepped back. "I don't like this version of you," she said quietly.

His smile faltered, and something sharper slid into his eyes. "No? You didn't like the furious one either. It seems you don't like the quiet version or the loud one… Tell me, Beatrix—" his voice dropped as he slurred, "—do you just not like me at all?"

She met his unflinching gaze. "I don't know who you are right now, August, and I think that frightens me more than anything. Come back when you're sober."

"If that's what you want." He slurred. His words were quiet, but the coldness in them lingered after he left.

***

Gus awoke in the chartroom. He struggled to open his eyes as the world swirled in front of him. His tongue was as dry as sandpaper, and his stomach seemed to roll with the rest of the room.

Callahan stood at the far end of the table with one hand braced on the wood and the other holding a pencil over the navigation chart. His eyes were fixed on Gus, not with anger, but with that steady, assessing look that never boded well.

"Morning," Callahan said. The sound of his voice rattled in Gus's head, even though he'd spoken in barely more than a whisper. "We're sailing blindly in a westwardly direction. You going to give me a heading, or are we drifting till your skull stops pounding?"

Gus rubbed at his temple and straightened slowly in his chair. "Any ports we need to stop in before we head back to Calverique?"

Callahan's pencil stilled on the chart. "No," he said shortly. "We took on enough in Bridgetown to last the journey twice over."

Gus nodded, reaching for a mug that had gone cold overnight. "Good. Then we—"

Callahan's voice cut in, low but tight. "That's all you've got to say after last night?"

Gus lifted his gaze and raised an eyebrow at his first mate. "We're well stocked, aren't we?"

"We are," Callahan said, his jaw working. "But if you think I'll stand by while you drink yourself blind and steer us into another storm, you're sorely mistaken."

"Just give the order," Gus commanded. The sound of his own voice ricocheted painfully in his skull.

Callahan's stare lingered for a beat too long before he turned and slammed the door behind him. The loud crack of it made Gus flinch.

He sat for a moment, rubbing the bridge of his nose. The ache in his skull throbbed in time with the ship's rhythmic creak. The taste of stale rum lingered in his mind like regret.

He pushed to his feet and made his way down the companionway toward their cabin. Each step was an effort of will.

Whatever awaited him behind that door, he had no wish to put it off any longer.

The door gave a quiet click as Gus eased it open. Beatrix was sitting up in bed. She looked rested, but the guarded way her eyes followed him said she had been waiting.

He shut the door behind him and stood there for a beat, uncertain whether to approach her or keep his distance.

Her fingers toyed absently with the chain of her locket. She didn't look at him.

"What happens now, Gus?" she asked at last. Her voice was even but edged with the kind of calm that comes after a storm has passed.

"We sail back to Calverique," he said without hesitation, as though the course had been set in his mind for days. "There are answers there...ones we've been chasing too long to abandon now."

Beatrix nodded slowly. Her eyes were fixed on the table rather than his face. "That's not what I meant."

His brow furrowed. "Then what did you mean?"

She looked up and met his gaze. "I want to know what happens now...with us."

Gus's expression softened, though there was a shadow in his eyes. "I hope," he said quietly, "that we can find our way back to where we were before Martinique... Before everything went so very wrong."

Her fingers twisted in the blanket. "Do you still feel that way about me?"

Something in his face changed. His expression softened, and he became less guarded and more certain. He crossed the space between them and sat beside her on the bed. Without a word, he drew her into his arms.

"I've never stopped," he murmured, his voice warm against her hair.

His lips brushed hers, tentative at first. Then the kiss deepened, gathering heat and urgency until it carried the weight of every unspoken word, every fear, and every longing they had endured since Ambrose had forced her hand in Martinique.

Beatrix let him kiss her. She rested her hands lightly against his chest. She returned the kiss, but with a measured slowness, as though testing whether she could trust this moment… and whether she could trust him. Her breath was unsteady when they finally parted.

"I don't know if we can marry," she whispered.

Gus's expression darkened for a moment, then softened into something almost weary. "I don't care if we ever stand in a church, Beatrix. I just want you right here, with me, always."

She stared at him as if he'd struck her. "You don't care? After everything we've been through, that's all you have to say?"

"It's the truth," he said, leaning closer. "I'd take you as you are, without vows, without papers—"

Her anger flared. "And leave me to live as what? Your mistress?"

"I'm offering you my life, Beatrix," he said, the words rough with conviction.

Her eyes searched his, unblinking. "Then why am I not worth your name?"

He drew in a slow breath, as if bracing against a blow. "It's not about worth—"

"It is to me," she cut in, her voice sharp and trembling. "If I'm good enough to share your bed, to risk my life beside you, then tell me why I'm not good enough to be your wife."

His gaze didn't waver, but his voice dropped low. "Because the law won't have it. Without proof that Ambrose is dead, no priest will wed us. We'd have to wait seven years before they'd even call you free."

She drew in air as though the world had stopped, and to her own shame, she felt tears sting her eyes. "Seven years?" she whispered, the words breaking.

"Beatrix, your marriage to him was real in the eyes of the world. You said the vows, you signed the registry, and you consummated—"

"No." She shook her head. He searched her eyes for meaning. "He touched me, yes—but he never… he never went through with it, Gus. He may talk like a cur, but in the end, he didn't want to force me, and after he realized you and I had… well, he never tried anything again. That has to matter, doesn't it? Couldn't we have it annulled?"

Relief swept through him, loosening muscles he had not realized were locked tight. He drew her into his arms, holding her close. "Thank God," he breathed. From Ambrose's taunts, he had imagined the worst—that his brother had claimed her in the most intimate way. At least that, he had not taken.

The moment of reprieve was brief. His gaze hardened. The warmth in his embrace gave way to the weight of unwelcome truth.

Gus looked as though he hated what he had to say. "It would matter if he stood beside you in court and admitted it. Without that, there's nothing to prove your claim. The law won't free you unless he agrees or he's proven dead."

Beatrix stared at him. Her pulse pounded in her ears. "Then we have to go back for him."

Gus blinked as though he hadn't heard her correctly. "Back?"

"Yes," she said, leaning forward. "If he's the only one who can free me, then we can't just leave him to rot on that island. We have to bring him back, make him stand in front of a magistrate, and tell the truth."

His jaw tightened. "You'd have him walking the decks again? Breathing the same air as you?"

"If it's the only way to be free of him forever, then yes."

Gus's eyes turned cold. "No."

She sat back, startled by the flatness in his voice. "Why not?"

"Because the moment he sets foot anywhere civilized, he'll find a way to twist free. He'll use our father's name, make bribes, and forge alliances. He could win, Beatrix, and you'd be forced to remain his wife." He chose each word judiciously, hoping she'd see reason. "I will not give him another chance to touch you."

Her hands curled in the bedclothes. "So, you mean for me to live in purgatory?"

His jaw worked, but his gaze did not waver. "Better to live in purgatory than with the devil."

Her hands clenched. The thought of Ambrose's hands on her again made her stomach churn. "I wouldn't have chosen to maroon him if I'd known…" She realized that by saving Gus from damning himself in Ambrose's dark and twisted game, she'd damned herself. "Let's turn back, right now. We can be sure he's dead. Maybe there'll be a body..."

Gus shook his head once, firm as iron. "No. We sail forward. We've left him to his fate, and I won't waste another breath chasing him."

Her breath came unevenly. Her eyes glistened with the tears she was trying desperately not to shed. "Then what do you expect me to do, Gus? Sit here and warm your bed for the next seven years?

Be your whore until the law says I'm free?" Her voice cracked on the last word, despite her efforts.

He flinched as if struck, but his jaw hardened. "I expect you to be with me, and to let me be with you."

"I won't do it," she said. Her voice was barely a whisper. She tugged his mother's ring from her finger and pressed it into his palm. "I won't spend another night in your bed, August."

He stared at the ring silently.

"I'll take the second officer's quarters until you see fit to put me ashore somewhere with a ship bound for Cornwall. I want to go home, and with Ambrose gone, there's no reason I shouldn't." Her chin lifted, daring him to argue. "Until then, we speak only when necessary."

She turned before he could answer. The cabin door shut hard behind her.

For a long moment, Gus sat on the bed where she'd left him. His mother's ring bit into his hand. He might have taken it to give to Aria, but he knew it belonged on Beatrix's finger. It was meant for her.

He was losing her, and he didn't know what to do about it.

CHAPTER 26

Callahan stood at the rail. His hands braced on the worn wood as he stared at the horizon. He turned at the sound of her footsteps. "You look like you've had the wind knocked out of you."

"I'm leaving," Beatrix said without preamble. "I'm going home."

His gaze sharpened. "And what will you tell your father when you arrive on his doorstep after months on the open sea with a crew of fifty men and no chaperone?"

"I'll tell him that I couldn't marry Ambrose, so I went to find Calverique," she replied, her voice steady despite the knot in her chest. "I'll tell him it was all a fairytale that my mother and Aria made up to entertain me as a child. I will tell him that Ambrose followed me, but now he's gone and won't trouble him again. I'll make it clear that I never intend to marry. I'll go home and be a spinster."

For a moment, silence stretched between them. Then Callahan let out a short, incredulous laugh. "Never marry? You? Lass, there'll be men lining up from Penzance to Edinburgh the moment you set foot ashore."

She shook her head. "Not if I can help it."

His smile faded, replaced by something closer to sorrow. "If you're sure you want to leave…" He exhaled slowly, glancing toward the captain's cabin. "I'll go with you. I can't stand to watch him burn down his life any longer."

A hush filled her chest instead of breath, but she managed a quiet, "Thank you."

***

Gus was bent over the chart table when the door swung open without a knock.

Callahan stepped inside, shutting the door with deliberate care. "We need to talk."

"If it's about the heading, we've already discussed it," Gus said without looking up.

"It's not about the heading," Callahan replied, his voice clipped. "It's about my commission."

That got Gus's attention. He straightened, and his grey eyes narrowed. "What about it?"

"I'm giving it up." Callahan's hands pressed flat to the table, braced as though keeping himself from striking something. "I'll not stand by and watch you drive her away—or drive yourself into perdition."

"You think walking away will stop me?" Gus's tone was icy.

"I think staying makes me complicit," Callahan said. "So, here's how it's going to be. We turn back to Bridgetown. I'll see her safely on a ship bound for Cornwall, and then I'm done."

Gus's jaw flexed. "You're asking me to sail back because she's angry?"

"I'm asking because she's leaving. You've finally driven her away, and it's not fair to keep her here to watch you go mad with rage, or guilt, or whatever it is that possesses you."

For a long moment, the only sound was the creak of timbers and the faint lap of water against the hull. Gus's gaze was hard as cut stone, but there was something wounded beneath it.

"Get out," he said finally. "Before I say something I won't take back."

Callahan's eyes searched his for a beat longer, as if looking for the man he'd followed for years buried behind his steely gaze, then he turned and left without another word.

The door had barely shut behind Callahan when a shadow filled its frame again.

O'Malley leaned in, hat in hand. "Begging your pardon, captain, but the helmsman wants the word. Are we still bound for Calverique, or…?"

Gus's fingers drummed once against the chart table before stilling. "Calverique."

O'Malley hesitated, his weathered face tightening. "Aye, sir. Just wanted to be sure. Wind's in our favor either way."

"Then make use of it," Gus commanded.

The quartermaster gave a short nod, but his eyes lingered on his captain a beat too long, as if weighing whether to say more. In the end, he settled for pulling the door behind him, leaving Gus alone with the charts, the empty rum bottle, and the ache in his head.

***

The deck lamps swayed gently overhead as the galley steward cleared away the last of the plates. Callahan leaned back in his chair, cradling a half-empty tankard. He studied the sad woman across the table from him.

"Thank you for joining me tonight," he said quietly. "I thought you might prefer some company."

Beatrix folded her hands in her lap. "I appreciate the thought."

He watched her with the sort of patience that invited honesty. "Will you tell me what happened? What made you finally decide to go home?"

She sighed, and her gaze drifted down to the table. "I need to make certain whether Ambrose is dead or alive. Gus won't turn back."

Callahan's brow furrowed. "Why would you need to go back? There was no escape, lass. You saw it the same as I did. He had no choice but to die."

"Because I can't be free of him without proof that he's dead. I didn't know that when we left him there."

"I assure you—"

"No, you don't understand," she interrupted. "If I don't prove he's dead, I can't marry for seven years. If he *is* alive, I'm still his wife in the eyes of the law." She stopped, shaking her head.

"I see," Callahan nodded.

"I asked Gus to turn around and go back to make certain Ambrose is dead; he refuses. He says it doesn't matter to him. He said that he doesn't care if we ever stand before a priest."

Callahan sat forward slowly, the tankard forgotten in his hand. "So that's what this is."

Beatrix met his eyes. Her voice was steady now. "Yes, that's what this is."

Callahan exhaled through his nose, setting the tankard down with a dull thud. "Beatrix, he loves you. I've known August for ten years, and I've never seen him look at anyone the way he looks at you."

Her lips pressed into a thin line. "He's never said so."

"You don't need the words to see it."

"I do," she said sharply. "I need more than his wanting me in his bed. I won't be his whore, Callahan."

The first mate studied her in the lamplight. His eyes were heavy with something between frustration and sympathy. "Then I suppose you've already made up your mind."

"I have," she said.

***

Callahan didn't knock when he stepped into the chartroom. Gus looked up from the map, and his expression immediately darkened.

"It's certainty that she wants," Callahan said, shutting the door behind him. "And she's right to want it. She deserves to know her own fate."

Gus's gaze hardened. "I told you—"

"You told me nothing that changes the fact that she's twisting in the wind. You left your brother on that beach without proof he's dead, now you mean for her to live seven years wondering if he's out there, waiting to claim her again? That's not a future, it's a sentence."

Gus's jaw flexed. "We're not going back."

Callahan planted his hands on the table, leaning in. "Then I'll see her there myself. I'll charter a vessel at the next port and take her to Dead Man's Cay so she can know for certain. She deserves at least that much truth."

The chart slammed against the wall, pinned there by Gus's fist. "You'll do no such thing."

Callahan's voice rose to match him. "If you cared for her half as much as you acted when you thought she was going to die, you'd turn this ship around yourself instead of drinking and pretending you've done right by her."

Gus stepped forward, every muscle taut. "You'll mind your tongue, or I'll see to it you're put ashore before you speak another word against me."

"I'll walk ashore gladly," Callahan shot back, "if it means she gets free of the madman you've become."

For a long moment, the only sound was the creak of the ship beneath them and the rasp of their breathing.

Gus's temper snapped. "God's blood, Callahan—make up your mind! I'm damned if I do, damned if I don't. First, you want me to be rid of him, and now you want me to go looking for him?" His voice roared through the chartroom, rattling the glass in the lantern. "What happens if he is alive? You think he won't charm half of whatever court we find to petition for the annulment? You think she won't be forced to his side again, no matter what either of us wants?"

Callahan's jaw set like stone. "I think she's strong enough to face whatever truth is waiting there, and I think you're afraid of it."

Gus's grey eyes flashed like summer lightning. "Afraid? I've bled for her, fought for her, held her in this life while the blood drained from her body—"

"And now you've locked her in a prison of your own making," Callahan cut in, his voice low but lethal. "And you can't even see it."

"Get out," Gus snarled.

Callahan didn't move. "August—"

"I said, get out!" Gus's shout cracked against the wood. His hand slammed down on the table hard enough to rattle the charts.

Callahan's stare lingered on him for a long moment before he turned sharply and strode out, slamming the door in his wake.

***

It was past midnight before Gus's temper cooled enough for him to seek his bed. On his way down the narrow hallway, a single sound broke him.

From behind the second officer's door came the faint, muffled sound of Beatrix's sobs. They were not loud or desperate. They were the quiet, breaking kind that clawed at the edges of a man's soul. He stood there with his chest tight and his hand curled into a fist.

He wanted to knock. God help him, he wanted to go in, gather her into his arms, and tell her he'd tear down the whole damn world to make things right, but his feet stayed rooted, and his hand refused the latch. He didn't want to hurt her any more than he already had.

Instead, he lowered himself to the floor beside her door with his back to the bulkhead. The lanterns swayed in the passage, casting shifting shadows over him as he drew his knees up and rested his forearms across them. He could hear her sobbing still, soft and steady. Each sound was a twist of the knife.

When exhaustion finally claimed him, he stayed there, guarding her from the wrong side of the door. It was the closest he could be to her without breaking her further.

***

Sunrise burst through the porthole windows in rays of warm gold. Beatrix eased the second officer's door open and blinked into the dimmer hallway light.

She nearly stumbled when she saw him. Gus was slumped against the bulkhead. His head was bowed, and one arm draped loosely over his knees. His coat had slipped from his shoulders during the night, and the shadows beneath his eyes told her he had not moved for hours.

For a moment, she simply stood there, torn between the instinct to touch him and the memory of their words the day before. She could still feel the sting of them. Yet there he was, sleeping like a sentinel outside her door, as if the simple act might keep the whole world from reaching her.

Her throat tightened. She crouched and brushed her fingertips lightly across his temple. The gesture was almost involuntary. His eyes flickered open, and for a brief, unguarded second, the steel in them softened into tenderness.

"You should be in your bed," she whispered.

"Couldn't," he said, his voice rough from sleep. "I just needed to know you were still here."

She drew back. The wall between them still stood, though a crack had formed in its mortar. "Get some rest, Gus," she murmured, holding back tears anew. "We both need the strength to let go."

He watched her walk onto the deck and said nothing. The echo of her touch lingered like the warmth of the rising sun. For the first time since leaving his brother on that island of the damned, his certainty in the decision wavered.

Gus shifted against the bulkhead. The stiffness in his neck made him wince. His coat was hanging uncomfortably from his forearms, constricting the blood flow to his hands. He pulled himself free of it, and something small thudded onto the planks. The compass that never pointed north—the one that had led him to Calverique—rolled once before settling on the floor, face down.

He picked it up and turned it over in his hand. It reacted immediately to the gold ring on his pinkie and pointed toward Calverique. Today it felt heavier, as if it carried every mile still between them and Calverique, about two to three days' journey away. His thumb brushed the worn edge, and a thought took hold: What if she never forgave him?

A door creaked open. Callahan stepped out, pulling his shirt straight, only to stop short at the sight of him. "Hell's bells, Gus... you slept here?"

Gus didn't answer right away. He closed his fist around the compass. "She was crying."

Callahan's gaze softened, but he kept his voice even. "Then give her what she's asking for. You can live with the truth, whatever it is. She can't live with not knowing."

For a moment, the only sound was the groan of the timbers as the ship shifted with the swell. Then Gus pushed to his feet, slung his coat properly around his shoulders, and placed the compass back in his pocket. "Change course. We're going back to Dead Man's Cay."

"Aye, captain," Callahan answered, recognizing his friend, finally, behind Gus's red and tortured eyes.

***

Beatrix was halfway through her tea in the galley when the shout came from above.

"O'Malley, bring her about!" Callahan's voice rang clear and loud through the morning air.

The words sent a ripple of movement through the room. Chairs scraped, boots thudded, and a few of the men hurried above decks. She set down her cup and followed at a slower pace.

Callahan stood at the rail. The wind ruffled through his hair. His gaze was fixed on the shifting horizon.

"What's happening?" she asked.

He glanced at her but didn't meet her eyes. "We're turning for Dead Man's Cay."

She searched his face for some trace of a jest but found none. "Why?"

"Because you deserve to know," he said quietly. "One way or the other."

Her eyes narrowed. The disbelief settled in her chest like a stone. "Gus agreed to this?"

Callahan's only answer was a slow nod.

She did not thank him. She simply turned on her heel and crossed the deck. The wind whipped at her skirts as she made for the chartroom. She found Gus there, one hand braced on the table, gripping a working compass over a sea chart.

"You're turning back," she said. Her voice was quiet but edged with urgency.

He lifted his gaze to hers. "Aye."

"Why?"

His mouth twitched as if he meant to give some glib answer, but instead he said, "Because I can't stand the thought of you locked in purgatory, crying yourself to sleep every night for the next seven years."

She stood in the doorway, searching his face. "If he's alive?"

The corner of his mouth curved without warmth. "Then I'll finish him."

She gave a single nod, no more. Without another word, she turned and left him there.

***

The next two days passed in a strange, uneasy truce. She kept to her cabin and avoided his eyes. Gus stayed in the chartroom or on the quarterdeck pretending to read or study charts. Even Callahan, usually a constant presence between them, seemed to sense the quiet and kept his distance.

Gus slept outside her cabin door each night. She heard the rustle of his coat as he lowered himself to the floor. The light that normally peeked below the door darkened. He didn't say a word, but she knew he was there.

When at last *The Tempest* dropped anchor in the shallows near Dead Man's Cay, neither she, nor Callahan, nor Gus dared to break the silence between them. They had learned too well how quickly their words could turn to weapons.

The chains creaked loudly as the longboat was lowered. Once again, they had armed themselves well. Gus had his sword strapped to one hip and his pistol strapped to the other. He had not bothered to wear his coat in the striking hot sun, but she suspected he had a knife hidden in his boot as well. Callahan had his musket slung across his back and a sword at his hip. Beatrix carried her knife in a belt around her waist.

Every pull of the oars sent them closer to the pale strip of sand where they had left Ambrose to die. The island loomed larger, but still bleak and desolate. Beatrix's pulse quickened as the longboat's bow grated against the sand.

Gus stepped out first with his pistol drawn. His boots sank deep into the warm, shifting surface. Callahan followed, reaching his hand out to help Beatrix out of the boat. She followed Gus with Callahan close at her heels.

The island was nothing but sand and stone, broken here and there by a handful of thin palms bending in the wind. There was no shade, no shelter, and no place to hide.

They moved slowly. Their boots left fresh tracks along the pale curve of the shore. The only sounds were the hiss of the waves and the rustle of palm fronds.

They walked the entire length of the island before turning inland and sweeping the middle. Gus's eyes squinted in the bright light as he searched for any movement, ready to strike at any sign of his brother.

Beatrix was the first to spot it; half-buried in the sand near the island's far side lay a boot. It was torn, and its leather was stained dark. She bent and lifted it. The metal trim at the top was dented, as though struck hard, and the heel was caked with dried blood.

"Here," she called softly.

Callahan came up beside her. His gaze drifted from the boot to a jagged trail etched into the sand. Long, uneven furrows led down toward the tide line.

"Chains," he muttered. "He dragged himself or was dragged. Either way, the sea's taken him."

Beatrix stared at the boot in her hands. Her throat felt tight, and her head began to swim. She knelt in the sand to keep from falling. Her fingers brushed the cracked leather. "It's definitely his."

Gus crouched beside her, taking the boot from her hands. The heel was dark with blood, and a jagged tear split the side.

"He's gone," Callahan said, his voice grim. "No man could swim from here, not with irons. I'll stand witness to it."

Gus looked between them. The boot was heavy in his hand. His brother was gone. His rage had softened over the past few days. It left behind a sort of sadness, or at the very least, reflection. He didn't mourn for his brother, exactly, but he felt loss all the same.

"We have the proof," he said at last. "We can head back to Bridgetown; there's a Vice-Admiralty Court there. They will declare him dead."

Beatrix closed her eyes and exhaled a breath she had been holding for days. Gus handed the boot to Callahan and stood. He reached for Beatrix's hand and led her back to the longboat.

Again, they traveled in silence. The oars dipped and rose with a steady rhythm. The island receded behind them; it shrank to a pale smear on the horizon.

Halfway to *The Tempest*, Gus broke the stillness. "We marry tonight." His words did not offer a question; they rang in the air like one of his orders on deck to his crew. "I have a plan."

Callahan's eyebrow twitched upward, but he said nothing. The only sound was the creak of wood and the hush of the sea. No one spoke again until they reached the ladder hanging from *The Tempest*'s side.

Part IV: The Cavern of Judgement

CHAPTER 27

When Gus stepped onto *The Tempest*'s deck, and the crew looked to him expectantly. He stood at the center with boots braced.

"Ambrose Drake is dead," he declared, holding up the bloody, torn boot like Perseus's prize, an ugly proof meant to turn the last of their doubts to stone.

"For the next day," he continued, his voice sure and carrying to the furthest mast, "I am no longer your captain. For tonight, I am simply a bridegroom."

A murmur of astonishment rippled through the men. Callahan, brows drawn, took a half step forward. "And who will see the ship through, while you play bridegroom?"

"You will," Gus replied without hesitation. "Until the sun sets on the marrow, the command is yours. You will see me wed to Beatrix before this night is over."

The crew's murmurs swelled into cheers. Some threw hats into the air. Gus's unreadable gaze never left Beatrix as he crossed to her. He extended his hand to her, palm open. She placed her fingers lightly in his, and he closed his grip around them.

Without another word, he led her to his cabin. The roar of the crew faded as the door closed behind them. In the quiet of the cabin, Gus released her hand only long enough to close the door. The distant shouts and laughter of the crew seemed a world away.

"On this ship," he began, "under my command, I make the rules. My rule tonight is this: You will become my wife."

Beatrix's brow arched, though she held her tongue.

"A captain may officiate a wedding in the absence of a priest or minister," he continued, stepping closer. "It is an old tradition, and one I intend to see honored. We will stand before the crew tonight, and in their witness, you will be mine."

She searched his face, her lips parting as though to speak, but he pressed on.

"In the autumn, we will have a proper wedding in my family's chapel at Merthwaite, unless you'd rather marry in your own family's chapel at Brackwater. It does not matter to me, but we will do this properly, with a bishop presiding, as befitting our stations."

"Gus—"

"I will write to your father when we reach Bridgetown and explain this to him. He gave me permission to marry Aria all those years ago, so I see no reason why he wouldn't give me his permission to marry you now. If my bastard brother was good enough for him, certainly the heir to the Earl of Falmouth will be. But I won't wait for his permission. You are of age, and I have no need of your dowry. Tonight, and forever more, you will be my wife."

His words hung between them. They were both an invitation and a decree.

Beatrix's pulse quickened, though not entirely from the warmth in his voice. The last weeks played through her mind—his rage, his reckless joy, and the darkness she had seen more often than not shadowing his eyes. She had only just begun to glimpse the man she loved, hidden beneath the storms, and now he was pulling her into another gale.

"It is all happening too quickly," she said at last. "I have not had enough time to know who you truly are now."

Something in him shifted. Gone were the half-smile and the teasing bravado. He caught both of her hands in his and held them as if they anchored him to the floor.

"Then know me by this truth," he said. His voice was rough with urgency. "I love you, Beatrix, passionately and completely. I have fought for you, bled for you, and—God forgive me—killed for you. I have prayed for you in the dark and cursed the heavens when they would not give you to me. There is nothing I would not do to keep you safe and nothing I would not give to see you happy. You are my heart, my compass, and my home. Without you, I am lost."

Beatrix was breathless. His words pressed against every wall she had built, and before she could summon another protest, he pulled her into his arms and captured her lips. His kiss was neither hurried nor rough, but certain. It was deep and unshakable in its claim.

Her heart pounded against his chest as she returned it. All her questions drowned beneath the tide of him. For this moment, there was no past to haunt them and no future to fear. There was only the warmth of his hands framing her face and the steady strength of his body holding hers.

When they parted, her cheeks were flushed, and her lips trembled. "Tonight?" she whispered, half in disbelief, half in surrender.

"Tonight," he vowed as he rested his forehead against hers. "And forever after."

Beatrix stepped back, still dizzy from his kiss, and tried to steady herself. "If I am to be a bride tonight, I will need something to wear."

A spark of boyish mischief lit Gus's eyes. "Then see what treasures the hold might offer you. I seem to recall a crate of goods we picked up in Bridgetown that we're meant to drop off for a shop in Saint Lucia. There's lace, silks, pearls, and perhaps even a gown worthy of your wedding day."

Her heart beat unevenly. She was torn between the absurdity of it all and the growing thrill in her chest. She kissed his cheek quickly, then slipped from the cabin. Her skirts swayed as she made for the companionway. She was already imagining what might be hidden beneath the tarpaulins below.

When she was gone, Gus found Callahan standing by the rail, overseeing the wedding preparations. Men were stringing lanterns and creating an aisle from barrels, bales of rope, and stools.

"First Mate," Gus greeted. His voice was lighter than it had been in weeks. "Or should I say… Captain."

Callahan's brows rose. "You're serious about this?"

"More so than I have ever been about anything," Gus replied. "You'll officiate the ceremony. We'll do a proper handfast, as old as the sea and binding enough until we stand in a church." Gus knew he had a long way to go to make things right with Callahan. His old friend was the bravest, most loyal man he knew, and Gus had let his rage and need for vengeance come between them.

"Tonight," Gus continued. "I want no quarrels and no shadows of Ambrose between us. That chapter is closed."

Callahan studied him for a long moment, then gave a slow nod. "Very well, but if we're doing this, we'll do it right. The crew will expect tradition."

Gus's mouth curved into a grin. "Then give them tradition, Captain Callahan. Bind our hands with rope, speak the old words, and let the sea itself bear witness."

***

By the time the glorious sunset bled into twilight, the deck had been transformed. Lanterns now swung from the rigging and cast a warm glow over the semi-circle of crew gathered on either side of the make-shift aisle before the quarterdeck. Callahan stood tall at the center. His coat was brushed and buttoned, and his red hair was slicked back into a neat tie at the base of his neck. His expression was solemn in his temporary captain's role.

A hush fell over the deck. The only sounds were the lap of the sea against the hull and the faint sigh of the wind through the rigging. Then, from somewhere near the bow, a lone fiddle began to play an old Irish tune, chosen by Callahan, "The Dawning of the Day." The melody was slow and lilting. Each note caught the salt breeze and carried across the gathering like a tender blessing. All eyes turned toward the companionway.

Beatrix stepped onto the deck, and every gaze turned toward her. She wore a bold crimson gown that fit as though it had been made for her. The low neckline bared just enough to tempt without crossing into vulgarity, while the silk clung in all the right places, shaping her narrow waist and the gentle curve of her hips. In the lanternlight, the fabric's sheen seemed to burn against the darkness. Her hair was swept into a crown of loose curls, and at her throat, the silver locket caught the light.

Gus stood waiting. His roguish smile softened into reverence as his gaze found her. For a long moment, he could only stare. The soft, unhurried tune seemed to wrap around him, drawing him into a place where the rest of the world ceased to exist. He held his breath as Beatrix moved toward him. Her eyes locked on his. She looked like no vision he had ever dared to dream. She was strong, beautiful, and entirely his.

He felt the press of a hundred eyes on them, but it made no difference. The fiddle's sweet, aching notes seemed to carry her straight into his keeping. By the time she reached him, he had the distinct, humbling sense that he would remember this moment for the rest of his life.

When she reached him, Gus offered her his hand. She placed her hand in his without hesitation. The song ended, and Callahan cleared his throat. His deep voice carried over the waves and wind.

"By the old custom," he began. "We stand before the witness of ship and sea. We bind the hands of these two in troth until a priest may bless their union."

O'Malley placed a length of braided rope in Callahan's hands. Gus lifted their entwined hands, and Callahan stepped forward to loop the rope loosely around them. Gus's fingers tightened around Beatrix's, and he saw her blush a little as his thumb brushed her palm in yet spoken promise.

"Speak your vows," Callahan said.

Gus's voice was steady, low, and meant for her alone, but the crew leaned in to hear, all the same. His eyes never left hers, so she could make no mistake that he meant every word.

"I give you my loyalty, my strength, and my life. I will guard you from all harm, stand with you in every trial, and lay down my sword before I let you go. Before these witnesses and the sea itself, I bind my fate to yours, Beatrix, from this night until my last."

Beatrix's lips trembled, but her voice did not falter. She took a deep breath and answered his vow with her own.

"I give you my trust, my heart, and my hand. I will meet you in every joy and weather every storm at your side. Before these witnesses and the sea itself, I bind my fate to yours, August, from this night until my last."

With the care of a man setting a sail in a storm, Callahan then crossed Gus's right hand over Beatrix's left, looping the rope between them. His fingers moved with the surety of years at sea, shaping the strands into a Carrick Bend. Two lines joined so they would hold fast under strain yet yield when the time came to loosen them. The knot lay flat and neat between their wrists, sealing their promises.

"By the word of your vows and the knot that binds you, you are husband and wife in the eyes of this ship, her crew, and all you meet upon tide and shore. As the sea is bound to the moon, so may you be bound to one another. Let no temptation, no tempest, nor the long watch through moonless nights ever part you."

Callahan gave a slight nod to Gus. He drew Beatrix into his arms. The kiss that followed sealed what neither court nor priest could yet undo. Cheers rose from the crew, and the deck sprang alive with shouts, laughter, and the thrum of boots on wood, but for Gus and Beatrix, the world had narrowed to the space between them.

The crew surged forward, clapping Gus on the back and sweeping Beatrix into the whirl of celebration. Fiddles struck up a jolly tune that Beatrix didn't recognize. Boots thudded in rhythm as lanternlight swayed over grinning faces.

Callahan stepped close to her and whispered, "You've got him now, lass; just hold him steady. He's been through storms most men wouldn't have survived. Try to keep him from sailing into another."

Beatrix met his gaze. She recognized the weight behind his words. She nodded once and tucked the promise away as Gus caught her hand and spun her into the dance. His laughter rang out over the music.

The music was quick and bright. Every note urged her feet to move. Gus held her as if he had never meant to let her go. For the first time in too long, she saw no shadow in his eyes. They shone with warmth and unsullied joy. The tension she had been carrying for weeks began to ease, and her steps fell naturally into his. They danced until her skirts swirled about them like a flame. The rest of the world blurred away in the rhythm of his hands and the music's pull.

As the last note from the fiddle faded, Gus held Beatrix's hand and led her toward their cabin. His crew cheered in a show of rum-soaked goodwill as the door shut softly behind them.

***

The air inside the cabin was warm, but not unpleasantly so. He took off his coat and slung it over a chair, then sat for a moment and removed his boots. He stepped toward her slowly, and his hands found her waist. "My wife," he murmured in awe. His thumb brushed the edge of her bodice, and she felt the tremor in his touch, not from uncertainty, but from the weight of the moment.

Her chest rose in a ragged hush when his lips met hers. His kiss was soft at first. His lips tasted of the rum and laughter they had shared on deck. The gentleness deepened, and the kiss grew warmer and more insistent. Her fingers slid into his sun-bleached hair, and she felt his breath catch at her touch.

He drew her closer, until there was no space left between them. She could feel his heartbeat against her own.

Without breaking the kiss, his fingers moved to the laces at her back. The silk made a soft, rustling whisper as he drew the crimson gown from her shoulders and let it fall in a slow cascade to the floor. He stilled when he saw what lay beneath—a corset of deep scarlet, trimmed in delicate black lace. She had found it in the same crate as her wedding dress, sitting on top as if it were meant to support the garment. The color was daring, almost wicked, and it made his eyes darken with desire.

"God help me," he breathed, brushing his knuckles along the curve of her waist. "You are a vision that even Helen of Troy would have envied."

Her cheeks flushed, but she met his gaze without lowering her eyes. She whispered, "Then let us be glad I belong only to you."

His smile deepened, and he bent to press his lips to the hollow of her throat, then lower. His lips traced a slow path of kisses along her collarbone. She felt the heat of his breath against her skin and closed her eyes against his touch as she caressed his back. Her hands found the hem of his shirt, and with unhurried care she drew it upward, baring the breadth of his chest to her eyes and hands.

She took a moment to admire the deep cut of his tight muscles. She splayed her fingers over them and felt the steady thrum of his heartbeat beneath her palm. Leaning forward, she pressed a soft kiss just above where she felt the rhythm, then moved her lips lower to kiss just above his navel, lingering there as if to lay her claim. A low sound rumbled in his chest. It was not quite a sigh, but not quite a groan. His hand came to rest at the small of her back, and he drew her closer, as though her touch was both his undoing and his salvation.

His fingers worked at the laces of her scarlet corset. Each pull loosened the fabric's hold until it slipped away entirely. She stood before him fully exposed. The rise and fall of her bosom betrayed the quickening rhythm of her breath. He lowered his mouth to her chest with a reverence that felt like worship. His lips lingered in unhurried devotion as he kissed and caressed each mound. When the soft heat of his mouth closed over one of her peaks, she threaded her fingers through his hair, drawing him closer and surrendering to the exquisite spell of his touch.

With her fingers still tangled in his hair, he lifted his head. His gaze was molten with longing. Without a word, he slipped his arms beneath her and drew her up against his chest. She gave a soft gasp, and her hands gripped his shoulders as he carried her across the cabin. He set her gently upon the bed. His touch lingered at her waist as though he were reluctant to let her go, even for an instant.

He stepped back just enough to let his hands fall to the fastening of his breeches. His eyes never left hers. One by one, the buttons gave way beneath his fingers. The garment slid down over his hips, and he stepped free of it. The warm lanternlight traced the powerful lines of his body. For a breathless moment, they simply looked at one another—two souls stripped bare in every sense. Then he moved to the bed. The mattress dipped as he settled beside her, and his hand found hers as though it had always belonged there.

He pressed her hand to his chest, and his gaze held hers for a breath before he leaned in and claimed her mouth. The kiss was no longer tender; it was hungry, steeped in need and the heat of all the moments they had been forced apart. His fingers threaded into her copper strands, holding her into the kiss as though the world might try to steal her away. She met him with equal fervor. Her breath mingled with his as the urgency between them deepened.

Her hands, eager and unafraid, traced the planes of his chest, gliding lower over the taut muscle of his abdomen until her fingers brushed the proof of his desire. His breath left him in a shudder, and for a moment he stilled beneath her touch, as if savoring the exquisite torment she stirred.

Then, with a low sound deep in his throat, he rolled toward her, gathering her into his arms as though he could draw her entirely into himself. His mouth found hers again, fiercer now, and his hand slid down her thigh to pull her closer still.

With a measured shift, he moved over her. His body was a warm, solid weight that surrounded her in the circle of his arms.

One hand cradled her cheek while the other wandered lower, stroking along the curve of her hip before settling between her thighs. His touch there was tender at first, as though he sought to memorize every shiver and breath she gave him.

Her lips parted on a quiet gasp. Her back arched in a silent plea as his fingers teased and explored her folds with patient skill. He watched her face as if her every reaction were a gift. When her hands clutched at his shoulders and her breathing turned ragged, he bent to kiss the hollow of her throat, murmuring her name like a vow. Only then did he guide himself to her and paused at the edge of joining. His eyes burned into hers.

He lingered there, just at the brink, as though savoring the final breath before surrender. One last kiss claimed her mouth—deep, unhurried, a mingling of warmth and promise—before he pressed forward. She drew in a sharp breath at the exquisite stretch. Her hands clutched his arms as he filled her in a slow, deliberate glide. His own breath left him in a shudder, and for a moment they simply stilled with hearts pounding in the same breathless rhythm.

His forehead came to rest against hers, and she felt the tremor of his restraint as he let her grow accustomed to him. When she shifted beneath him, welcoming him more fully, his low groan was half devotion, and half need. He began to move then. Each thrust was measured, deep, and threaded through with the kind of care that spoke as loudly as any vow they had taken that night.

His movements found a rhythm that was unhurried yet impossibly consuming. Each one drew a soft sound from her lips that made his pulse quicken. Her fingers trailed along his back, urging him closer still, as though she could fuse them into one.

He kissed her again. His mouth captured every sigh and every whispered plea, until her body arched to meet his in perfect time. The heat between them built in steady waves. His control was fraying with every rise and fall of her hips beneath him. Her nails curled against his skin.

"Beatrix…" He breathed her name like a prayer. His voice was rough with the strain of holding back. She felt it too—the gathering tide that would not be held at bay much longer—and her breath grew ragged as she clung to him, ready to be swept into it with him.

The tension broke all at once. A rush of sensation stole her breath and set her every nerve alight. Her cry was muffled against his shoulder as fierce, unrelenting pleasure surged through her. He followed her into it with a shudder. His arms tightened around her as though he could anchor them both against the force of it. For a heartbeat, they moved together in that perfect, breathless unity, neither willing to let go. Then the rhythm slowed, and he drew her into his chest. Their hearts still raced in time.

They lay entwined in the quiet. Her cheek rested over his heart, and she was lulled by its steady, slowing beat. His fingers traced idle patterns along her spine with a touch so light that it felt like a secret.

"Every wave, every wind, and every star has led me to you," he murmured, his voice rough with emotion. "And I will follow them all again, for as long as I draw breath, if it means I end each journey here—in your arms."

"And I will meet you here, always," she whispered, her voice steady despite the rush of emotion between them.

He tipped her chin so their eyes met. Whatever shadows had lingered between them seemed to fall away in that moment. He brushed a final soft, reverent kiss to her lips before drawing the blanket over them both. With her body tucked securely into his, she let her eyes close, feeling for the first time in months that she could truly rest.

CHAPTER 28

The three days to Bridgetown were the sweetest Beatrix could remember. *The Tempest* sailed under a forgiving sky. Her sails were full and the wind was warm, as she carried them ever closer to port.

By day, she and Gus dined alone on the quarterdeck. The sea breeze lifted the curls at her temples while he poured her wine and teased her with stories from his youth. They walked the deck together in the golden light of late afternoon. They paused often to lean on the rail and watch the foam slip away behind them. Sometimes, in the shaded quiet of the chartroom, they read aloud from *Robinson Crusoe*, trading chapters until laughter blurred the words.

They spent their nights wrapped in each other's arms. They took their time exploring each other's bodies. Each delighted to learn what touch or movement brought pleasured moans and gasps to the other's lips.

On the final afternoon before they reached port, Gus and Beatrix sat in the chart room to compose the letter to her father.

"Dear Lord Wrenwood, your daughter pretended to be a lad and stowed away on my ship. Since I discovered her presence, I have ravished her unceasingly with a riotous passion that would burn down a village..." Gus teased, miming his quill on the parchment.

Beatrix giggled and bent over him to pull the utensil from his hand. He caught her hand and pulled her into his lap. She threw her arms around his neck.

"What would you have me say, my love?" He asked, nuzzling his nose against hers playfully.

"Maybe something formal and elegant? He doesn't need to know the details."

"How about... 'Dear Lord Wrenwood, your daughter has captured my heart completely. I couldn't wait for your blessing to make her my wife, so we married at sea. We shall return to Cornwall in the Fall, where we will say our vows anew before whatever clergy member happens to be in town upon our arrival. Yours Truly, August Drake.'"

She wrinkled her nose. "Maybe..." He sighed and shifted her to one knee. He took the quill and dipped it into the ink this time.

"Dear Lord Wrenwood," he said aloud. His voice was serious this time as he composed the words. "I am writing to inform you that your daughter, Beatrix, is safe in my care."

"That's good..." she said as she watched him make his marks on the parchment.

"My brother has perished at sea. His death will be recorded in Bridgetown, Barbados, before you receive this letter."

"You're sure that's true? I don't know what to expect tomorrow." Her eyes were downcast. He lifted her chin to meet his tender gaze.

"I promise you that I will bribe whoever it takes to assure his name is recorded among the deceased when we get to Bridgetown." She looked away. He continued his letter.

"Your daughter has given me her hand in marriage. We were married at sea in a traditional hand-fasting ceremony before more than 50 witnesses." He stopped for a moment and turned to her.

"Would you rather hold our blessing ceremony at your estate or mine?" he asked.

"Mine, I think," she answered after a brief contemplation. Merthwaite was older and grander than Brackwater Hall, but she knew his relationship with his father was strained. His quill began moving again.

"We will return to Cornwall later this Autumn and will repeat our vows in your chapel at Brackwater. We are eager to have our union blessed and recorded by the church. Signed, your son-in-law, Lord August Drake, Viscount of Alverdon."

"Oh, so *there* you use your title." She teased.

"I use it when I need to," he quipped, then his tone turned serious. "If you want that life, Beatrix, I will give it to you. There will come a day when I have to take over my father's estate, but if you're done with the sea now, we could go home and settle. I own property in my own right in Ireland, as well as a townhouse in Mayfair, or I could buy you an estate wherever your heart desires."

"I just want to be by your side, wherever you go," she said softly, then her tone turned teasing again, "Though I would like to be the great Lady Alverdon when we're in port."

"Ah, yes, the grand Lady—and one day, you'll be even grander as the Countess of Falmouth."

"Oh la la! Do you think your crew will curtsy to me then?"

"I doubt it, but Callahan might give you a little bow." She giggled again. Things between Gus and Callahan had started to thaw, and the entire mood of the ship was better for it.

Gus folded his letter and sealed it with wax pressed with his signet ring. He never wore it, but this particular correspondence needed the weight of his heraldry.

O'Malley knocked on the chartroom door and waited until Gus answered to step inside. He blushed when he saw Beatrix balanced on his captain's lap.

"Uh, just wanted to let you know, captain. We should dock in Bridgetown late tonight." The old sailor couldn't meet her eyes and focused instead on the chart laid out on the table.

"Excellent. We will conclude our business there quickly, I believe." Gus said.

"Aye, captain." O'Malley said as he ducked back out the door.

"Dinner, my love—I mean, Lady Alverdon?" He said to her with mock grandeur.

"I thought you'd never ask, My Lord." She smiled and stood, and he rose from the chair behind her and offered his arm. She took it, and they enjoyed one more evening of newly-wedded bliss.

***

The Vice-Admiralty Court in Bridgetown smelled faintly of ink, wax, and dampness. Its high windows let in slanted bars of sunlight that fell across the polished oak bench where the magistrate sat. His wig was powdered and pristine. His gaze was sharp and narrowed as it swept the three of them.

"Captain August Drake," he said, his voice carrying in the hushed chamber, "you claim to have evidence regarding the presumed death of one Ambrose Drake, formerly master of *The Resolute*?"

Gus inclined his head. "We do, sir. This is my first mate, Mr. Callahan, and Lady Beatrix Wrenwood Drake, the deceased's lawful wife."

The magistrate's quill scratched as he made a note. "Proceed."

Callahan stepped forward first, placing the torn and bloodied leather boot upon the bench. His voice was steady as he described finding it half-buried in the sand of Dead Man's Cay. He described the telltale marks in the sand from shackles still fresh in the tide-washed shore. Gus's tone was grave as he corroborated each word.

The magistrate looked to Beatrix last. "You were present, my lady?"

"I was," she said softly. "We searched the island. He could not have survived without a ship, fresh water, or shelter."

The magistrate regarded them for a long moment before dipping his quill again. "This Court finds sufficient cause to rule that Ambrose Drake lost at sea and presumed dead. The declaration shall be entered into the registry this day and recognized by the Crown."

Beatrix held her breath.

"This judgment," the magistrate continued, "frees Mrs. Drake of all marital obligations and renders her free to marry again, should she choose."

Gus's hand found hers beneath the table. His thumb pressed against her knuckles with quiet, fierce assurance in the middle of the solemn room.

"Let the record show," the magistrate concluded, "that the matter is closed."

***

The heavy doors of the Vice-Admiralty Court closed behind them with a resonant thud. Outside, the air was bright and hot. The harbor spread before them. Beatrix exhaled, as though only now releasing the breath she had held while the magistrate decided her fate.

Gus reached for her hand. His grip firm and warm. "It's settled," he said quietly. "The law may still wait for a blessing, but in every way that matters, you are my wife."

She didn't look up.

His thumb brushed over her fingers. "Paper and priest won't make you more mine than you are now. We'll have both, in Cornwall, before your father and God, but nothing could bind us tighter than what we already share."

Some of the tension eased from her shoulders, and though she did not smile, the look she gave him was soft enough to make his chest ache.

***

The galley smelled of roasted fish and fresh bread that night. Gus sat at the head of the narrow table, with Beatrix at his right, and Callahan and O'Malley opposite them. The clink of cutlery and the low hum of the sea outside gave the meal a rare sense of calm. Most of the crew were ashore, enjoying the pleasures of Bridgetown.

"St. Lucia's next on our manifest," Callahan said between bites. "After that, we've ports lined from Grenada to Guadeloupe. All of it pays well enough."

"Aye," O'Malley agreed. He wiped his mouth with the back of his hand. "Wouldn't hurt to keep our schedule. Cargo's worth more delivered on time."

Gus set down his fork. The scrape of metal on tin drew every eye to him. "After St. Lucia, we sail for Calverique."

Beatrix's hand froze around her cup. "Calverique?" she asked quietly. "Gus, whatever is there…it may be better left buried."

Callahan's gaze darkened. "She's right. You remember what it was like last time. We don't know what's waiting inside that island. Sometimes the sea swallows things for a reason."

Gus leaned forward with determination. His voice was edged like drawn steel. "And sometimes it swallows what was never meant to be lost. That cave called to me, even when Beatrix was bleeding out in my arms. Do you think I've forgotten? I almost went inside, and you—" he jabbed a finger toward Callahan—"had to drag me back. I can still hear it. I still dream about what might be behind that wall of stone."

Callahan's expression tightened. "I remember, Captain. I also remember thinking you'd lost your damn mind."

Beneath Gus's shirt, the silver locket warmed against his skin. A faint pulse of light bled through the linen like the heartbeat of something waiting in the dark. Beatrix's eyes darted to it, but before she could speak, she saw Callahan's gaze follow hers. His expression sharpened.

"Then promise me," she said, her voice low, "if we go back, we go together, and if we find something dangerous, we leave it be."

Gus's jaw flexed. "Together, yes; but I won't turn away again."

The table fell quiet. Conversation sputtered out, and though the meal went on, the name *Calverique* seemed to hang in the lantern-lit air.

***

After dinner, Callahan, Gus, and Beatrix moved to the chartroom to determine their course to Saint Lucia and then to Calverique. The lantern swayed overhead, throwing shifting light across the chartroom table where three maps lay side by side: *The Tempest's* delivery map, Gus's navigational charts, and the worn map Beatrix's mother had left her.

Gus leaned over them. His fingers traced the faded marks. "We never recovered the last clue," he said, tapping the inked circle over Saint Lucia. "We could work on that while we're in port in Saint Lucia."

"We don't need to," Beatrix interrupted. Both men looked at her quizzically.

Her hands rested on the edge of the table. Her grip turned her knuckles pale against the wood. "I already found it…with Ambrose."

Gus's voice was careful. "You…found it? What was it?"

"It was a watch, lined with constellations," she said quietly. "With the glow from my locket, I could read the hidden stars on its face. That's how I navigated Ambrose's ship to meet you in Calverique."

Callahan's head snapped toward her. "A watch?"

Her brows drew together. "You know it?"

He hesitated. "The day Ambrose shot you in Calverique…when we brought you aboard, something fell from your dress pocket. I picked it up without thinking. I thought—" He turned abruptly to his desk, rifling through drawers. "I thought I still had it."

The search grew more frantic. He tore through papers, lifted logbooks, and yanked open the small chest in the corner. "It should be here."

"Where did you last see it?" Gus asked, his tone sharpening.

"In my coat pocket," Callahan muttered. "I meant to give it back to Beatrix, but never had the right chance. Then, I forgot about it. I don't know how long it's been gone."

The room went still.

"Is it possible," Beatrix asked, "that someone took it?"

"By someone, do you mean…Ambrose?" Gus asked.

"I was never alone with the man," Callahan stumbled through his words. His Irish accent thickened in his panic.

"Well, if he did have it, it's washed out to sea with him," Gus said with finality. "Luckily, we don't need the watch to get to Calverique." He pulled the compass out of his pocket and held it in his palm. It responded immediately to the gold ring he wore on his pinky finger. Its needle snapped into position and pointed towards Calverique.

"Gus…are you certain—" Beatrix began.

"Yes." His declaration came louder than he intended. The locket lit again at his chest. It pulsed a moment, then dimmed as his expression softened.

"We won't linger in Saint Lucia, then. We will exchange cargo and then sail immediately for Calverique."

"Aye, captain," Callahan answered wearily. Gus held out his hand to Beatrix and led her to their cabin.

***

The lantern's sway cast fleeting shadows as they readied for bed. Gus's shirt fell away, and her linen dress slipped to the floor. In moments, they were beneath the sheets. He kissed her with quiet certainty, and she melted into the familiar strength of his arms.

They moved together in a gentle, passionate rhythm. Their breaths tangled, and their hearts beat as one. Each movement drew them closer to that shared, aching release until the world beyond the cabin ceased to exist.

As his passion spilled over and she shuddered beneath him, he drew her tightly against his chest. It was then she felt it—the faint, steady pulse of golden light from where his locket rested against her skin.

Beatrix stilled. The glow was soft yet insistent, as if it breathed with a will of its own. Her gaze lifted to Gus's face, but he was lost in the moment. His eyes were half-lidded, oblivious of the light.

A strange weariness began to seep into her bones. It carried a subtle pull, as though an unseen tide had taken hold of her and was drawing her toward some far, shadowed shore. The hum came next; it was low, resonant, and growing louder until it filled her skull. Then, clear and sweet as moonlight, *The Compass Waltz* began to play in her mind.

The melody was no longer just sound; it was a voice, coaxing her to follow. The pulse of the locket quickened, keeping time with the music. Her breath slowed, her muscles loosened, and for a dizzying instant she felt herself slipping—falling—into the song's embrace.

Calverique was calling her again.

Her eyes flew open. With a hard blink, she forced the melody into silence. She clung to the feel of Gus's body against hers. Her hand rose to trace the strong line of his jaw, seeking the anchor of his touch.

He seemed already half-asleep, but she could not shake the thought that perhaps the locket's siren call had reached him, too.

"Gus?" She whispered.

"Sleep, my love," he murmured absently. His voice was warm against her temple.

She closed her eyes, but the slow, steady pulse of the locket lingered in her mind long after.

CHAPTER 29

Saint Lucia faded into the horizon behind them. The scent of traded spices and fresh provisions still lingered in the galley. *The Tempest* cut through the waves with a familiar ease as her crew worked in practiced rhythm.

They knew the way to Calverique well enough to bring her near, but the final approach was Gus's alone to make. For three days, O'Malley and Callahan took turns following the path they had traveled weeks prior. Both were apprehensive as they remembered all too well the limp, bleeding figure Callahan had carried from the island, but neither questioned their captain. They knew all too well that it was a losing battle.

Late on the third night of their voyage, the sea lay still as glass. Callahan and O'Malley exchanged a wary glance; no map or star chart could guide them any closer. All they could do now was watch as Gus stepped to the helm with the compass resting in his palm. The needle moved at once and quivered as if it knew the way by memory alone. This close to the island, its tip began to glow. It gave a steady, golden pulse, like the first notes of a half-remembered melody, beckoning them toward the shore none of them could see.

Beatrix joined Callahan at the quarterdeck rail. Her gaze fixed on Gus as she observed the set of his shoulders and the way his fingers curled around the brass casing as though it were an extension of himself.

At first, nothing seemed amiss. He adjusted the wheel with his eyes fixed on the needle's slow, deliberate swings. Then his movements grew too precise. His gaze never lifted from the compass, and his lips parted slightly as though he listened to something neither she nor Callahan could hear.

The ship answered him like a living being. It glided into each new bearing with uncanny smoothness.

"Callahan..." Beatrix's voice was low.

"I see it," he murmured grimly. "That's no navigation. That's the damned island pulling him in."

She felt the truth of it in her bones. The same pull she had fought in the cabin days ago now gripped Gus with relentless force. He no longer stared down at the compass. His eyes, usually sharp and alive, were distant and fixed on something beyond the horizon.

"Gus?" she called.

He did not answer.

The wheel spun in his hands. *The Tempest's* sails strained in the sudden shift. They could see nothing in the blackness of the night, yet Gus continued to steer towards something completely unseen. The golden light from the compass and his locket cast his sun-browned skin in a spectral pallor. Beatrix's lungs forgot their rhythm; he looked less like the man she loved and more like some ancient mariner answering the call of a forgotten god.

Beatrix took a step toward him, but Callahan caught her arm. "If you break him from it too soon, we could lose our heading—or worse, wreck her outright. Let him get us close."

Her pulse pounded in her ears. Every slow rotation of the wheel, every measured breath he took felt like the tolling of a bell, each note pulling them closer to something neither of them was ready to face.

Then, through the thinning veil of mist ahead, the jagged silhouette of Calverique rose from the dark waters. The island's cliffs caught the moonlight in silver flashes. Only then did Gus blink, as though waking from a dream. His knuckles were white on the wheel, and his breathing was ragged, but the compass lay quiet in his hand. Its glow faded into shadow.

The cliffs loomed larger by the moment. Callahan's eyes met hers, and she read the same unspoken thought that gripped her own mind.

We've made it, but at what cost?

Gus tucked the compass into his coat and turned toward them. His eyes were bright and alive with something that made Beatrix's breath hitch.

"We're here," His voice was almost wistful. "I could feel it—like the island was drawing me in. Every turn…it was as if the sea itself moved for me."

Beatrix's stomach knotted. "You…liked it?"

A slow smile touched his mouth. "Liked it? I'd follow that pull forever if it meant steering like that again. I've never felt so certain of a course in my life."

Callahan's brow furrowed. "And if that course had run us into the rocks?"

Gus replied, not with arrogance, but with absolute conviction. "It wanted me to find it. I could feel the welcome in it."

The certainty in his tone chilled Beatrix more than the night air. She glanced at Callahan, but neither of them found words to answer him.

The cliffs loomed higher with each passing minute. They were jagged silhouettes carved against the moonlit sky. Gus stood at the rail, eyes fixed on the narrow mouth of the cove.

"Bring her in slow," he ordered. "No sails snapping, no loose rigging to give us away."

Callahan moved to his side, his gaze sweeping the shoreline. "You're not going in there alone. After what happened last time, we will take a full landing party."

Gus shook his head. "It should be just me and Beatrix."

Callahan crossed his arms. "That isn't happening. I'm coming with you, and I'm not asking permission."

The muscles in Gus's jaw flexed. "I don't need—"

"You do," Callahan cut in sharply. "The last time we stood in that cave, I nearly had to knock you senseless and haul you out by your hair. Now, after watching you at the helm, I'm not about to let whatever's in there sink its claws in."

Beatrix had been silent until now. She stood just behind them with her arms wrapped around herself against the night breeze.

"I agree with Callahan," she said softly, though her voice carried enough weight to make both men turn. "You weren't...yourself at the helm, Gus. I've never seen you like that."

His eyes smoldered with banked fire. "I had us on course. Perfectly."

"That's what frightens me," she replied. "You weren't steering us—you were answering something. I don't know if I can follow you into that cave if I think it might call you away from me."

Gus's gaze softened for a heartbeat, but his answer came steady. "I need to see what's inside, and I need you with me."

"Then you'll have me," she said, glancing toward Callahan, "but you'll have him, too, whether you like it or not."

The faintest curve tugged at Callahan's mouth, though it never reached his eyes. Gus gave one short nod, the kind that was half agreement, half surrender.

"Fine. We go at first light," he said, turning back toward the cove. "The three of us, and no one else."

***

Beatrix curled against Gus beneath the sheets. She rested her cheek over his heartbeat, and its steady rhythm soothed her. Then the light from the lockets grew so brightly that she could not ignore them.

Even through the thin linen of her shift, her locket's light seeped like moonlight through fog, pulsing with a slow, unearthly certainty. His own shone faintly against her, and when the silver surfaces brushed, they almost hummed.

"Do you feel it?" she whispered.

"I'd have to be dead not to." His voice was quiet, threaded with something that chilled her—a quiet hunger, almost rapture. "It's…beautiful."

Her pulse quickened. "It's dangerous."

He shook his head faintly. "It's calling us home."

The pull grew stronger as *The Compass Waltz* threaded into the silence as quiet as memory, but as insistent as the tide. She closed her eyes, but the image of the cave's black mouth rose unbidden, waiting.

"I don't think I can sleep," she murmured.

"I don't want to," he murmured, and his lips found hers.

At first, it was only a kiss. It was slow and deep—warm with the promise of the tenderness that was quickly turning towards the conviction of their building bond. Slowly, with every heartbeat, the light from the lockets flared brighter, until it spilled across the bed in glittering gold. *The Compass Waltz* swelled, threading into the rhythm of their mouths and into the rise and fall of their breath, until it seemed the song was kissing her through him.

She felt his hand cup the back of her head, holding her as though he could keep her there forever. The pull of the island slid into her bones, making her dizzy, and still he kissed her. His breath mingled with hers in a heat that was no longer entirely his own.

"Gus," she whispered against his mouth, trying to draw back.

He did not move. His eyes were open, yet unfocused, with pupils blown wide until they nearly swallowed the silver-grey flecks she knew so well. The golden light spilled across his cheekbones, jaw, and throat. Each pulse kept time with the music only they could hear.

Her heart pounded. She pressed her palm to his chest, and she could feel the steady thud of his heart beneath the unnatural light. "Gus—stop."

It was as though the word barely reached him.

She took his face in both hands, forcing his gaze to hers. For a long, breathless moment, he looked straight through her, as though he were already standing in the cave's mouth, staring into the dark beyond.

With a sudden shudder, he blinked. The glow retreated to a faint throb, and he drew in a ragged breath, as if he had run a great distance. "I'm here," he rasped, pulling her into a fierce embrace.

Beatrix could still feel the echo of the pull in her bones, and she knew it had not truly let him go.

***

Neither of them slept. The golden pulse lingered in the corner of her vision, beckoning her. At the first hint of dawn, they dressed quickly as the island's shadow began to rise on the horizon.

Callahan was waiting on deck when they emerged. The morning light glinted off the pistols strapped across his chest and the sword at his side. A brace of knives was tucked into his belt, and another was sheathed along his boot. He looked ready to take on an entire regiment.

Gus, by contrast, appeared entirely untroubled. He wore only his sword. The scabbard swayed against his thigh as he strode toward the longboat. "It's a short row," he said, as if that explained everything.

Without a word, Callahan drew one of his knives and pressed it into Beatrix's palm. His eyes met hers, the unspoken message clear: *stay alert.*

She closed her fingers around the hilt and followed them down the gangway. The three settled into the longboat, and oars dipped into the calm water as *The Tempest* receded behind them. The cave's black mouth drew nearer with each pull.

The longboat scraped against the sand, and Callahan jumped out first to drag it higher on the beach. Beatrix steadied herself, expecting Gus's hand to reach back for her. It never came. He had already leapt into the shallows. His boots struck the sand in long, purposeful strides. His gaze never wavered from the black mouth of the cave. The glow from the locket beneath his shirt bled faintly through the fabric, pulsing like a heartbeat as it urged him onward.

By the time Beatrix stepped into the surf, he was nearly at the base of the cliff. Callahan caught up beside her. His voice was low and grim. "We'll lose him if we're not careful."

They followed in his wake. The sound of their footsteps was lost beneath the distant, haunting hum that seemed to come from the stone ahead of them.

The air within the cave was cool and damp, and it hit them like a gust of wind as Callahan and Beatrix entered the cave. Their footsteps echoed against the stone as they chased after the sound of Gus's voice.

"Beatrix! Hurry!"

She rounded a curve in the passage and saw him. He was already standing in the center of the cave at the stone plinth. Two indentions glowed at the top, ready to receive the lockets.

"Put yours here," he urged, his voice sharp with urgency. "Now."

Her pulse stumbled. "Gus—"

"Do it!" He was already pressing his own locket into place. The chain slid over his fingers. "It needs both of them."

Callahan's hand brushed her arm in warning, but the air was thrumming now. The same siren hum she had fought against the night before was now relentless. The light seemed to reach for her, tugging her forward.

Her fingers curled tightly around the locket at her throat, but it was no use. She felt herself stepping forward. Each pace was stolen from her will. Her arm lifted as though guided by some invisible hand.

"No," she whispered, but the word had no weight.

The cool silver of the chain slid across her skin as she removed it. Her own locket found the waiting indentation beside Gus's. The moment it touched the stone, the golden light swelled. It was blinding in its intensity. The carvings on the plinth shimmered as though molten. The hum grew to a deep, resonant chord that shook the air.

"Bloody hell," Callahan cursed and threw an arm across his eyes.

The light built and built until it was all they could see. It burned away the shadows, the cave, even her sense of her own body…and then was gone. Silence crashed in its place.

The plinth stood unchanged, just as it had the last time they had tried to unlock it. For a long, heavy moment, none of them moved. The only sound was the slow drip of water from the cavern roof.

"There's nothing here now," Callahan said at last. "We should go."

"There is," Gus shot back. His tone was sharp with certainty. "It's still here—I can feel it." His gaze locked on Beatrix. "Last time, you held both lockets and sang the song."

Before she could protest, he seized the lockets from the plinth and forced the cool silver into her palms. His hands closed around hers with unyielding pressure. "Sing the song," he ordered.

She shook her head. Fear and frustration tightened her voice. "Gus, you have to stop this madness."

His grip tightened. "Sing it!" His voice rang against the cave walls. He was desperate and commanding all at once.

Callahan moved to her side in a single stride. His hand rested lightly but unmistakably on her arm. "Take a breath, August," he said. His tone was level but edged with warning. "You're not hearing yourself."

Gus's jaw clenched. His eyes were still fixed on Beatrix as if Callahan's presence were nothing more than a passing shadow. "We're too close to turn back."

"You're too far gone to see straight," Callahan countered. "Let it go."

Beatrix's fingers curled instinctively around the cool silver. The moment both lockets touched, light flared between them and spilled over her hands in molten gold. It pulsed with a rhythm that was not her own. It seeped up her arms, wound into her chest, and settled like a weight behind her ribs.

Her breath hitched. She tried to speak. She tried to tell Gus she would not do this, but the sound that emerged was not her own voice. *The Compass Waltz* slipped past her lips. It was soft at first, then grew fuller and richer until the notes filled the cave.

The light swelled and painted the stone walls in rippling gold. Gus leaned toward her. His eyes were alight, as though the very air were answering his call. Callahan squinted against the brightness. His hand hovered near his sword.

The final note died on the air. The glow from the lockets snuffed out as if some unseen hand had closed a shutter. The plinth stood bare before them. The cave was silent.

Gus's breath came fast. He let go of Beatrix's hands and moved towards the plinth as though willing it to stir. "It's here," he said. His voice was fervent. "I can feel it. Just as before. Something's missing."

Callahan shifted, placing himself squarely between Gus and Beatrix. "What's missing is the sense God gave you. There's nothing here, Gus. There's nothing but rock and shadows."

Gus shook his head. His eyes never left the stone. "No, I remember. The last time…you were bleeding," he said. He turned toward Beatrix with a strange, almost fevered light in his eyes. "It answered then. *Blood will find its line.* You have to give it your blood."

Beatrix recoiled. Her fingers tightened around the lockets. "You cannot be serious." The words were sharp with disbelief. Her voice clanged against the cave walls.

Callahan's stance hardened, and he braced a hand on her shoulder. She trembled slightly beneath his touch. "You've lost your bloody mind if you think I'll let you lay a finger on her. Whatever's in this place is twisting you into something I don't care to recognize."

Gus's hand went to his sword hilt in a slow, deliberate motion. The steel whispered free. The sound was unnervingly calm against the echo of the cave.

"Gus," Beatrix whispered. Her voice trembled.

He stepped toward her. The golden light from the lockets glinted along the blade. "Just a drop," he murmured, as though the words alone might soothe her fear. "It will answer us."

Steel rang again, this time sharper, as Callahan drew his own sword and moved without hesitation.

"Not another step," Callahan said. His tone was cold enough to frost stone. He reached back with one hand and guided Beatrix behind him. His stance was wide and unyielding. The two men locked eyes with blades poised.

Gus's jaw went rigid. "You don't understand—"

"I understand enough," Callahan cut in. His blade lifted just enough to make the threat plain. "You're so bloody certain this cave holds your answer that you'd spill her blood to get it. That's not a husband or even a captain speaking. It's a man gone to madness."

The plinth began to glow again. Its golden light danced over Gus's face, illuminating the fevered hunger in his eyes. "It's not madness; it's *truth*. It's here, calling to me. I can feel it in my bones."

"And I can feel your blade," Callahan shot back. "So, choose, captain—are you the man I'd follow into hell, or the poor bastard I put in the ground myself?"

Gus's gaze locked on Callahan's, then, with a suddenness that made Beatrix's heart seize, he lunged. Steel rang as his blade met Callahan's. The clash echoed off the stone walls.

Callahan shoved her back, never breaking his guard. "Run!" he barked.

She turned and darted toward the mouth of the cave, but the uneven stone caught her foot. She pitched forward, and her palms scraped against the rock before her temple struck the ground with a dull crack. White light flared behind her eyes, and the sound of the duel blurred into a distant roar.

Gus pressed forward. His strikes were brutal and relentless. Each one forced Callahan to yield ground toward the plinth. The golden light from the lockets spilled over them, gilding the sweat on their faces and the feral intensity in Gus's eyes.

"You don't see it!" Gus snarled between blows. "You don't hear it calling!"

"I hear you losing yourself," Callahan snarled. Steel rang against steel. "And by God's blood, I'll not let you drag her to damnation with you."

"She has to bleed," Gus shot back as he pressed forward with a force that nearly drove Callahan to his knees. The golden light flared, catching the sharp planes of his face. He looked half-man, half-phantom. "It's the only way."

"The hell it is." Callahan twisted, knocking Gus's blade aside. "You'll spill her blood over my corpse."

The words landed like a gauntlet, and Gus answered with a ferocious swing meant to end it. Steel clashed and sparks scattered across the stone floor. The clang of steel became a furious rhythm: thrust, parry, riposte. Finally, Callahan caught Gus's blade on a hard block and slid it aside. He stepped in, hooking the guard of his sword over Gus's hilt and wrenched it from his grip. The weapon clattered to the stone floor.

In a heartbeat, Callahan's point was at Gus's throat. His chest heaved. "It ends here, August," he said, his voice low but edged with iron.

The tip of Callahan's blade hovered at Gus's throat, and the silence between them was thick enough to choke on. Then Gus's gaze shifted past him, and his breath stopped.

Beatrix lay sprawled near the cave's mouth. Her hair fell loose over her face and one arm twisted beneath her. She was grimly still. Callahan glanced over his shoulder and saw her.

"Saints preserve us," Callahan breathed, the words torn between prayer and fury. He barely had time to react before Gus shoved past him.

Gus dropped to his knees beside her. He brushed back her tangled hair to find a deep gash at her temple. Blood trailed down her cheek.

"No…no, no, no." His voice was raw. He brushed away the blood on her cheek with his hand. "Trix, wake up."

Callahan crouched at her side. He sheathed his sword with a harsh motion. He held a hand gently against her chest. "She's breathing. We need to get her out of here, now."

Gus nodded as he reached for the lockets lying on the stone where she had dropped them. His fingers closed around the silver, and the blood on his hand smeared across the metal. The instant it touched, the light flared, and with a deep, grinding rumble, the mouth of the cave yawned open behind them. Gus rose to his feet.

"Christ on a crooked cross, what have you gone and done?" Callahan barked, the words echoing off the stone as the golden glow spilled across the cave walls.

Beatrix lay motionless. The faint trickle of blood from her temple glistened in the light.

Gus did not look back at her. His eyes were locked on the widening gap beyond the plinth; the glow painted his face in molten gold. "I knew it," he breathed. He leaned down to pick up his sword from where Callahan had disarmed him just moments ago.

Callahan stared up at him. "What's the plan, then? Walk right into hell and hope it serves you tea?"

Gus's gaze never left the cave. "I'm going in."

Callahan's jaw worked as if he were biting down on every curse he knew. "Go on, then. If you're set on walking into the devil's gullet, I won't stop you."

Without waiting for another word, Gus walked forward. He slipped both lockets around his neck as he stepped toward the opening. Their glow pulsed in time with his heartbeat as the darkness swallowed him whole.

The glow faded from the chamber, leaving only the cave's cold dampness. Callahan gathered Beatrix into his lap with surprising gentleness.

"Come now, lass," he murmured, brushing the blood from her temple with the back of his hand. "You've been through worse, haven't you? Just open those eyes for me."

A soft breath escaped her lips. Her brow knit faintly, and she stirred against his chest.

Her lashes fluttered, and she drew in a shallow breath. "Callahan…?"

"Aye, I've got you," he said, steadying her as she tried to lift her head. "Easy now."

She blinked, and the dim cave walls swam into view. "Where's Gus?"

Callahan's gaze flicked toward the black maw of the passage. "Gone inside."

She struggled in his hold, but he kept an arm firm across her back. "No—"

"Beatrix, you can't follow him in there," he said. His voice was low but unyielding. "Not in your condition—and not after the way he just acted."

The distant hum of *The Compass Waltz* seemed to seep from the tunnel. It was faint but insistent as it curled into the air like a siren's breath. Her pulse quickened. "He shouldn't be in there alone."

"I know," Callahan said as he glanced toward the darkness. "But we've no choice now but to wait for him to come out…or for whatever's in there to spit him back."

Beatrix's eyes were fixed on the cave's mouth. "If he keeps going, we'll lose him. Not for an hour…for good." Her voice shook. "I can't let that happen."

Callahan wasn't budging. "Lass, he's just tried to carve me in two. He left you out here for dead. If he's that far gone, let him go."

Her chin lifted and her eyes blazed. "If it were you in there, he'd go after you. You know he would."

That landed. Callahan's jaw worked, but he said nothing for a long moment.

"No," she pressed on. "That's not him. That's this place. It's pulling at him, and he can't resist it."

He blew out a slow breath, shaking his head. "You think walking into its jaws is the answer? I've no taste for another fight with your husband, especially in the dark."

"Then don't fight him," she said. Desperation edged into her tone. "Help me bring him back."

"God's blood," Callahan muttered. His eyes narrowed on the black maw ahead. Finally, he gave a short, grim nod. "We stay together, and if I say we turn back, we turn back."

She nodded without argument. Callahan rose first, then bent to help her to her feet. He kept his arm braced for her to steady herself. She took it gratefully. Together, they stepped into the cave's cool, damp breath.

The golden light from the lockets had faded, leaving only the dim flicker of Callahan's lantern to push back the blackness. The stone walls pressed close, slick with moisture. They swallowed every sound except the soft echo of their boots.

"Gus?" Beatrix's voice rang out brittle against the oppressive quiet. No answer. They pressed deeper, and her heart pounded louder with every step.

"August?" She called to him again.

This time, the darkness answered with a raw, ragged scream that was distant but sharp enough to slice through the stone labyrinth.

She froze. "That was him."

Callahan's expression betrayed his worry. "Aye, and if he's in pain, that means there's more in here than shadows."

They moved faster, but the tunnel twisted and forked like a serpent. Each turn was littered with jagged rocks and sudden drops. Twice, Callahan pulled her back just before she stepped into a near-invisible snare line strung across the path. The second time, he muttered, "Bloody hell. It's booby trapped."

"Damn and blast!" They could hear Gus's cursing in the darkness ahead. They followed the sound as they wove through the narrowing passage until the walls funneled them toward the echo of his voice.

"Gus!" she called again.

This time, his reply came, "Here!"

They pushed forward, then Callahan's boot pressed down on a stone that shifted under his weight with a sharp click. His instincts fired faster than thought.

"Down!" he barked as he shoved Beatrix low as an arrow hissed past in the darkness, so close he felt the wind of its passage. It splintered against the wall behind them.

He kept her tucked beneath him, scanning the shadows above. "Well, that's one way to keep the uninvited out."

They pressed on slowly, taking every step with care. Still, the traps came. A section of the floor gave way to a pit of jagged stakes. A cluster of loose stones released a cascade of rocks from the ceiling. Each trap brought them closer to the sound of Gus's voice, until it was no longer echoing from everywhere at once, but from directly ahead.

They rounded a bend and stopped dead. Gus hung several feet off the ground, tangled upside down in a woven net of coarse rope. His sword lay on the ground beneath him, just out of reach. The contents of his coat pocket were strewn about below him: The compass, Ambrose's signet ring, and his black opal, now shattered into pieces.

"Beatrix!" he called when he saw them.

Callahan's hand shot out, barring her path. His voice was edged with warning. "We don't know if that's him talking or the damned island."

Her pulse jumped. "It's him."

"Prove it," Callahan barked toward Gus. "Say something only I'd know."

Gus's mouth curled in a wry half-smile. "Havana. Five years ago. You got so deep in your cups you woke up with a mermaid tattooed on your arse. She was bare-breasted, and winking, no less."

Beatrix blinked at Callahan. Her lips twitched despite the tension. "Is that true?"

Callahan handed her a knife. "Get him down before I let him hang here and rot," he muttered.

As they cut through the ropes, Gus dropped lightly to his feet. His smirk faded the moment his eyes found the cut at Beatrix's temple. The dried blood against her skin was a stark reminder of how she had been hurt, and how dangerously he had behaved.

"I—" He swallowed, stepping closer but not quite touching her. "I didn't mean for any of this… Beatrix, I'm sorry."

Her gaze softened for only a heartbeat before she looked away.

Gus drew a slow breath and, perhaps to mask the heaviness in the air, said, "She's got a fine smile, your mermaid. You ever name her?"

Callahan shot him a glare. "Augustina. I thought it fitting at the time."

Beatrix arched a brow. "After him?"

"After a lot of rum," Callahan said shortly. He strode ahead before either could press the point.

Gus chuckled under his breath as he picked up his fallen sword. "I'll take it as a compliment." He picked up the compass and his brother's ring, then Beatrix bent to pick up the black opal's pieces.

"Where did you get this?" she asked him.

"It was with Ambrose's things after the crew threw him in the brig." He answered.

"Ambrose stole this. Aria had put it in a letter to you, and Ambrose took it." As she touched the broken pieces, they began to turn color from black to white. "I think it must be…cursed."

"Why would Aria send me a cursed stone?" He asked.

"I don't think she would have. Ambrose must have corrupted it in some way." She gathered the pieces and slipped them into the pocket of her dress. They had all turned white now, so whatever curse or power they held was broken.

"August! Beatrix!" Callahan called for them from the darkness. They followed the winding passage towards his voice until they caught up to him. The air grew cooler as the darkness pressed closer. Callahan's lantern cast its shadows in strange, stretching shapes along the damp walls.

Gus kept pace at her side. His expression was taut. "I never meant to hurt you," he said quietly. "Not then. Not now. Whatever this place does to me, I will fight it. You have my word."

She stopped, forcing him to halt beside her. "Your word," she said, her voice low but cutting, "didn't stop you from drawing your sword to cut me. It didn't keep you from trying to hack your best mate to bits. It didn't keep you from leaving me bleeding on the ground so you could chase your obsession. If Callahan hadn't been there, I might still be lying there."

He flinched but didn't look away.

She stepped closer. The faintest ghost of a smile curved her lips, though her eyes stayed cold. "Hear me, August Drake, if you let anything bewitch you or make any move to mistreat me again, Callahan won't need to run you through." She pulled the sword from his waist in one quick movement and held the tip to his chest. "I'll do it myself."

For a long moment, the only sound was the drip of water somewhere deeper in the cave. Then he gave a slow nod. "Fair enough." She flipped the sword to hand him the hilt. He immediately sheathed it. "Will you allow me a kiss—in truce, if nothing more?"

Her eyes narrowed, weighing him. Then she gave a slight nod. "One, but don't think it means I've forgiven you."

The kiss he gave her was not the light touch of someone seeking absolution; it was deeper and lingering. It stole the breath from her lungs before she could stop him. For a heartbeat, the heat between them drowned out everything else: the stone, the damp, and the shadow of danger.

A low cough came from behind them. "If you two are quite finished," Callahan said dryly, "we've still got a bloody riddle to solve before this cave decides to kill us."

Callahan's lantern lifted to illuminate an oval indentation carved into the stone. The shape was different from the others they'd encountered. Around the carving, a ring of Latin words had been chiseled deep into the stone.

Beatrix stepped forward; her fingers brushed the inscription. "Duo corda divisa… cor unum pulsare debent… Una vox domum canat… Argentea luna… bibit rubrum aestum." She looked over her shoulder at Callahan and Gus. "Two hearts divided must beat as one. One voice must sing the song of home. The silver moon drinks the crimson tide."

"Two hearts divided must beat as one…" Gus's voice trailed as he repeated the first line.

"It has to refer to the lockets. We've never had a clue where the lockets weren't used as a key," she said.

Gus lifted the lockets from around his neck. He studied them in the dim golden glow. "You've never opened yours, have you?"

She shook her head slowly. "Nor you?"

"Not once." He turned hers over in his hand, then his, as though weighing a thought. "What if…"

He stepped closer and held both lockets before him. The edges were almost identical. The silverwork was precise in its curves and filigree. When he pressed their flat backs together, the pieces slid into place with a soft click, forming one perfect oval. The seam vanished into the design, as though they had never been apart.

Beatrix gasped. "They were one all along."

"And they're meant to be again." Gus proclaimed.

Callahan scowled. "I don't like that last bit of the riddle—*the silver moon drinks the crimson tide*. It sounds like blood."

"It is blood," Beatrix said softly.

"We're not doing that again." Callahan's voice was fierce and commanding.

Gus stepped closer to the stone. "It doesn't say whose blood."

Beatrix's brow knit. "What are you suggesting?"

"That I try mine," Gus said with an ease that made her shiver.

Callahan met his gaze with exasperation. "Or we all try walking away and leaving the bloody door shut."

Gus was already drawing his sword. He set the joined lockets into the stone circle. Then he turned his wrist and cut his palm with a quick, deliberate stroke. The blood ran freely. He pressed his hand to the silver surface.

"Sing, Beatrix," He bade.

Her voice was soft and lilting as she sang each word clearly. For a heartbeat, nothing happened, then the locket flared with golden light, brighter and brighter until it burned in their vision. The glow spilled into the carved seams of the stone.

With a deep, resonant click, the mechanism released. Stone ground against stone, and a great door shuddered open. They stepped forward as one—and stopped; silence swallowed their breath.

Before them, a valley unfolded like something from a daydream. Sunlight poured over the rooftops of gilded stone. Every building was a masterpiece of an age long past. Sweeping colonnades stood beside timbered facades. Moorish arches stood beside Renaissance domes. They all gleamed as if they were newly built.

The air carried the scent of blooming gardens. Beatrix could pick out the scent of roses, gardenias, and even lavender. Somewhere in the distance, a fountain's tranquil drizzle mingled with the trill of unseen songbirds.

High cliffs and jagged mountains walled the valley on all sides, concealing the valley entirely from the sea. They had walked through the heart of Calverique's mountain and found an entire world waiting on the other side.

The sound of hoofbeats broke their stunned silence. From between two gilded arches, a white horse emerged. Its mane was braided with golden ribbons. The rider was a woman dressed in green silk and brocade in a fashion from a century past. Her bearing was regal as her long, unbound red hair trailed behind her as she rode toward them. She drew the horse to a graceful halt and dismounted with the ease of one long accustomed to command.

Beatrix gasped with disbelief. The woman's face was striking—so like her mother's that for a moment she could not speak. She looked older than her mother. The lines of her face told of years weathered, but the resemblance was undeniable.

"Arabella?" Beatrix's voice trembled.

A warm smile curved the woman's lips. "Please, call me Auntie, my dear." She stepped forward and gathered Beatrix into her arms. She held her tightly in a warm embrace.

Beatrix felt Arabella's hand slip from around her shoulders as the woman turned to Gus. "August," she said with a smile that seemed to carry the weight of years. "We have been waiting for you." She clasped his hand; the affection in her eyes was unmistakable. She then turned to Callahan.

"Cormac Callahan," she said, greeting him as though they were old friends reunited at last. She took his hand. "Welcome home."

The three of them stood rooted to the spot awestruck. Beyond Arabella, the valley was bathed in gold; its spires and arches gleamed like the hidden cities of legend—the kind Odysseus might have glimpsed on some far shore before the gods veiled it from mortal eyes.

Arabella's smile deepened. "We have much to discuss. Shall we have tea?"

EPILOGUE

Ambrose Drake lay slumped against a weathered palm. His lips were split, and his tongue was thick and useless in his mouth. The chains at his wrists had rubbed the skin raw, and the tide licked at his bare feet like a slow, mocking clock. He had stopped counting the days.

The heat had stolen his will hours ago, and he almost laughed when he saw her. Softly, like a midnight lover, her footsteps came—Death's promise was dressed in moonlight.

She emerged from the shallows like some sea-born goddess. Water slipped in rivulets over her sun-brown skin. Long, dark hair clung to her shoulders in damp waves, framing the kind of face poets would immortalize, though none could catch the way it shifted one moment in warm invitation, and the next as untouchable as starlight. Her eyes—dark, cobalt blue and impossibly bright—found him and held him fast.

If death looks like this, Ambrose thought, *I will follow it willingly into the dark*. She had come at last to claim him, not with a scythe, but with lips that could tempt saints into the fire. Her eyes held him spellbound, as if they could burn the very soul from his body. If she meant to lead him to hell, he would follow her into the flames, unrepentant, if it meant her touch would be his everlasting torment.

She knelt beside him and reached down to touch his face. His eyes closed as he readied himself for the great hereafter, but her hand felt solid, warm, and shockingly alive against his jaw.

"Lazarus," she murmured. Her voice was deeper than he would have imagined and accented in French. The name curled through him; its truth wrapped around his muddled mind.

Ambrose opened his eyes to see steel flash in the moonlight. Her curved dagger sliced through his shackles as if they were made of string. He was still alive…and free. His pulse kicked hard.

"You've risen from the grave," she proclaimed. Her voice was velvet-rich and threaded with a wicked amusement that curled down his spine. She extended her hand, not in mercy, but in invitation—the sort a man would be a fool to refuse.

He caught her wrist and immediately felt the warm, rapid beat of her pulse against his thumb. Something inside of him roared back to life. With a single, unrelenting pull, he drew her down to him.

She breathed in sharply an instant before his mouth claimed hers in a kiss that was fierce, starved, and unapologetic. Salt and heat exploded between them in a rush that consumed the thirst, the sun, the endless days of dying. She tasted of the untamed sea and some darker promise that spoke of sin dressed as salvation.

Her lips moved against his with an answering fire, as though she, too, had been starved for centuries and had finally found the feast. She was Persephone, emerged from the underworld to claim him as her own. She was heat and shadow, tempest and flame, with a touch as binding as the chains of Hades. Her fingers threaded into his hair with the unyielding claim of a siren who had already chosen her mortal. Time dissolved, leaving only the pull of her mouth and his impossible certainty that if this really was hell, he would walk willingly into her fire and let it consume him for all eternity.

The kiss broke, though only because she willed it. Her breath came fast, and her lips still parted as if reluctant to let him go. For a heartbeat, she studied him. Her cobalt eyes gleamed with something perilously close to admiration.

"Come, Lazarus," she whispered. Her cobalt gaze was alight with sin. "We sail for danger, for gold…and for pleasures you've yet to imagine."

He smiled faintly, still tasting her salt and lust on his lips. She was real. He was alive. Hades could keep his kingdom—Ambrose Drake had better places to be.

***

To Be Continued in *The Devil's Dagger: Legends of Calverique, Book Two*

About the Author

Katarina D'Beers is an award-winning instructional designer and longtime college English and Humanities instructor. She has taught since 1998, sharing her passion for Literature and storytelling with generations of students. A native of Central Florida, she now divides her time between the Sunshine State and the mountains of East Tennessee. When she is not writing, she plays the harp and enjoys the lively company of her poodles. This is her debut novel.